PENGUIN BOOKS

MY HEART IS BROKEN

Mavis Gallant was born in Montreal and worked as a feature writer there before giving up newspaper work to devote herself to fiction. She left Canada in 1950 and after extensive travel settled in Paris. Her novels and collections of short stories include *The Other Paris, Green Water/Green Sky, A Fairly Good Time, The Pegnitz Junction, The End of the World, From the Fifteenth District, Home Truths, Overhead in a Balloon,* and *In Transit.* She is a regular contributor to *The New Yorker* and currently is working on a major account of the Dreyfus case and on a novel.

Mavis Gallant

My Heart
Is
Broken

PENGUIN BOOKS

PENGUIN BOOKS
Published by the Penguin Group
Viking Penguin, a division of Penguin Books USA Inc.,
375 Hudson Street, New York, New York 10014, U.S.A.
Penguin Books Ltd, 27 Wrights Lane,
London W8 5TZ, England
Penguin Books Australia Ltd, Ringwood,
Victoria, Australia
Penguin Books Canada Ltd, 2801 John Street,
Markham, Ontario, Canada L3R 1B4
Penguin Books (N.Z.) Ltd, 182–190 Wairau Road,
Auckland 10, New Zealand

Penguin Books Ltd, Registered Offices:
Harmondsworth, Middlesex, England

First published in the United States of America by
Random House, Inc., 1964
Published in Penguin Books 1991

1   3   5   7   9   10   8   6   4   2

PUBLISHER'S NOTE
These stories are works of fiction. Names, characters, places, and
incidents either are the product of the author's imagination or
are used fictitiously, and any resemblance to actual persons, living
or dead, events, or locales is entirely coincidental.

(CIP data available)
ISBN 0 14 01.5228 8

Printed in the United States of America

To William Maxwell

Contents

My Heart Is Broken

Acceptance of Their Ways

Prodded by a remark from Mrs. Freeport, Lily Littel got up
and fetched the plate of cheese. It was in her to say, "Go get
it yourself," but a reputation for coolness held her still.
Only the paucity of her income, at which the *Sunday
Express* horoscope jeered with its smart talk of pleasure
and gain, kept her at Mrs. Freeport's, on the Italian side of
the frontier. The coarse and grubby gaiety of the French
Riviera would have suited her better, and was not far away;
unfortunately it came high. At Mrs. Freeport's, which was
cheaper, there was a whiff of infirm nicety to be breathed,

a suggestion of regularly aired decay; weakly, because it
was respectable, Lily craved that, too. "We seem to have
finished with the pudding," said Mrs. Freeport once again,
as though she hadn't noticed that Lily was on her feet.

Lily was not Mrs. Freeport's servant, she was her
paying guest, but it was a distinction her hostess rarely
observed. In imagination, Lily became a punishing statue
and raised a heavy marble arm; but then she remembered
that this was the New Year. The next day, or the day after
that, her dividends would arrive. That meant she could
disappear, emerging as a gay holiday Lily up in Nice. Then,
Lily thought, turning away from the table, then watch the
old tiger! For Mrs. Freeport couldn't live without Lily, not
more than a day. She could not stand Italy without the
sound of an English voice in the house. In the hush of the
dead season, Mrs. Freeport preferred Lily's ironed-out Bays-
water to no English at all.

In the time it took her to pick up the cheese and face
the table again, Lily had added to her expression a perma-
nent-looking smile. Her eyes, which were a washy blue, were
tolerably kind when she was plotting mischief. The week in
Nice, desired, became a necessity; Mrs. Freeport needed a
scare. She would fear, and then believe, that her most
docile boarder, her most pliant errand girl, had gone forever. Stealing into Lily's darkened room, she would count
the dresses with trembling hands. She would touch Lily's
red with the white dots, her white with the poppies, her
green wool with the scarf of mink tails. Mrs. Freeport
would also discover—if she carried her snooping that far
—the tooled-leather box with Lily's daisy-shaped earrings,
and the brooch in which a mother-of-pearl pigeon sat on a
nest made of Lily's own hair. But Mrs. Freeport would not
find the diary, in which Lily had recorded her opinion of so
many interesting things, nor would she come upon a single
empty bottle. Lily kept her drinking to Nice, where, anonymous in a large hotel, friendly and lavish in a bar, she let
herself drown. "Your visits to your sister seem to do you so

much good," was Mrs. Freeport's unvarying comment when
Lily returned from these excursions, which always followed
the arrival of her income. "But you spend far too much
money on your sister. You are much too kind." But Lily had
no regrets. Illiberal by circumstance, grudging only because
she imitated the behavior of other women, she became,
drunk, an old forgotten Lily-girl, tender and warm, able
to shed a happy tear and open a closed fist. She had been
cold sober since September.

"Well, there you are," she said, and slapped down the
plate of cheese. There was another person at the table, a
Mrs. Garnett, who was returning to England the next day.
Lily's manner toward the two women combined bullying
with servility. Mrs. Freeport, large, in brown chiffon, wearing a hat with a water lily upon it to cover her thinning
hair, liked to *feel* served. Lily had been a paid companion
once; she had never seen a paradox in the joining of those
two words. She simply looked on Mrs. Freeport and Mrs.
Garnett as more of that race of ailing, peevish elderly children whose fancies and delusions must be humored by the
sane.

Mrs. Freeport pursed her lips in acknowledgment of
the cheese. Mrs. Garnett, who was reading a book, did
nothing at all. Mrs. Garnett had been with them four
months. Her blued curls, her laugh, her moist baby's
mouth, had the effect on Lily of a stone in the shoe. Mrs.
Garnett's husband, dead but often mentioned, had evidently
liked them saucy and dim in the brain. Now that William
Henry was no longer there to protect his wife, she was the
victim of the effect of her worrying beauty—a torment to
shoe clerks and bus conductors. Italians were dreadful;
Mrs. Garnett hardly dared put her wee nose outside the
house. "You are a little monkey, Edith!" Mrs Freeport would
sometimes say, bringing her head upward with a jerk,
waking out of a sweet dream in time to applaud. Mrs.
Garnett would go on telling how she had been jostled on
the pavement or offended on a bus. And Lily Littel, who

knew—but truly knew—about being followed and hounded and pleaded with, brought down her thick eyelids and smiled. Talk leads to overconfidence and errors. Lily had guided her life to this quiet shore by knowing when to open her mouth and when to keep it closed.

Mrs. Freeport was not deluded but simply poor. Thirteen years of pension-keeping on a tawdry stretch of Mediterranean coast had done nothing to improve her fortunes and had probably diminished them. Sentiment kept her near Bordighera, where someone precious to her had been buried in the Protestant part of the cemetery. In Lily's opinion, Mrs. Freeport ought to have cleared out long ago, cutting her losses, leaving the servants out of pocket and the grocer unpaid. Lily looked soft; she was round and pink and yellow-haired. The imitation pearls screwed on to her doughy little ears seemed to devour the flesh. But Lily could have bitten a real pearl in two and enjoyed the pieces. Her nature was generous, but an admiration for superior women had led her to cherish herself. An excellent cook, she had dreamed of being a poisoner, but decided to leave that for the loonies; it was no real way to get on. She had a moral program of a sort—thought it wicked to set a poor table, until she learned that the sort of woman she yearned to become was often picky. After that she tried to put it out of her mind. At Mrs. Freeport's she was enrolled in a useful school, for the creed of the house was this: It is pointless to think about anything so temporary as food; coffee grounds can be used many times, and moldy bread, revived in the oven, mashed with raisins and milk, makes a delicious pudding. If Lily had settled for this bleached existence, it was explained by a sentence scrawled over a page of her locked diary: "I live with gentlewomen now." And there was a finality about the statement that implied acceptance of their ways.

Lily removed the fly netting from the cheese. There was her bit left over from luncheon. It was the end of a portion of Dutch so dry it had split. Mrs. Freeport would have the cream cheese, possibly still highly pleasing under its coat of pale fur, while Mrs. Garnett, who was a yoghurt fancier, would require none at all.

"Cheese, Edith," said Mrs. Freeport loudly, and little Mrs. Garnett blinked her doll eyes and smiled: No, thank you. Let others thicken their figures and damage their souls.

The cheese was pushed along to Mrs. Freeport, then back to Lily, passing twice under Mrs. Garnett's nose. She did not look up again. She was moving her lips over a particularly absorbing passage in her book. For the last four months, she had been reading the same volume, which was called "Optimism Unlimited." So as not to stain the pretty dust jacket, she had covered it with brown paper, but now even that was becoming soiled. When Mrs. Freeport asked what the book was about, Mrs. Garnett smiled a timid apology and said, "I'm *afraid* it is philosophy." It was, indeed, a new philosophy, counseling restraint in all things, but recommending smiles. Four months of smiles and restraint had left Mrs. Garnett hungry, and, to mark her last evening at Mrs. Freeport's, she had asked for an Italian meal. Mrs. Freeport thought it extravagant—after all, they were still digesting an English Christmas. But little Edith was so sweet when she begged, putting her head to one side, wrinkling her face, that Mrs. Freeport, muttering about monkeys, had given in. The dinner was prepared and served, and Mrs. Garnett, suddenly remembering about restraint, brought her book to the table and decided not to eat a thing.

It seemed that the late William Henry had found this capriciousness adorable, but Mrs. Freeport's eyes were stones. Lily supposed this was how murders came about— not the hasty, soon regretted sort but the plan that is sown from an insult, a slight, and comes to flower at temperate speed. Mrs. Garnett deserved a reprimand. Lily saw her, without any emotion, doubled in two and shoved in a sack. But did Mrs. Freeport like her friend enough to bother teaching her lessons? Castigation, to Lily, suggested love. Mrs. Garnett and Mrs. Freeport were old friends, and vaguely related. Mrs. Garnett had been coming to Mrs. Freeport's every winter for years, but she left unfinished letters lying about, from which Lily—a great reader—could learn that dear Vanessa was becoming meaner and queerer by the minute. Thinking of Mrs. Freeport as "dear Vanessa" took flexibility, but Lily had that. She was not "Miss" and not "Littel;" she was, or, rather, had been, a Mrs. Cliff Little, who had taken advantage of the disorders of war to get rid of Cliff. He vanished, and his memory grew smaller and faded from the sky. In the bright new day strolled Miss Lily Littel, ready for anything. Then a lonely, fretful widow had taken a fancy to her and, as soon as travel was possible, had taken Lily abroad. There followed eight glorious years of trains and bars and discreet afternoon gambling, of eating éclairs in English-style tearooms, and discovering cafés where bacon and eggs were fried. Oh, the discovery of that sign in Monte Carlo: "Every Friday Sausages and Mashed"! That was the joy of being in foreign lands. One hot afternoon, Lily's employer, hooked by Lily into her stays not an hour before, dropped dead in a cinema lobby in Rome. Her will revealed she had provided for "Miss Littel," for a fox terrier, and for an invalid niece. The provision for the niece prevented the family from coming down on Lily's head; all the same, Lily kept out of England. She had not inspired the death of her employer, but she had nightmares for some time after, as though she had taken the wish for the deed. Her letters were so ambiguous that there was talk in England of an inquest. Lily accompanied the coffin as far as the frontier, for a letter of instructions specified cremation, which Lily understood could take place only in France. The coffin was held up rather a long time at customs, documents went back and forth, and in the end the relatives were glad to hear the last of it. Shortly after that, the fox terrier died, and Lily appropriated his share, feeling that she deserved it. Her employer had been living

on overdrafts; there was next to nothing for dog, companion, or niece. Lily stopped having nightmares. She continued to live abroad.

With delicate nibbles, eyes down, Lily ate her cheese.
Glancing sidewise, she noticed that Mrs. Garnett had closed
the book. She wanted to annoy; she had planned the whole
business of the Italian meal, had thought it out beforehand.
Their manners were still strange to Lily, although she was
a quick pupil. Why not clear the air, have it out? Once
again she wondered what the two friends meant to each
other. "Like" and "hate" were possibilities she had nearly
forgotten when she stopped being Mrs. Cliff and became
this curious, two-faced Lily Littel.

Mrs. Freeport's pebbly stare was focussed on her
friend's jar of yoghurt. "Sugar?" she cried, giving the
cracked basin a shove along the table. Mrs. Garnett pulled
it toward her, defiantly. She spoke in a soft, martyred voice,
as though Lily weren't there. She said that it was her last
evening and it no longer mattered. Mrs. Freeport had made
a charge for extra sugar—yes, she had seen it on her bill.
Mrs. Garnett asked only to pay and go. She was never coming again.

"I look upon you as essentially greedy." Mrs. Freeport
leaned forward, enunciating with care. "You pretend to eat
nothing, but I cannot look at a dish after you have served
yourself. The *wreck* of the lettuce. The *destruction* of the
pudding."

A bottle of wine, adrift and forgotten, stood by Lily's
plate. She had not seen it until now. Mrs. Garnett, who was
fearless, covered her yoghurt thickly with sugar.

"Like most people who pretend to eat like birds, you
manage to keep your strength up," Mrs. Freeport said.
"That sugar is the equivalent of a banquet, and you also eat
between meals. Your drawers are stuffed with biscuits, and
cheese, and chocolate, and heaven knows what."

"Dear Vanessa," Mrs. Garnett said.

"People who make a pretense of eating nothing always

stuff furtively," said Mrs. Freeport smoothly. "Secret eating is exactly the same thing as secret drinking."

Lily's years abroad had immunized her to the conversation of gentlewomen, their absorption with money, their deliberate over- or underfeeding, their sudden animal quarrels. She wondered if there remained a great deal more to learn before she could wear their castoff manners as her own. At the reference to secret drinking she looked calm and melancholy. Mrs. Garnett said, "That is most unkind." The yoghurt remained uneaten. Lily sighed, and wondered what would happen if she picked her teeth.

"My change man stopped by today," said Mrs. Garnett, all at once smiling and widening her eyes. How Lily admired that shift of territory—that carrying of banners to another field. She had not learned everything yet. "I *wish* you could have seen his face when he heard I was leaving! There really was no need for his coming, because I'd been in to his office only the week before, and changed all the money I need, and we'd had a lovely chat."

"The odious little money merchant in the bright-yellow automobile?" said Mrs. Freeport.

Mrs. Garnett, who often took up farfetched and untenable arguments, said, "William Henry wanted me to be happy."

"Edith!"

Lily hooked her middle finger around the bottle of wine and pulled it gently toward her. The day after tomorrow was years away. But she did not take her eyes from Mrs. Freeport, whose blazing eyes perfectly matched the small sapphires hanging from her ears. Lily could have matched the expression if she had cared to, but she hadn't arrived at the sapphires yet. Addressing herself, Lily said, "Thanks," softly, and upended the bottle.

"I meant it in a general way," said Mrs. Garnett. "William Henry wanted me to be happy. It was nearly the last thing he said."

"At the time of William Henry's death, he was unable

to say anything," said Mrs. Freeport. "William Henry was my first cousin. Don't use him as a platform for your escapades."

Lily took a sip from her glass. Shock! It hadn't been watered—probably in honor of Mrs. Garnett's last meal. But it was sour, thick, and full of silt. "I have always thought a little sugar would improve it," said Lily chattily, but nobody heard.

Mrs. Freeport suddenly conceded that William Henry might have wanted his future widow to be happy. "It was because he spoiled you," she said. "You were vain and silly when he married you, and he made you conceited and foolish. I don't wonder poor William Henry went off his head."

"Off his head?" Mrs. Garnett looked at Lily; calm, courteous Miss Littel was giving herself wine. "We might have general conversation," said Mrs. Garnett, with a significant twitch of face. "Miss Littel has hardly said a word."

"Why?" shouted Mrs. Freeport, throwing her table napkin down. "The meal is over. You refused it. There is no need for conversation of any kind."

She was marvelous, blazing, with that water lily on her head.

Ah, Lily thought, but you should have seen me, in the old days. How I could let fly . . . poor old Cliff.

They moved in single file down the passage and into the sitting room, where, for reasons of economy, the hanging lustre contained one bulb. Lily and Mrs. Freeport settled down directly under it, on a sofa; each had her own newspaper to read, tucked down the side of the cushions. Mrs. Garnett walked about the room. "To think that I shall never see this room again," she said.

"I should hope not," said Mrs. Freeport. She held the paper before her face, but as far as Lily could tell she was not reading it.

"The trouble is"—for Mrs. Garnett could never help

giving herself away—"I don't know where to *go* in the autumn."

"Ask your change man."

"Egypt," said Mrs. Garnett, still walking about. "I had friends who went to Egypt every winter for years and years, and now they have nowhere to go, either."

"Let them stay home," said Mrs. Freeport. "I am trying to read."

"If Egypt continues to carry on, I'm sure I don't know where we shall all be," said Lily. Neither lady took the slightest notice.

"They were perfectly charming people," said Mrs. Garnett, in a complaining way.

"Why don't you do the *Times* crossword, Edith?" said Mrs. Freeport.

From behind them, Mrs. Garnett said, "You know that I can't, and you said that only to make me feel small. But William Henry did it until the very end, which proves, I think, that he was not o.h.h. By o.h.h. I mean *off his head.*"

The break in her voice was scarcely more than a quaver, but to the two women on the sofa it was a signal, and they got to their feet. By the time they reached her, Mrs. Garnett was sitting on the floor in hysterics. They helped her up, as they had often done before. She tried to scratch their faces and said they would be sorry when she had died.

Between them, they got her to bed. "Where is her hot-water bottle?" said Mrs. Freeport. "No, not that one. She must have her own—the bottle with the bunny head."

"My yoghurt," said Mrs. Garnett, sobbing. Without her make-up she looked shrunken, as though padding had been removed from her skin.

"Fetch the yoghurt," Mrs. Freeport commanded. She stood over the old friend while she ate the yoghurt, one tiny spoonful at a time. "Now go to sleep," she said.

In the morning, Mrs. Garnett was taken by taxi to the early train. She seemed entirely composed and carried her

book. Mrs. Freeport hoped that her journey would be comfortable. She and Lily watched the taxi until it was out of sight on the road, and then, in the bare wintry garden, Mrs. Freeport wept into her hands.

"I've said goodbye to her," she said at last, blowing her nose. "It is the last goodbye. I shall never see her again. I was so horrid to her. And she is so tiny and frail. She might die. I'm convinced of it. She won't survive the summer."

"She has survived every other," said Lily reasonably.

"Next year, she must have the large room with the balcony. I don't know what I was thinking, not to have given it to her. We must begin planning now for next year. She will want a good reading light. Her eyes are so bad. And, you know, we should have chopped her vegetables. She doesn't chew. I'm sure that's at the bottom of the yoghurt affair."

"I'm off to Nice tomorrow," said Lily, the stray. "My sister is expecting me."

"You are so devoted," said Mrs. Freeport, looking wildly for her handkerchief, which had fallen on the gravel path. Her hat was askew. The house was empty. "So devoted . . . I suppose that one day you will want to live in Nice, to be near her. I suppose that day will come."

Instead of answering, Lily set Mrs. Freeport's water lily straight, which was familiar of her; but they were both in such a state, for different reasons, that neither of them thought it strange.

Bernadette

On the hundred and twenty-sixth day, Bernadette could no longer pretend not to be sure. She got the calendar out from her bureau drawer—a kitchen calendar, with the Sundays and saints' days in fat red figures, under a brilliant view of Alps. Across the Alps was the name of a hardware store and its address on the other side of Montreal. From the beginning of October the calendar was smudged and grubby, so often had Bernadette with moistened forefinger counted off the days: thirty-four, thirty-five, thirty-six . . . That had been October, the beginning of fear, with the trees in the garden and on the suburban street a blaze of red and yellow. Bernadette had scrubbed floors and washed walls in a frenzy of bending and stretching that alarmed her employers, the kindly, liberal Knights.

"She's used to hard work—you can see that, of course," Robbie Knight had remarked, one Sunday, almost apologizing for the fact that they employed anyone in the house at all. Bernadette had chosen to wash the stairs and woodwork that day, instead of resting. It disturbed the atmosphere of the house, but neither of the Knights knew how to deal with a servant who wanted to work too much. He sat by the window, enjoying the warm October sunlight, trying to get on with the Sunday papers but feeling guilty because his wife was worried about Bernadette.

"She *will* keep on working," Nora said. "I've told her to leave that hard work for the char, but she insists. I suppose it's her way of showing gratitude, because we've treated her like a human being instead of a slave. Don't you agree?"

"I suppose so."

"I'm so tired," Nora said. She lay back in her chair with her eyes closed, the picture of total exhaustion. She had broken one of her nails clean across, that morning, helping Bernadette with something Bernadette might easily have done alone. "You're right about her being used to hard work. She's probably been working all her life." Robbie tried not answering this one. "It's so much the sort of thing I've battled," Nora said.

He gave up. He let his paper slide to the floor. Compelled to think about his wife's battles, he found it impossible to concentrate on anything else. Nora's weapons were kept sharp for two dragons: crooked politics and the Roman Catholic Church. She had battled for birth control, clean milk, vaccination, homes for mothers, homes for old people, homes for cats and dogs. She fought against censorship, and for votes for cloistered nuns, and for the provincial income tax.

"Good old Nora," said Robbie absently. Nora accepted

this tribute without opening her eyes. Robbie looked at her, at the thin, nervous hand with the broken nail.

"She's not exciting, exactly," he had once told one of his mistresses. "But she's an awfully good sort, if you know what I mean. I mean, she's really a good sort. I honestly couldn't imagine not living with Nora." The girl to whom this was addressed had instantly burst into tears, but Robbie was used to that. Unreasonable emotional behavior on the part of other women only reinforced his respect for his wife.

The Knights had been married nearly sixteen years. They considered themselves solidly united. Like many people no longer in love, they cemented their relationship with opinions, pet prejudices, secret meanings, a private vocabulary that enabled them to exchange amused glances over a dinner table and made them feel a shade superior to the world outside the house. Their home held them, and their two daughters, now in boarding school. Private schools were out of line with the Knights' social beliefs, but in the case of their own children they had judged a private school essential.

"Selfish, they were," Robbie liked to explain. "Selfish, like their father." Here he would laugh a little, and so would his listeners. He was fond of assuming a boyish air of self-deprecation—a manner which, like his boyish nickname, had clung to him since school. "Nora slapped them both in St. Margaret's, and it cleared up in a year."

On three occasions, Nora had discovered Robbie in an affair. Each time, she had faced him bravely and made him discuss it, a process she called "working things out." Their talks would be formal, at first—a frigid question-and-answer period, with Robbie frightened and almost sick and Nora depressingly unreproachful. For a few nights, she would sleep in another room. She said that this enabled her to think. Thinking all night, she was fresh and ready for talk the next day. She would analyze their marriage, their lives, their childhoods, and their uncommon characters.

She would tell Robbie what a Don Juan complex was, and tell him what he was trying to prove. Finally, reconciled, they were able to talk all night, usually in the kitchen, the most neutral room of the house, slowly and congenially sharing a bottle of Scotch. Robbie would begin avoiding his mistress's telephone calls and at last would write her a letter saying that his marriage had been rocked from top to bottom and that but for the great tolerance shown by his wife they would all of them have been involved in something disagreeable. He and his wife had now arrived at a newer, fuller, truer, richer, deeper understanding. The long affection they held for each other would enable them to start life again on a different basis, the letter would conclude.

The basic notion of the letter was true. After such upheavals his marriage went swimmingly. He would feel flattened, but not unpleasantly, and it was Nora's practice to treat him with tolerance and good humor, like an ailing child.

He looked at the paper lying at his feet and tried to read the review of a film. It was hopeless. Nora's silence demanded his attention. He got up, kissed her lightly, and started out.

"Off to work?" said Nora, without opening her eyes.

"Well, yes," he said.

"I'll keep the house quiet. Would you like your lunch on a tray?"

"No, I'll come down."

"Just as you like, darling. It's no trouble."

He escaped.

Robbie was a partner in a firm of consulting engineers. He had, at one time, wanted to be a playwright. It was this interest that had, with other things, attracted Nora when they had been at university together. Robbie had been taking a course in writing for the stage—a sideline to his main degree. His family had insisted on engineering; he spoke of defying them, and going to London or New York.

Nora had known, even then, that she was a born struggler and fighter. She often wished she had been a man. She believed that to balance this overassertive side of her nature she should marry someone essentially feminine, an artist of some description. At the same time, a burning fear of poverty pushed her in the direction of someone with stability, background, and a profession outside the arts. Both she and Robbie were campus liberals; they met at a gathering that had something to do with the Spanish war —the sort of party where, as Nora later described it, you all sat on the floor and drank beer out of old pickle jars. There had been a homogeneous quality about the group that was quite deceptive; political feeling was a great leveler. For Nora, who came from a poor and an ugly lower-middle-class home, political action was a leg up. It brought her in contact with people she would not otherwise have known. Her snobbishness moved to a different level; she spoke of herself as working-class, which was not strictly true. Robbie, in revolt against his family, who were well-to-do, conservative, and had no idea of the injurious things he said about them behind their backs, was, for want of a gentler expression, slumming around. He drifted into a beer-drinking Left Wing movement, where he was welcomed for his money, his good looks, and the respectable tone he lent the group. His favorite phrase at that time was "of the people." He mistook Nora for someone of the people, and married her almost before he had discovered his mistake. Nora then did an extraordinary about-face. She reconciled Robbie with his family. She encouraged him to go into his father's firm. She dampened, ever so gently, the idea of London and New York.

Still, she continued to encourage his interest in theatre. More, she managed to create such a positive atmosphere of playwriting in the house that many of their casual acquaintances thought he *was* a playwright, and were astonished to learn he was the Knight of Turnbull, Knight & Beardsley. Robbie had begun and abandoned many plays since college. He had not consciously studied since the creative-writing course, but he read, and criticized, and had reached the point where he condemned everything that had to do with the English-language stage.

Nora agreed with everything he believed. She doggedly shared his passion for the theatre—which had long since ceased to be real, except when she insisted—and she talked to him about his work, sharing his problems and trying to help. She knew that his trouble arose from the fact that he had to spend his daytime hours in the offices of the firm. She agreed that his real life was the theatre, with the firm a practical adjunct. She was sensible: she did not ask that he sell his partnership and hurl himself into uncertainty and insecurity—a prospect that would have frightened him very much indeed. She understood that it was the firm that kept them going, that paid for the girls at St. Margaret's and the trip to Europe every second summer. It was the firm that gave Nora leisure and scope for her tireless battles with the political and ecclesiastical authorities of Quebec. She encouraged Robbie to write in his spare time. Every day, or nearly, during his "good" periods, she mentioned his work. She rarely accepted an invitation without calling Robbie at his office and asking if he wanted to shut himself up and work that particular night. She could talk about his work, without boredom or exhaustion, just as she could discuss his love affairs. The only difference was that when they were mutually explaining Robbie's infidelity, they drank whiskey. When they talked about his play and his inability to get on with it, Nora would go to the refrigerator and bring out a bottle of milk. She was honest and painstaking; she had at the tip of her tongue the vocabulary needed to turn their relationship and marriage inside out. After listening to Nora for a whole evening, agreeing all the way, Robbie would go to bed subdued with truth and totally empty. He felt that they had drained everything they would ever have to say. After too much talk, he would think, a

couple should part; just part, without another word, full
of kind thoughts and mutual understanding. He was afraid
of words. That was why, that Sunday morning toward the
end of October, the simple act of leaving the living room
took on the dramatic feeling of escape.

He started up the stairs, free. Bernadette was on her
knees, washing the painted baseboard. Her hair, matted
with a cheap permanent, had been flattened into curls that
looked like snails, each snail held with two crossed bobby
pins. She was young, with a touching attractiveness that
owed everything to youth.

"*Bonjour, Bernadette.*"

" *'Jour.*"

Bending, she plunged her hands into the bucket of soapy
water. A moment earlier, she had thought of throwing herself down the stairs and making it seem an accident.
Robbie's sudden appearance had frightened her into stillness. She wiped her forehead, waiting until he had closed
the door behind him. Then she flung herself at the baseboard, cloth in hand. Did she feel something—a tugging,
a pain? "*Merci, mon Dieu,* she whispered. But there was
nothing to be thankful for, in spite of the walls and the
buckets of water and the bending and the stretching.

Now it was late December, the hundred and twenty-
sixth day, and Bernadette could no longer pretend not to be
certain. The Knights were giving a party. Bernadette put the
calendar back in the drawer, under her folded slips. She had
counted on it so much that she felt it bore witness to her
fears; anyone seeing it would know at once.

For weeks she had lived in a black sea of nausea and
fear. The Knights had offered to send her home to Abitibi
for Christmas, had even wanted to pay her fare. But she
knew that her father would know the instant he saw her,
and would kill her. She preferred going on among familiar
things, as if the normality, the repeated routine of getting
up in the morning and putting on Mr. Knight's coffee and

Mrs. Knight's tea would, by force of pattern, cause things to be the way they had been before October. So far, the Knights had noticed nothing, although the girls, home for Christmas, teased her about getting fat. Thanks to St. Joseph, the girls had now been sent north to ski with friends, and there was no longer any danger of their drawing attention to Bernadette's waist.

Because of the party, Bernadette was to wear a uniform, which she had not done for some time. She pressed it and put it back on its hanger without trying it on, numb with apprehension, frightened beyond all thought. She had spent the morning cleaning the living room. Now it was neat, unreal, like a room prepared for a color photo in a magazine. There were flowers and plenty of ashtrays. It was a room waiting for disorder to set in.

"Thank you, Bernadette," Nora had said, taking, as always, the attitude that Bernadette had done her an unexpected service. "It looks lovely."

Nora liked the room; it was comfortable and fitted in with her horror of ostentation. Early in her marriage she had decided that her taste was uncertain; confusing elegance with luxury, she had avoided both. Later, she had discovered French-Canadian furniture, which enabled her to refer to her rooms in terms of the simple, the charming, even the amusing. The bar, for example, was a *prie-dieu* Nora had discovered during one of her forays into rural Quebec just after the war, before American tourists with a nose for a bargain had (as she said) cleaned out the Province of its greatest heritage. She had found the *prie-dieu* in a barn and had bought it for three dollars. Sandpapered, waxed, its interior recess deepened to hold bottles, it was considered one of Nora's best *trouvailles*. The party that evening was being given in honor of a priest—a liberal priest from Belgium, a champion of modern ecclesiastical art, and another of Nora's finds. (Who but Nora would have dreamed of throwing a party for a priest?)

Robbie wondered if the *prie-dieu* might not offend

him. "Maybe you ought to keep the lid up, so he won't see the cross," he said.

But Nora felt that would be cheating. If the priest accepted her hospitality, he must also accept her views.

"He doesn't know your views," Robbie said. "If he did, he probably wouldn't come." He had a cold, and was spending the day at home, in order to be well for the party. The cold made him interfering and quarrelsome.

"Go to bed, Robbie," said Nora kindly. "Haven't you anything to read? What about all the books you got for Christmas?"

Considering him dismissed, she coached Bernadette for the evening. They rehearsed the handing around of the tray, the unobtrusive clearing of ashtrays. Nora noticed that Bernadette seemed less shy. She kept a blank, hypnotized stare, concentrating hard. After a whole year in the household, she was just beginning to grasp what was expected. She understood work, she had worked all her life, but she did not always understand what these terrifying, well-meaning people wanted. If, dusting a bookcase, she slowed her arm, lingering, thinking of nothing in particular, one of them would be there, like a phantom, frightening her out of her wits.

"Would you like to borrow one of these books, Bernadette?"

Gentle, tolerant, infinitely baffling, Mr. or Mrs. Knight would offer her a book in French.

"For me?"

"Yes. You can read in the afternoon, while you are resting."

Read while resting? How could you do both? During her afternoon rest periods, Bernadette would lie on the bed, looking out the window. When she had a whole day to herself, she went downtown in a bus and looked in the windows of stores. Often, by the end of the afternoon, she had met someone, a stranger, a man who would take her for a drive in a car or up to his room. She accepted these adventures as inevitable; she had been so overwarned before leaving home. Cunning prevented her giving her address or name, and if one of her partners wanted to see her again, and named a time and a street number, she was likely to forget or to meet someone else on the way. She was just as happy in the cinema, alone, or looking at displays of eau de cologne in shops.

Reduced to perplexity, she would glance again at the book. Read?

"I might get it dirty."

"But books are to be read, Bernadette."

She would hang her head, wondering what they wanted, wishing they would go away. At last she had given in. It was in the autumn, the start of her period of fear. She had been dusting in Robbie's room. Unexpectedly, in that ghostly way they had, he was beside her at the bookcase. Blindly shy, she remembered what Mrs. Knight, all tact and kindness and firm common sense, had said that morning: that Bernadette sometimes smelled of perspiration, and that this was unpleasant. Probably Mr. Knight was thinking this now. In a panicky motion her hand flew to "L'Amant de Lady Chatterley," which Nora had brought from Paris so that she could test the blundering ways of censorship. (The English version had been held at customs, the French let through, which gave Nora ammunition for a whole winter.)

"You won't like that," Robbie had said. "Still . . ." He pulled it out of the bookcase. She took the book to her room, wrapped it carefully in newspaper, and placed it in a drawer. A few days later she knocked on the door of Robbie's room and returned "L'Amant de Lady Chatterley."

"You enjoyed it?"

"*Oui. Merci.*"

He gave her "La Porte Etroite." She wrapped it in newspaper and placed it in a drawer for five days. When she gave it back, he chose for her one of the Claudine series, and then, rather doubtfully, "Le Rouge et le Noir."

"Did you like the book by Stendhal, Bernadette?"

"*Oui. Merci.*"

To dinner guests, Nora now said, "Oh, our Bernadette! Not a year out of Abitibi, and she was reading Gide and Colette. She knows more about French literature than we do. She goes through Stendhal like a breeze. She adores Giraudoux." When Bernadette, grim with the effort of remembering what to do next, entered the room, everyone would look at her and she would wonder what she had done wrong.

During the party rehearsal, Robbie, snubbed, went up to bed. He knew that Nora would never forgive him if he hadn't recovered by evening. She regarded a cold in the head as something that could be turned off with a little effort; indeed, she considered any symptom of illness in her husband an act of aggression directed against herself. He sat up in bed, bitterly cold in spite of three blankets and a bathrobe. It was the chill of grippe, in the center of his bones; no external warmth could reach it. He heard Nora go out for some last-minute shopping, and he heard Bernadette's radio in the kitchen.

"*Sans amour, on est rien du tout,*" Edith Piaf sang. The song ended and a commercial came on. He tried not to hear.

On the table by his bed were books Nora had given him for Christmas. He had decided, that winter, to reread some of the writers who had influenced him as a young man. He began this project with the rather large idea of summing himself up as a person, trying to find out what had determined the direction of his life. In college, he remembered, he had promised himself a life of action and freedom and political adventure. Perhaps everyone had then. But surely he, Robbie Knight, should have moved on to something other than a pseudo-Tudor house in a suburb of Montreal. He had been considered promising—an attractive young man with a middling-good brain, a useful background, unexpected opinions, and considerable charm.

He did not consider himself unhappy, but he was beginning to wonder what he was doing, and why. He had decided to carry out his reassessment program in secret. Unfortunately, he could not help telling Nora, who promptly gave him the complete Orwell, bound in green.

He read with the conviction of habit. There was Orwell's Spain, the Spain of action and his university days. There was also the Spain he and Nora knew as tourists, a poor and dusty country where tourists became colicky because of the oil. For the moment, he forgot what he had seen, just as he could sometimes forget he had not become a playwright. He regretted the Spain he had missed, but the death of a cause no longer moved him. So far, the only result of his project was a feeling of loss. Leaving Spain, he turned to an essay on England. It was an essay he had not read until now. He skipped about, restless, and suddenly stopped at this: "I have often been struck by the peculiar easy completeness, the perfect symmetry as it were, of a working-class interior at its best. Especially on winter evenings after tea, when the fire glows in the open range and dances mirrored in the steel fender, when Father, in shirt-sleeves, sits in the rocking chair at one side of the fire reading the racing finals, and Mother sits on the other with her sewing, and the children are happy with a penn'orth of mint humbugs, and the dog lolls roasting himself on the rag mat. . . ."

Because he had a cold and Nora had gone out and left him on a snowy miserable afternoon, he saw in this picture everything missing in his life. He felt frozen and left out. Robbie had never been inside the kitchen of a working-class home; it did not occur to him that the image he had just been given might be idyllic or sentimental. He felt only that he and Nora had missed something, and that he ought to tell her so; but he knew that it would lead to a long bout of analytical talk, and he didn't feel up to that. He blew his nose, pulled the collar of his dressing gown up around his ears, and settled back on the pillows.

Bernadette knocked at the door. Nora had told her to prepare a tray of tea, rum, and aspirin at four o'clock. It was now half past four, and Bernadette wondered if Mr. Knight would betray her to Mrs. Knight. Bernadette's sleeves were rolled up, and she brought with her an aura of warmth and good food. She had, in fact, been cooking a ham for the party. Her hair was up in the hideous snails again, but it gave her, Robbie thought, the look of a hard-working woman—a look his own wife achieved only by seeming totally exhausted.

"Y a un book, too," said Bernadette, in her coarse, flat little voice. She put the tray down with care. "Je l'ai mis sur le tray." She indicated the new Prix Goncourt, which Robbie had lent her the day it arrived. He saw at once that the pages were still uncut.

"You didn't like it?"

"Oh, oui," she said automatically. "Merci."

Never before had a lie seemed to him more pathetic, or more justfied. Instead of taking the book, or his tea, he gripped Bernadette's plump, strong forearm. The room was full of warmth and comfort. Bernadette had brought this atmosphere with her; it was her native element. She was the world they had missed sixteen years before, and they, stupidly, had been trying to make her read books. He held her arm, gripping it. She stared back at him, and he saw that she was frightened. He let her go, furious with himself, and said, rather coldly, "Do you ever think about your home in Abitibi?"

"Oui," she said flatly.

"Some of the farms up there are very modern now, I believe," he said, sounding as if he were angry with her. "Was yours?"

She shrugged. "On a pas la television, nous," she said.

"I didn't think you had. What about your kitchen. What was your kitchen like at home, Bernadette?"

"Sais pas," said Bernadette, rubbing the released arm on the back of her dress. "It's big," she offered, after some thought.

"Thank you," said Robbie. He went back to his book, still furious, and upset. She stood still, uncertain, a fat dark little creature not much older than his own elder daughter. He turned a page, not reading, and at last she went away.

Deeply bewildered, Bernadette returned to the kitchen and contemplated the cooling ham. She seldom thought about home. Now her memory, set in motion, brought up the image of a large, crowded room. The prevailing smell was the odor of the men's boots as they came in from the outbuildings. The table, masked with oilcloth, was always set between meals, the thick plates turned upside down, the spoons in a glass jar. At the center of the table, never removed, were the essentials: butter, vinegar, canned jam with the lid of the can half opened and wrenched back, ketchup, a tin of molasses glued to its saucer. In winter, the washing hung over the stove. By the stove, every year but the last two or three, had stood a basket containing a baby—a wailing, swaddled baby, smelling sad and sour. Only a few of Bernadette's mother's children had straggled up past the infant stage. Death and small children were inextricably knotted in Bernadette's consciousness. As a child she had watched an infant brother turn blue and choke to death. She had watched two others die of diphtheria. The innocent dead became angels; there was no reason to grieve. Bernadette's mother did all she could; terrified of injections and vaccines, she barred the door to the district nurse. She bound her infants tightly to prevent excess motion, she kept them by the flaming heat of the stove, she fed them a bouillon of warm water and cornstarch to make them fat. When Bernadette thought of the kitchen at home, she thought of her mother's pregnant figure, and her swollen feet, in unlaced tennis shoes.

Now she herself was pregnant. Perhaps Mr. Knight knew, and that was why he had asked about her mother's kitchen. Sensing a connection between her mother and herself, she believed he had seen it as well. Nothing was too farfetched, no wisdom, no perception, for these people.

Their mental leaps and guesses were as mysterious to her as those of saints, or of ghosts.

Nora returned and, soon afterward, Robbie wandered downstairs. His wife had told him to get up (obviously forgetting that it was she who had sent him to bed) so that she could tidy the room. She did not ask how he felt and seemed to take it for granted that he had recovered. He could not help comparing her indifference with the solicitude of Bernadette, who had brought him tea and rum. He began comparing Bernadette with other women he had known well. His mistresses, *faute de mieux*, had been girls with jobs and little apartments. They had in common with Nora a desire to discuss the situation; they were alarmingly likely to burst into tears after lovemaking because Robbie didn't love them enough or because he had to go home for dinner. He had never known a working-class girl, other than the women his wife employed. (Even privately, he no longer used the expression "of the people.") As far as he could determine now, girls of Bernadette's sort were highly moral, usually lived with their parents until marriage, and then disappeared from sight, like Moslem women. He might have achieved an interesting union, gratifying a laudable social curiosity, during his college days, but he had met Nora straightaway. He had been disappointed to learn that her father did not work in a factory. There was an unbridgable gap, he had since discovered, between the girl whose father went off to work with a lunch pail and the daughter of a man who ate macaroni-and-cheese in the company cafeteria. In the midst of all her solicitude for the underprivileged, Nora never let him forget it. On the three occasions when she had caught him out in a love affair, among her first questions had been "Where does she come from? What does she do?"

Robbie decided to apologize to Bernadette. He had frightened her, which he had no right to do. He no longer liked the classic role he had set for himself, the kindly educator of young servant girls. It had taken only a glimpse of his thin, busy wife to put the picture into perspective. He allowed himself one last, uncharitable thought, savoring it: Compared with Bernadette, Nora looked exactly like a furled umbrella.

Bernadette was sitting at the kitchen table. The ham had been put away, the room aired. She was polishing silver for the party, using a smelly antiseptic pink paste. He no longer felt the atmosphere of warmth and food and comfort Bernadette had brought up to his room. She did not look up. She regarded her own-upside-down image in the bowl of a spoon. Her hands moved slowly, then stopped. What did he want now?

Before coming to Montreal, Bernadette had been warned about the licentious English—reserved on the surface, hypocritical, infinitely wicked underneath—and she had, in a sense, accepted it as inevitable that Mr. Knight would try to seduce her. When it was over, she would have another sin to account for. Mr. Knight, a Protestant, would not have sinned at all. Unique in her sin, she felt already lonely. His apology sent her off into the strange swamp world again, a world in which there was no footing; she had the same feeling as when they tried to make her read books. What was he sorry about? She looked dumbly around the kitchen. She could hear Nora upstairs, talking on the telephone.

Robbie also heard her and thought: Bernadette is afraid of Nora. The idea that the girl might say something to his wife crossed his mind, and he was annoyed to realize that Nora's first concern would be for Bernadette's feelings. His motives and his behavior they would discuss later, over a drink. He no longer knew what he wanted to say to Bernadette. He made a great show of drinking a glass of water and went out.

By evening, Robbie's temperature was over ninety-nine. Nora did not consider it serious. She felt that he was deliberately trying to ruin the party, and said so. "Take one good stiff drink," she said. "That's all you need."

He saw the party through a feverish haze. Nora was on top of the world, controlling the room, clergy-baiting, but in the most charming manner. No priest could possibly have taken offense, particularly a nice young priest from Belgium, interested in modern art and preceded by a liberal reputation. He could not reply; his English was limited. Besides, as Nora kept pointing out, he didn't know the situation in Quebec. He could only make little grimaces, acknowledging her thrusts, comically chewing the stem of a cold pipe.

"Until you know this part of the world, you don't know your own Church," Nora told him, smiling, not aggressive.

The English-Canadians in the room agreed, glancing nervously at the French. French Canada was represented by three journalists huddled on a couch. (Nora had promised the priest, as if offering hors d' oeuvres, representatives of what she called "our chief ethnic groups.") The three journalists supported Nora, once it was made plain that clergy-baiting and French-baiting were not going to be combined. Had their wives been there, they might not have concurred so brightly; but Nora could seldom persuade her French-Canadian finds to bring their wives along. The drinking of Anglo-Saxon women rather alarmed them, and they felt that their wives, genteel, fluffy-haired, in good little dresses and strings of pearls, would disappoint and be disappointed. Nora never insisted. She believed in emancipation, but no one was more vocal in deploring the French-Canadian who spoke hard, flat English and had become Anglicized out of all recognition. Robbie, feverish and disloyal, almost expected her to sweep the room with her hand and, pointing to the trio of journalists, announce, "I found them in an old barn and bought them for five dollars each. I've sandpapered and waxed them, and there they are."

From the Church she went on to Bernadette. She followed the familiar pattern, explaining how environment had in a few months overcome generations of intellectual poverty.

"Bernadette reads Gide and Lawrence," she said, choosing writers the young priest was bound to disapprove of. "She adores Colette."

"Excellent," he said, tepid.

Bernadette came in, walking with care, as if on a tightrope. She had had difficulty with her party uniform and she wondered if it showed.

"Bernadette," Nora said, "how many children did your mother have?"

"Thirteen, Madame," said the girl. Accustomed to this interrogation, she continued to move around the room, remembering Nora's instructions during the rehearsal.

"In how many years?" Nora said.

"Fifteen."

"And how many are living?"

"Six, Madame."

The young priest stopped chewing his pipe and said quietly, in French, "Are you sorry that your seven brothers and sisters died, Bernadette?"

Jolted out of her routine, Bernadette replied at once, as if she had often thought about it, "Oh, no. If they had lived, they would have had to grow up and work hard, and the boys would have to go to war, when there is war, to fight—" About to say, "fight for the English," she halted. "Now they are little angels, praying for their mother," she said.

"Where?" said the priest.

"In Heaven."

"What does an angel look like, Bernadette?" he said.

She gave him her hypnotized gaze and said, "They are very small. They have small golden heads and little wings. Some are tall and wear pink and blue dresses. You don't see them because of the clouds."

"I see. Thank you," said Nora, cutting in, and the

student of Gide and Colette moved off to the kitchen with her tray.

It ruined the evening. The party got out of hand. People stopped talking about the things Nora wanted them to talk about, and the ethnic groups got drunk and began to shout. Nora heard someone talking about the fluctuating dollar, and someone else said to her, of television, "Well, Nora, still holding out?"—when only a few months ago anyone buying a set had been sheepish and embarrassed and had said it was really for the maid.

When it was all over and Nora was running the vacuum so that there would be less for Bernadette to do the next day, she frowned and looked tired and rather old. The party had gone wrong. The guest of honor had slipped away early. Robbie had gone to bed before midnight without a word to anybody. Nora had felt outside the party, bored and disappointed, wishing to God they would all clear out. She had stood alone by the fireplace, wondering at the access of generosity that had led her to invite these ill-matched and noisy people to her home. Her parties in the past had been so different: everyone had praised her hospitality, applauded her leadership, exclaimed at her good sense. Indignant with her over some new piece of political or religious chicanery, they had been grateful for her combativeness, and had said so—more and more as the evening wore on. Tonight, they seemed to have come just as they went everywhere else, for the liquor and good food. A rot, a feeling of complacency, had set in. She had looked around the room and thought, with an odd little shock: How old they all seem! Just then one of her ethnic treasures—a recently immigrated German doctor—had come up to her and said, "That little girl is pregnant."

"What?"

"The little servant girl. One has only to look."

Afterward, she wondered how she could have failed to notice. Everything gave Bernadette away: her eyes, her

skin, the characteristic thickening of her waist. There were
the intangible signs, too, the signs that were not quite
physical. In spite of her own motherhood, Nora detested,
with a sort of fastidious horror, any of the common refer-
ences to pregnancy. But even to herself, now, she could
think of Bernadette only in terms of the most vulgar expressions, the terminology her own family (long discarded,
never invited here) had employed. Owing to a "mistake,"
Bernadette was probably "caught." She was beginning to
"show." She was at least four months "gone." It seemed to
Nora that she had better go straight to the point with
Bernadette. The girl was under twenty-one. It was quite
possible that the Knights would be considered responsible.
If the doctor had been mistaken, then Bernadette could
correct her. If Bernadette were to tell Nora to mind her
own business, so much the better, because it would mean
that Bernadette had more character than she seemed to
have. Nora had no objection to apologizing in either instance.

Because of the party and the extra work involved,
Bernadette had been given the next afternoon off. She
spent the morning cleaning. Nora kept out of the way.
Robbie stayed in bed, mulishly maintaining that he wasn't
feeling well. It was after lunch, and Bernadette was dressed
and ready to go downtown to a movie, when Nora decided
not to wait any longer. She cornered Bernadette in the
kitchen and, facing her, suddenly remembered how, as a
child, she had cornered field mice with a flashlight and
then drowned them. Bernadette seemed to know what was
coming; she exuded fear. She faced her tormentor with a
beating, animal heart.

Nora sat down at the kitchen table and began, as she
frequently had done with Robbie, with the words "I think
we ought to talk about a certain situation." Bernadette
stared. "Is there anything you'd like to tell me?" Nora said.

"No," said Bernadette, shaking her head.

"But you're worried about something. Something is wrong. Isn't that true?"

"No."

"Bernadette, I want to help you. Sit down. Tell me, are you pregnant?"

"I don't understand."

"Yes, you do. *Un enfant. Un bébé.* Am I right?"

"*Sais pas*," said Bernadette. She looked at the clock over Nora's head.

"*Bernadette.*"

It was getting late. Bernadette said, "Yes. I think so. Yes."

"You poor little mutt," said Nora. "Don't keep standing there like that. Sit down here, by the table. Take off your coat. We must talk about it. This is much more important than a movie." Bernadette remained standing, in hat and coat. "Who is it?" said Nora. "I didn't know you had   . I mean, I didn't know you knew anyone here. Tell me. It's most important. I'm not angry." Bernadette continued to look up at the clock, as if there were no other point in the room on which she dared fix her eyes. "Bern*adette!*" Nora said. "I've just sked you a question. Who is the boy?"

"*Un monsieur*," said Bernadette.

Did she mean by that an older man, or was Bernadette, in using the word "*monsieur*," implying a social category? "*Quel monsieur?*" said Nora.

Bernadette shrugged. She stole a glance at Nora, and something about the oblique look suggested more than fear or evasiveness. A word came into Nora's mind: sly.

"Can you . . . I mean, is it someone you're going to marry?" But no. In that case, he would have been a nice young boy, someone of Bernadette's own background. Nora would have met him. He would have been caught in the kitchen drinking Robbie's beer. He would have come every Sunday and every Thursday afternoon to call for Bernadette. "It it someone you *can* marry?" Nora said. Silence. "Don't be afraid," said Nora, deliberately making her voice

kind. She longed to shake the girl, even slap her face. It
was idiotic; here was Bernadette in a terrible predicament,
and all she could do was stand, shuffling from one foot to
the other, as if a movie were the most important thing in
the world. "If he isn't already married," Nora said, "which
I'm beginning to suspect is the case, he'll marry you. You
needn't worry about that. I'll deal with it, or Mr. Knight
will."

"*Pas possible*," said Bernadette, low.

"Then I was right. He *is* married." Bernadette looked
up at the clock, desperate. She wanted the conversation to
stop. "A married man," Nora repeated. "*Un monsieur*." An
unfounded and wholly outrageous idea rushed into her
mind. Dismissing it, she said, "When did it happen?"

"*Sais pas*."

"Don't be silly. That really is a very silly reply. Of
course you know. You've only had certain hours out of this
house."

The truth of it was that Bernadette did not know. She
didn't know his name or whether he was married or even
where she could find him again, even if she had desired
such a thing. He seemed the least essential factor. Lacking
words, she gave Nora the sidelong glance that made her
seem coarse and deceitful. She is so uninnocent, Nora
thought, surprised and a little repelled. It occurred to her
that in spite of her long marriage and her two children,
she knew less than Bernadette. While she was thinking
about Bernadette and her lover, there came into her mind
the language of the street. She remembered words that had
shocked and fascinated her as a child. That was Bernadette's fault. It was Bernadette's atmosphere, Nora thought,
excusing herself to an imaginary censor. She said, "We
must know when your baby will be born. Don't you think
so?" Silence. She tried again: "How long has it been since
you . . . I mean, since you missed . . ."

"One hundred and twenty-seven days," said Bernadette. She was so relieved to have, at last, a question that

she could answer that she brought it out in a kind of shout.

"My God. What are you going to do?"

"*Sais pas.*"

"Oh, Bernadette!" Nora cried. "But you must think."
The naming of a number of days made the whole situation
so much more immediate. Nora felt that they ought to be
doing something—telephoning, writing letters, putting
some plan into motion. "We shall have to think for you,"
she said. "I shall speak to Mr. Knight."

"No," said Bernadette, trembling, suddenly coming to
life. "Not Mr. Knight."

Nora leaned forward on the table. She clasped her
hands together, hard. She looked at Bernadette. "Is there a
special reason why I shouldn't speak to Mr. Knight?" she
said.

"*Oui.*" Bernadette had lived for so many days now
in her sea of nausea and fear that it had become a familiar
element. There were greater fears and humiliations, among
them that Mr. Knight, who was even more baffling and
dangerous than his wife, should try to discuss this thing
with Bernadette. She remembered what he had said the day
before, and how he had held her arm. "He must know,"
said Bernadette. "I think he must already know."

"You had better go on," said Nora, after a moment.
"You'll miss your bus." She sat quite still and watched
Bernadette's progress down the drive. She looked at the
second-hand imitation-seal coat that had been Bernadette's
first purchase (and Nora's despair) and the black velveteen
snow boots trimmed with dyed fur and tied with tasselled
cords. Bernadette's purse hung over her arm. She had the
walk of a fat girl—the short steps, the ungainly little trot.

It was unreasonable, Nora knew it was unreasonable;
but there was so much to reinforce the idea—"*Un monsieur,*" and the fact that he already knew ("He must know,"
Bernadette had said)—and then there was Bernadette's
terror when she said she was going to discuss it with him.
She thought of Robbie's interest in Bernadette's education.

She thought of Robbie in the past, his unwillingness to remain faithful, his absence of courage and common sense. Recalling Bernadette's expression, prepared now to call it corrupt rather than sly, she felt that the girl had considered herself deeply involved with Nora; that she knew Nora much better than she should.

Robbie had decided to come downstairs, and was sitting by the living-room fire. He was reading a detective novel. Beside him was a drink.

"Get you a drink?" he said, without lifting his eyes, when Nora came in.

"Don't bother."

He went on reading. He looked so innocent, so unaware that his life was shattered. Nora remembered how he had been when she had first known him, so pleasant and dependent and good-looking and stupid. She remembered how he had been going to write a play, and how she had wanted to change the world, or at least Quebec. Tears of fatigue and strain came into her eyes. She felt that the failure of last night's party had been a symbol of the end. Robbie had done something cheap and dishonorable, but he reflected their world. The world was ugly, Montreal was ugly, the street outside the window contained houses of surpassing ugliness. There was nothing left to discuss but television and the fluctuating dollar; that was what the world had become. The children were in boarding school because Nora didn't trust herself to bring them up. The living room was full of amusing peasant furniture because she didn't trust her own taste. Robbie was afraid of her and liked humiliating her by demonstrating again and again that he preferred nearly any other woman in bed. That was the truth of things. Why had she never faced it until now?

She said, "Robbie, can I talk to you?" Reluctant, he looked away from his book. She said, "I just wanted to tell you about a dream. Last night I dreamed you died. I dreamed that there was nothing I could do to bring you back, and that I had to adjust all my thoughts to the idea of going on without you. It was a terrible, shattering feeling." She intended this to be devastating, a prelude to the end. Unfortunately, she had had this dream before, and Robbie was bored with it. They had already discussed what it might mean, and he had no desire to go into it now.

"I wish to God you wouldn't keep on dreaming I died," he said.

She waited. There was nothing more. She blinked back her tears and said, "Well, listen to this, then. I want to talk about Bernadette. What do you know, exactly, about Bernadette's difficulties?"

"Has Bernadette got difficulties?" The floor under his feet heaved and settled. He had never been so frightened in his life. Part of his mind told him that nothing had happened. He had been ill, a young girl had brought warmth and comfort into his room, and he wanted to touch her. What was wrong with that? Why should it frighten him so much that Nora knew? He closed his eyes. It was hopeless; Nora was not going to let him get on with the book. Nora looked without any sentiment at all at the twin points where his hairline was moving back. "Does she seem sort of unsettled?" he asked.

"That's a way of putting it. Sometimes you have a genuine talent for irony."

"Oh, hell," said Robbie, suddenly fed up with Nora's cat-and-mouse. "I don't feel like talking about anything. Let's skip it for now. It's not important."

"Perhaps you'd better tell me what you consider important," Nora said. "Then we'll see what we can skip." She wondered how he could sit there, concerned with his mild grippe, or his hangover, when the whole structure of their marriage was falling apart. Already, she saw the bare bones of the room they sat in, the rugs rolled, the cracks that would show in the walls when they took the pictures down.

He sighed, giving in. He closed his book and put it beside his drink. "It was just that yesterday when I was feeling so lousy she brought me—she brought me a book.

One of those books we keep lending her. She hadn't even cut the pages. The whole thing's a farce. She doesn't even look at them."

"Probably not," said Nora. "Or else she does and that's the whole trouble. To get straight to the point, which I can see you don't want to do, Bernadette has told me she's having a baby. She takes it for granted that you already know. She's about four months under way, which makes yesterday seem rather pointless."

Robbie said impatiently, "We're not talking about the same thing." He had not really absorbed what Nora was saying; she spoke so quickly, and got so many things in all at once. His first reaction was astonishment, and a curious feeling that Bernadette had deceived him. Then the whole import of Nora's speech entered his mind and became clear. He said, "Are you crazy? Are you out of your mind? Are you completely crazy?" Anger paralyzed him. He was unable to think of words or form them on his tongue. At last he said, "It's too bad that when I'm angry I can't do anything except feel sick. Or maybe it's just as well. You're crazy, Nora. You get these—I don't know— You get these ideas." He said, "If I'd hit you then, I might have killed you."

It had so seldom occurred in their life together that Robbie was in the right morally that Nora had no resources. She had always triumphed. Robbie's position had always been indefensible. His last remark was so completely out of character that she scarcely heard it. He had spoken in an ordinary tone of voice. She was frightened, but only because she had made an insane mistake and it was too late to take it back. Bravely, because there was nothing else to do, she went on about Bernadette. "She doesn't seem to know what to do. She's a minor, so I'm afraid it rather falls on us. There is a place in Vermont, a private place, where they take these girls and treat them well, rather like a boarding school. I can get her in, I think. Having her admitted to the States could be your end of it."

"I suppose you think that's going to be easy," Robbie

said bitterly. "I suppose you think they admit pregnant unmarried minors every day of the year."

"None of it is easy!" Nora cried, losing control. "Whose fault is it?"

"It's got nothing to do with me!" said Robbie, shouting at her. "Christ Almighty, get that through your head!"

They let silence settle again. Robbie found that he was trembling. As he had said, it was physically difficult for him to be angry.

Nora said, "Yes, Vermont," as if she were making notes. She was determined to behave as if everything were normal. She knew that unless she established the tone quickly, nothing would ever be normal again.

"What will she do with it? Give it out for adoption?" said Robbie, in spite of himself diverted by details.

"She'll send it north, to her family," said Nora. "There's always room on a farm. It will make up for the babies that died. They look on those things, on birth and on death, as acts of nature, like the changing of the seasons. They don't think of them as catastrophes."

Robbie wanted to say, You're talking about something you've read, now. They'll be too ashamed to have Bernadette or the baby around; this is Quebec. But he was too tired to offer a new field of discussion. He was as tired as if they had been talking for hours. He said, "I suppose this Vermont place, this school or whatever it is, has got to be paid for."

"It certainly does." Nora looked tight and cold at this hint of stinginess. It was unnatural for her to be in the wrong, still less to remain on the defensive. She had taken the position now that even if Robbie were not responsible, he had somehow upset Bernadette. In some manner, he could be found guilty and made to admit it. She would find out about it later. Meanwhile, she felt morally bound to make him pay.

"Will it be expensive, do you think?"

She gave him a look, and he said nothing more.

Bernadette sat in the comforting dark of the cinema.
It was her favorite kind of film, a musical comedy in full
color. They had reached the final scene. The hero and
heroine, separated because of a stupid quarrel for more
than thirty years, suddenly found themselves in the same
night club, singing the same song. They had gray hair but
youthful faces. All the people around them were happy
to see them together. They clapped and smiled. Bernadette
smiled, too. She did not identify herself with the heroine,
but with the people looking on. She would have liked to
have gone to a night club in a low-cut dress and applauded
such a scene. She believed in love and in uncomplicated
stories of love, even though it was something she had never
experienced or seen around her. She did not really expect
it to happen to her, or to anyone she knew.

For the first time, her child moved. She was so astonished that she looked at the people sitting on either side of
her, wondering if they had noticed. They were looking at
the screen. For the first time, then, she thought of it as a
child, here, alive—not a state of terror but something to be
given a name, clothed, fed, and baptized. Where and how
and when it would be born she did not question. Mrs.
Knight would do something. Somebody would. It would be
born, and it would die. That it would die she never doubted.
She was uncertain of so much else; her own body was a
mystery, nothing had ever been explained. At home, in
spite of her mother's pregnancies, the birth of the infants
was shrouded in secrecy and, like their conception, suspicion of sin. This baby was Bernadette's own; when it died,
it would pray for her, and her alone, for all of eternity. No
matter what she did with the rest of her life, she would
have an angel of her own, praying for her. Oddly secure in
the dark, the dark of the cinema, the dark of her personal
fear, she felt protected. She thought: *Il prie pour moi.* She
saw, as plainly as if it had been laid in her arms, her child,
her personal angel, white and swaddled, baptized, innocent, ready for death.

The Moabitess

Elderly Miss Horeham, though timid and poor, did not shrink from a row on that account, particularly when she imagined that something was expected of her. It was she, in the end, who cornered Mme. Arnaud in the passage and complained about the noise the Oxleys made. The others marveled at her nerve, for she was known to be someone who wouldn't say boo to a goose. But then, Miss Horeham had the room next to the Oxleys, with only the thin wall between, and she had probably had enough.

"It's a disgrace, you know," Miss Horeham whispered,

blinking, drawing rapid little breaths between words; she really was excruciatingly timid, and this business of going outside herself took all her strength.

Mme. Arnaud said she did not understand. She did not understand what Miss Horeham meant by disgrace.

Well, it was the way the Oxleys quarreled in the night, said Miss Horeham, apologizing with her eyes for having to bring up that sort of thing. It was the things they said—particularly Mr. Oxley. You could hear them all over the floor. Mr. Wynn had heard them. Mme. Brunhof had heard. Those people from Liverpool had probably heard, too.

It was all so clear to Miss Horeham, this picture of the *pension* tenants roused and trembling in their rooms. But Mme. Arnaud still screwed up her eyes and frowned. She folded her hands on her filthy apron. She said, *"Et alors?"*

Mrs. Oxley, Miss Horeham whispered, bending close, Mrs. Oxley might find life hard, but she was a married woman. If she didn't want to be a married woman, if she didn't care about . . . that side of life . . . why did she marry? There were plenty of women who didn't care about life . . . about that side of life . . . and they simply never married.

All this was more than she had intended to say, and she would never have brought it all out so courageously, especially that last bit about marriage, if she hadn't had the wine at lunch. Departing guests, the nice Lawrences from Wimbledon, had left her the remains of their wine —half a litre of red. So now there was a grape-colored flush on Miss Horeham's cheeks, and she was saying everything that came into her head.

"If you don't like your room, I can move you back to the attic," said Mme. Arnaud. The passage was dark and smelled of the cauliflower they had been given for lunch, and all at once Mme. Arnaud, with her dirty apron, and the black mustache on her upper lip, seemed the dark wielder of power Miss Horeham had known as a child, after her mother died and delivered her into servants' hands.

"I meant change their room, not mine," she said faintly.

Mme. Arnaud pushed by her and went into the kitchen. She had other things to do, such as disguise the remains of the cauliflower so that it could be served up again that night. It was November, out-of-season on the Riviera; she had few enough people as it was, without offending the Oxleys for the sake of mad Miss Horeham.

"We are at their mercy," Miss Horeham said, stepping into the lounge. The encounter had stimulated her and widened the world, usually limited to her room and her own face in the glass. "We are at the mercy of hotel-keepers. And with all the decent places closed until Christmas, we are obliged to stay here and suffer the inconveniences."

Nobody replied. There was no assenting ripple from among the stuffed chairs and potted ferns. Mr. Wynn didn't so much as lower the *Daily Telegraph*. For one thing, Mrs. Oxley was in the room—the very person complained about; it couldn't have been more tactless. And then they had known that Mme. Arnaud would never take Miss Horeham's word. Everyone knew that she paid next to nothing, and that every summer, in the good season, she was moved to a small kiln of a room under the roof. The poor thing had lived abroad too long to be eligible for a pension at home; it was really a shame. Mr. Wynn had tried to do something about it, but even the welfare state had its rules.

Miss Horeham walked once about the lounge, as if seeing the travel posters on its walls for the first time, then sat down in her usual place, on a stone-hard upholstered sofa adrift in the room, away from lamps and footstools and magazines. This did not trouble her in the least, for she came to the lounge only to see the others, and the position of the sofa was such that the rest could escape her gaze only by swiveling around with their backs to her, and no one ever had the courage to do this. They were down from their afternoon naps now. There was Mr. Wynn with the

Telegraph, and little Mrs. Oxley reading *Vogue*, and Mme. Brunhof writing a letter. The people from Liverpool— father and mother and nearly grown sons—stood at separate windows, looking with mute despair at the rain, which came off the Alps in gusts, like gray veils, to merge with the gray fog on the sea. Buses, wet and cold as toads, crawled along the sea road. The last of the zinnias in the garden were being battered into the ground.

"It usen't to rain like this before the war," said Miss Horeham, fixing her eyes on Mr. Wynn's paper, but without seeing it. She had a small, particular field of vision, as if her eye were eternally pressed to a knothole. Everything else was quite blurred. "It never rained at the villa in the old days," she said in a droning voice. "When father died, I gave it up. The villa was called La Bella. That was for me." She stuttered so at the memory that the others thought she would choke.

Mr. Wynn rustled the *Daily Telegraph*. He knew all about La Bella by now. "Do read us something," said little Mrs. Oxley, putting down her *Vogue*. "Some interesting bit."

He read where his eyes rested, if only to put a halt to that droning voice. "The Queen wore mauve, while the Queen Mother . . . trimmed with fox . . . Rain failed to dampen the spirits of a large crowd . . ."

Temporarily stilled, Miss Horeham contemplated them all with grave good will. She had fought their battle with Mme. Arnaud, as she used to battle for her father in the old days, in the war. She had been straight as an arrow— not a gray hair until she was forty-three. The curls around her face were yellow-gray now, her eyes were sunken, and the skin around them was dark. She wore long-sleeved dresses in gray, violet, or brown. Most of her dresses had been given her, and although many of the castoff things that came her way were gay and bright, she felt she oughtn't wear anything cheerful. She felt as if "Charity" should be written on her in letters four feet high, so that wherever her father was, in whatever dark passage of the

dead, he might see the word and doubly perish with shame.
If there was another annihilation after death, then let it
come to Mr. Percy Horeham, who had irresponsibly de-
parted from life in 1946 and left his maiden daughter not
a penny, not a franc, nothing but debts. She had nursed
him through the war, through the Occupation, under the
very noses of Italians and Germans—all those strangers!
She had walked seven miles to buy him an egg! And still
she had had no allowance but had had to beg for everything
from the locked box under the bed, so that all her life she
had no idea of money, of what things ought to cost. She
did not doubt that the dead knew what went on among the
living. Let him see now what had become of the remnants
of his house—a solitary daughter in castoff dresses in the
lounge of a third-class *pension*. Let him see! Let him
perish!

Thinking this, she smiled, and Mrs. Oxley thought,
She's not a bad old thing. It must be awful to be alone . . .
Mrs. Oxley had not only a husband to quarrel with but also
a son of four. "Do you like being read things?" she said to
Miss Horeham, when Mr. Wynn had stopped about the
party in the rain.

"At the villa we never read—only the Bible," said Miss
Horeham, which was true. There wasn't another book at
La Bella, aside from her prizes from school, put away in a
box. But there was the Bible, and the two of them had
known it by heart.

Miss Horeham moved her lips to say again, "We are
at their mercy," but she had lost the thread, and only liked
the Biblical sound it made. She went on smiling. She was
thinking of the Bible and the old days, and of what a nice
time of year this was; in spite of what she had said about
its being off season, it was really the period she liked best.
When the rain stopped, the sun came out, unnaturally large
and bright, like a flower forced into bloom. But it was never
high in the sky, and the shadows of people walking in the
pension gardens stretched like the long shadows of a sum-

mer evening; noon was a brilliant evening. In Miss Hore-ham's vision of life this was the climate in which everything took place. On November nights, the world closed comfortably in. They were the same people in the same lounge, but at night they were held by the dark corners of the room, drawn together in the dim pools of light from the low-watt lamps beside their chairs: Mr. Wynn, pensioned from the Admiralty, and Mme. Brunhof, who lived here between invitations to the houses of rich old friends, and little Mrs. Oxley with her son. Mr. Oxley, that disturbing influence at night, disturbed Miss Horeham even more by not staying quietly in the lounge after dinner. He and the Liverpool lot, who had imagined the Riviera as being very different, would make off straight after their meal, down the road to the Bar du Midi. They never came back until just before twelve, when the *pension* door was locked. What fun was there in the bar? There was nothing to see from there but the sea and the odd, starry light of a fishing boat, or the moon rising over an Alp. "When you've seen it once, you've seen it forever," Mr. Wynn always said. And as for the bar itself, there was no one English there; you couldn't even talk.

Mrs. Oxley sat in a large armchair with little Tom on her lap. He was afraid to stay alone upstairs, and she had to wait until he was sound asleep and then carry him up. Sometimes kind Mr. Wynn carried him for her. She was twenty-six and plump, with skin like an apricot. Her eyes, her fat little hands, her full lips suggested she was the last person in the world to deny that side of life, but even without Miss Horeham to inform them the others would have understood that things were not well with the Oxleys. "Don't wake me up when you come in," she would tell her husband as he started out for "just a turn down the road." A quick resentful look would pass between them. He was a fair man with light-blue eyes, and he colored easily. Pink with anger, he would stride off, wearing flannels and a blazer with the crest of an obscure school. The Oxleys lived in South Africa because of his job, and were in Europe for a leave of three months.

"When Tom was born, I nearly died," Mrs. Oxley once said, after her husband had gone. The others took this to mean she knew they heard the night quarrels and wanted to give a decent explanation.

Mrs. Horeham nodded her yellow-gray curls, as if she knew all about that. "They are dreadful," she murmured vaguely, but whether she meant men or births or quarrels she was not quite sure. Her eyes turned to Mr. Wynn—to his fine white hands, his cropped gray hair, his colorless lips. She watched the delicate way he inserted a cigarette in an amber holder. She admired the white of his cuffs. Even his newspapers seemed cleaner and crisper than other people's. She remembered a dream of a union that had nothing to do with quarrels at night or damp bath towels on the floor or someone using your comb. It was an ancient girlhood dream, small and removed now, and she had to dig under the leaves of her memory to find it—an early dream of living with someone rather like Mr. Wynn and sharing with him a cold immaculate bed. But the dream retreated. It was small and bright and slipped under the leaves again. She knew about living in the same house with men; she had nursed her ailing father for years and years.

Mr. Wynn loved children. "Isn't it time for me to carry little Tom upstairs?" he would ask. And Mrs. Oxley, who would not have surrendered him to anyone else, would let Mr. Wynn take Tom from her arms. "It's a wonderful age," he would say, looking down on the flushed, sleeping child.

"I wish he needn't grow up. I never want him to change."

"No, he mustn't."

They would go up the stairs together, quietly, so as not to wake Tom, and after a few minutes Mr. Wynn would descend alone and pick up his paper again. Sometimes it was Mme. Brunhof who got up to go first, leaning on her cane. She was an Englishwoman, in spite of her name.

"Who is she?" Mrs. Oxley had asked.

A direct question of this sort plunged Miss Horeham into uncertainty. She struggled to emerge. "Mme. Brunhof —Well, you see, she *is* English. Oh, very English indeed." It was so difficult to find the right words, the most delicate explanation. "Mme. Brunhof was closely associated for many years—years ago, of course—with an *important person*. We believe it to have been—oh, someone very grand." Her love of established order rose and checked the disloyal suspicion. She could not bring it out.

Mr. Wynn gave an irritated cough and told the royal name.

"Goodness," said Mrs. Oxley, but without real interest. It was all so long ago. She stretched one of Tom's brown curls. It sprang back.

"He married her off to this Brunhof, after he was fed up with her," said Mr. Wynn, who could be surprisingly coarse. "An Austrian count."

"An Alsatian baron," said Miss Horeham, making a fluttering motion with her hands at being obliged to contradict.

"She must have been good-looking," Mrs. Oxley said. "You can see the traces still. She must be seventy-five."

"Eighty," gasped Miss Horeham.

"You're all I care about in the whole world," Mrs. Oxley whispered.

Miss Horeham suddenly blinked and peered sharply out of the small universe in which she lived. Did she mean Tom, or Mr. Wynn? She meant Tom, of course, for she was rocking him gently in her chair.

Night after night, November went on like this, and it was the best season, even though there were fewer people to give Miss Horeham old dresses and half bottles of wine. The world drew into itself, became smaller and smaller, was limited to her room, her table in the dining room, her own eyes in the mirror, her own hand curved around a glass. Dreams as thick as walls rose about her bed and sheltered her sleep—unless the Oxleys quarreled. Then she would lie awake in the dark, her heart ticking rapidly and dryly, like her father's old watch.

What made this peaceful order stop? Why did it stop? What made Mr. Oxley quarrel with kind Mr. Wynn? Miss Horeham had never heard anything like it. There was Mrs. Oxley out in the hall or on the staircase—probably in her nightdress, for it was very late—wailing "Oh, it's a mistake! He came to see Tom!" and Mr. Oxley yelling until they heard him in the basement. Mme. Arnaud came out and shouted louder than anyone else. From Mr. Wynn there was no sound. Oh, it was terrible; the harsh night broken with shouts, like being taken on a night journey when one was a child: the flashing lights, the strange voices, the names of unknown stations swimming by. Miss Horeham lay flat on her back and recited at random from Proverbs: "A virtuous woman is a crown to her husband: but she that maketh ashamed is as rottenness to his bones." It was the first thing that came into her head. What came next? "He that tilleth . . ." No, that came later. "The thoughts of the righteous are right." She repeated this until the noise had stopped, and then she fell back into sleep.

In the morning she was sure she must have dreamed it, but at breakfast Mr. Wynn was not at his place, and at the Oxleys' table there were only Mr. Oxley, looking mulish, and little Tom, perfectly calm but hugging a girl's doll. Mme. Brunhof did not say good morning to Mr. Oxley. Mme. Arnaud was siding with Mr. Wynn. She said that Mr. Oxley had been drunk, and that she would not have South Africans again. Miss Horeham tried not to see anything; she tried to pretend nothing had happened at all. But then in the garden she had to run into the Oxleys, and see Mrs. Oxley sitting bolt upright on a wrought-iron chair, and Mr. Oxley standing with Tom.

"Don't take him away from me today!" said Mrs. Oxley. "I ask as a special favor. Don't take him today. He's never been away from me for a minute."

"He's going to be five," said Mr. Oxley. "He can go with his own father to the beach."

"Where's my dolly?" said Tom.

"You're too big," his father said. "Forget it."

"He's not yet five!" cried Mrs. Oxley in a kind of wail.

"He's not to have it," said Mr. Oxley, suddenly very red, for he saw Miss Horeham, hands clasped to her heart, all in gray-brown today, like a little thrush.

"You're taking it out on him," said Mrs. Oxley. She had not yet seen their witness.

Mr. Wynn was not down to lunch, or to dinner. Miss Horeham kept glancing at his table. It was upsetting, like a day with no post. The Oxleys were all together, eating in silence. That evening, father and son were both red in the face, because they had been sitting on the beach.

Tom had brought a colored stone from the beach. He held it in one hand and ate with the other. Suddenly, as if he had been good too long, he flung the stone across the room, and it hit Miss Horeham on the arm and fell on the carpet. She bent down and picked it up. "Naughty boy," said both parents, but without much heart behind it. They seemed both of them worn out with this day.

"What a charming present," Miss Horeham said. "Everyone gives me things."

The Oxleys went up to their room after dinner. Then Mme. Brunhof went, and the Liverpool people, and then, since there was nothing to stay up for, Miss Horeham left her sofa and sadly climbed the stairs. There was a light under the Oxley's door and a light under Mr. Wynn's, but there was no sound. From her own room, Miss Horeham could hear the Oxleys, talking in low voices of ordinary things. They talked about the end of their leave in Europe, and of the things they had bought and now regretted—a white nylon pullover that had gone yellow in the wash, a bathrobe of toweling, four butter plates shaped like vine leaves, with butter knives to match.

"Give it all to the old trout," said Mr. Oxley.

Miss Horeham meekly bowed her head, although there was no one to see. Beggars couldn't be choosers, she knew. But the gifts came into the small, clear field of light, moved across it, and vanished into the blur.

An hour later, the house was so quiet you could hear the maids leave the kitchen and crunch down the gravel path in the garden on their way home. It was quieter than it had been since the arrival of the Oxleys, yet Miss Horeham could not settle down to sleep. There were woolly knitted bootees on her feet, and she wore a warm nightdress, and she had no aches or pains, and had not forgotten to pray. She tried to send herself off with Proverbs, but could not. At last she rose and turned on the light and drew on a dressing gown. Tom's stone was on the table by her bed. I had better put it away, she thought. It was a present, and besides it might be rare. She removed two cushions from what appeared to be a window seat, and revealed a small trunk. The key to the trunk hung around her neck on a string. Kneeling, she opened the trunk and began to take out her treasures—all the secret things she could have sold for pounds and pounds and pounds. Oh, how they would die if they knew—all those people who left her wine and dresses and gave her stones! How they would simply die! But none of them knew —not the sleeping Oxleys, or Mme. Brunhof, nor Mr. Wynn. Perhaps he was awake and brooding over last night's misunderstanding; a scene of that sort must have been dreadful for a man like Mr. Wynn. But he was already removed to the blurry world beyond her field of vision, and the little beam she had thrown in his direction flickered out.

She removed the first tray. There was her father's old collection of butterflies in a glass box; they must be worth something. At any rate, they were very gay. There was the scarf from Sicily, and the broken amber beads in a little cardboard box, and the box of Christmas soap, so precious it had never been used. There were the smoked mother-of-pearl buttons from her grandfather's waistcoat, and nineteen prewar stamps from India and Ceylon. She began to empty the trays still more rapidly. Three gold sovereigns in a leather bag. An orange stuck with cloves and tied with velvet ribbons; you never saw those now. The head of the "Madonna of the Chair," painted on ivory. A pewter plate with a date scratched on its back. Her prize books from school, with her name inside. A locket of garnets on a silver chain. A Spanish shawl, heavy embroidery on pink silk. A box from Italy inlaid with little colored stones and "Perugia" spelled in green. A bundle of clippings about the 1937 Coronation. Her father's letters to her, when she was still in school: "Dearest Girl . . ."

She stroked the striped Sicilian scarf and lifted it out of its tray and put it over her head. Mme. Arnaud grumbled at that locked trunk, when it had to be moved to and from the attic room. But she never dreamed of what it contained—not for one moment.

Miss Horeham sat down at the dressing table and solemnly regarded herself in the glass. Sometimes with that scarf on she looked like Ruth the Moabitess, and sometimes Bath-shebah, and sometimes even Rebekah, for Rebekah on seeing Isaac had put up her veil. But it was as Ruth that she fancied herself, a Moabitish woman with hoops in her ears and a red-green-black striped veil. "Dearest Girl," he had written when she was young; and how they had acted out the glorious stories—Samson and his traitress, and Boaz and Ruth. Well, it had all been harmless and a secret, and gave them the feeling that something rich was being lived at La Bella, something nobody knew. They had never read anything other than the Bible together. Not even the *Daily Mail*. And then his illness, and the slobbering, and having to shave him, for he wouldn't have anyone else, and even that wasn't the worst. In the end he hadn't known her, but then he opened his dying eyes and called her Ruth. He looked old and evil and cunning, going into his death. But he still knew her as Ruth, with hoops in her ears and the green-red-black striped veil.

It was only a Sicilian scarf, of course, bought on such an innocent holiday years ago. Staring in the mirror, she did not see her dressing gown or the yellow-gray curls. She saw her own eyes, until she was dazzled by the very sight of them. Everything else fell away. Her eyes were the center of the house, of the world. And there in the next room lay the Oxleys, and never guessed what Miss Horeham was really like. Mme. Brunhof never guessed, or Mr. Wynn. Nobody guessed at all. She smiled at herself, for of everyone in the house only Miss Horeham had favor in the sight of the Lord.

Oh, how they would all die if they knew! Oh, how they would all of them die!

Its Image on the Mirror

A SHORT NOVEL

What is love itself,
Even though it be the lightest of light love,
But dreams that hurry from beyond the world
To make low laughter more than meat and drink,
Though it but set us sighing? Fellow-wanderer,
Could we but mix ourselves into a dream
Not in its image on the mirror!
from "The Shadowy Waters"
William Butler Yeats

Its Image on the Mirror

I

My last sight of the house at Allenton is a tableau of ges-
ticulating people stopped in their tracks, as in those
crowded religious paintings that tell a story. Usually everyone points, and there are gross signs of doom and dismal
virtue: Judas counts his money, Daniel indicates the wall,
the Prodigal and his father are applauded by cheerful
servants. Our picture, on the afternoon of a July day in
1955, was this: my mother sat beside me in my car, the
back of which was filled with sweaters and winter coats,
the overflow of the moving. Behind us, at the wheel of my

parent's old Chevrolet, my father looked grim and aggrieved. He had been asked by my mother to keep an eye on her precious Staffordshire figurines. Across the street, the driver of a vanload of furniture bound for storage in Montreal slammed the doors. Half a dozen French-Canadian children straggled along the sidewalk. They are the new tide. French-Canada flows in when English-Canada pulls away.

The faces of the unknown children, like ours, are turned to the house. On the west lawn, where the copper beech has shed a few leaves, a tall priest in black points. We can see, through the trunk of the tree gone transparent, the statue of St. Therese of Lisieux that will stand in its place very soon.

Mr. Braddock, the real estate agent, opens the front door for a cleaning woman. We have never seen her before.

A gardener kneels before a row of stones, painting them white. Nearby is the pile of gravel with which the new owners of the house intend to kill the grass.

My mother says I saw nothing of the kind. She says the priest had called in the morning, but was nowhere around when we left. She says she remarked: "I suppose they'll have the typical institutional garden, phlox with white stones," and that I imagined the gardener because of that. As for Mr. Braddock and the cleaning woman, my mother had simply observed that the house was clean, and she hoped all those priests would find it clean enough.

Nothing remains now in Allenton to remind me of the past. I have been told that a bright aluminum-painted fence surrounds what used to be the lawn. The tree is down, and the gravel trodden into the dead grass. I do not have to see to remember the murmuring seminarists and their pale tormented faces. The windows of our house are shut tight in all seasons. Glassy white curtains cover the panes. On summer nights an unshaded light shines on the front porch, where the older priests sit in a row. They have kept the custom of the towns they come from, and they sit and rock and watch the cars passing by.

To be truthful, from home to institution wasn't an abrupt change. Even before the house was sold, before it became the dormitory annex of a seminary, it began to die. Three of the bedrooms were anonymous and empty, used as storage places. Ghosts moved in the deserted rooms, opening drawers, tweaking curtains aside. We never saw the ghosts, but we knew they were there. We were unable to account for them: no one had lived here but our family, and none of us had died in Allenton. The house was built for my parents, when they married, in 1913. It resembled the other Allenton houses of that period, with the two porches screened in summer and double-glassed in winter, and the lightning rod on the roof, and the Virginia creeper surrounding the windows, pressing behind the shutters. A hedge parted the lawn and vegetable garden. The house next behind ours was a farm, and our garden backed into a cornfield. Now the field is a development of bungalows, and I doubt if the farmhouse exists. Some of the bungalows are in Quebec and some stray over the border to Vermont, but nearly everyone in the development speaks French. When my sister and my brother and I were children we thought there was a difference in physical substance between people who spoke English exactly as we did, and the rest of mankind. I think my parents still believe it, for nothing else can explain the expression of honest dumb-foundedness that comes over my father's face when he meets someone decent, moderate, conservative and polite, and discovers that this acceptable person is not English or Scottish or Protestant—all that one can be; and I feel sorry for my father when this happens, for it seems hard to have your views shared by everyone around you all your life and then confounded in your old age.

My mother lived much as she ever had in the expiring house. There were flowers in the rooms, and a fresh book from the library beside her chair. She would never have tolerated the unmade bed, the picnic supper taken with television, the jam jar and mustard pot astray on the dining room table; but the ghosts moved on the stairs, and she knew that her existence was a draught of air too feeble to blow them away. When I visited my parents for a week-end, a ghost in my old bedroom watched me watching myself in the glass. It was not mischievous, but simply attentive, and its invisible prying seemed improper rather than frightening. My mother must have felt that way too. The ghosts outnumbered the survivors. Nothing could bring back Frank, my brother, killed in the last war, or Isobel, my sister, married, and in Venezuela, and equally lost.

My mother's selling the house to a religious order was a gesture of total renunciation. She pushed our past and our memories of Allenton as an Anglo-Scottish town over a cliff. It meant she would never be tempted to go back.

If she had been challenged about it, she would have said that it was a quick sale, and that since Allenton is all Catholic and all French-speaking now, what is one more dormitory, one more sleeping place for embryo priests? Once the sale was arranged we had to find an apartment for my parents in Montreal. My mother, unexpectedly old and trying, said she wanted to be near stores but away from traffic. She wanted sun, but preferred the ground floor. She did not want windows on a busy street and she did not want windows on a court. Before discovering this marvel, my husband and I had to invite my parents to live with us, and they had to refuse. My mother then sent Isobel a cordial note, explaining that the old house was sold, and asking if Isobel wanted any of the furniture, carpets, curtains, china or silver before they vanished, perhaps forever, into a storage warehouse.

My mother knew perfectly well that Isobel wanted nothing from Allenton, but the letter had one unexpected result: Isobel answered. She said nothing about spoons or teacups. Her vain and immature handwriting covered four sheets of paper. She talked about her two children, and her husband, and on the last page said that her husband was attending a medical conference in Boston in August, that she and the two boys were coming with him, and that we would all meet at my parents' lakeside cottage on Labor Day weekend.

There was something touching and innocent in Isobel's assumption that our parents still lived on a rhythm of school holidays, with Labor Day weekend at the lake the last episode of summer. My mother seemed bemused by the letter. She said it had been written with a cheap ball point pen, and that the paper didn't match the envelope. That was all she found to say about a letter from a daughter she had not seen, and scarcely heard from, in six years. Isobel is married to an Italian doctor none of us had then set eyes on. She seemed young when she left us, but now—I counted—must be all of thirty-three. My mother says "poor Isobel" when she mentions her just as she says of our dead brother "poor Frank."

When I say that Isobel's marriage was unfortunate, or that my mother was distressed by it, it is only because I am shy before words like "calamity," or "catastrophe" or "disgrace." Isobel had been married once before, and we had lavished our fund of disapproval on the first husband —the bumptious, the unspeakable Davy Sullivan. We were too worn out to insult Alfredo, even in secret. Nothing in mother's experience could account for that second marriage. She said she guessed Isobel had married an Italian because she wanted to live abroad; but if she wanted to travel all that much, my mother said, why not marry someone we could be proud of—an attaché of some kind? She could have been photographed with him and their normal-looking children on a Canadian-looking lawn, no matter where the government sent them. There was also the question of Isobel's happiness; I think my mother did care about it, and truly believed that only a Canadian—and not just any Canadian—was good enough. Look at the miserable girls who married Polish officers after the last war, my mother commanded! Were those girls happy now,

with the husbands drunk as owls every night of the week
in the White Eagle of Pilsudski Club? Look at the girls
who fell in love with the Free French and the Free Norwegians! Free was the word: every one of them had a
wife back home. It wasn't just that Isobel had deceived her
family, which never paid, but she had probably made herself wretched as well.

What my mother did not say aloud was that Isobel
had tricked us by not dying. She had been dying of a
kidney infection and we were told to pay our last visits.
Her face was smooth and round and babyish on the pillow.
Between puffed lids her eyes were slits. She had gone well
away from us by then and seemed amused at something
too personal to share. I thought she was telling me, "You
think you've always known all about me, but you don't
know this; you can't follow me here." Once I thought that
when Isobel died I would surely die too. I would kill her cat,
Barney, because no one else would look after him for her,
and I would sit in an armchair and close my eyes and
rest my hands on my lap and never move again. This
thought lasted no longer than the time it takes to see the
weather in the sky; for, in the space of the same thought,
cloud into cloud, I knew that Isobel's death would end the
problem of my sister forever, and that if she died I had
every reason to live. Her death would remove the ungov-
ernable daughter for my parents and the unattainable for
my husband. Dead-and-buried Isobel, under a heap of snow,
or a rectangle of grass, would be harmless Isobel, the
pretty Duncan sister, taken too soon to her Maker. We
cried, all of us, when we thought she was lost. We spoke
of feelings for her and for each other we have certainly
never mentioned since: and then Isobel recovered, and left
us all looking like fools.

She had met Alfredo in the hospital. He had nothing
to do with her case, and no business in her room. On a
gray June day we drove her to Allenton for her convales-
cence. She was docile and sweet, then, only half returned

from dying. She lay in a garden chair, and ate what was put before her, and looked at the books my mother placed in her hands. For a short time my mother had the submissive daughter she had always dreamed of. Then Isobel began taking short trips to Montreal to visit me, and at the end of August, during one of those journeys, she married Alfredo in the sacristy of St. Patrick's Church. She left for Caracas by plane the same day, after ringing and asking me, in a light fluty voice, if I would mind telling our mother she was married. I was pregnant with my second child then, and stupid with heat and summer; I said, "Alfredo who?" It was the fourth summer after the end of the war. It seemed to me I had waited years for life to begin and that the false start of after-war was all there had been to wait for. The shape of life was pressed on stones in the form of ferns and snails, immutable. Yesterday, tomorrow: stones had picked up the pattern and there was nothing I could change. Isobel had broken a stone. She was married (so was I), but she was leaving for Caracas: I was here.

"Well, at least she didn't turn Catholic," my mother has said since. My mother went to St. Patrick's to inquire, and thanked God for a small favor. There must have been a fair amount of messing round with priests, all the same; that was my father's contribution.

My mother was upset because Isobel must have been married in the clothes she had worn for her shopping trip to Montreal—shopping had been the pretext for the journey, and the lying girl had said she was meeting me. She was last seen wearing a green and white cotton frock and open sandals. She was carrying a straw bag. Her legs and head were bare.

"She wasn't wearing stockings," my mother said. "She wasn't even wearing a hat." She reflected on it, and then said, rather pathetically I thought, "Do you think Isa had just brains enough to get some stockings and buy herself a hat?"

"I can't imagine her wearing a hat," I said.

"Oh, that child!" my mother burst out. "As if Davy Sullivan wasn't enough to put us through."

Yes, I thought, and Alec Campbell, and Tom. It has so often been in my power to destroy my sister—to destroy, that is, an idea people might have about her—but something has held back my hand. I think it is the instinct that tells me Isobel will betray herself; there will always be the hurt face of her admirer turning slowly to me, as if to tell me, So you were the good one, after all. And then, because Isobel *is* my sister, there is the other restraint, for the vision of my sister delivered, my sister undone, is totally repugnant. When she flew off to Caracas I thought, Well, she will never want to see any of us again, but instead of rejoicing I felt as though my own life drained away with her. I was left face down on a beach with no one to get me to my feet but a muddling trio of husband, mother, infant son. Isobel was in romantic Caracas, which I began to construct, feverishly, as a paradise of coral islands. I could not have found it on a map, and confused it with Bermuda.

Six years later, when the Allenton house was sold, and my mother asked me to spend a weekend with her so as to help with the packing, my husband said, "Your mother ought to leave you alone. She's always after you for something." I answered meekly, "I know, but she only has one daughter now. There's only me." He could not know that her bothering me was a victory. I was the only daughter: I had won.

Tom was right; that weekend was a bother. There were the children to be left, and the long drive on crowded roads. Trust my mother to summon me on a weekend, with her wonderful certitude that life outside the family never matters, even if all life is just where you want to be—thronging the highways and beaches and eating-places. I found her in panic, for she had dawdled all summer as if the sale weren't taking place, and the need for moving unreal: now she had to pack and be out in three days. I kissed her, a bird peck on the cheek, and we began to work in silence. As I grow older I see that our gestures are alike. It touches me to notice a movement of hands repeated—a manner of folding a newspaper, or laying down a comb. I glance sharply behind me and I know I am reproducing my mother's quick turn of head. Our voices are alike. We have the flat voice of our part of the country; our r's fall like stones. I am pleased to be like her. There is no one I admire more.

We took down and folded green rep curtains bleached white in streaks. We rolled carpets that showed frayed bars straight through the weave. Removing pictures, we saw what the walls had been like. A breath would have crumpled the rooms. My father rescued rubbish as we threw it away. He made a private store of pots and pans, and the Elsie Dinsmore books, and a vegetable dish so cracked it could never be used for anything. "It will do for the church," he said. There are only a handful of Protestants in Allenton now, and most of the Old Presbyterians went into the United Church of Canada years ago. "Don't bother Father," said my mother sharply when I saw him walking resolutely out and toward the Old Presbyterian Church with an oil painting of a child feeding ducks under his arm. "He thinks that picture was a wedding present from his side of the family. Let him give it to the minister, if he wants to."

That weekend of packing must have been anguish for her. She was leaving the house she had lived in forty-two years, and the town where she had spent her life. She said not a word about it, and expected no embarrassing behavior from me. When it was over, and the vans were loaded, and two of them gone, she stood out on the porch, before the locked door, and handed the keys to Mr. Braddock.

She was small, commanding, and permitted no backchat. My mother has lived every day of her life as if it were preparation for some kind of crisis. You could look straight through her and find not a sand-grain of weakness or compassion or pity: nothing to start up emotional rot. She looked calmly past Mr. Braddock to the French-Canadian children loitering on the sidewalk.

"I don't know these children's names, and I don't know who their parents are," she said. "That's what Allenton has become. At least in Montreal I shall *expect* people to be strangers."

I wanted to put my arms around her, but even without Mr. Braddock she would have hated it, and it would have been wrong: it would have been an attempt to put myself in her place, think for her, sense what she ought to feel. This was the house of my childhood, but not my home. Here, I might have spent my life, creeping in my mother's small shadow, welcomed as companion and errand girl, despised as a sexual failure, if marriage, the only rescue possible, had not taken me away. I was twenty-four when it happened. It was a late marriage, in our terms. My husband thinks he married too young, but too young for him was almost too late for me. Twenty-one was the limit for girls, and my mother must have spent many anxious seasons wondering what would become of me. Isobel married Davy Sullivan when she was eighteen.

I brought out of our common past two dozen fish knives and forks my mother insisted I have, and a pile of children's books. In one of the books was a snapshot of Frank and Isobel and me sitting on the lawn, all three in dark woolen bathing suits. It must have been taken the summer of 1926. We look happy enough; I am thankful to say we look unremarkable. "Happy families are all alike," Davy Sullivan used to say, unpleasantly, because he thought we weren't happy, but pretending. "All's well with the Duncans" was one more of his taunts. I sometimes heard his voice, like a record, repeating, "Happy families are all alike, and all's well with the Duncans," and I thought Davy odious but clever until I opened Isobel's *Anna Karenina*. "Happy families are all alike" came from there.

It is just at the beginning, first thing on the first page. Davy wasn't clever about anything.

In the snapshot Isobel is chubby, flaxen-haired, the baby of the family. She was three years younger than Frank (grave and skinny here, aged about seven) and five younger than me. Even her baby face is secretive, although no one would think that except me. I pick up a book with her autograph inside, or a striped towel with her boarding school name tape, and I remember that she was evasive and stealthy, and that I used to imagine she knew something she was too careless or indifferent to tell. I believed that one day she would speak, and part of my character hidden from everyone but her would be revealed. She might have spoken, but our dialogue was cut short. Our family is open, blameless, and plain. Anything she cares to say, now, would be spiteful but harmless. Perhaps she has been silent because she respects us. I can't believe she is afraid.

"You people are going to haunt this house," said Mr. Braddock, as the advance guard of new occupants fanned out on the lawn. They were a priest, a gardener with a paintbrush and bucket of white paint, and a boy with a barrow of gravel.

"The house is full of ghosts as it is," my mother said pleasantly. "There wouldn't be room for ours."

The gardener began painting stones, and the boy spilled his barrow of gravel on the lawn. He raked the gravel into swirls and scrolls. How long did it take them to kill the grass? (My mother says I did not see this.)

The rector of the seminary climbed three front steps, paying his courtesy call. He stared with a cold suspicion my father fully rendered. My mother addressed the rector in unstressed French, and he replied in their curious English. This exchange in opposing languages was the extreme limit of mutual politeness and contempt. "Quebec Highlander," muttered my father, giving the old wartime invective for a priest. I was grown before I realized that the difference between my parents was apparent in the use of a phrase like this. My mother would never have said it.

"He's going to have the beech down," my mother remarked, as we were leaving. She sat in the car beside me and said, "The priest told me. He said so this morning. He says the leaves make a mess and the place is neater without trees." She began to speak about something else. I have seen her cry twice, once when Frank was little and said something dreadful about sex, and once when Isobel was dying. She wept as I imagine a doll could, with a still face, and a slow gathering of moisture on an eye so wide it might have been painted. She was dry-eyed, now, and scornful, holding her shabby alligator purse. We drove down the main street of Allenton, strange and bustling and full of people whose names my mother didn't know, hot in the hot afternoon, and presently she said, "We won't be getting down to the lake much any more." Now, at this I felt a shock of real nostalgic panic. We had spent all our summers there. We went to the lake every summer—every summer for years and years. "If Tom wants to buy it," my mother went on, "he can have first choice. Do you think he'd be interested?"

"He might be." I knew better. He was deeply attached to his family's summer house in Muskoka. He wanted a repetition of his childhood summers for his own children.

"He ought to have another look at the cottage," my mother said. "A buyer's look. He can think about it when you come down on Labor Day. We'll talk about it then. Tom can take his time. There is no great rush."

"Isa will be there," I said.

"Oh, yes, of course. Naturally Isobel will be there," said my mother, as if my sister came every year.

A car hooted behind me, wanting to pass, and I thought if that car has a Texas license Tom will buy the cottage. It had a Texas license, and I burst out laughing. I felt gay and light-headed. I said, "I'm just laughing at myself."

"I like to think you weren't laughing at me," my mother said.

We had lost my father miles back. He was driving like a snail because he was being careful with the figurines. I could imagine his plaintive face over the wheel. My mother suddenly said she had been trying to imagine the best thing in the world and it had taken the form of a dry martini. We stopped at the next place we saw and waited for my father. We were tired, and silly and innocent as girls. Those were the good times with my mother. They were rare, but when they occurred we were so close, so similar, that I would think, Life with her could have been all right; and I would remember everything I had done to make my marriage happen; just so that I could get away. My father caught up, and we three sat down at a shaky table covered with beer rings.

In my father's family women do not drink in public and men drink their beer at home. I could tell that he was wondering how it was that a woman as irreproachable as my mother could sit in this filthy atmosphere and ask her married daughter (another decent woman) if she thought the martinis would be fit to drink. We chose beer, and my father and mother suddenly fell silent and stared straight before them in a way I hope observers didn't consider too dramatic. For the first time in my life, I saw my parents holding hands. My father's hand lay on the table, and my mother placed her small freckled hand over his. It was the singularity of the gesture that made me uneasy. Their tenderness seemed a sign of their defeat. Searching for an excuse—why should they hold hands here?—all I could think was, All's well with the Duncans. Happy families are all alike. Frank was dead and Isobel gone and the house sold. I had been called Price for many years. I was Jean Price. I had four children, and although I wasn't tough enough to control them as mother had hers, they were mine. They were the Price children, another clan. I got up from the table and looked at postcards. When I turned back to my parents they were still staring straight before them. The public handholding had not been a mistake or an illusion: their hands were now palm to palm. No one was looking at them: I cast a quick glance about to make sure. I was cold with shame, and I remember saying to myself, I'm not like either of them, really. My children will be different too.

"Isobel wouldn't like this place. She wouldn't think anything of it," I heard my mother say. She stared round and back at me, the old madwoman, and said, "She would never have brought me to live here."

2

On Labor Day weekend we drove to the lake with our usual accoutrements. The car looked as if we had lived, eaten and slept in it all our lives. In the back seat, three of the children devoured an emergency picnic, while Hughie, the youngest, proud of his reputation for being carsick, tried his best to vomit into a plastic pot. My parents had gone down to the cottage a few days earlier, and Isobel and her family had been with them overnight. We made poor time because of the holiday traffic. I rang my mother from a filling station when we were still an hour away. "Don't hurry," she said pleasantly, as if we could.

At half-past one, with my children uproariously hungry again, we turned off the lake road onto our gravel drive. Beds of perennial flowers were picked out in thick colored wool. The sun striking off the lake made me blink. Parked so that we could not get by it was a caramel Chrysler with foreign license plates—Isobel's! We abandoned our own car behind it and the next thing I saw was a pair of child's underpants drying on a bush. Then Isobel came towards me leading a little boy who wore nothing but a shirt. I have forgotten what she said. Her tone was childish and light, and the brush of her cheek against mine like a whisper. We tried to introduce our children, but they were shy as animals. Suddenly shy as well, I looked down at her baby, and her thin hand.

My mother, following Isobel down the drive, walked in a strange way, as if she were wandering on spongy ground. Isobel's elder boy clung to her.

"This is Claud," said my mother firmly.

"Claudio," said my sister, making *Cloudio* of it.

The half-naked baby was Franco. I supposed he had been named for our dead brother, Frank. Claudio, who had evidently taken a fancy to my mother, strained up at her, gabbling incomprehensibly, and then fell into a hostile silence, sulking and hanging his head. He was a detestable little boy. Franco, all belly under his shirt, trotted close to my sister as he ran about, clad in his shirt, urinating with pride on the steps or in the flowers. My three elder children found this unbelievably funny. I expected Isobel to put a stop to it, but she was the mother one might have expected.

My mother wore an expression that might have been suitable if lightning had got in the house. When Alfredo appeared she could not speak. She could not as much as say our names. A gesture was all she could manage: here he is. I shook hands with the dashing doctor from Caracas who had carried my sister away. He was a shad fly of a man, dressed for a hot summer day in town. At lunch, he fretted about mosquitoes, and declared that he liked comfort and air-conditioning. In his opinion, the only places worth living in were Caracas, Rome, Mexico City, and New York. My mother had now lost any power to react normally. I think she smiled and nodded happily, as I certainly did. It is difficult to explain why, but an admission that one really liked New York was all of a piece with his towny shoes. We smiled and said we agreed with him, perfectly.

My children, sitting at their table across the room, sensed that something had gone wrong. The eldest boy, Jamie, stared thoughtfully at his bantam uncle-by-marriage. He knew, already, that Alfredo was something one must never become. Jamie then looked at me, to see if I agreed, and we had a moment of complicity before I told him sharply to turn around and get on with his food. My mother finally selected a tone. She asked Alfredo tenderly if Caracas was a social sort of place. Alfredo said it might well be, for all he knew, but that he was busy with his medical practice. "I am a busy man," he said, with a perhaps foreign emphasis on the "I." He had been at a university in the States—I think in California. His accent was not one my mother would like, but I doubt if he would have cared.

Franco and Claudio had refused to eat with the children. One sobbed, the other screamed, and their parents seemed to take it for granted we wanted them with us. An extra chair was squeezed in so that Claudio could sit next to my mother, while Franco sat on my sister's lap and picked bits from her plate with his fingers. He was now wearing the damp underpants I had seen drying in the bush. I wondered if the child had made the journey from Caracas in his underclothes. From across the room my Jamie began taking an interest again.

"Do you like sailing?" he asked Alfredo.

"Not on your lake," said Alfredo. "Too many speedboats."

"Do you like swimming?"

"Jamie, that's enough," I said.

"I like to swim where the water is clean and not too cold," said Alfredo. "I don't *object* to swimming if I have the conditions I want. Your lake is full of sewage because the land around is overdeveloped. Not only is the water here disgusting," Alfredo continued, addressing himself only to the child, "but the lake is too far north and too cold."

"I think so too," said Jamie, who had never been south of this cottage. He sounded like Tom. "But if you won't sail and you won't swim there's nothing to do around here."

"Jamie, do you want to leave the table?" I said. Tom and I both detest pert, precocious children; also, I was hurt to realize that Jamie was bored at the cottage. Our complicity vanished; I saw him in league with Tom, who would not buy the place. That "nothing to do" carried a familiar whine.

My sister said softly, "And so in the end he did nothing at all, but sit on the shingle wrapped up in a shawl." She was smiling to herself, as if alone in the room except for the unruly baby on her lap.

"Don't let that child eat all your lunch," my mother said to her. The ex-family favorite glanced at my mother, still smiling. She had become accustomed to the unshared reference, the solitary joke. I had not dared to look at Isobel until now. She was dry and frail as a leaf.

Alfredo and Isobel did not exchange a word or a glance. It occurred to me that the only contact in the room had been between Jamie and Alfredo.

Alfredo's eyes now went to the screen door. Outside the door, sitting on the floor of the porch, was Poppy Duncan, my dead brother's daughter. She was neither child nor grownup and, because we had tried to make her sit at the children's table, she had decided not to eat. She appeared to be wearing a hideous wig, for she had dyed her hair that summer and then cut most of it off. Alfredo was obviously the source of his sons' table manners: he held a slice of bread flat on his hand and buttered it as if he were painting it, and then, without asking my mother's opinion, carried this bread outside and offered it to Poppy. He sat down beside her on the floor of the porch. I had a view of their two heads. Poppy's was rusty-orange and slightly larger than his.

My mother said swiftly, "He might have taken it for granted we know Poppy better than he does."

"He likes girls," said my sister, smiling, eyes down.

My mother was less shocked by the meaning of the remark than astonished that anyone could find Poppy likable.

After lunch my father removed his hearing aid and

went to sleep. My mother lay back in a deck chair, and my husband and I sat at her feet. My youngest child had been put to bed, and the others, united for once instead of wrangling and quarreling, sat in a ring with the neighbor's children, the MacBains. They were charming, there, in the porch, playing jacks. The harmony wouldn't last an hour, but it made a pretty picture.

From the house came a crash and a roar: the Shostakovich Fifth.

"Turn it down, Poppy," said my mother, unheard. Poppy has always been a trial to us all. She has been a trial since her conception. When she came to Canada, a little thing of seven months, Frank was already dead, and Poppy's mother a war widow. The child's name is unfortunate, but she was christened in England. Her mother remarried years ago and went back there. Poppy used to think of her mother as a fairy princess. She would threaten to run away and join her. "Go, by all means," my mother would reply. "Go, if you think you will be welcome." My mother was always fair. She would fetch pen and paper and let Poppy sit at her desk. "Write and tell your mother when to expect you," she would say, and leave Poppy to it. Poppy must have thought she would not be welcome, for her letters were only of the "Dear Mother, I am fine" sort. When she ran away from camp or school, it was always back to my mother.

Poppy's mother gave her up when Poppy was still an infant. She talked to me about it and while she was talking she stabbed a pen in her hand. "There's nothing I can do," I remember her saying. "She's strong and I'm weak." She meant that my mother was strong. We stared at the blue hole below the cushion of her thumb, where the point of the pen had gone in. Poppy's mother hadn't a cent of her own, and was an incompetent girl. My mother had done the only thing possible.

Right or wrong, my mother has had the worst of it, for Poppy has been more scandal and strain than her three children put together. I saw next to nothing of her when she was growing up. She was at camp in summer and in boarding school all winter. There were stray periods when she had run away and we were looking for another school, and of course we had her about at Easter and Christmas. She is unlike any of us. At eleven she wore orange lipstick. Once, banished to a school in Vancouver, she was found by the police in Detroit. On this Labor Day weekend she was between camp and school. She spent the last days of summer mooning around, all dyed hair and bangle bracelets, playing Shostakovich and Sibelius and writing us up in her diary.

I felt, that afternoon, the closest feeling I have to happiness. It is a sensation of contentment because everyone round me is doing the right thing. The pattern is whole. Even Poppy, with her music and her vague adolescent longings and hates, seemed correct. I was proud of my children and pleased with my mother and husband. The Sunday papers lay on the grass. There was the slightly sad atmosphere that hangs in the air between summer and autumn. This may be our last weekend here, unless Tom buys the cottage. All at once my gaze fell on my sister, whom I had forgotten. She sat apart from the rest of us, on the dock, with her husband and her two monkey-babies. The husband had changed to swimming trunks; his clothes were neatly folded beside him, as if he were in a dubious hotel and could not trust the staff. He was a stray animal here. Daunted by our family likeness, our solidarity, he kept his things nearby. He lay prone, his face on his folded arms. One of the boys sat on Isobel's lap, the other in a moored rowboat.

My sister was straggly and unkempt—the aging bohemian. Her dress was saffron colored; she wore with it a belt that belonged to some other frock. On her feet were elaborate sandals with high heels. She seemed washed-out, rather than fair, and gaunt instead of slim. Isobel had never

cared for her untidiness. My mother had dressed her until
she rebelled, and I suspected that Alfredo chose her dresses
now. He must have dressed her with another woman in
mind: her dress and her shoes would have suited someone
Latin, plump, and jeweled. She wore her hair just as she
had at eighteen—long and straight, with a band to hold it
back from her forehead. When she was young, she had
reminded everyone of a Tenniel Alice. From the lawn,
against the luminous yellow haze on the lake, she looked
thin and sallow and all of a color with her saffron dress. As
for her sons, curly-haired, eyes too liquid, eyebrows too
dark, they might have been adopted. She and her family
were isolated and lost, and although I could not help comparing her children with mine, and Alfredo with Tom, I
was so filled with pity for her and her children that the pity
was a physical pain; I started up from the grass and went
toward her, pushed by the old feeling that she might want
me and need me. As I drew near, walking softly on the long
grass, her shad-fly husband rolled on his back, sat up, and
began to speak. Isobel laughed, shrugged, examined her
sandals, kissed the monkey-boy on her lap. Everything
about her spoke of wretchedness. She could laugh all she
liked, but I knew my sister: her tense shoulders were elo-
quent. It was incredible that Isa, blessed at the cradle,
should be unhappy.

I was intensely conscious of my appearance as I ad-
vanced, composing in my mind's eyes the picture they
would have of me. As my mother had been saying for some
time, I was nearer forty than thirty, but the signs of aging
that had begun so young with me stopped when Isobel
married. My hair had grown no grayer than it had been
when I was thirty-two; I had the same faint cobweb
lines from eye to temple I had noticed in my twenties.
I wore a blue denim skirt with zippered pockets, a white
cotton shirt, and tennis shoes. I wore a watch with a
plain strap, and if there was an aura around me it was of
Yardley talcum powder. I knew that my expression was

kindly and my waist slim. I looked like any other woman of my age and my condition. I was part of my mother and father, and my children were part of me. I had succeeded in that, and Isa had failed.

Isobel and her family looked like excursionists from a factory town in New England, plumped down on our dock by mistake. They looked like forlorn picnickers, hating the countryside, littering the lakeshore with beer cans, wishing they had gone to a movie instead. I would never have sought revenge for myself, for the past, but I had it now through my children, who would never be mistaken for anything except themselves; and that was true justice, or vindication—call it whatever it is. I was near enough now to hear Alfredo say "Why didn't you warn me about the food?" I heard Isobel's laughter, but not her reply. She saw me. The laughter stopped, her eyes darkened, and then I remembered how she had looked when she was dying. She summed me up. Her total tallied with mine, but failed to daunt her. My pride in my children was suddenly nothing. I was part of a wall of cordial family faces, and Isobel was not hurt by her failure, or impressed by my success, but thankful she had escaped. I approached; we spoke. Alfredo complained about the towel he had been lying on. He said it was too rough for his skin.

They left that afternoon. I think Alfredo had had enough. My mother made a mild suggestion he leave Isa and the children for a bit, but that brought on a puffed chest and the statement that Venezuelans do not abandon their wives. Heaven knows who or what that was aimed at. Everyone seemed to have a private perplexity, to judge from our expressions. We stood in a knot near the caramel Chrysler. Isobel was going, and had said nothing to me. She had not spoken at all. There was no limit to the size of the world and we would never find each other in it again. Their car vanished, and the world contracted. Left behind, the rest of us were a family again. The children began to rush about and quarrel as if released, and I heard Poppy accuse someone of reading her diary. No one answered. We had all read it, often.

"Funny little guy," said my husband, casually, as we walked back.

I was tempted to repeat what Alfredo had said about the food, but the realization that Isobel would expect nothing better of me—would expect me to gossip—kept me still. Besides, I knew what Alfredo had meant. At lunch, our parents had sat at opposite ends of the table. My mother, presiding over covered vegetable dishes, received the passed-along plate on which my father had placed a dry slice of salmon loaf. The vegetable dish covers were removed to reveal creamed carrots, and mashed potatoes piled like a volcano, with a pat of salty butter melting inside the crater. The ritual of mealtime mattered to us more than food. None of the women in our family could cook, and we felt that women who worried about what they were to eat or serve were wanting in character: I did bother about it, once, and even took a Cordon Bleu course, but then I had Jamie and lost interest in cooking. Nothing on a plate seems attractive after you have fed children and tried to push into their reluctant mouths puréed spinach and sieved yolk of egg. "Food" came to mean the soggy remnants of their cornflakes, or the sliced apple gone yellow. I had the habit of spooning up their leftovers—fruit salad from which they had carefully picked out with their fingers the slices of banana and maraschino cherries.

The day had turned cold, and we went indoors. The children were given their tea, tea moved into our Sunday night supper. My husband built a fire in the fireplace and after the children were asleep we sat round it.

"Do you think Isa is happy?" I ventured. She and Alfredo had not been spoken of since Tom's remark.

"I should think so," said my mother. "Why wouldn't she be?"

"I suppose she is, as much as most people," said Tom.

There was a depth of satisfaction under his voice. I think he has what he wanted in life. He wanted children, and he has them. He sees his own boyhood, which he says was happy, in our children's lives: the same kind of house, the same schools, the summer in the country. He has repeated his parent's cycle—family into family: the interlocking circles. I see the circles too, for happy families are all the same, and only the unhappy families seem different.

My mother said nothing for a minute or two. She frowned and stared into the fire. Then she told us that Alfredo was maniacally jealous of Isobel. Their servant had orders to report the telephone calls that came to the house when he was away. If a strange man looked at Isa on the street, Alfredo made a scene that went on all day. If Isa had to shop, or pay a bill, or take the children to the dentist, Alfredo went with her and waited for her in the car. As I had suspected, he chose Isobel's clothes.

"Did Isobel tell you that?" I asked.

"Not *she*," said my mother with pride. She was proud of Isa for keeping her secrets. No, an Allenton neighbor had gone to Caracas to visit her son. The son, who had known Isobel as a child, had tried to meet Isa and Alfredo, but Alfredo was impossible, he said. As for Isobel, she was so sloppy and untidy that she could not be invited anywhere. By a stroke of fortune, they had hired a cook whose last employer had been Alfredo. The cook had told all this, and it came back to Allenton and my mother. The most astonishing thing was not the story itself, which I might almost have put together without help, but that my mother had waited two years before telling it. "I thought it might have been just gossip," she said. "I knew some day I'd be able to judge for myself. Poor old Isa," said my mother quietly.

"She ought to put her foot down," said Tom. "She used to be tough enough."

"Maybe she doesn't mind," I said. "Maybe that's why she married him, so she'd have somebody to think for her, and make all the decisions for her," but everyone laughed at that, and my mother said, "Don't complicate a simple situation." If we are to assume that Isobel likes having her dresses chosen by Alfredo and keeping servants who spy, then we get to what my mother calls "the unnecessary side of life." My husband probably agrees. He would never be the one to complicate a simple situation, either. "Bad things don't happen to decent people," he once said to me, seriously, when we were both of us much younger.

"Funny little guy," said Tom again, vaguely, perhaps bored with it now.

"He's not little," said dreadful Poppy, suddenly speaking up from a couch, where, lying on her stomach, she was reading the comics spread on the floor. It was odd how one forgot that child, then suddenly there she was—loud as life, saying her piece. "He's taller than Aunt Isobel, and she's tall."

"I didn't mean that the gentleman was short," said Tom, who always talked to Poppy in a mocking pedantic way. "Alfredo is quick, nervous, and thin, and his constant hopping around gives him a grasshopper look that—"

"He's better looking than you," said Poppy, turning a page.

"Poppy, you are a horror," I said. "Besides, it isn't true."

"Thanks," said my husband.

"Anyway, that's what I'm going to be when I grow up," said Poppy.

"Handsome?" my husband said.

"No," said Poppy, swinging round and sitting up on the couch. "Married to some person like Alfredo."

"I don't doubt that," my mother said.

"But first I'll fall in love," said Poppy.

We all laughed as if it were a fate we were fortunate to have escaped. I tried to meet my husband's eyes, to see what it had been for him to have Isobel here again; but he was already thinking about something else. He was probably trying to find the right words with which to refuse the cottage. When the words came, finally, they were Alfredo's. "I think the place is overdeveloped now," he said. "And the water's not too clean."

"We're all still alive," my mother answered.

I blame Alfredo unfairly. Tom would have turned it down in any case. Every inch of shore is built on now. The lake is criss-crossed with speedboats, radios scream, there is a shoddy camp for children at the far end of the lake; although none of that was mentioned, I knew Tom thought the value of the place was dropping every year, and that something should be knocked off the price for a son-in-law. He didn't say so. Nothing was said, after that day. The less said the better, always; and, as my mother had pointed out, we were still alive.

3

When our father caught Frank reading *The Yellow Fairy Book* down at the lake one Sunday, long ago, he snatched the book and threw it in the water. Frank must have been ten or eleven then. He was the only boy, and our father was afraid he would become girlish under the influence of two sisters. My brother had been a pretty baby with yellow curls, our mother's pet, but when he was three she suddenly relinquished him, saying she knew nothing about the upbringing of sons. His curls were shorn, and our father took him over. He said Frank had got off to a bad start, but that he, our father, was going to make a man of him. Frank must have had a miserable time. He was an undistinguished little boy, slow in his reactions, rather dull. Although suspicious of Isobel and me, he was a born dupe, and we teased him wickedly.

Our father had only a short period in which to admire the product of his training. Frank was killed young. I suppose he was manly enough to please our father, but during the very few years he had of life as a man he seemed to me severe rather than strong. There was something disapproving and spinsterish in his behavior. He was on the side of discipline and hanging and all the rest of that—not brutally, but as disappointed elderly women sometimes are. When he was angry his voice became tight and sharp. Far from resenting the past, and our father's heavy hand, he seemed to be grateful. I often heard him boast about his upbringing, and describe broken promises, the supperless nights, the frequent beatings, with self-satisfaction, as if they had made him the excellent person he was.

Those beatings, so alarming in retrospect, never disturbed our family life. Like *The Yellow Fairy Book* they sank below the surface. Hearing Frank catching it in an upstairs room, I never pitied him, but was simply glad I was not a boy. His punishments were a masculine ritual, like a religious mystery. I remember our father going round the house, closing the windows so that the neighbors wouldn't hear, while Frank, crying before he was touched, howled incoherent tear-laden promises from cellar to attic. He never tried to run away and never tried to hide. I wish I could say that compassion or loyalty had kept Isobel and me from tormenting and betraying him, but his nervous rages made us laugh, and Isobel was particularly skilful at making him lose control. He was the weeper in our dry household. "The more you cry the less you ll pee," said our beautiful sister in her elegant voice. That was because no amount of punishment could make him stop wetting his bed.

Isobel ruled Frank. She was three years younger than he, but twice as quick. She spent her pocket money on herself, and then appropriated his. In Frank's books you will find Isobel's name. She went through a period of signing in a round back-slanting hand, never using capital letters, and drawing globes instead of dotting her *i*'s. That was a sign of vanity, our mother said. She never failed to point out some flaw in her best-looking child, but her tone was complacent. Now she implied that Isobel could afford to be vain. Vain or not, she was persistent: in one of Frank's old books I found curly lower-case "isobel duncan" twenty-seven times.

It was our mother who used to buy those Christmas albums from England—the boys' stories that were supposed to make a man of Frank, and the boarding school tales for Isobel and me. The girls' books, solemnly read by Frank, contained stories of plucky children named Gillian and Monica. The illustrations had them rushing in a half crouch with field-hockey sticks in their hands and cantaloupe hats on their innocent heads. They were honest girls, if plain, and they had our brother's entire approval. He may have wanted his sisters to be more like Gillian and Monica —wholesome and fair instead of annoying and rude. Years later when I met Frank's bride, Poppy's mother, I remembered the girls in the books, their speech, their spines, their upper lips, and saw he had carried his old admiration on into love. What fascinated Isobel in the English stories was the unfamiliar slang, which seemed to us pallid and coy, and the obsession with eating. "They must be half starved over there," she said, with sympathy. Nothing less than national famine could account for the delight in jelly and custard and little pieces of cake.

I don't know why our mother wanted us to steep in books so removed from Canadian life. She may have been trying to counteract the comics and the radio—the American influence. As long as I can remember there has been a preoccupation with that. Also, in those days being English-minded was respectable. In my Allenton public school I sang:

> Oh dearest island far away
> Beyond the ocean wide
> Our hearts are true to thee alway'
> Whatever may betide.
> We love our own dear native land
> Home of the brave and free

But we are part of England
The ruler of the sea.

Anything from England was elegant. The newspaper
photograph of the chaste engagement kiss exchanged by
the Duke of Kent and Princess Marina was shown to Isobel
and me and compared with those disgusting creatures
embracing in Hollywood. When the time came for us to
marry, our mother implied, we would know how to behave.
My mother may have had more fantasy in her nature than
I suspect, all the same, for she did buy us the fairy books.
When Isobel asked her point-blank, once, if mermaids existed, she replied without hesitating that they certainly did,
but not in Canada. I believed it briefly, and Isobel believed
it for years. She was confident it was only a matter of finding the right country. Isobel and I must have been dumb
little girls. My children would never have asked the question, or accepted my mother's reply. There is no special
country, and they were born knowing it. They inherited
from me the assurance that there are no magic solutions.
They were not to inherit the house at Allenton, or the cottage at the lake, but I did give them that.

It was when I brought our old books out of Allenton
that I thought of all this. I remembered, for instance, that
I had once believed that planets were small and cold, and
melted like ice cubes. An instant later I knew I had never
thought anything of the kind, but that *Isobel* had. The
truth was I had preferred the Monica-Gillian stories and
scarcely ever finished reading a fairy tale in my life. A
prince of a country: what country? Which castle? I never
understood; I was always putting myself in my sister's
place, adopting her credulousness, and even her memories,
I saw, could be made mine. It was Isobel I imagined as the
eternal heroine—never myself. I substituted her feelings
for my own, and her face for any face described. Whatever
the author's intentions, the heroine was my sister. She
was the little Mermaid, she was Heidi; later she was

Gatsby's Daisy. She was Anna Karenina with the velvet
dress and the little crown of pansies on her head.

"isobel duncan," twenty-seven times: what a vain,
silly child she must have been! Yet when I traced her signa-
ture with my finger I felt the old unquietness, as if I must
run after her into infinity, saying, "Wait, I am not the person you think at all." Even if I were to catch her, the meeting would be incomplete, like the Labor Day disaster at
the lake. Even when we were young I silenced her. She
would catch my eye (the hopeful, watching, censor's eye)
and become silent, "behaving," as our family called it, and
nothing could bring her back except my departure. People
said I was a heavy presence for Isa to support. She was
another person when I wasn't there. I don't know why. I
loved her.

My children fell on Isobel's books (we might as well
call them hers, since her name is everywhere). We went
through an old-book period until the children were bored. I
read aloud, and that was good for me. Addressing my
audience of small, intent faces, I lost Isobel's perception
and held onto my own. Mine told us that fairy stories are
stupid and a bore. My children liked a few. They liked
best a story about a woman surpassingly beautiful (Isobel
again) married to a man wretchedly poor. The husband,
downcast because he cannot give his wife the gowns and
jewels her beauty deserves, meets an old man in a magic
shop in one of those unexplained forests. The old man
offers him a purse that can never be emptied of gold in
exchange for the husband's sense of beauty and the wife's
sense of humor. The husband accepts. He can buy his wife
the most exquisite dresses imaginable, but her absence of
humor permits her to go about like a peacock, while the
husband, who now lacks all feeling for beauty, finds her
only absurd. At last they take the purse back to the forest,
reclaim their lost senses, and live happily ever after.

"Did they keep the jewels, though?" Jamie asked.

Was it only the humorless woman that made me think

of Isobel? The husband was surely a man I had known.
That man would have kept the purse. He was mean to the
marrow; and if I had been in the story I would have advised
him to keep the purse, because my sister had little humor to
lose or regain. It is one of the things we can say about
people whose characters differ from ours: they have no
sense of humor, they don't know what it is to worry, they
have never been unselfish. I said all of that about her, once.
I remember saying, "She can't have much sense of humor,
or she wouldn't keep falling in love." I was the humorless
one then; I can see myself, glum-faced, apprehensive,
barely in sight of my sister's secrets, creeping round the
edge of her life. She never asked me to worry about her.
Except once, she never asked anything of me except to be
let alone.

Her humorless love was for Alec Campbell. He would
have kept the purse. I can see him any day of the year, for
he lives not far away and is assistant headmaster of
Hughie's school. Sometimes he drives by, and I catch a
glimpse of his failed poet's face concave with discontent,
and the Macintosh scarf above the collar of his coat. (His
mother must have been a Macintosh; he would always be
punctilious about details like that).

Last autumn he and I had an interview about Hughie.
The school sent for me. Why should a child with plenty of
pocket money steal?

We talked about Hughie as if we had never met.
Gradually our tone changed, as if the room had been filled
with witnesses, and the witnesses were disappearing,
leaving us free to speak. He tried to set a tone of comrade-
ship: we are modern, we are not stuffy. He is modern in
the doom-laden manner of the 'thirties. To him the Spanish
war is going on. *Ash-Wednesday* was published recently,
and Spender and his friends are mischievous leftwing
sprites. Years ago his Englishness in Montreal was an
asset. He assumed a cultural superiority I am certain he
felt. He was politically important: if he had not actually
fought in the Spanish war, he had surely thought about it.

I am positive he was somewhere near the Spanish frontier part of the time. I expect he wouldn't want his old Spanish feelings known, now. He is assistant headmaster of a conservative school. He has a pinched, bewildered look, as if the apple had been snatched away. I don't pity him. He must have wanted everything he has—this desk, and this room, and the colored picture of the Queen in full fig on the wall, and the black-and-white picture of the founder of the school. Above Alec's head is a framed text of the school founder's moral code: "Let me do my duty always for I shall pass through this world but once." Seeing Alec sitting between the Queen and the Founder I saw Isa defeated, Isa betrayed, and I thought, Be unhappy, you deserve it, you built your unhappiness—the little worms gnawing the closed box.

"How are your kids?" he said.

"Growing," I said. "As for Hugh, you seem to know more than I do."

"It's funny," he said, "how quiet the town is now. The city's cleaned up. This mayor's made a difference. The men with the big cigars have gone back to the States. I'm just as glad," said my sister's love, suddenly one with the creed of the Founder. His children are grown. At least one must be in college.

"Kids are quieter now," I said, meaning people in their twenties.

He smiled the rueful smile of the tamed rebel. He was well in his middle-life when Isa loved him, but I expect he thinks she was part of an extreme and heedless youth. "*You* weren't noisy," he said. He may have wanted to lead the talk on to Isobel, but I had to get away. I know something I could tell him, because I know what she became. I saw her on Labor Day weekend, 1955. Why should I tell Alec anything? He never confided in me. Besides, think of the absurdity of our conversation, if we'd tried having one: a failed poet and a middle-aged matron on the subject of love.

Once I followed Isobel down a busy street during the

noon rush hour. It was a hot April day, I think in 1944. I
remember the moist heat, the snow melted and rushing in
the gutters, and the winter clothes weighing pounds on
one's back. My sister wore a belted raincoat. Her ankles
were thin and her shoes fitted badly. She stumbled along
in her careless way as if she had never been shown how
to walk. I remember that a man turned to stare at her. It
shocked me to have him look at my sister, for I shared the
Allenton belief that the purity of a decent girl showed in
her demeanor, and that no man, however ill-mannered,
could make a mistake. Isobel had our family features, after
all, even though she had come out of the mold better than
Frank or me. Why should a man look at her and not at
her sister?—not that I wanted him to! Isobel seemed childish, younger than her age. She was a child in grownup
clothes—a corrupt, untidy child. Men who knew her
slightly found her enchanting. Her love for Alec Campbell
was known, but because he was older than Isobel he was
blamed. Corrupted innocence had a quality of attraction I
could not understand, believing, as I did, that only prosti-
tutes and movie stars provoked desire. She told me once
that men sometimes spoke to her on the street. It was never
the compliment she might have heard in a Latin country,
but a puritan insult, or an obscenity, as if the attraction of
her child's face aroused resentment and hate. That day, she
stopped and turned and saw me. It should have been easy to
smile and talk. I could have said, "I've been trying to catch
up with you," but she would have known the truth, which
was "I am trying to catch you." "Come on," she said, that
day, and we walked on together, Isa the besieged, I the
sister-pest.

    It should have been easy, but I *was* her sister, and that
was the barrier. There was between us a wall of family
knowledge. No people are ever as divided as those of the
same blood; yet we were alike, and our sameness was
stamped on our faces and spoke in our breath: Eastern
Canadian. Protestant, Anglo-Scot. The seed of our char-

acters came from another continent. Like the imported
daisies and dandelions, it was larger than the parent plant.
Flowering in us was the dark bloom of the Old Country—
the mistrust of pity, the contempt for weakness, the fear of
the open heart.

In those days, Isobel and I lived in Montreal. It was
wartime and our husbands—Tom, and Davy Sullivan—
were overseas. We could have lived the life our mother, in
Allenton, suggested when she said, "The girls are up in
Montreal with war jobs." It could have meant sharing an
apartment, attending the same Red Cross meetings, and
baking cakes together to send our husbands. To our mother,
war was a good occasion for everyone's keeping busy. For
Isobel and me it was an excuse to leave home, and for Isa
to get away from home and husband and me. If I think
the word now—war—it is just emptiness, empty streets.
War is an old house with the furniture out and the hangings down and the women left to click their heels along
the floor. The day I followed Isobel was the day of my
twenty-seventh birthday. I thought she might say something about it, but I suppose she forgot. That night I saw
a spider's web of lines take form at the corner of my eyes.
I saw it growing. I got up to take aspirin because I had a
headache, and I leaned my head against the mirror of the
medicine chest. I drew back, looked at my face, and I saw,
spreading, the indelible web.

Was it that night or another I knew that news of my
husband's death would be a release? That any news would
do, providing it put a stop to the emptiness of the city, the
passage of time, the length of winter? My nights were long
and uneasy and full of ugly thoughts. Daytimes I was busy
and sensible as my mother would have wished. I worked in
the industrial research office of a railway. I painted sewers
and waterworks on maps of cities. It was fine detailed work
that strained my eyes, and must have been responsible for
my headaches at night. Apart from my work, I had a busy
life. Twice a week I went to meetings of my war-work

committee. There, I often sat near Alec Campbell's wife. My sister's lover's wife: those two possessives terminated in the person of Bitsy Campbell, short and merry, with a head of sheared curls, like a wig of Persian lamb. She was named Bitsy because she had been unable to say Elizabeth as a child: I can't think how many times she explained it, or how important she seemed to consider the explanation. She had been one of the dimpled girls of the 'thirties. Her mouth was a narrow bow, and her eyes blinking and bright. Bitsy Campbell and I wrapped each other up in bandages (what to do after the air raids) and once we collected salvage in her car. While we drove up and down wintry streets collecting newspaper and old pots and pans, my sister was somewhere with Bitsy's husband. I was swollen with my secret: I knew. I realize now that Bitsy knew too. She must have known. She may not have realized the enemy was my sister, but her nails were bitten to the skin and her dimpled face was frozen and hard. She had dignity, all the same; she collected salvage and got ready for air raids and kept her troubles to herself.

I wrote to my husband every Sunday, Tuesday and Thursday. Saturdays I sent him either a box of candy or five hundred cigarettes. Sometimes he wrote asking me to post parcels to Dutch or English families who had been kind to him. I was conscientious about this. I washed my clothes and shampooed and set my hair twice a week. I spent one weekend a month at Allenton, and dined with my husband's married sister every two weeks. Sometimes I was invited to a party by a girl named Suzanne Moreau, the only friend in the world Isobel and I had in common. Suzanne was even stranger to me than my sister, but as there was no blood tie between us I expected her to be odd. She accepted me as she thought I was, whereas Isobel (turning and finding me behind her on the street) never laid eyes on me without wishing I were someone else. At Suzanne's parties I would see my own sister in the room, among strangers, and she would treat me as if I were just anyone. I would go up to her then and insist on talking about home, giving her news of Frank, forcing her to recognize me as kindred if she would not let me into her life. I wanted her to say, You and I are alike, and we are not like any other person in this room. But, of course, she never did.

I wish I could say I had spent those years, when I had time and a vacant mind and freedom to do what I liked, learning something useful. I think with astonishment that I complained I had time on my hands. No matter how busy I was, I still had time. I could have learned a foreign language: Suzanne and Isobel both tried Russian, and at Suzanne's I met a Red Army officer who was later arrested in his own country—an event that made us feel close to history. I could have attended evening classes in world literature. It would have improved my mind. Unlike my sister and brother I had not been sent to college, and I was ignorant. I might have read the newspaper and mapped the progress of the war with colored thumbtacks. None of it interested me. In those days I had one pursuit, and that was my sister's life. No mystery could have drawn me as much as the mystery of the plain rooms she lived in. No romantic story of my own (if ever I'd had one) tormented me as much as her story with Alec Campbell. Her denial of me was as entire as she could make it without an open breach. I know what she thought of me, and even now, knowing I have succeeded and she has failed, I am still troubled. She was wrong about me, but this is what she thought: she thought I was flat-minded, emptily optimistic, and thoroughly pleased with myself. She despised my safe marriage to a man my mother liked, and my war work, and even my job. I was the pattern of life discarded, the route struck off the map, the possible future. She walled herself away from me. There were gaps through which I could come in; there were times when, shameless, I forced my way. When she was ill, for instance, in the depths of one of her winter bouts of tonsillitis, I would hear about it in a letter from Allenton. I would remember that Isobel had always doctored her colds with a special honey from a shop in the east end of the city. I would spend my lunch hour traveling to and from the shop by tram. I would stop off and buy her a magazine, and arrive, finally, my hands cramped with cold, bearing the honey and the magazine as an excuse for my presence. Isobel might be up, smoking (the worst thing in the world for her throat, and I would tell her so) wearing a flowered crêpe dressing gown too short for her long legs. Most of her clothes looked as if they had belonged to someone else first, like the cut-down dinner dresses and ratty fur bits women passed on to their maids. The very sight of me, cold and sniffling, seemed a reproach. She would say, in a kind of comic despair, "Oh, why do you bother? It isn't a command, if I once say I like something." Her voice was nervous and rapid, and a little hoarse because of her bad throat. She would laugh, but her laughter was false. I think she knew it, then. She must have sensed it. I had to bother. I warmed my hands at her life. I cherished any reason for visiting her apartment, staring at the Matisse drawing torn from a magazine and pinned to the wall, seeing the envelopes of letters, the harsh wartime paper of letters from overseas, the ends of cigarettes she had smoked with a stranger, the four yellow tulips drooping in a milk bottle on the window sill. In illness she was weak. She had been delicate as a child—she and Frank were what our old Allenton doctor called TB types—and she gave up easily. Feverish, depressed, she could not prevent my changing the water in the milk bottle, emptying the ashtray, rinsing the sticky beer-smelling glasses I found in the kitchen. She must have sensed that I was drawn, curious, although I made it seem so ordinary—one sister visiting another.

"Are you moving again soon, or do you think you'll stay for a while?" I asked, keeping busy, chattering.

"I don't know. It depends."

She worked for a real-estate firm with one foot outside

the law. She changed apartments often—it was part of her job. Isobel signed the lease, and the firm then sublet the apartment, furnished. Moving was easy for her. She owned nothing except a coffee pot and a cat named Barney. Barney owned more than she did: he had a cushion, a tennis ball, a cake tin, a plate, a teacup, and pieces of string to which Isobel had tied buttons. When she moved, she took Barney and Barney's possessions and the coffee pot and her clothes, and left everything else behind. She left magazines, books, cups, plates, can openers, paper napkins, bottles, hand lotion, Kleenex, needles and thread, shoe polish, scissors, and ashtrays. She did not keep or collect the odds and ends that seem to me, now, the symbol of women: I mean the chocolate box containing lipstick brushes, hair curlers, imitation pearls, lighters without wicks, a glove, a stamp from Finland. She did not keep buttons, or match folders with something scribbled inside. I had all of that then, and have it now. I cannot throw away the single earring for fear I might afterward discover its mate. I am sure that the left-hand blue suede glove will be returned to the Lost and Found department of the store where I think I left it three years ago. Well, she and I were very different. Our friends were different too.

When I remember all the foreigners Isobel knew I wonder why I found them so strange. There are so many around, now, since the last war. The Germans have their own newspaper, the *Montrealer Nachrichten*. In those days, a foreigner was either a workman or a refugee. Now, of course, it is quite different. My husband has German and Belgian and Norwegian colleagues—all thoroughly decent, with charming wives. Our children have been taught One World (although not *too* much). They have learned that a tailor in Oslo is the same as a tailor in Montreal, and I suppose believe it. I know that an engineer from Oslo is just the same as an engineer from Montreal. He gets just as drunk. His children are as spoiled. His wife disappears from the party to have a good cry in the bathroom, and some other woman has to fetch her and bring her back, murmuring, "He didn't mean it"—just like one of us. If I were to meet one of Isobel's friends now I might not find him so odd. But then! She knew Greeks, Italians, refugees, Jews; people from the north end of the city who could not pronounce "*th*" and never would. She knew French-Canadians—not foreign, but young, sullen and blasphemous; my generation, but a class unknown to me.

In Isobel's apartment, with honey in my hand, my excuse for being there, I encountered her friends. I remember the faces full of mobility and impatience, the bad accents, the false promises, the talk of getting away. It was never clear where anyone was going, but to hear them go on there wouldn't be anyone left here the minute the barrier of war was up. Those faces, those ambitions, my mother would have dismissed at once. Such people were unplaceable, and that was that.

To Isobel's friends I was wonderfully placeable. I see myself arriving and I see myself in their eyes. They imagine the world of bland blond faces I have come from; they invent my evenings of movies and innocent dinners with the girls from my office. I see myself arriving, and finding my sister up, smoking. One of her friends sprawls on the unmade bed. He is a dark boy of twenty. Why isn't he in uniform, I think, enjoying my mother's certain reaction. It may have happened dozens of times; it may have happened once. There are years between then and now. I have four children, and Isobel vanished to Venezuela in 1948. Some people think she died in a sailing accident (her companion was drowned that time) and others think she died of a kidney disease, and some confuse us, thinking that Jean made a bad marriage, or Jean is dead. They have forgotten who was good and who was bad. This is a small memory, of no importance: one sister visits another. Words are omitted, and the wrong things said—wounding, hopeless, inevitable.

Say that it happened once, my arrival on a winter day

with the jar of honey and the magazine. I leave my coat to
shed its snow on the radiator in the hall. Isobel's apartments are all the same: hall, arch, living room, cube of
kitchen, smell of paint, plaster falling like snow. I step out
of my snow boots and pad into the living room in stocking
feet. Isobel throws me her scuffed moccasins which are
dirty and too big for me. She wears knitted after-ski socks
on her feet and looks ridiculous, with the printed wrapper
on her back. My eyes water, my nose runs. This is a bad
climate for women. There is the friend, young, unknown,
sure of himself, shedding ashes on the floor.

"That your sister?" he says, or, "I didn't know you had
a sister." Isobel might have spared me that.

Isobel's sister, Jean Price, sits down, crosses her
ankles, clasps her hands, smiles. She is not rude, and says,
How do you do? The stranger takes her in. She is shorter
than Isobel, has small feet, is neater. Her hair is a sensible
length (Isobel's straggles over the wrapper) and she is
well polished, as if the surface of body, hair, skin, eyes,
nails, were of a single substance, a thin shell. There is a
faint web of lines at the outer corner of each eye, but no one
but Jean has seen them. Isobel makes coffee, and pours me
a cup. She stands, feet apart, and gives me the cup without
a saucer. She does this with a grand air, as if bestowing a
treasure. Suzanne Moreau has said that Isobel really thinks
she is giving something splendid when she hands one a
cup of coffee or a light for a cigarette. Suzanne has said
that Isobel is lavish; she has painted a portrait of my sister curiously decorated, trailing feathers and loops of
colored stones. The face in the picture is ugly and sharp.
Isobel in the picture reminds me of a bird; Suzanne has
called it "Personnage aux Plumes."

"Well, I'm sure it's very interesting," I said when it
was shown me.

No one has ever painted me as a personage with
plumes.

Isobel's sister, unlavish, is decent in an old-rose cash-

mere sweater and matching cardigan knitted by an aunt in
Scotland. She wears a brown tweed skirt, pearls (husband's
family's wedding present) and husband's fraternity pin.

"So you're Isobel's *sister*?" Mocking little face.

"I'm afraid I am. She certainly keeps her family in
the dark." Flat, the flat Allenton laugh. Isobel gives me a
look. The friend, suddenly impatient, wants me to go so
that he can get on with his conversation. When I am there
Isobel will not speak. Into this social vacuum (I shall not
go) I make conversation. I speak of the season; of my
job. They've never had a girl in that job before. It used to
be reserved for graduate engineers. My husband was in
that department, but after the war I don't think he'll go
back. It will seem tame after everything he's been through.
What do I do? Well, I take industrial maps of all these
cities and . . . its painstaking work. If I keep on, I shall have
to get glasses. The fluorescent lighting is bad. Some people say it makes you depressed. A man I know lost his sight.
A man I heard about tried to kill himself with iodine.
Some people have been in the same department thirty years
and they say they've definitely been more depressed since
the fluorescent lighting was put in. They can't change it
now. With a war on, where would they get anything else?

"God, you sound like Mother," my sister says.

The young man seems to become larger at this. He
relaxes, smiles, scatters more ashes on the floor. He asks
me questions now: what do I feel about the Russians?
Not what do I think, mark you: he takes it for granted
that I am all instinct and prejudice. He fancies I am an earnest conservative and hopes I am a Protestant bigot. He has
heard about them, but thinks they will soon be extinct.
Isobel, silent, making faces when she swallows coffee because it hurts her throat, is no help to me. Panic. I fall back
on my mother, on her innocent assumption that the other
person is waiting for her to set the tone. Something new
enters my manner. I sit up. I examine him, kindly. The
stranger feels it. My manner fills the room: whatever it is,

it will daunt him all his life. His father is a tailor on Tupper Street. He never got beyond public school. He has a talent for poetry, but who has not? His father is a chauffeur in Vancouver, but no one in Montreal must know. He was in a reformatory from the age of fourteen. His sister has an illegitimate child. Vicissitudes, the troubles we call handicaps, rise like waves. He is a German refugee and his father was a professor of philosophy but he is nothing under a kind Canadian stare. He will never make it; if he marries, his children will never fit in.

Do you see how difficult it was? And here was I, anxious to be friendly, quite without pride. No wonder my sister despised me. In the end we were all three apart, for inevitably Isobel became impatient with the cringing stranger too. But the greatest distance was between us, the sisters. In the end I said something petty or aggrieved, and put on my coat and boots and went back to my office. All afternoon I would think, she didn't even thank me. I would tell my mother about it next time I spent a weekend in Allenton. I would tell the whole story, ending with, "She didn't even say thanks."

"Isa is selfish," my mother would say, with the complacency that meant Isobel could afford to be. "Looks aren't everything," she might add. That made it worse. Isobel lives in Venezuela now, in a climate I can only imagine. I think of her in winter and darkness, in the black January of Montreal. When I dream of her she stands bareheaded, her coat flying open. She wears her fur-topped Russian boots, and holds a handbag slung over one shoulder by a buckled strap. The face is evasive, turned away. She has nothing to say. She will not speak to me out of her death, or out of my dreams, where, in theory, I ought to have things as I want them. She walked toward me out of the dark once: I was about to say, "She looked like that the first time I saw her"—I don't know why, for we had been seeing each other all our lives. The city was silent and abandoned; nothing moved. Because of the gasoline ra-

tioning there were few cars at night, and after a fall of
snow the streets were white and untouched as country
roads. I was plodding westward along Sherbrooke Street
after a dinner with my husband's sister. My head was down,
against the wind. The wind dropped, and I looked up and
saw Isobel and Alec Campbell. They emerged out of the
dark and took form as a couple. Isobell was tall as he. She
listened to something he was telling her. They leaned in-
ward as they walked, as if both had recived an injury and
were helping each other stand up. Isobel's face was a
flower. Everything wary and closed, removed and mistrust-
ful had disappeared. I wondered what he was telling—he
was so tweedy, plaid-scarved, ordinary. He was an ordinary
looking man, but that made their love affair seem all the
more extraordinary, as if there were something I should
see, clear as morning. Alec was secretive, like Isobel. They
had that in common: I imagined they told each other that
they were special, like no lovers who had ever existed.
Whenever I tried to imagine the conversation of lovers it
was like that. I was twenty-seven and married but fanciful
as a little girl. I had an idea about love, and I thought my
sister knew the truth. Until the time of my own marriage
I had sworn I would settle for nothing less than a certain
kind of love. However, I had become convinced, after
listening to my mother and to others as well, that a union
of that sort was too fantastic to exist; nor was it desirable.
The reason for its undesirability was never plain. It was
one of the definite statements of rejection young persons
must learn to make; "Perfect love cannot last" is as good
a beginning as any.

When Isobel saw me her face closed. She probably
knew that I was coming from my ritual meal with my
sister-in-law and that, if nothing else, would have annoyed
her. She may even have believed I was out in the snowy
street at half-past eleven at night purposely to irritate her.
Alec, who was simpler, looked uneasy. He was a teacher,
married, a father, and penniless. "She sure can pick men,"
our brother Frank had said, when I told him about Alec.

Neither of us had liked her husband, Davy Sullivan, either. Alec may have known that I saw his wife twice a week at our work committee. Only two nights before, Bitsy had set my arm after an imaginary air raid, and said that if I accidentally swallowed poison, having lost my reason under the bombs, she would prescribe flour and water to make me vomit. Upon which she received a further badge or certificate of some sort. I had done my share too. I had treated Bitsy for an imaginary epileptic seizure. I had stuck a pencil across her tongue so that she wouldn't swallow the tongue and choke. She had bitten the pencil in a spasm of giggles. I had the pencil now, in my purse, with tiny indentations in the yellow paint.

Isobel's lips were chapped. She shook back her light ribbons of hair, and revealed her cold and slightly swollen pink ears. She had never prized her beauty. Our mother, who had dreamed of having a pretty daughter she could dress, had been given a pretty daughter who positively did not wish to be dressed.

"Come and have a drink with us," said Alec, who was kind. Our breath hung between us in white clouds and there was something marble and monumental about the group we formed in our winter clothes on the white street. Alec tried gently to pull away from my sister's arm, but she tightened her hold, and he smiled. All of that was secret and I'm sure they thought I didn't see. "I'll see that you get home," he said, as if that were the reason for my hesitating, keeping them still on the frozen street. Isobel gave no sign. The last faint trace of her smile was dying. I knew that I must not follow them to a bar. I could pry into my sister's life, but not when he was there. He would sense it. Besides, they were such a solid being that I would be invisible beside them. They were the lighted window; I was the watcher on the street.

In an excess of chattiness I said that I was walking home, all the way. We were stamping and shuffling like horses. I knocked one hard solid snow boot against the other. "I don't seem to be sleeping well," I said seriously.

"I find that walking at night sort of helps. I'm against taking pills, aren't you?"

Alec gave me the shadow of a look of interest—all the interest he could spare from my sister, from the pressure of her arm, from her presence on the dark street—and said, "Try not to think you can't sleep. The more you're afraid the harder it is to sleep."

Isobel glanced at me too, almost with curiosity. No, it was pity. All at once I felt as if the absence of love in my life, my solitude, my chastity, were visible and ugly as a disease. I felt dreary and defiled before these sinners. They were right and I was wrong. The figure I represented, historically permitted, morally correct—the wife of the soldier, untouched, waiting his return—I would have thrown away in a minute for a fragment of their mystery. The cleanliness of my clothing, my washed hair, my washed, deodorized, unwanted person, even the coldness of the night, with its white suggestion of purity, mocked my condition. I saw no end to it, and I knew I could not stay near Alec and my sister. I walked on, brusquely, smiling back at them, saying something like, "See you soon," (untrue) or "Have a good time"—as if they needed my wishes.

What I had told Alec was absurd. It would not have occurred to me to walk every night. The city at night was too cold, too silent. The light lay under street lamps in pools of blue. I was afraid of purse-snatchers. When I couldn't sleep I took a sleeping pill. That night, however, I did walk home, all the way, and it was late before the anguish awakened in me by the sight of them died down. I thought that my sister ought to have helped me, but even now I don't see what she could have done.

4

I am afraid I have given two misleading impressions: one that I was jealous of my sister, the other that I married

without love. At twenty-four I was ready to love anyone.
I had never left home. I had not been sent to boarding
school, like Isobel and Frank, and when I was ready for
college, and in robust health, my mother decided I was
delicate and would never stand the strain.

It was Isobel who brought Tom Price to the family.
She invited him for a weekend at the lake. I remember
the car stopping and Isobel jumping out and running along
the drive as if escaping. Her friend, the stranger, seemed
deliberate and slow. He rolled up the windows because it
was a gray afternoon and put the car keys in his pocket.
If I were to see him now, for the first time—as he was then,
as I am now—I would think, Young army captain, loves
his uniform, loves the war. Then, I thought, He looks too
old for his rank. He was thirty-three.

My mother instantly saw in Tom a man who would
do. He would do for either daughter. He had the cautious
humor, the stern but reassuring face she admired in men.
All weekend Isobel bothered us about a cat—a deaf, mangy
cat named Julie my mother had had destroyed. That is,
my mother had given the cat to the grocer in the village
down at the end of the lake and asked him to find Julie
a good home. A day later M. Robineau, the grocer, said
Julie had disappeared. My mother translated this to mean
"ran away."

"She ran away because you brought her down here,"
said Isobel. "Cats always run away from strange houses.
She's trying to get back to Allenton. She's walking all those
miles. She's so old . . . she doesn't know where we are."

I have said that we are not a family of weepers. The
dryness of Isobel's face is before me now. I think of her
that Saturday and Sunday calling "Julie, Julie," bumping
along the shore in a boat, calling into strange cottages.
Children mocked her: "Julie, Julie," came to us in a chorus
of young voices as we sat inside the cottage late Sunday
afternoon. Light rain spattered on the window netting.
Isobel closed the screen door behind her and said, "Julie's

drowned. The Robineau kids took her out in their boat and threw her in the lake. They hit her with an oar but she was still alive when they left her there."

"Julie ran away," said my mother, knitting.

There might have been a kinder way of putting old Julie to sleep, but my mother could hardly be blamed because French-Canadian villagers are cruel to animals. She had handed Julie in a basket to M. Robineau and said, "Find it a good home." For my mother the matter ended there. Isobel was always collecting animals, and Julie was the worst of the lot: in spite of her age she still inundated us with litters.

Isobel sat down and pretended to read. She picked up the first book she saw and opened it anywhere. In an atmosphere of extinguished quarrels Tom, her guest, began to pay attention to me. He looked at me with Isobel there, in the same room. Isobel was presumptuous. She judged us, the adults. She was eighteen but she thought she was fifty. My mother glanced at me and then at Tom. She was knitting for Frank, who was overseas. Tom would do for either daughter and he was likely to choose me. The weight of her personality, her moral strength, her contempt for men and her knowledge of their weaknesses, were now on my side. My mother backed the winner. Tom answered her gentle questions: he was a civil engineer; he had one married sister; both parents were still living; he worked in the industrial research office of a railway; he was going overseas, he supposed, any day now. Once, when her scrutiny of him ceased, when he thought he was not being watched, he sighed and relaxed and rubbed the back of his neck.

"Isobel is a rude child, I'm afraid," said my mother placidly, testing his interest, as though Isobel were out of earshot.

"I guess she feels badly about her cat," he said. If Isa had looked up at him then he would never have married me. She turned a page, indicating that she had heard but wanted no part of us. My mother and I were cold and still. I felt our unity. She and I were grown women. We knew what we were doing. Isobel was a silly girl.

She was a silly girl, there, with her legs bent under her, curled in an armchair, pretending to read. She was older than I was in one kind of experience—she had already had a lover. I knew, because Frank had found out and there had been an unholy row between them, which I overheard. Frank considered himself guardian of his sisters' virtue, but as I listened—they were in Frank's room, I on the stairs—I was astonished to realize that his principal objection was only Isobel's choice.

"Are you going to marry him?" said Frank.

"Of course I'm not," said Isobel. "I'm seventeen, for God's sake. I don't want to marry anybody and even if I did it wouldn't be him. I wouldn't marry someone just because of *that*."

"Don't get yourself caught," said Frank. "Don't tell Jean."

"Jean!"

I was poised, a little below Frank's door, hand on the bannisters. "Don't tell Jean": that was unkind of them, but no matter. "Are you going to marry him?" should surely have been, "Do you think he'll want to marry you now?" Isobel ought to be beaten. If she were my sister I'd take a strap to her: I mean—correcting the thought—if I were her brother.

That had been nearly a year ago. Now Frank was in England, Isobel was eighteen, and Tom (was he the lover?) was taking notice of me. He had never been her lover: I learned that later. He had wanted to marry her, though. My mother told me, after Tom and I were married, after he was overseas. He had proposed to Isobel that weekend, on the way down to the lake, and Isobel had refused him. Isobel said "No," and darted out of the car in search of her cat. She told Tom she never wanted to marry. She was not going to marry him, or Davy Sullivan. She did not want

children, because mothers were abominable and she did
not intend to be one. Those were her ideas at eighteen. It
must have been a shock to poor Tom. He did not expect
girls to have ideas about anything.

The night he asked me to marry him, a few weeks
after this, I went to my mother's room and knelt by her
bed and said, "Tom's smashed up his brother-in-law's car.
We aren't hurt, so don't worry. We want to get married
right away because he's going overseas." She sat up in bed,
two pillows behind her. She closed the book she had been
reading but held her finger between the pages. My marriage was a temporary interruption; she would go on
reading for years after I left. She seemed amused. In the
pupil of her eye I thought I saw a door closing, far down a
tiny corridor.

She's thrown Tom and me together, I thought. She's
wanted this.

It was months before I understood that pinpoint
amusement—before she told me he had proposed to Isobel
first. Isobel had refused him because he was too old, too
old, repeated my mother (he still thinks he married too
young) and because she was passionately in love with
Davy Sullivan and intended to marry no one but him.

Both versions of what Isobel had to say came from my
mother. Perhaps Tom told her one story and Isobel another; perhaps she made the whole thing up. I ought to
put the two accounts before Tom and let him take his pick.
When he was overseas, at the beginning of our marriage,
I imagined all the questions I would ask when he came
back; but then the personal nature of marriage made it too
difficult. I could pour out my life to a stranger—at least I
did, once—but with Tom I was shy. There are questions I
could ask, even now, if I thought I was safe. It was a long
time ago, his having wanted Isobel, but the wrong question
might still pull down the house. You can never be certain
of that house, even if it has been standing twenty years.

Did he ask me to marry him so that he could be near

her? Of course he would say no. The question is childish. Did he think he would wake up one day and find my sister instead of me in his bed? Did he believe I could lose five years, grow four inches, speak with a different voice? Did he think I would become bored with Jean and decide to be Isobel? No, no and no, he would say. It is better not to ask, even now; for what if he said no, but thought to himself yes, yes. The house could still come down. When we thought she was dying we talked out of character, and sounded deranged. We admitted we loved her—we who dread the word. We would rather say we adore: it is so exaggerated it can't be true. Adore equals like, but love is compromising, eternal. When my sister lay dying Tom said, "She always smelled of gardenias." Isobel never wore perfume. I don't know what he meant; it was an extraordinary thing for Tom to have said.

He proposed to me after an automobile accident. He was spending a forty-eight hour leave with us, again at the lake—no longer Isobel's guest, but a family friend—and on our way back from a party he ran his brother-in-law's car into the wall of a garage. The wall came out of the dark. I thought, That's what it's like to be killed. Tom says I seemed to be sleeping and then I opened my eyes and said calmly, "All we can do is leave the car here and walk home." The tension between us during the walk made it clear something would happen. It was the first shared experience: the accident. I know of marriages that keep going on less than that. We stumbled in the dark, holding on to each other. I was closer to him than I had ever been to my father or brother, and I was not afraid of him. I was never afraid of Tom. We swam in the lake and made love on the dock. I knew what I was doing, I was not afraid of him, or of the shock part of the accident. I knew he would marry me. I decided to love him with a determination I had never shown about anything else. He asked me to marry him after we were dressed; not as an afterthought, but perhaps part of the accident too. He said he wanted to get married as quickly as possible because he was going overseas. I crept to my mother's room and knelt by her bed. In the morning Tom and I were not clandestine lovers, like Davy and Isobel, but an engaged couple with everyone's blessing. We did not make love again until after we were married. There wasn't time, we were seldom alone, and I avoided it because of the pain. Days afterward I was seized by pain that doubled me in two. I told him that. I was not afraid to tell him about the pain, or about the stains on the dock I had to scrape away with a knife. I could tell him that, even at the beginning. He always listened to me, but there was this—he never said that he loved me, and I was too shy to ask if he did.

At my wedding in Allenton Isobel was center of things. Her escapade with Davy Sullivan had been discovered and they were to be married, and soon. She had told Frank she would never marry "because of *that*" and yet she did. Her wedding took place two days before her nineteenth birthday, but some people said she was seventeen, or even sixteen. At her wedding any number of uninvited guests crowded in. No one approved of Davy, but everyone wanted to see what he was like.

Tom went overseas almost at once, and I moved to Montreal. First I stayed with my sister-in-law, who was still distressed about the smashed car. "You young people drink so much nowadays," she said, as if I were Isobel. Then, my first act of independence, I rented a room in a boarding house and went there, and then I shared an apartment on Queen Mary Road with a girl who worked in my building. I had a job, now, in Tom's old office. I met Alma Summer there. She could never have been mistaken for one of my mother's daughters, but my mother liked her well enough. It was Alma who found the apartment, and, as I had never lived in an apartment, except for the few weeks with my sister-in-law, I thought it seemed a bohemian, almost glamorous thing to do. Alma told me that if it weren't for the war, and the scarcity of places to live, she would never have signed the lease. She read the names on

the mailboxes and declared we must surely be the only
Protestants. "We're a little island here, Jeannie," she said.
"Look at them—Gordeaux, Magione, Brondfield, Leroux,
Godl, Dupay, Eschmann, Skiba, Thibeouf, di Gorbio . . ."

"Nonsense," I said. "There's a White, and a Jones."

"I don't trust them," said Alma.

From our kitchen we heard the services bellowed over
a loudspeaker from St. Joseph's Oratory, and we saw the
pilgrims going up the steps of the shrine on their knees.
Armies of pilgrims with uniformed brass bands came from
outside the city and they all climbed on their knees. "If
they're so crazy about uniforms," Alma said, "why don't
they join up? They could get into real uniforms and do
something. There's a war on." I said nothing; I had been
brought up not to say what I thought. Alma, who was from
a small Ontario town, believed that Catholics sent a quarter of their incomes directly to the Pope. "It's a shame," she
said, "when you think of how poor they are." She watched
them from the kitchen window. The windowsill, with its
soot and grit and ration books and milk tickets and parsley
in a tumbler of water, was her protection against the Oratory and all the horrors it contained: pilgrims' crutches,
and one hideous relic—a man's heart in a bottle. I'm sure
she would have set a machine gun on the window sill if
she could—not in attack: in defense. She was a plump girl
with gentle eyes. She could not pronounce the letter "*r*"
and had been encouraged to use a baby lisp by her closest
friend, Mr. Callwood. I never saw a photograph of him,
never heard his voice on the telephone, and never learned
his Christian name. "Mr. Callwood says . . ." Alma would
begin, and turn pink with love and distress. She slept in
our living room, where a revolving electric log in the
grate made her feel cosy. Most of our furniture was Alma's,
and so were the rules by which we lived. She had always
lived with women, and it was she who explained about taking turns with the cleaning, the shopping, and carrying
the garbage out.

Our rooms were separated by a curtain on a rod, and

it comes to me now that she had taken the door off its hinges because it was unfriendly and could be shut. I remember the gradual slackening, the hysterical untidiness that soon prevailed. I, who at Allenton would not have emerged from my room with a pin in my hair, now faced Alma at breakfast with cream still on my face and my head a helmet of snails. Our conversation turned on the thoughts of idle or unloved women: we were spellbound by the condition of our skin, the fragility of our fingernails, our cramps, our aches, our migraine headaches, our dreams, our pre-and post-menstrual depressions; we brewed hot water bottles and fed each other aspirin. We had nothing in common except that we were women, and we had to make that do.

From this Sargasso of scarves, stockings, lipsticks, damp towels, pins, uncapped toothpaste tubes, we emerged every morning side by side, clean, smooth, impeccable as eggs. Side by side we descended the stairs, emerged on the street, and waited for our streetcar. We traveled to work, still talking about skin, nails, pains and dreams. Arriving at our building we went at once to the third-floor washroom to powder the wings of our noses and comb our hair. Our energies were spent making certain that our teeth gleamed, our eyes shone, and that we did not under any circumstances smell of sweat. We were not beauties, mind you: all that effort was required just to keep us moderately decent. In summer our short cotton dresses were rigid with starch. Our skirts were lampshades. Our damp hands were encased in spotless gloves. Home again, we became like our rooms. We assumed the shaplessness, the deliberate sloppiness of rooms shared by women whose hopes are somewhere else. The feeling here was of waiting, as the feeling in Allenton, years later, was of death.

Alma was waiting for Mr. Callwood's wife to die of diabetes. Sometimes when Mrs. Callwood was in hospital, undergoing treatment, or visiting her old mother in Nova Scotia, Alma abandoned Queen Mary Road and lived in Mrs. Callwood's house. She would return full of sniffy criticism of Mrs. Callwood's housekeeping. Her plants were puny and untended, her bedsheets yellow, her preserves more ersatz than they need be even in wartime. "Don't the neighbors notice you?" I asked her once. Alma thought that a poor question. We could discuss Mrs. Callwood's bedsheets but we had to pretend Alma had never been in Mrs. Callwood's bed. I remember about Alma two things more: she had twenty curved imitation tortoise-shell combs, each with a bow ribbon of different color attached. Once a month she washed and ironed and retied all the ribbons and then wore a new comb every day, over a small, straying chignon. Once she remarked in a helpless, frightened way, "Believe me, Jean, you never know what goes on any place once the door's closed."

Alma tried to kill herself in 1952. I think she went to live with a niece in Windsor—we lost track. If I had known more about depression I would have guessed she might try to do something foolish. Often when I came in at night after a movie or from my war-work meeting I would find the living room dark and Alma fast asleep. She lay on her divan, fully dressed, under her gray squirrel coat. I would take off my boots and pad past the couch where she breathed like someone with a heavy cold. She would speak with great clarity and unhappiness phrases like "my red cable-stitch sweater" and "got off at the wrong stop." The room would be cold and stale. She had forgotten to disconnect the revolving log that sent bubbles of orange light over the ceiling and walls, over sorrowing unconscious Alma, over Churchill disguised as a bulldog sitting on the Union Jack. I would push aside the mulberry curtain and switch on my bedside lamp. The bar of light falling on her face made Alma turn to the wall, and I could extinguish the bubbling log. Hours later I might hear her groan, rise, undress, and crawl back to bed. We never talked about it. I know that when I was away, weekends, she took a pill that gave her five hours' sleep. If she woke up and discovered it

was still Sunday she wandered drowsily into the bathroom
and swallowed another five hours' oblivion. She revealed
this to me in a casual remark, but we did not go on with it.
Our greatest intimacy was probably the sight of each
other's underwear drying in the bathroom. With mutual
prudery we never asked favors, and never had debts.

I had been living with Alma three years when her
cousin, a girl in the Air Force, passing through on her way
to Halifax and overseas, asked if she could spend the night
with us. Alma went to endless trouble, combining our ration
books to buy a little roast of veal, which she rolled up with
bread and onion stuffing to make it seem more. She bribed
the grocer for beer, which was scarce, and laid dinner on
a card table in front of the fireplace. There was a wrapped
present before her cousin's plate—an Elizabeth Arden
traveling kit, I think it was: something Alma thought her
cousin would never find in England. We worked all day
that Sunday making the apartment neat, putting stray objects behind cushions and just generally out of sight. Alma
talked about her cousin in an odd way, as if she were expecting a man. When Mona Summer walked in that evening, so emphatically uniformed that the uniform might
have been ambling by itself, I wondered if Alma had connected "uniform" and "Air Force" and "overseas" to create
a phantom airman and not her cousin at all. She hesitated
before kissing Mona. Mona was only a girl. Why had we
cleaned the apartment, bribed the grocer, stuffed a roast?

Mona stalked about and flung herself into chairs like
an adolescent boy. She was a woolly-headed girl of nineteen with enormous teeth. She drank like a man and had a
man's way of holding a cigarette and glass. The uniform
was cruel: the skirt seemed a sack, and the tunic a bolster
stuffed with straw. She had the feminine military face:
round cheeks, snub nose, large mouth and piggy, impudent
eyes. I remember her grubby hands and her bulging calves.
She could have been the comic Air Force girl-chum in a
brave English film. Alma now gave her cousin the sober

reverence due to a hero. If Mona was not a pilot, we would continue to treat her like one. She was a stenographer, and going overseas to do the same job Alma performed here, in Montreal. All the same I could see that Alma felt inferior, as if her own life were without direction. She told Mona that I was the wife of an officer and the sister of an airman and that my sister's husband had been wounded in Italy. This was said with an air of offering me. Mona gave me a hard and impertinent stare.

The log revolved. We ate the veal and drank the beer. Mona spoke of her commanding officer—her ma'am. Ma'am had a code of honor; she had ideals. She could tell whether you were lying by looking in your eyes. "Our Ma'am is a real Christian, not like some," said Mona.

After dinner, when Alma and I were clearing away the plates, we decided in rapid whispers that Mona would sleep with me. Alma's couch was even narrower than my small bed. In cheerful proximity Mona and I undressed and hung our skirts on hangers. The hostess, I offered cream, Kleenex, and bobby pins. We put up our hair. We washed stockings, and brushed our teeth. I opened the window, letting in the noise of streetcars and a tide of black winter air. We got into bed and lay like mummies, side by side. Her rayon underwear, all strings and straps, had been dropped on the carpet. She turned in bed and yawned and stuck her little flanneled rump against my hip.

"Don't you want to sleep spoons?" she said. "The bed's so small."

"No, I don't."

"Well, don't mind me if I'm all over, then," said Mona, not in the least offended. "Ma'am says I'm just awful." After a silence she said in the dark, "I wish she was here to say goodnight." She gave another carefree boyish yawn. In the next room poor Alma, who had taken a pill, sank and murmured into sleep under her gray squirrel coat. "Have you got a boy friend?" Mona said.

"Mona, go to sleep," I said.

"I can't sleep," said Mona. "The bed's too small." She turned her head slightly and whispered, "You can't sleep, either. Do you want to play?"

"Go to sleep," was all I said.

When I awoke in the morning merry Mona was clambering over me on her way to breakfast. It was a quarter past seven on a winter day and the day was dark. I decided not to get up. I would stay here, at home, in my own bed, to which I had an unqualified right. The railway could flourish and the war be won without my aid. I lay with my hands behind my head and I remember this: I stared at the dark and hated Isobel. I hated Tom because he had gone away and left me with the Almas and Monas, but what Isobel had to do with that morning is not clear. I suppose I thought she was having a better time.

5

My father, who has become too deaf to listen to reason, bores us with news of the weather. We have lost the sense of seasons; our climate has been degenerating since the first nuclear explosion in Nevada a generation ago. He remembers that radioactive clouds traveled from Nevada to upstate New York and that all the exposed negatives in the Kodak laboratories in Rochester were damaged. He says he saw a news item about it in an early edition of a Montreal paper, but that in the later editions it had been left out. Did we read it then? Do we think about it now? He has also noticed that salt is less salty than it used to be and that sugar has lost its sweetness. When Tom and I lunch with my old parents my father begs us to taste the salt and sugar and say we agree. Tom, who is rational, argues. I cannot be made to remember. My father is old and talkative. My mother is quiet. Her brown-spotted hands tighten and flex, and I can see she is full of silent answers.

Salt, sugar, and the seasons: our summer is cold smoke in air-conditioned rooms, our autumn a summer misplaced. Autumn was spring, a false promise, in the old days. The first metallic morning reminded us that everything could change, and with this false beautiful expectation we were tricked into winter. By Christmas I knew the promise had been a lie, and in January, when the heart of the city was slow as the heart in sleep, I knew I would not survive. Every spring I was alive and had survived. One February day in 1945 I was still living and had nearly emerged from the winter alive. The days drew out by two minutes every twenty-four hours. Mr. Prescott, the Chief Engineer of the Industrial Development section of the railway office where Tom had worked, and where I now performed a superfluous but patriotic task, said that this was so. At any moment I might become Tom's widow. The ambition of eight chattering stenographers at the far end of the room was to become like me: each of them wanted to marry a brave boy, live for a few days and nights with him—every day and night the last—and then write letters to him for ever and ever. A translucid comb of icicles hung at the window next to my desk. Looking into the comb of the wavy gray winter sky and the wavy brown office building next to ours, Mr. Prescott said, "We're gaining two minutes a day now. It's nearly spring." The day I had news that my brother had died Mr. Prescott said, "Look at that sky, Mrs. Price," and through the now dazzling icicles I saw blue, plain blue, a sky like a plate.

In our overheated office thirty people idled, cast up by the war. There were middle-aged men, veterans of that earlier war they never stopped describing, and a veteran of the present war, Wing-Commander Meadmore, who wore the Air Force uniform and a shabby greatcoat he was no longer entitled to, but no one thought less of him for that. We were accustomed to Majors and Colonels from the other, boring war. I remember their bristling mustaches and unbrushed suits. They stank of beer and strong tea. Elderly Major Currie kissed my mouth at an office party and called me "little girl." It was like being held one second too long by an old family friend. Children know when a kiss must end, but I was twenty-eight and had better manners and fewer defenses than a child. Wing-Commander Meadmore, our recent veteran, sharing my lunch of hard-boiled egg sandwiches one day, said, "I felt funny just then."

"What do you mean?"

We sat facing each other at an empty drawing table. The lights were thriftily dimmed on this dark winter noon. Wing-Commander Meadmore's skin became lumpy and porous and his smell unclean. He turned away, raised an arm slowly as if to bless me, and uttered a cry. I heard Julie drowning in the lake, hit by an oar. Having nursed Bitsy Campbell in a make-believe fit, I was able to prevent Wing-Commander Meadmore from swallowing his tongue. Afterwards he said, "I fainted." An invocation was required, but instead of an exorcist we had Jean Price, possessor of a First Aid certificate. I treated him so carefully and with such tact that anything he, or his possessed soul, might have revealed to me was stilled. I was not consciously avoiding the Devil: I would have been just as tactful with God. We permitted the existence of God without discussing Him, and He existed without the Devil. I put a pencil over Wing-Commander Meadmore's tongue, undid his tie and collar, and slipped my rolled cardigan beneath his head. The stenographers and the office boys eating sandwich lunches said he put them off their food. He smelled as if he were rotting. Presently two of the men helped him to the infirmary—"Come on, kid, you're fine"—where he slept and wakened to say, "I fainted." We ventilated the office and opened the windows to the wind and soot and gray-wool sky. I washed my hands to rid them of the corruption they had touched, and rubbed them with Hind's Honey and Almond lotion.

"Do you think he knows?" said Mr. Prescott.

"No," I said, without wondering if it were true. "It's better that way."

"Poor chap had a knock on the head," said Mr. Prescott.

"In my personal opinion," said young Moray Mackenzie, called up and leaving in a fortnight, "the company shouldn't be forced to take back just any vet, just because he is a vet. If I come back and I'm not fit for a good day's work I won't expect to be kept on out of charity."

"Hear, hear," said Mr. Prescott.

Moray Mackenzie only a month ago would have been squashed by any of us if he had introduced an opinion about anything. Now, leaving us, he was the office hero. He lounged, smoking, knocking ash on the floor. Standing before me he said, "I'm middle class and proud of it"— surely not in argument. I would have never said anything that could provoke an unpleasant answer. We must have been in deep accord.

The third-floor washroom, where, under running water, I cleansed my hands of Wing-Commander Meadmore, overlooked the harbor. Moray Mackenzie has passed on a story that German spies spent their time there, watching the movements of ships. He was reprimanded for spreading rumors, but Alma heard about it and was alarmed. She longed to catch Peter Lorre or Eric von Stroheim peering out of the window of the Ladies', but never did. The fact that the harbor was closed in winter failed to console Alma. She would have preferred a harbor open the year round, and spies continually at work. If the spy had been with me now he would have seen a narrow street and gritty snow and a dark Greek restaurant. Even when the street was busy, rattling with streetcars, it had the empty look of a place where nobody lives. At night migrations of rats took place. Our toothless night watchman, who wore his decorations from the Boer War, said it was a sight you could never forget: The rats crossed the street from cellar to cellar. It occurred to me that South African and Indian and Australian railways were run from buildings like this and that they had the same night watchmen and invisible spies and the same armies of rats. That was the trace of Empire: the dark brown buildings, the old men with their medals. This street seemed to me to belong to an extremely ancient period of history. I had never seen anything older and it did not enter my head that a single stone or pediment or Victorian gargoyle could ever vanish or be replaced.

"The girls are up in Montreal with war jobs," my mother liked to say. Every morning I was given a supply of industrial maps of the cities of Canada served by the railway, and I painted the sewers and waterworks yellow and mauve. I had a box of water colors for my exclusive use, and four fine brushes in a jam jar. I had clean cloths, a cold cream pot for fresh water, stacks of blotting paper, and a pad on which to rest my hand so that it would not soil the map. An envious stenographer was ordered to see that my supplies never ran short. Before the war, during the depression, a degree in civil engineering had been required for this post. Now, with a shortage of qualified men, the railway was happy to have me. My qualifications for this or any job were that I had taken lessons in geography and ancient history from an old friend of my mother's and had also been taught to play the violin.

I painted mauve and yellow pipelines all day, and scarcely ever let the brush slip out of the guide drawn for me. I sat, perched high on a draftsman's stool, my hair falling in smooth plaques as I bent my head. In a heap at the upper lefthand corner of my desk were my watch, my charm bracelet, my engagement ring, and Tom's fraternity pin. The dressing and doffing ritual took place in the morning, before and after lunch, and at half-past five. No one thought it odd of me, for nearly every person there depended upon some finicky personal ceremony before the day's work could begin. One sharpened pencils, another watered the sweet-potato plant that grew out of a peanut-butter jar on a windowsill. Mr. Prescott cut up the morning paper and filled little envelopes with mysterious clippings.

The older men were fretful about possessions no one must touch: slide rules, calendars, graph paper, and in one inexplicable case, a colored photograph of the Dionne quintuplets as infants. I would swear today, and would have certainly sworn then, that everyone in the room was harmless and sane. The office was overheated, the lighting system hard on the nerves, and we were cast up by the war. Safe and high and dry was Wing-Commander Meadmore, the possessed, who spent his working time tracing the cabooses that American railroads were forever pinching from Canada and then abandoning on sidings in the Middle West. The wartime shortage of cabooses obliged him to search for each like a missing friend, by number, through grimy, fifth-carbon leading-sheets. Aloud he muttered numbers, and sometimes the names of towns: Stony River, Chicoutimi.

When Frank was killed, the days were drawing out by two minutes in twenty-four hours, and the sky was blue as a plate. The telephone on Mr. Prescott's desk rang for me. It was my mother, in Allenton. She asked about my health and gave me news of hers before mentioning that Frank was dead.

"But he's just got there," I said, for it was barely five weeks since Isobel and I had seen him before he left for Halifax and "there." Frank was intended to survive this war, and someone like Davy Sullivan to be killed; but a mistake was made, for Frank was never seen again and it was Davy who came back. My brother had been overseas, and repatriated to Canada after typhoid fever. After a long leave he volunteered to return. He wanted to marry an English girl.

"Can you leave your job?" I heard, shrill and faint. Even now my mother maintained the legend of Isobel and me in natty uniforms with red crosses on our berets. "I think your father would like it if you girls could come down for a couple of days." Frank had been our father's child. It was our mother who wanted the daughters now.

"Is he killed or missing?" This was the crisis, and this

was the manner bred since the cradle. All our training was directed towards the emergency, towards how to behave when the moment came. It was for this conversation that I had learned to go blank in the presence of worry and pain, and had been taught it was foolish to weep.

"Killed," said the insect voice, with a hint of melancholy triumph, as if to say it could not have been otherwise. She knew, but did not tell me then, that Frank died in a foolish accident. A coping stone fell on his head. He was on leave in Brighton, with his bride, It might just as easily have been someone else.

"I'll get Isa. We'll come down on the six o'clock."

"It's a slow train. I'll keep dinner for you," my mother said.

The stenographers had stopped rattling the wrappers of their candy bars. I saw on Major Currie a look of soft indecent concern. Every day he read the Killed-Wounded-Missing columns in the *Montreal Star* aloud, tracing the names with his finger. "There's a Duncan," he said once. "Would that be your brother, Mrs. Price?" I learned over the telephone and spoke to Mr. Prescott, who had opened a drawer and pretended to rearrange its contents the instant I said "killed."

"It's about my brother," I said softly. "He's been killed, but I don't know anything more. I think my sister and I should go home."

"Oh, yes." He looked up, unwillingly, with kind, worried eyes. "Take all the time your people need." Adopting my tone, he lowered his voice, as though we were discussing something shameful, a scandal, something no decent family would want known. After I had gone he might stroll across to one of the engineers—perhaps Wing-Commander Meadmore—and say, "It was her brother." The answer would be that it was too bad, but what could you expect in times like these. From "I felt funny just then" to "I fainted" was the truth about times like these, but Wing-Commander Meadmore had never seen himself, and could not know that he died before our eyes, and smelled of his death. I often heard him say, "It's the chance he took," when evil Major Currie came upon a Killed-Wounded-Missing name one of us knew. When Mr. Prescott's son had been killed in the invasion of Europe, the summer before, Mr. Prescott stayed away from the office ten days, giving as an apologetic excuse, "My wife is taking it hard." When he returned he said to me mildly, "I suppose you know about the boy." Months afterwards, he told me with the same gentle discretion that he had established contact with his son through a medium in Rosemount. The lad told the medium he was happy on the other side. "I'm glad, for the wife's sake," Mr. Prescott said.

"What did he expect?" Wing-Commander Meadmore asked me. "What did he go over there for?" Wing-Commander Meadmore, he of the upraised arm and dying animal cry, had expected it. We all expected it, of course. Mr. Prescott developed a tic after his son was killed, an almost imperceptible flutter of the lid of an eye.

I had to fetch Isobel. That was now the most important thing. I would arrive at her office unannounced and bring her the news.

She worked in the maid's room of a large and dirty flat that had been let, furnished, to Czechoslovakian refugees. Madame Adele Tessignier, Isobel's employer, lived in the room and used it as an office, giving her tenants the housing shortage as reason. The refugees must have thought that was the way things were done in Canada, for they never complained.

The building was full of grime and mirrors, and the elevators moved on frayed ropes: but the block had been fashionable thirty years earlier, and the flats were still sought after and highly priced. I saw stiff elderly couples and had glimpses of firescreens. "Rooms full of candy dishes," Isobel had said once, describing as best she could.

I did not think about Frank. I walked, in my snow boots, under a cloudless sky, and thought about Isobel, and

Madame Tessignier, and our friend Suzanne Moreau, who
was giving a party that night; and when I arrived at the
dark and sooty place where my sister worked, I thought,
she'll wonder what I'm doing here like this, in the middle
of the day.

The maid's room, the office, had its own entrance.
From the dark hallway I heard my sister's voice, rapid and
light, saying obviously into a telephone, "Is there a garage?
Are you leaving the linen and dishes?" I was astonished
years later when Davy Sullivan said, "Madame Tessignier
is a crook. In any town but Montreal she'd have been in
jail years ago. Isobel's a crook too. She loved the job. She
was made for it." I protested, reminding Davy of Isobel's
poverty, of the corners she could get into where a dollar-
fifty made all the difference. He said that Isobel wasn't
interested in money, but in being near someone who was
dishonest; it excited her; it excited her to lend her charming face and pretty voice to the business of duping refugees
and families who would pay anything for a roof. Davy
always went too far. There was a wartime shortage of
apartments just as there was of cabooses, and if Isobel
hadn't taken that job someone else would. It couldn't have
been much fun for her, moving from place to place with
Barney, losing half her husband's letters because her address changed so often. I told Davy so, but it was impossible
to make him ashamed.

I knocked on the door, and Madame Tessignier, whose
bed was behind it, and who spent her time on that bed,
let me in. Her fat arm, covered with blue satin—she lived
in dressing gowns—barred the way for a moment, and
then she recognized me and said, "Eesa, it's your little
soeur." In the new role of little soeur I stepped inside, falsely
smiling, and Madame Tessignier said, "You have brought
in the cold of the street." She lay down on the bed, and
drew an eiderdown from the feet up to her chin. On the
shelves surrounding her bed were files, magazines, lists of
inventories of furnished apartments, and a photograph of

Jean-Claude, a sullen adolescent son. Isobel knew little about Monsieur Tessignier, except that his wife had him followed by detectives for the dismal pleasure she took in reading their reports. She had no intention of granting him the divorce he had urgently been demanding for years, and the detectives were the only financial extravagance she allowed herself. Isobel made a sign to me, a vague wave of the hand, and went on with her inquiry.

"The war is nearly over," said Madame Tessignier, "and the Jews are taking everything."

She seemed deeply unhappy, so small, fat, and round, her hair dyed blue, her face pink, pressed into shape like soft wax.

"Sit on the bed, dear Jean," she said. "I would offer you a chair, but I cannot afford to buy one, and besides the office is so crowded I wouldn't know where to put it. Don't sit too close to me. There, at the foot of the bed. Let us not interrupt sweetest Isobel, who has discovered a completely furnished house. The owners have been called to Ottawa. The house will make many people happy. We can easily get three couples into it. Sweetest Isobel will get them to leave everything behind. That child is an angel."

I sat as far from her as I could, remembering her fear of microbes and germs from the street. Madame Tessignier's clothes were in cases under the bed. One of the filing cabinets was full of hoarded food. On Isobel's desk were a buttery knife and some greasy papers, the remains of a private feast. Sometimes Madame Tessignier was obliged to live in one of the apartments she intended to sublet—during the holidays, for instance, when Jean-Claude had to be decently housed. The prospect terrified her; every day was torment when she thought of the money lost. She was as incompetent as my sister at assembling even the rudiments of living—say, a bed, a table, a chest of drawers—and she always scuttled back to the office and maid's room with relief. Once I remember her in a large new building, living in five rooms with nothing but a bed and a grand piano. She complained that she had to take all her meals standing up, because she used the piano as a table, and that she could not understand why people lived in apartments when an office was so obviously the best place to be.

Isobel put down the telephone. I said, so casually that I knew Isobel would forever despise me, "Mother's just called. Frank's been killed. She'd like us to come down tonight. There's that slow train around six. We might as well get it."

From Isobel's slight frown she might have been thinking about nothing except the train. Madame Tessignier gave a puppy cry. Her mouth widened, her eyes stared, and she put her fat hands to her ears, as if to prevent their receiving further horrors. Instead of applauding the performance Isobel gave her employer a look of great irritation and said, "I'm going to wash." She slammed into the maid's bathroom—where Madame Tessignier kept more food, and a number of coats and dresses on the shower rail—and only then did Madame Tessignier remove her hands. Her first words for Frank were, "Oh my poor Jean-Claude. I am a mother, dear Jean." Jean-Claude was young, and safe in boarding school. Once when Isobel visited the school, he led her into the chapel and kissed her and tried to put his hand inside her sweater. He begged her never to tell—not about the kiss, but about her being in the chapel. It had never been defiled by a woman's presence before.

Isobel returned. She took her coat and scarf from the top of a filing cabinet, where they were rolled in a ball, and sat down to pull on her snow boots. She suddenly pressed her head on the metal surface of the filing cabinet. "I feel sick, I feel so sick," she said softly.

"She loved her brother," said Madame Tessignier, as if I were a stranger.

Frank and Isobel had never got on. Isobel was younger than he, but tougher, a bully. They had often been torn

apart in grim and frightening physical quarrels when they
were small. When Isobel was only seven she stuffed his
mouth full of dirt and grass, and, later, Frank was pun-
ished by our father for not defending himself. They had in
common one memory: they had both been delicate in
health as children, subject to pneumonia and bronchial
complaints. Consequently, they spent two winters with a
relation of our father who had a small hotel in the Lauren-
tian mountains. This relation, a woman my mother considered friendly but common, promised to be a second
mother to them. However, it became increasingly evident
from the children's behavior that they were running wild,
and that our father's relation had no notion of what a
mother ought to be. Our mother also felt that Isobel's character was suffering because she dominated Frank (no one
thought of what it was causing Frank) and they were
eventually decreed cured, no longer TB types, and des-
patched to separate boarding schools in Ontario. They had
in common a memory of winter and sun; of choosing whatever they wanted to eat in the hotel dining room—I believe
this shocked our mother more than anything else. They
could speak French, of a sort, and had experienced a
rhythm of life foreign to me. Only occasionally some word,
or gesture, would bring them together within this memory,
and they would glance at each other, in accord. My mother
never encouraged this; but still the memory must have
persisted for Isobel, and the person who could share it had
gone. So I thought that if Isobel was now feeling sick, it
was because in losing Frank she lost two winters of childhood.

Madame Tessignier lay back on her dirty pillows and
spoke as if describing monuments to war, motherhood, and
the future of nations. She squeezed out a tear—the first
I saw shed for Frank. There was a silence. Isobel wound
her scarf around her collar, picked up her gloves, and said,
"There."

"You know, little Jean," said Madame Tessignier,

"business is terrible. There isn't much time. The war will be over soon, everyone says so, and the Jews are taking everything."

I responded. Business was bad? Did she think the war nearly over?

"As a matter of fact," my sister said, "business is good. And the Jews are taking what you've left." She swept oddments off her desk into her open handbag. "Collusion pays."

"I say nothing, because you are suffering," said Madame Tessignier, closing her eyes. "I say only this: the war will soon be over, and we will look back on these years as the happiest of our lives."

"Well, goodbye," said Isobel. She stood with her feet apart, like a child. "I'll be back soon."

Madame Tessignier began to weep, seriously this time. "How can I manage without you?" she said.

"It doesn't matter, does it, if business is over and the Jews have taken everything?" said Isobel.

"Sweetest Jean," said Madame Tessignier to me. "Tell your mother that another mother sends her heart. Her *heart*."

"Thank you," I said, and I did feel guilty about leaving the poor weeping woman alone.

Isobel, without looking at me, began to speak with an intensely pronounced, "Listen!" as if she could not be ᐧcertain of my attention. "Listen, don't you feel sorry for *her.* You ought to see some of the places she rents to Jews —to refugees, I mean. If there's an ironing board and an egg-beater she says it's a furnished apartment. You should see the key money they pay. She finds out what they've got in the bank. I don't know how. She knows everybody. And then she says the price of the lease, just the lease, not counting the rent, will be just that—whatever she knows they've got. They're used to paying for leases in Europe and they think it's done that way here too. They don't think it's legal, but they're not used to anything being legal. Well, she's got a big rival now. He's a refugee and a lot of the

refugees go to him because they think he's safer than a
Canadian. Don't worry about *her*. He's smart, but she knows
everybody. She'll win. I've met him. He's a snake, but she's
a fat little squirrel with sharp little teeth and she'll . . ."

She stopped abruptly. The building was full of squeaks
and the hum and wheezing of ancient elevators. The elevator bell, after I had pressed it, left a coating of grease
on my finger. A hunchback in uniform let us in. We pretended not to see him. The other passenger was a servant
wearing a windbreaker over her cotton dress. "Listen,"
said Isobel again, "we're supposed to go to Suzanne's tonight. At least I am, and I guess she invited you too. It's
her birthday. Twenty-three."

"No, twenty-four," I said.

"We're the same age," said Isobel. "I talked to her
this morning."

"All I can say is, she was twenty when I met her four
years ago, but have it your own way." I sounded like our
mother: flat and calm and certain I was right.

It was part of the quality of that day that we should
discuss Suzanne Moreau all the way out and into the street,
and through a series of short-cut alleys to the street where
Isobel lived. We walked on cinders and garbage and snow
that looked winters old. From the basement kitchen of a
restaurant rose a smell that made me cover my face with
my gloved hands. We kept on about Suzanne Moreau, saying we must call her, yes, that one of us must ring and
explain why we could not be at her party that night; and
yet the "why" was left out of our talk. My sister was still
pale and the skin around her eyes seemed bruised. She
talked as if she were trying to use her breath, be rid of it,
as people do when they fear that an intake of cold air will
make them sick. She let me into her flat and kicked off her
boots, and dropped her coat on the floor. She had lived here
three months without being obliged by Madame Tessignier
to move on. I had never known her to stay as long as that
anywhere. In these rooms we had last seen Frank: he had
spent his last days of leave in Montreal with Isobel.

I picked up her coat and placed her boots neatly in the hall closet.

"I suppose business *is* bad, or Madame Tessignier would have rented this place by now," I said.

"No, it's blackmail, just blackmail. I don't care where I live, but I like scaring her. It's a game. I know so much about her, you see. Her sister has a call house. Suzanne— it's a coincidence—is on the call house party line. She doesn't know it's Madame Tessignier's sister, but I know. I don't care, I don't care about other people's business." She meant that I did, I suppose. She laughed, telling me this. The telephone was on the floor and she knelt down to it, dialing Suzanne's number. We smiled at each other. I had forgotten why we had left our offices—our war jobs —in the middle of the day. I was in Isobel's flat without a false excuse, and could observe the bed, the books, the traces of her life.

"Doesn't answer." She padded around the room in stocking feet, pulling out drawers, opening cupboards. Searching for something—a suitcase?—she pulled our wet snowboots out of the hall closet and dropped them on the polished floor. Her boots were huge, fur-lined; mine were small, the black velvet white where snow had stained it. They lay, ugly, in spreading pools of melted snow. I found myself worrying about the effect on the polished floor, but knew that if I said so Isobel would call me the worst appellation in her vocabulary, an Allenton Mum.

She slept more or less on the floor, on a thin mattress and springs Madame Tessignier had lent her. With half-understood prudishness I sat down on the floor with my back to this bed; it had something to do with Isobel and Alec, and it was something I didn't want to consider too specifically lest my thoughts show on my face. I took the telephone now and called Suzanne. The telephone rang and rang. Isobel had found a paper shopping bag with the name of a grocery store printed upon it. Into this she crammed a toothbrush wrapped in a bit of Kleenex, and

wildly folded pajamas. Looking round, distracted, evidently
wondering if more objects were required for an absence
of four days, she rolled up a sweater and a blouse and
thrust those into the bag too. Satisfied, she picked up
Barney, who, aware of disaster, had been sitting on the
windowsill. He had been moved about so often he had lost
his instinct of fear, but not of apprehension. When Isobel
picked him up, now, to bear him away to the janitor, he let
himself go limp, resigned.

"A fatalist. A Slav, this cat," said Isobel.

The telephone rang in Suzanne's empty rooms. I
imagined her kitchen table covered with empty bottles and
piles of magazines, and the record albums left behind by
her friends. I imagined her towering and surrounded by a
multitude of tiny refugees, pin-sized, with anxious pin-
sized faces. I saw the paintings on the wall and the frames
stacked on chairs. Her bedroom was the size of a cupboard
and nearly filled with an unmade bed. It must be curious,
empty, except for the emphatic telephone now. "Of course
Suzanne's studio is unspeakably filthy," I felt obliged to
explain to my invisible mother. The ringing filled the
kitchen and the bathroom, where sheets soaked in a rimmed
tub. I had never seen her bathtub when it was not being
used as a laundry. I could not imagine Suzanne in a per-
fumed bath; the smell of her bathroom was of Javel water.

I heard Isobel in the kitchen now collecting Barney's
sandbox and drinking bowl. I let the telephone ring three
times more and hung up. If Suzanne was home, and not
answering, she must have been cursing richly in two languages by this time. It was just as well that I hadn't reached
her: I would have stumbled in my explanation about Frank.
Suzanne looked at the war as an English-Canadian affair
and the death of our brother would be our doing—our col-
lective error, our guilt. Yet she was married to an army
private who was in Europe, too. He was a prisoner of war.
She was called by her maiden name, Moreau, and scarcely
anyone realized she had ever been married. I had never

seen his photograph. He had been taken prisoner at Dieppe, in 1942, and vanished from her life. I think she forgot him because she could not imagine where he was. She had never been out of the Province of Quebec, and her mind's eye could not reach the real place we had seen as a make-believe country in films. She could not see the barracks of a prison camp because she had already seen them, gray and white, with film stars suffering and escaping and look-ing like no one she knew. Surely there was a true land-scape—gray, flat, spotted with gray trees and gray wooden houses, where foreign people with gray faces walked in the rain? We all received letters that were real enough, but the letters told us that everything we saw and read was a lie. Davy, Isobel's husband, saw a documentary film about Italy and even though it was a truthful film, and he saw himself, a glimpse of himself, he wrote that it was a lie. "I went out and puked," said Davy's letter—the only letter of his my sister ever showed me. It was Suzanne's husband's bad luck to have disappeared into a sham land-scape. The men we knew dissolved in a foreign rain. I think she did not expect ever to see him again.

"Suzanne doesn't answer," I said, when Isobel re-turned.

"Never mind. We'll call from home tonight."

"I've got to go and pack now," I said.

"You don't need anything," said Isobel. "You can buy a toothbrush. We'll miss the train."

Now that was unreasonable, for it was only a little after four o'clock. Isobel simply could not be bothered coming with me to Alma's apartment. She was irritated by its red maple furniture and the picture of Bulldog Churchill. She knew it was Alma's taste, but blamed me. I hadn't Isobel's advantages, I now thought meanly. I couldn't afford to live alone, and had no one to blackmail into letting me have a free apartment.

"Don't come, we can meet at the station," I said.

She was so self-centered, so unconcerned, with her

love and her cat and her good looks and her shopping bag. All she wanted was to get me out of the way so that she could call Alec and tell him she was leaving; and that was enough to silence and humble me, it seemed so important. Isobel followed me to the door as if I had said nothing.

"We'll take a taxi to your place," she said. "I'll pay." I interpreted this as an insult, knowing she considered me avaricious. I was saving money against my husband's return. We had already discussed this. Why need I always defend myself, when I was in the right?

Two hours had now passed since our mother had called me. My sister and I ground up Côte des Neiges Road in an overheated taxi. One of the chains around the tires had broken and made an irregular beating sound. Even that was enough to distract me.

It seemed wrong when I thought of it later. I scarcely mourned my brother; it seems to me now that I ought to pay for my indifference. But that series of incidents, feeling nagged by the need to cancel a party, or being offended when there was no cause for it, or thinking about the beating of a broken chain on the road, continued to drag on and away from the reason for my being out and alone with my sister on a working day. I withdrew from my brother's death into a living country of wrangles and arrangements and sharing taxis; of packing and snatching Alma's stockings from the towel rack instead of my own; of leaving Alma a note; of buying magazines and cigarettes and tickets for a train: all of it took Frank's share of my time. Although I speak now of his death, his death did not occur. What happened was that he was never seen again. He disappeared, like Suzanne's husband, in an unfamiliar landscape, under cinema rain, and we never saw him again.

At the station Isobel bought chewing gum because she thought she might be trainsick. Then it was dark, and the blackened windows of the train gave her boned face back like a dramatic photograph. "I feel sick, I really do," she said, leaning back and closing her eyes. I bought candy

from the vender—Commando Crunch, which was all he
had left—but Isobel asked me not to unwrap it in her presence. She said the smell of ersatz chocolate would finish
her. We discussed why this should be so. These diversions
occupied us. I ate my patriotic candy, and proved to Isobel
that she was not really sick. When we reached Allenton we
found our mother bound with trifles and worries, the
crumbs of life, and there we were, an ordinary family,
wondering only how it was that we were together at such
an odd time of the week, and at such an unlikely time of
the year. We spoke of the train journey, and arranged
where we were to sleep. Our parents now slept apart, and
my mother occupied what was still called the girls' room.
Isobel was put in a spare room full of jam jars and apples
on shelves. "You'll sleep well there," my mother said.
"Apples give you pleasant dreams." I was to have Frank's
bed. I unpacked in his room as if it were the most natural
place to be. We were so busy with the details involved by
our simply being here, at home, together, that it was some
time before we spoke about him at all.

6

"Poor Frank," our mother said. That was the principal
change when we did speak about him: the new little word
"poor." Our mother walked about the glassed-in sun porch,
where she had lighted a kerosene stove not so much for
our comfort as to assure the survival of her plants. She
seemed to be walking with a reason for walking, not simply
drifting or nervously pacing. She walked up and down,
past the wicker sofa and the wicker table, and pulled dead
bits off the geraniums, and she sighed, and said, "Poor
Frank." It was half-past six o'clock, too dark for reading.
The pattern of the pierced stove, like a hoop of bright embroidery, became distinct on the ceiling. Isobel read, her
face nearly pressed to the book. She was reading *Anne of
Green Gables,* which had belonged to both of us, but had

her name on the flyleaf. Our mother said, "You're a silly girl, you'll ruin your eyes," and, stopping by the door, where the light was, suddenly revealed the porch in its winter shabbiness and our father in his wretchedness. He sat, physically shrunken, at the far end, where a draught seeped through the ill-fitted double windows. The panes went black and reflected us: Isobel reading, our mother erect by the door, our father mourning and small. We were in a lighted cage. We could be seen from the street. Anyone going by in the snow would think, The Duncans have lost their boy, the girls are down from Montreal.

"There's a kind of inner serenity about you," dear Alma Summer had once said to me. Was there, now? I smiled at myself in the black glass.

"Would you girls eat floating island for dessert tonight?" our mother said. "Because if you'd like it, I'll make it right now." We considered it. I could not help considering it. Floating island? Isobel looked up from her reading and lowered the book to her lap. It was so important. "Isa," our mother went on, "I want you to give me all your sweaters tomorrow, everything you've brought. I don't know what you've been washing that sweater with, but it wasn't Lux."

Across the snowy lawn we saw into our neighbors' lighted living room. The neighbors were careful not to look at us, but they must have said, "The Duncans have lost their boy."

The ghost in the Allenton house cannot be Frank's. If Frank had left part of himself there I would have felt him then, that night. He left no trace; nothing of him came back.

We had sat here, Isobel and I side by side, at Christmastime. There were evergreen wreaths with electric candles in three of the windows, and a Christmas tree in the bay window of the room behind us; and we had looked straight over the lawn to our neighbor's tree. Frank was here, on embarkation leave. Light haired, stiff shouldered,

sharp nosed, he sat in the middle of the porch on a wicker
chair and was polite to aunts. The aunts, our mother's sisters, talked about their own sons, who had done well in
the war and were higher ranking than Frank. Everyone
they knew had done well in this war; they knew a milkman
who was a major. Isobel smoked one cigarette after the
other because she knew it would annoy our father's
mother, our least-liked relation. Our father was being
dreary over Ypres. Whenever anyone spoke to Frank, our
father butted in with a reminder of the war he had been
in, and boasted about the lice, the rats, and the dirty water,
and rolled his eyes at the mention "France." "*Auprès de ma
blonde*," our staid father intoned, and my mother's glance
met mine; her look told me that he'd had too much to
drink, but that this was a permissible occasion and she was
not going to do anything about it.

Our mother was behaving strangely too. She seemed
to have mixed, tumultuous feelings about Frank now that
it appeared he might be killed after all. She had always said
she knew nothing about the training of boys; they were
boisterous, hard to understand, and inevitably faithless.
She would have wanted an ideal daughter, as pretty as
Isobel and tractable as Jean. In a way she had nothing, and
was about to lose the boy. Her odd behavior that day took
the form of brusque assaults of tenderness that sent Frank
pale with dismay. We said little about his leaving then,
just as now, six weeks later, we said next to nothing about
his death. At Christmas we spoke of the dinner we had
eaten, and the snow weighing the branches of the trees,
and of the coal shortage. We spoke of Frank's journey as
if he were going to a football game in another town. Isobel
was restless on the creaking wicker sofa; she crossed her
long legs and blew cigarette smoke so that our least-liked
grandmother could go through an exaggerated pantomime
of having to beat it away. Isobel looked severely from face
to face. "Being direct" was her preferred expression then
—I think she had it from Suzanne—and I suppose she

wanted everyone to make a statement, as in one of those plays where every character suddenly says what he thinks in the most disconcerting manner imaginable. If Frank had never given us great cause for pride, he had never until recently given us cause for alarm: I expect she wanted statements made about that. Our mother should have said, "I have never loved you enough," and our father, "I love you but I am envious." Frank, stiff, silent Frank, ought to have said—if one were to complete the deranged dialogue—"I don't want to go back. I've had enough. But appearances are in favor of my going. I secure my parents' position. I assure myself of their esteem. Besides, I am bored here and have nothing to do, and I have a girl in England who must be married."

Our upright brother had left behind a girl whose daughter had since been born. We spoke of Enid decently as his fiancée. News of her misfortune had passed through the family from hand to hand, like a forfeit. The event ought to have satisfied our father once and for all about Frank's possible girlishness, but he seemed taken aback and never mentioned it. Enid was already writing our mother her first stoic letters about hardship and destruction, mentioning her own troubles in such a delicate way that she seemed to avoid and take them for granted all at once. Our mother, far from innocent, almost never taken in, said that Enid was plucky, and that those English girls couldn't be having much fun, what with all the rationing and the danger. "They've got our men," I said once, suddenly, not knowing I had an opinion about it until the words were out. My mother answered in a low, intense, and anxious voice, as close to passion as I had ever seen her. England was a permitted emotional channel; one could be as worked up as one liked over the white cliffs of Dover. Enid was of the same race as Churchill and the King and Queen. She was excused.

Dutiful Frank stayed in Allenton twelve days of his leave. On the thirteenth and next to last day he was sent

up to Montreal like a bundle of laundry, our mother having
announced that what he wanted now was the company of
his sisters. She had no qualms about deciding what other
people wanted, and the odd thing was that they usually
ended up wanting what she had decided. Frank arrived
in Montreal announcing that he wanted to see his sisters.
He had seen us ten days before, at Christmas, and we had
said goodbye then. Isobel and I had a scrambled discussion
by telephone about where he was to stay. Unexpectedly
Isobel said she would have him. They quarreled so much
when they were together that I often forgot they were
really close friends. Isobel's apartment was small, but she
could put a camp cot in the hall, which she would borrow
from some other Tessignier hovel.

I met Frank at the station on Saturday afternoon. He
was leaving Monday. He kissed me solemnly and gave me
news of our parents. I explained about his staying with
Isobel; he was instantly suspicious.

"What's her place like?"

"All right, but bare. It's not hers. It's one of Madame
Tessignier's so-called furnished apartments. Isa lives
around in these places till they're rented. She moves every
few weeks. She doesn't pay any rent or gas or light. Don't
tell Mother."

"That's darned nice, about the gas and light," said
Frank.

I told him that the apartment was over a garage, and
sometimes the noise from the garage drove everybody but
Isobel mad. It was sunny (I was answering Frank's questions) and Isobel could see cheerful happenings on the
street: drunks beating their girls, and American tourists
looking for butter and meat. I had realized that morning
that Frank was the head of the family, for even Isobel had
been in panic about what he might think of her way of
life. She had borrowed a red counterpane from Suzanne,
a remnant of Suzanne's homespun old Quebec period, and
begun painting the kitchen cupboards. I had collected for

her a pillow, a blanket, a lamp, and a blue glass bowl that had been one of my wedding presents. Isobel was grateful for everything. We were both of us nervous as birds.

She was warm and cheerful when I returned with Frank, and threw her arms around him. "I've got a huge bottle of rye," she said to him "All for you, only you have to drink it here."

The camp cot lay in pieces on the hall floor, with my folded blanket. "I hope to God you know how to put that thing up," she said, "because I don't." The room smelled of fresh paint, of the apples she had put in my blue glass bowl, and of Isa's own blond fragrance. I remember now why Tom said she smelled of gardenias. There were four long yellow tulips in a milk bottle on the windowsill; they threw their shadows on the bare floor, in a rectangle of pure winter sun.

"It looks almost furnished," I said. "There's even a chair."

"A friend of mine made it," said Isobel proudly. It was canvas chair shaped like a hammock on tiny wire legs. Frank sat down on its edge and was immediately toppled back into it. I got him a chair from the kitchen, a sensible wooden upright chair, and he sat down on that. He looked at Barney, curled on the bed, and offered the information that our mother disliked cats.

"Has she ever liked anything, except this damned war?" said Isobel, pouring rye into three tumblers lined up on the windowsill.

"Now, Isa," said Frank, comfortably, in a male head-of-family role. When the three of us were alone he took on this air. He thought his sisters' destinies depended on his strength of character and his judgement. If he could, he would have put us under glass bells, protected from dust and the elements, until he could decide what was to be done. He did not consider us married. Our husbands had never been there, except as pictures. Frank was too mild to believe that women should be driven, but there was no doubt he was convinced they ought to be led. "Why don't you get Mum to send you some furniture?" he said, looking around the room. This was his way of commenting on the canvas chair.

"The apartment isn't hers," I said. "I told you."

"I guess you can't buy much stuff now," he said.

"There's a war on," I said primly, sitting on the bed, trying to stroke Barney.

"All the same, you'd think they would . . ." Either Frank often forgot to finish his sentences, or I forgot to listen to the end. He sniffed the fresh paint and said, "Is it safe to sleep here?" Then he said, "This is a new place, isn't it? I mean, it's remodeled. It's funny, this Mrs. Tessignier getting permission to remodel a building in wartime. A whole apartment house."

"She just has this one apartment," I said.

"The Carters at home couldn't even get permission to build a garage. Who owns this place, anyway?"

"Madame Tessignier," I said.

"She rents it. Who does she rent it from?"

"A man called Farrow," Isobel said, adding ice and water to our drinks.

She turned to the telephone a split second before it rang. She picked it up from the floor and put it on the windowsill; she leaned on the sill, partly screened from me by her long hair, her eyes absently looked away, out the window, into the sunny, frozen day. All the roads that separated her from Frank, from me, led her to Alec; I was sure it was he. Her voice, after the first words, dropped, became gentle and trusting. I sat on the red counterpane, warmed by the sight of the oblong of sun on the floor, and told myself I was warmed by the sudden presence of love. To my horror and shame, tears came to my eyes, but then Barney jumped on my lap, and I stroked him and bent my head while Isobel talked. Frank picked up a book, discovered it was verse, and put it down. Isobel was removed from us to a warmer world, to a climate I could sense but not capture, like a secret, muddled idea I had of Greece, or the south, or being warm. What she said was ordinary enough. She said:

"Frank's here. He's on his way overseas. He's sleeping here for the weekend. No, I think he likes the idea. Jean's here. We're going to take him to Suzanne's. Oh, one of her parties. It'll be either for a refugee or a pansy, they're the only people she knows these days. You know, it happened again. I knew the phone was going to ring. Oh, about half a second before. ESP. No, don't laugh. It *is* ESP. I'll tell you when I see you. Soon. Soon, soon. What? Are you alone? Well, I thought so. That remark. Yes, soon. Goodbye. Soon. Goodbye."

When she turned back to us we had had time to adjust our faces and perhaps our thoughts. Frank had picked up the book again and opened it, and I was able to look with no question in my eyes.

"Which Farrow is that?" said Frank.

"Farrow?" said Isobel.

"Who owns this place," said Frank patiently. "Farrow, did you say, or Farrell?"

"The Farrows of Upper Galicia," said Isa, still smiling, still in the voice she had used with Alec, as if the break could not be made all at once. "Of Upper Galicia. A special branch."

"I thought so," my brother said, with great satisfaction. He put the book down. "That's exactly what I thought. The names they take! I don't know why the real Farrows don't sue."

He was driving Isa away. She looked absent, indifferent, now, as she did at Allenton, retreating from the family, "behaving." She handed Frank his glass rather abruptly, and gave me mine with a gesture less brusque.

"Farrow," said Frank, as if determined to drive her still farther off. If it had been in my power to make a decision of that sort, I might have hit him with the blue glass wedding present.

"Don't bother about it," I said, stroking the cat, slowly. "The real money behind this place is all Scot.

Farrow's only a small partner, a midget. The money is a man called MacKenzie Hamilton."

"I don't believe it," said Frank. Nevertheless he was silent for half a minute. It was difficult for him to find fault with the integrity of a Scot. Our father believed that Scottish blood was the best in the country, responsible for our national character traits of prudence, level-headedness, and self-denial. If anyone doubted it, our father said, the doubter had only to look at the rest of Canada: the French-Canadians (political corruption, pusillanimity, hysteria); the Italians (hair oil, used to bootleg in the 'twenties, used to pass right through Allenton); Russians and Ukrainians (regicide, Communism, pyromania, the distressing cult of nakedness on the West Coast); Jews (get in everywhere, the women don't wear corsets); Swedes, Finns (awful people for a bottle, never save a cent); Poles, hunkies, the whole Danubian fringe (they start all the wars). The Irish were Catholics, and the Germans had been beyond the pale since 1914. The only immigrant group he approved of were the Dutch. A census had revealed that although there were a quarter-million of them in the country, they were keeping quietly to themselves on celery farms in Western Ontario, saving money, not setting fire to anything, well-corseted, and out of politics. Their virtue, in fact, was that until the census one needn't have known they existed.

Frank continued to eye me suspiciously. Isobel was completely absent, sitting in the canvas chair. I said, "Farrow's hard working. He's only been in Canada three years, but he's got all his kids in good schools." (Frank would love that.) "But this MacKenzie Hamilton, now, he's only been here seven months, and he owns most of Peel Street."

There was a long silence. Frank mulled this over; he looked at the white wall and moved his lips. Like our father, Frank respected people who had made money, providing they were not Italian, Irish, Ukrainian and so forth, in which case the rise in wealth was put down to political chicanery and the complete absence of any sort of moral sense. Frank could not criticize the Galician Farrow without involving MacKenzie Hamilton as well. I had invented MacKenzie Hamilton, which poor Frank suspected.

"This Farrow," said Frank, finally. "Why'd he come to Canada?"I could see straight into the thicket of Frank's thinking to the tiny, sunlit clearing he had now discovered. The Scot had come to Canada willingly, because it was a country with a great future: MacKenzie Hamilton stood with his head tilted back and his hands outspread, on a background of pigmy pines. Galician Farrow had come here because he had nowhere else to go. Why wasn't he in uniform, fighting for Galicia?

Isobel suddenly woke up. She said, "Frank, for God's sake cut it out. I get enough of that from Madame Tessignier. If you start about the refugees I'll tell you about my unhappy childhood, and it'll bore you as much as you're boring us now."

"I haven't anything against anybody," said Frank.

"Don't be Christly," said Isa.

"There'll be refugees at the party tonight," I said. "Suzanne has discovered Europe."

"I'm sorry I bored you," said Frank earnestly. "We had exactly the same childhoods, so I don't see how yours could have been unhappy."

He wore his uniform as if he had never worn anything else. With his sandy hair, thin face, blue eyes, he looked as if he had been born to be photographed, in uniform, for the *Montreal Star*. We emptied the bottle, slowly, and the oblong of sun moved over the low red bed, over Barney, over me, and the room grew pale with the winter afternoon, then dark, and Isobel lit the lamp I had brought her that morning. In the new light we seemed softened by the experience of the day. The ashtrays were heaped. Instead of emptying them Isobel brought plates from the

kitchen. We played Isobel's Charles Trenet records on a
record player I'd never seen before. I guessed that it was
a Christmas present from Alec. We played Noel Coward
songs for Frank, who was drunk and solemn. He grew protective; assertive; we were his sisters. He observed that I
was too pale and Isobel thin. He wondered if it was safe
to sleep here, with the smell of paint, but this time his concern was for Isobel and not himself. He said the word
"sister" as if it were a figure he had to explain. He looked
pleading. All he demanded of us was that we be exactly
like the sister he was describing. It was all he demanded of
any human being: to be nothing more than a word suggested—sister or mother or husband or friend. A concern
for some new, personal idea (brother-in-law) now made
him look around the room and ask about Davy's picture.
Isobel had put her husband's picture away. It was an enlarged snapshot of a funny clownish boy. She had put it
away because it had been taken when he was eighteen and
she found that she was writing year after year to a grinning
boy instead of to a man of twenty-four. She could not
understand the letters she received, and so she supposed he was writing to a much younger girl too. I would
never have dared ask the question about Davy's picture. Isobel told Frank why she had put it away as if Frank
were her conscience.

"Yes, I know what you mean," said Frank. "But just
the same I'd leave it out somewhere. This way, it looks as
if you didn't care."

Presently—I must have gone to sleep on the bed—I
heard Frank say, "I don't know why, but I never liked a
book like I liked *Butterfield 8*."

"You can't say 'like a book like I liked,'" said my sister.
The pupils of her eyes were huge. "I don't know what you
are supposed to say but I know it isn't 'like a book like I
liked.'"

Frank said, "Yes, and you know something else? A
book like that, I wouldn't give it to my mother to read."

"Neither would I," said Isobel. "If I had a mother I wouldn't let her read anything. Look at Jean, sound asleep with her eyes open."

"Ears too," said Frank, but I must have dreamed that Frank said this, for it was superimposed with the words, "The bottle's killed." My memory after that is our being all three in a restaurant, eating fried chicken, on the way to Suzanne's party. It was January 1945. We sat in a booth in a restaurant. Snow fell heavily on the street outside. I have forgotten if any important historical events were then taking place.

My concern was the party, and whether Frank would like Suzanne. I think that was how it was. I am the only person who can tell the truth about anything now, because I am, in a sense, the survivor. Suzanne is still alive, but I never see her. She must be in her forties. I imagine her thin and hard with hard dyed hair. She was twenty-three then. I was proud of her because Isobel liked her, and because I had met her first. We had lived in the same boarding house when I came up to Montreal, the summer I was married. I had never in my life lived in a city during a heat wave. In this worn and dusty house I heard gusts of words and music, the creaks and slams and the dropped hangers and vague exclamations that seemed to me all of life. Sitting by the window one breathless July night I recognized for the first time the feeling of a city. Suzanne had never known anything else. She was so fierce, white-skinned, black-haired, that if she had not spoken to me first I would never have had enough courage to say hello. She was just out of Beaux-Arts and living on her husband's service allowance and a part-time job as a waitress. She crashed through life, like the farmers in the north of Quebec who, settling on new land, cut every tree in sight just because nothing must stand. Suzanne crashed on, dragging with her a younger sister, Huguette, who was sweet-faced and barely literate, cutting down everything

she saw standing. The two girls were out of a slum in the
east end of a city I could barely imagine.

I remember Suzanne's telling me straight away that
she had a lover. He was a professor who had lost his post at
the Beaux-Arts owing to some intrigue I was unable to
follow. He had a second mistress, who satisfied certain
needs for the professor Suzanne could but partially gratify.
She did not say what they were and I had no idea even
approaching the sexual reality she was talking about.
Suzanne had a simple view of life and love then; she
thought a man of genius had a right to as many women as
he appeared to need. Her feelings toward him were almost
maternal. I once accompanied her on a Sunday morning.
The professor having been on a bender of three or four
days with the second mistress, Suzanne began to fret in
case he hadn't found time to eat during these busy hours,
and we traveled miles by streetcar in order to leave a
loving message and a bit of raw steak in his apartment
mailbox. Years later I was disappointed to meet the professor at one of her parties. He sat in a corner, wan and
moth-eaten, gray-haired, dressed with a Sunday air like
a local farmer in town for the weekend. That, indeed, was
his origin, and a long prewar residence in Paris had done
nothing to modify his looks. Suzanne, furious with me for
saying so, remarked that I was a hopeless provincial and
would never be anything else, since I lacked imagination
and could rely on nothing but the evidence of my experience. I begged her forgiveness and admitted she was
right. I had never been to Paris and could only imagine
how people there might differ from farmers.

Suzanne met Isobel through me (oh, the pride of that
introduction!) and it was Isobel who found Suzanne her
studio on Oxenden Street—two north-facing rooms so dank
and ratridden that even Madame Tessignier could not
disguise them as nests for refugees or servicemen. Slowly,
Isobel and Suzanne became friends. A pattern of friends
and encounters took form, and after a time I saw Isobel
only at Suzanne's parties.

"Isa won't get in any trouble there," I remember saying to my mother. "Suzanne only knows pansies." In relation to my mother, something always compelled me to be disloyal to my friends. Suzanne's friends, now, were young refugees. They seemed to me alike, and examined me in the same tense-mouthed manner. I was considered the symbol of English Canada. I told my mother so, and we laughed. Then I was ill with remorse, for Suzanne had been abrupt but generous with me always. I remember her thrusting into my hands a drawing of hers I had liked, or a pair of nylon stockings some man, perhaps one of her sister's racketeer boy friends, had given her. I remember walking away from her studio down a curved, foggy street, while flower-shaped lamps came out of the fog, and the cobbles of the street shone as if they had risen from the sea; I held the little parcel of whatever it was she had given me—stockings, or a rolled-up sketch—and I remember thinking, Now, this is the happiest moment of my life, I shall never be happier than now.

I hoped that in the presence of Frank Suzanne would not be too openly ironic about the war. Her new cult of refugees had taught her to say "anti-fascist," but she could not get over her idea of war as a social event for the English. I needn't have worried. Frank was given the same wary care as visiting parents in boarding school. One of Suzanne's new friends offered him a cigarette with trembling hands. In that atmosphere, where everyone represented something other than himself, Frank in his uniform was simply heroic. The uniform represented the fight for democracy and the betterment of mankind, and his physical coloring gave him the Anglo-Saxon appearance required for decent fighting. He was off to rescue any number of less fortunate people, many of them darker than himself. His conventional manners stood for order, and his unloquaciousness was the modesty of the doomed. Family instinct compelled me to stay by his side until Suzanne suddenly emerged and said, "Can't I talk to this boy?" She took his arm and guided him around the studio, making people move when they were in his way. "Did you paint all this?" I heard Frank say. Suzanne scarcely ever showed anyone her paintings in this way, but perhaps she had never known anyone like Frank. She looked at him from time to time as they circled the room, saying little. She was not mocking, as she often had been with me, but almost supplicating. Was Frank the person she wanted to reach? I was certain he would say "What are they supposed to be?" of her pictures, but to my astonishment he thought that everything looked like something. It was the first abstract art he had seen, except in magazines, and that was what he thought: everything looked like something. He saw a beach scene with children playing, Japanese women crossing a bridge, a plane smashed on a mountain, a table and window and somebody's frightening head at the window. He saw a fish in a bowl with flowers behind the bowl.

"Good," said fierce Suzanne, showing her white teeth when she laughed. She was a black and white girl: white teeth, white skin, black hair, a black scowl. She was dirty: I mean by that physically dirty. She slipped her arm around Frank, an incredible mark of her favor; but he moved slightly when she touched him, and I wondered for the first time what Enid was like.

My sister lay on the double bed in the next room, her head on her hand, her straight hair covering the hand, and stared at a boy from Halifax who was reciting, from memory, the opening sentences of his novel. The party was being given for him. "I thought he was a genius," said Suzanne. "My mistake." The new boy, the mistake, looked miserable. He sat beside Isobel, and droned on: "He walked through the hall. A rose fell. Roses, he thought. Blood." He would not have Isobel to himself for long. In a few minutes she would be surrounded by the men to whom she was nearly a legend: the young mistress of a middle-aged man to whom she was completely faithful. She looked as if love absorbed her so completely that she hadn't time for the ordinary cares of life. I observed her cracked, scuffed moccasins, and the blouse slipping out of the band of the skirt. She looked at the novelist with great kindness.

"I want to ask you a question," said an unknown man. "Why'n't you ever get tight? Why'n't you let yourself go?" Earnest, red-eyed, watery-kind—I have no idea who he was. I said crossly, "Well, I am tight, if you want to know," but he thought I was making fun of him.

Suzanne showed Frank a poem written by the boy from Halifax. The boy was still clinging to Isobel, as if he knew by now that Suzanne considered him a mistake. Suzanne read aloud: "And wash my sweating face."

"Lousy, eh?" she said, but Frank thought it was good. He said she had never been in the service and knew nothing about sweat.

"I've been poor, I've lived where there wasn't any water," said Suzanne, who was proud of this.

Frank was entranced, polite, and receptive. I had never known him. I heard Suzanne telling him about her party line, which was connected with a call house on Pine Avenue. She had once heard a distinguished lawyer say to a distinguished colleague, "Come right away, she's got high school girls." Frank smiled, a grave, friendly smile I had never seen, as if he might have been either of those two men. It was a pity I could not see him for the first time, now, without knowing he resembled our father, or had been bullied, and had left in England an illegitimate child.

Some of Suzanne's refugees had formed a circle, sitting on the floor, with their beer glasses inside the magic ring. They sang softly, "Freiheit." There was a girl with them, a little blonde girl who had fallen in love with one of them. Her hand was in his and she swayed, her eyes closed, and sang "Freiheit." I knew in an instant that Frank wouldn't like this. The refugees could sing anything they chose, but not the Canadian girl. He looked at the girl and his mouth closed as if on a secret. Suzanne noticed nothing. She and Frank sat side by side on a table and I stood before them. She went on telling him about the party line. It would seem curious to him, subversive even, to sing freedom during a war. The very idea was anti-duty. One could be anti-duty or anti-government or even anti-war if one were a crackpot, but one had better not be anti-circumstance. It was against the circumstance to sing of freedom now. *"Freiheit"* said the little blonde girl emphatically, eyes shut, swaying.

We were nearly the last to leave. We walked in snow, our arms linked, and in the curtain of snow Frank said, "Good party. That Suzanne, she's got a sense of humor." He shook his head at the memory of her, smiling and secretive. Snow lay thicker and thicker on our shoulders and our hair and the stuff of our coats. Frank suddenly said, "Did you see the girl singing?"

"Which one?" said Isobel.

"On the floor, singing in German. A little blonde."

"I was in the other room," my sister said.

"I saw her," I said.

"Well, she looks like Enid," said Frank. "That's what she looks like, the same hair and all. Enid can sing too."

"I'll ask Suzanne who she is," said Isobel.

His answer was, "You know what I said before? About Davy's picture? I'd leave it out if I were you. This way, it looks bad. Whatever your personal feelings are you shouldn't make it look as if you don't care."

They put me into a taxi then, and Frank instructed the driver to drive with care; he was taking over my destiny again. He and Isobel walked on in the snow. I slept through the next day, Sunday, and when I rang Isobel's number in the evening there was no reply. They had gone to a movie. On Monday he went to the station alone. We did not say goodbye, and I never saw him again.

In February, from the train that was taking Isobel and me to Allenton, we saw another lighted train pass with such speed that we might have been standing still. The drawn-out sweeping whistle rushed by the windows. It was the Boston train, which had seemed to me on winter nights before I married the sound of hope and escape. Afterwards it was the sound of nostalgia, as if there were a journey I had once made and now remembered. "Oh, you know, he isn't better off!" Isobel cried as if I had said it were possible. She said it to our reflections in the train window. It was all I ever heard her say about Frank.

7

Our period of family mourning continued for three days. One night I saw, or thought I saw, or may have dreamed, that my father sat on the stairs weeping. Our mother stood a few steps below him so that their faces were nearly level. She was in a flannel dressing gown, a plait of gray hair undone and over one shoulder. Patient, waiting, she held a glass of water to his lips as if control could be taken like a pill. Everything in that scene, which I must have dreamed, spoke of the terror of pity. "The girls are home," she said, for fear that we wake and see him and join him in grieving aloud.

On the last night Isobel came into Frank's room. I was sitting up in Frank's bed writing to my husband. Tom was in Holland. I wrote to a legendary husband, in a place I assumed must exist. Both of us wrote frequently, as if we wanted to say, "I am doing my best, I am not to blame." I had curled the ends of my hair and tied round the curls a coral chiffon scarf I had found in my overnight case. It must have been a scarf belonging to Alma, snatched from the towel rack together with Alma's stockings. Isobel peered round the door; I think she smiled. "Can I come in for a minute? Wait, I'll shut the window." She crossed the room and disappeared behind the drawn curtains. "There's snow all over the floor," she said, emerging. "How do you stand it, sitting there in the cold?" Her voice was light and full of life. I never could match the breathless child's voice with someone who seemed to me so closed and careful.

That day my mother and I had listened to a radio interview with a returned soldier. "What are your first impressions of good old Montreal?" asked the bright announcer.
"The girls have these awful voices," said the new repatri-
ate. "Thank *you*," my mother said, turning him off.

Isobel sat down, shivering, at the foot of the bed.
Her hair was streaky and dark at the roots, as if it had been
dyed. Our mother had mentioned it that evening: "Isa,
when did you last give your head a good wash?"

"The other day," my sister said, indifferently. "It's all
going dark. I must be getting a cold or something."

"Fine hair is a curse," our mother said, with the pride
one owed a divine affliction.

Isobel propped her elbow on the iron bedstead and
dropped her head on her hand. It was a romantic pose—
knees bent, one hand palm upward on her lap. She resembled the tired figures named "Hope" and "Waiting" on
colored postcards of the First World War. She moved,
sighed, smiled at me, and for a moment I saw why Suzanne
had called Isobel lavish. *Personnage aux Plumes.* A golden
bird. How foolish all of that was, when I think of it soberly!
She was a tall, slouching, untidy girl in a faded dressing
gown. There was no limit to my delusions then. They were
fed in solitude, on the wildness of people like Suzanne. I
had no reason then to live in reality, as I have now. Looking back and down from reality, I can correct the story
about plumes: Isobel was considered attractive, though
not a perfect beauty, and she was not lavish, and not
golden, and not a bird. Those are fancies.

"What do you do when you can't sleep?" Isobel said.
I had asked Alec about sleeping once, on Sherbrooke
Street.

I said, "Alma gives me a pill."

"Where does she get them?"

"From the nurse at the office infirmary. That nurse is
insane," I said. "She gives out phenobarb and codeine like
candy. Some of the old girls in the company live on it."

"Listen," Isobel said. "I'm pregnant. That's why I feel

sick all the time. I think being sick is only being frightened. I'm two months. I knew it when Frank was here. I wasn't certain but I knew."

"Don't tell Mother."

"Mother! Why do you think I'm telling you?"

She hadn't shut the window properly. I felt a draught of thin snowy air.

From that moment I stopped being the stranger on the dark street and I moved into the bright rooms of my sister's life. The doors were opened to me; everything had been leading to my entrance, my participation. Frank's old room, with his faded collection of butterflies and his maps and his schoolbooks in a glassfront case, disappeared with his memory. If Isobel needed me, then I had overcome the common inheritance, the family walls. I was up and closing the window against the draught before she had finished speaking. On my way back to bed I pulled a corner of the blanket over her bare feet. She seemed to have the lassitude of pregnancy, the droop of wrist, the relaxed fingers. She did not notice that I had covered her feet. The dressing gown she wore had belonged to both of us years before. It was inches short for her long arms. She said, "When we were kids we couldn't get away with a midnight talk, could we? We'd hear 'Jean-an-Isa. Isa-an-Jean. Quiet. It's late.' You know, for years I thought Mother could read our minds and see through walls."

"I still think it."

"I hate nicknames," Isobel said. "Isa. Isn't that ugly? Jean, now, that's plain."

"Mother thought I'd be plain."

"Mother didn't think anything. She named you after Granny Stewart, only Granny Stewart left it all to charity. Plain names are better, and there mustn't be nicknames. I say Alec, not Al. I'm the only person who does. I think his wife says Al, when she doesn't say 'My husband, Mr. Campbell.' Al sounds like somebody's no-good brother drinking beer in a tavern."

Our wishes are granted when we are least ready. How

often had I prowled around her house, waiting for a word, a half-open door, a sleeping sentry, so that I could see what it was to be Isobel, to have Alec, to be loved? The door opened, but I was unprepared.

It wasn't easy, this business with Alec, said Isobel calmly. He had the wife to support, and the children. When Isobel and Alec married—as of course they would—Isobel would have to keep on working. She knew she would work all her life for Bitsy and Bitsy's children. She didn't mind. There was Davy. She didn't want me to think she didn't care about Davy. She knew I disliked him, but did I know him, really? Wasn't I a bit prejudiced? What had he ever said to me that was impolite? She wrote Davy all the time, but she was writing to a kid. With Alec it wasn't the same thing. Alec was older. When she measured Davy against Alec she saw that Davy wasn't growing. He hadn't moved. Of course it wasn't his fault. The army was adolescent. Alec said so. Did I know, Davy still had that business about Thomas Wolfe? Yes, still, and he went on about Wolfe in nearly every letter. Wasn't he ever going to read anything else? Davy was still where they had been a long time ago. How many years? She had loved Davy, but Davy couldn't help her now. He needed help himself. He was a little peculiar, a little too young; and she was a little crazy too, so it would never do, she and Davy together. Alec had said so. Had I never noticed she was a little crazy? Well, she was. She knew it. Sometimes she had to stop while she was doing something ordinary, some commonplace thing like brushing her hair or looking for a postage stamp, and she had to say, "Is this the right thing to be doing? Am I right?" and she would be full of fear in case she had been about to do the wrong thing. Every step she took might be a step in a trap. Am I right? she had to keep saying. Is this all right? Am I doing what I ought to be doing? Alec knew. He kept her sane. He was the rock. As long as he was there she could behave like other people. She might have spent her life being a little weak, a little

frightened, if it hadn't been for him. It was the only kind
of love, Isobel said calmly. Alec had told her so. He had
said it was the best thing in the world for her, this secret.
You need to have someone between you and the rest, she
said; someone between you and the others, blotting out the
light.

She may not have said "blotting out the light," and I
may distort the remembered scene if I say she put up her
hand, flat, to indicate the kind of shutting out.

This had been spoken in the most simple tone. There
was no intensity, and no drama in her voice. Nevertheless
I had the feeling that I had been listening to something
completely astonishing and greatly intimate. I understood
as I had just before the automobile crash with Tom the
inevitability of dying: I experienced again the pool of saliva
under the tongue and the swollen lips. The words I had
thought then came back now: That is what it is like. I
understood she had told me something I wanted to know.
I would have gone once more to the window, for the sake
of something to do, but there was no real reason for moving. I sat straight, knees bent, and clasped my knees with
hands as thick as pieces of wood. What had troubled me?
The words, Someone between you and the rest? The wall
suddenly there, immovable, in the headlights of the car?

Presently I thought she had said everything and I
allowed my hands to come apart. The movement brought
Isobel to life. "I'm afraid of Alec's children," she said. "They
frighten me. I saw them once in his car. He was driving
and he saw me, but he didn't know me. He saw me but he
didn't *know*. When he's not with them he doesn't know anyone *but* me." More silence. She sighed, smiled, played with
the edge of the blanket I had turned over her feet. I had a
vain reaction. I began to undo the coral chiffon scarf, which
I knew was making me very homely, and take the pins out
of my hair. Isobel would come and live with me. Alma
would have to go. She would pack her ribboned combs and
her red maple furniture and go.

"You know why I've told you, don't you?" Isobel said.
"I don't need just an address. I don't need just good advice."

"You don't need any address except mine. You don't
have to go anywhere except with me."

"I don't need an address," Isobel said again. "I can get
that from Suzanne. I don't need advice about drinking gin
or taking boiling-hot baths. I need somebody's whole attention."

"Who else is there?" I said, creating a fantasy that we
were sisters, therefore confidants, therefore friends.

She gave me an exasperated and deliberately wounding glance. "There's Suzanne," she said. "She's sensible,
she minds her own business, she doesn't preach. But that
works both ways. She minds her own business when you're
in trouble too. Madame Tessignier can pray for me. But
I want somebody's whole attention. I don't want to be
alone."

"What about him?" I said bravely.

"There's nothing he can do, is there? I'm not going to
tell him until it's over." She spoke in the obstinate way
our mother detested. She was afraid. I thought again,
Someone between you and the rest. There was a flaw in
the story, just as some people said there was a flaw in her
face. Isobel was watching me now. We were sisters, rather
alike, in our brother's room, having a midnight talk. Isobel
watched me, with the expression one of Suzanne's refugees
wore when he was trying to explain in faulty English how
things had been at home. Someone who has lost his language wears that look, that despair. Fear, despair: despair
is too loud for the quiet night. Remove the word, leave
Isobel with cheek on hand, eyes gone yellow in the light
of the lamp.

It was plain and simple: She was in trouble and
needed me. Pretend I had never circled her life, been the
stranger on the street, afraid to meet the eyes of another
stranger looking out. "Afraid" is too loud, too. There remains Isobel, then, cheek on hand, a little tired. I remain

bolt upright in bed, hugging my knees. Forget despair, fear. We were very ordinary. Leave us there, with the lamp like a ship and the anchors round the shade, and the map on the wall with the Empire in pink, and my sister and I at opposite ends of the bed, with our childhoods between us going on to the horizon without a break. It was so plain and simple; and I thought that unless we could meet across that landscape we might as well die, it was useless to stay alive. She was the most beautiful girl I had ever known, even now, with her hair dark at the roots, her eyes yellow and circled; she was still the most elusive, the most loved. I moved forward, kneeling, in the most clumsy movement possible. It was dragging oneself through water against the swiftest current, in the fastest river in the world; I knelt on the bed near my sister and took her thin relaxed hand in mine. We met in a corner of the landscape and she glanced at me, then slid her hand out of mine and said, "Oh, don't."

I said, "I only meant I would give you what you said, you know, my whole attention."

"I know that," said Isobel. She tried to smile and I tried to return the smile, but I had attempted something beyond our capacities. I drew back and got under the blankets again. Isobel groped with her feet for her slippers. "I didn't bring them," she said to herself. She bowed her head. "I know you'll help me," she said. "That's why I told you. Everything is easy for you. You've got all the wheels turning."

She stood up, shivering as her feet touched the cold floor. She closed the door behind her and I sat still. Her movements cried her defeat. She wanted my attention, and would pay for it. She would tell me about Davy and Alec and life and love. She would tell me everything I wanted to know. She would never shut the door again and leave me on the street. Neither Suzanne nor Alec could give her what she could have from me: the whole attention. She needed it, and she would pay.

I left the scarf and pins on Frank's night table. It no longer mattered whether my hair was straight or curled. I saw the curtains tremble in the draught and went to the window. There is no condition of snow I have not observed, from the first fall to the mild deceptive stillness at night, close to the end of winter, when a dark breath, indrawn and held, warns that death is returning after all. I opened the window to this held breath and knew that winter was still here and might never come to an end.

I continued my letter to Tom. I wrote: "Mother is taking it well, as you might expect from her, but Dad feels it. Isa . . ." It wouldn't hurt to tell him about her. Why not describe the visit to my room and say that she needed me? It would be something to write into the void. Reading my letter in Holland (what was Holland?) he might remember something about me he had forgotten. His memory is for dates, not for feelings; even today he will insist that we last saw Isobel in 1958 and not 1955, as I tell it. He might realize he had not known me well, and he might write, "I was interested in your letter because . . ." It wouldn't hurt. Had he not loved her before proposing to me? Had she not refused him in the car that June day when she was eighteen and in love with Davy Sullivan? Why not tell him that Isobel and I could not look at each other? I wrote: "I don't think I've ever told you, but poor Isa is having a bad time. She's been having an affair with a married man and now she thinks she's pregnant. Don't mention it to anyone." That was how it was. If I sent the letter, the strangeness would be in having written, "Poor Isa," but it would be Isobel delivered, Isobel destroyed. The story could wait. It would always be there to tell. I might never tell it, but there is something in waiting for the final word. One day Isobel might be "poor Isa" in Tom's eyes. He would see and judge for himself.

He would see and judge providing he was not killed; providing the winter ended and we had survived. Madame Tessignier hoped it would never end—the night, the winter, the war. I suspected, then, sitting in Frank's unhaunted room, that all of us, save my brother, were obliged to survive. We had slipped into our winter as trustingly as every night we fell asleep. We woke from dreams of love remembered, a house recovered and lost, a climate imagined, a journey never made; we woke dreaming our mothers had died in childbirth and heard ourselves saying, "Then there is no one left but me!" We would waken thinking the earth must stop, now, so that we could be shed from it like snow. I knew, that night, we would not be shed, but would remain, because that was the way it was. We would survive, and waking—because there was no help for it—forget our dreams and return to life.

The Cost of Living

Louise, my sister, talked to Sylvie Laval for the first time on the stairs of our hotel on a winter afternoon. At five o'clock the skylight over the stairway and the blank, black windows on each of the landings were pitch dark—dark with the season, dark with the cold, dark with the dark air of cities. The only light on the street was the blue neon sign of a snack bar. My sister had been in Paris six months, but she still could say, "What a funny French word that is, Puss—'snack.'" Louise's progress down the steps was halting and slow. At the best of times she never hurried, and now she was guiding her bicycle and carrying a trench coat, a plaid scarf, Herriot's "Life of Beethoven," Cassell's English-French, a bottle of cough medicine she intended to exchange for another brand, and a notebook, in which she had listed facts about nineteenth-century music under so many headings, in so many divisions of divisions, that she had lost sight of the whole.

The dictionary, the Herriot, the cough medicine, and the scarf were mine. I was the music mistress, out in all weathers, subject to chills, with plenty of woolen garments to lend. I had not come to Paris in order to teach *solfège* to stiff-fingered children. It happened that at the late age of twenty-seven I had run away from home. High time, you might say; but rebels can't always be choosers. At first I gave lessons so as to get by, and then I did it for a living, which is not the same thing. My older sister followed me— wisely, calmly, with plenty of money for travel—six years later, when both our parents had died. She was accustomed to a busy life at home in Australia, with a large house to look after and our invalid mother to nurse. In Paris, she found time on her hands. Once she had visited all the museums, and cycled around the famous squares, and read what was written on the monuments, she felt she was wasting her opportunities. She decided that music might be useful, since she had once been taught to play the piano; also, it was bound to give us something in common. She was making a serious effort to know me. There was a difference of five years between us, and I had been away from home for six. She enrolled in a course of lectures, took notes, and went to concerts on a cut-rate student's card.

I'd better explain about that bicycle. It was heavy and old—a boy's bike, left by a cousin killed in the war. She had brought it with her from Australia, thinking that Paris would be an easy, dreamy city, full of trees and full of time. The promises that led her, that have been made to us all at least once in our lives, had sworn faithfully there would be angelic children sailing boats in the fountains, and calm summer streets. But the parks were full of brats and quarreling mothers, and the bicycle was a nuisance everywhere. Still, she rode it; she would have thought it wicked to spend money on bus fares when there was a perfectly good bike to use instead.

We lived on the south side of the Luxembourg Gardens, where streets must have been charming before the motorcars came. Louise was hounded by buses and small, pitiless automobiles. Often, as I watched her from a window of our hotel, I thought of how she must seem to Parisian drivers—the very replica of the governessy figure the French, with their passion for categories and their disregard of real evidence, instantly label "the English Miss." It was a verdict that would have astonished her, if she had known, for Louise believed that "Australian," like "Protestant," was written upon her, plain as could be. She had no idea of the effect she gave, with her slow gestures, her straight yellow hair, her long face, her hand-stitched mannish gloves and shoes. The inclination of her head and the quarter-profile of cheek, ear, and throat could seem, at times, immeasurably tender. Full-face, the head snapped to, and you saw the lines of duty from nose to mouth, and the too pale eyes. The Prussian ancestry on our mother's side had given us something bleached and cold. Our faces were variations on a theme of fair hair, light brows. The mixture was weak in me. I had inherited the vanity, the stubbornness, without the will; I was too proud to follow and too lame to command. But physically we were nearly alike. The characteristic fold of skin at the outer corner of the eye, slanting down—we both had that. And I could have used a word about us, once, if I dared: "dainty." A preposterous word; yet looking at the sepia studio portrait of us, taken twenty-five years ago, when I was eight and Louise thirteen, you could imagine it. Here is Louise, calm and straight, with her hair brushed on her shoulders, and her pretty hands; there am I, with organdy frock, white shoes, ribbon, and fringe. Two little Anglo-German girls, accomplished at piano, Old Melbourne on the father's side, Church of England to the bone: Louise and Patricia—Lulu and Puss. We hated each other then.

Once, before Louise left Paris forever, I showed her a description of her that had been written by Sylvie Laval. It was part of a cast of characters around whom Sylvie evidently meant to construct a film. I may say that Sylvie never wrote a scenario, or anything like one; but she belonged to a Paris where one was "writer" or "artist" or "actor" without needing to prove the point. "The Australian," wrote Sylvie, in a hand that showed an emotional age of nine, "is not elegant. All her skirts are too long, and she should not knit her own sweaters and hats. She likes Berlioz and the Romantics, which means corrupt taste. She lives in a small hotel on the left bank because [erased] She has an income she tries to pass off as moderate, which she probably got from a poor old mother, who died at last. Her character is innocent and romantic, but she is a mythomaniac and certainly cold. This [here Sylvie tried to spell a word unknown to me] makes it hard to guess her age. Her innocence is phenomenal, but she knows more than she says. She resembles the Miss Bronty [crossed out] Bronthee [crossed out] Brounte, the English lady who wore her hair parted in front and lived to a great old age after writing many moral novels and also Wuthering Heights."

I found the notes for the film in a diary after Sylvie had left the hotel. Going by her old room, I stopped at the open door. I could see M. Rablis, who owned the hotel and who had been Sylvie's lover, standing inside. He stood, the heart of a temper storm, the core of a tiny hurricane, and he flung her abandoned effects onto a pile of ragged books and empty bottles. I think he meant to keep everything, even the bottles, until Sylvie came back to settle her bill and return the money he said she had stolen from his desk. There were Javel bottles and whiskey bottles and yoghurt bottles and milk bottles and bottles for olive oil and tonic water and medicine and wine. Onto the pile went her torn stockings, her worn-out shoes. I recognized the ribbons and the *broderie anglaise* of a petticoat my sister had once given her as a present. The petticoat suited Sylvie —the tight waist, and the wide skirt—and it suited her even more after the embroidery became unstitched and flounces began to hang. Think of draggled laces, sagging hems, ribbons undone; that was what Sylvie was like. Hair in the eyes, sluttish little Paris face—she was a curious friend for immaculate Louise. When M. Rablis saw me at the door, he calmed down and said, "Ah, Mademoiselle. Come in and see if any of this belongs to you. She stole from everyone—miserable little thief." But "little thief" sounded harmless, in French, in the feminine. It was a woman's phrase, a joyous term, including us all in a capacity for frivolous mischief. I stepped inside the room and picked up the diary, and a Japanese cigarette box, and the petticoat, and one or two other things.

That winter's day when Sylvie talked to Louise for the first time, Louise was guiding her bicycle down the stairs. It would be presumptuous for me to say what she was thinking, but I can guess: she was more than likely converting the price of oranges, face powder, and Marie-biscuits from French francs to Australian shillings and pence. She was, and she is, exceptionally prudent. Questions of upbringing must be plain to the eye and ear—if not, better left unexplained. Let me say only that it was a long training in modesty that made her accept this wretched hotel, where, with frugal pleasure, she drank tea and ate Marie-biscuits, heating the water on an electric stove she had been farsighted enough to bring from home. Her room had dusty claret hangings. Silverfish slid from under the carpet to the cracked linoleum around the washstand. She could have lived in comfort, but I doubt if it occurred to her to try. With every mouthful of biscuit and every swallow of tea, she celebrated our mother's death and her own release. Louise had nursed Mother eleven years. She nursed her eleven years, buried her, and came to Paris with a bicycle and an income.

Now, Sylvie, who knew nothing about duty and less about remorse, would have traded her soul, without a second's bargaining, for Louise's room; for Sylvie lived in an ancient linen cupboard. The shelves had been taken out and a bed, a washstand, a small table, a straight chair pushed inside. In order to get to the window, one had to pull the table away and climb over the chair. This room, or cupboard, gave straight onto the stairs, between two floors. The door was flush with the staircase wall; only a ravaged keyhole suggested that the panel might be any kind of door. As she usually forgot to shut it behind her, anyone who wanted could see her furrowed bed and the basin, in which underclothes floated among islands of scum. She would plunge down the stairs, leaving a blurred impression of mangled hair and shining eyes. Her eyes were a true black, with the pupil scarcely distinct from the iris. Later I knew that she came from the southwest of France; I think that some of her people were Basques. The same origins gave her a stocky peasant's build and thick, practical hands. Her hand, grasping the stair rail, and the firm tread of her feet specified a quality of strength that had nothing in common with the forced liveliness of Parisian girls, whose energy seemed to me as thin and strung up as their voices. Her scarf, her gloves flew from her like birds. Her shoes could never keep up with her feet. One of my memories of Sylvie—long before I knew anything about her, before I knew even her name—is of her halting, cursing loudly with a shamed smile, scrambling up or down a few steps, and shoving a foot back into a lost ballerina shoe. She wore those thin slippers out on the streets, under the winter rain. And she wore a checked skirt, a blue sweater, and a scuffed plastic jacket that might have belonged to a boy. Passing her, as she hung over the banister calling to someone below, you saw the tensed muscle of an arm or leg, the young neck, the impertinent head. Someone ought to have drawn her—but somebody has: Sylvie was the coarse and grubby Degas dancer, the girl with the shoulder thrown back and the insolent chin. For two pins, or fewer, that girl staring out of flat canvas would stick out her tongue or spit in your face. Sylvie had the voice you imagine belonging to the picture, a voice that was common, low-pitched, but terribly penetrating. When she talked on the telephone, you could hear her from any point in the hotel. She owned the telephone, and she read *Cinémonde*, a magazine about film stars, by the hour, in the lavatory or (about once every six weeks) while soaking in the tub. There was one telephone and one tub for the entire hotel, and one lavatory for every floor. Sylvie was always where you wanted to be; she had always got there first. Having got there, she remained, turning pages, her voice cheerfully lifted in the newest and most melancholy of popular songs.

"Have you noticed that noisy girl?" Louise said once, describing her to me and to the young actor who had the room next to mine.

We were all three in Louise's room, which now had the look of a travel bureau and a suburban kitchen combined; she had covered the walls with travel posters and bought a transparent plastic tablecloth. Pottery dishes in yellow and blue stood upon the shelves. Louise poured tea and gave us little cakes. I remember that the young man and I, both well into the age of reason, sat up very straight and passed spoons and paper napkins back and forth with constant astonished cries of "Thank you" and "Please." It was something about Louise; she was so kind, so hospitable, she made one want to run away.

"I never notice young girls," said the young man, which seemed to me a fatuous compliment, but Louise turned pink. She appeared to be waiting for something more from him, and so he went on, "I know the girl you mean." It was not quite a lie. I had seen Sylvie and this boy together many times. I had heard them in his room, and I had passed them on the stairs. Well, it was none of my affair.

Until Louise's arrival, I had avoided meeting anyone

in the hotel. Friendship in bohemia meant money borrowed, recriminations, complaints, tears, theft, and deceit. I kept to myself, and I dressed like Louise, which was as much a disguise as my bohemian way of dressing in Melbourne had been. This is to explain why I had never introduced Louise to anyone in the hotel. As for the rest of Paris, I didn't need to bother; Louise arrived with a suitcase of introductions and a list of names as long as the list for a wedding. She was not shy, she wanted to "get to know the people," and she called at least once on every single person she had an introduction to. That was how it happened that she and the actor met outside the hotel, in a different quarter of Paris. They had seen each other across the room, and each of them thought "I wonder who that is?" before discovering they lived in the same place. This sort of thing is supposed never to happen in cities, and it does happen.

She met him on the twenty-first of December in the drawing room of a house near the Parc Monceau. She had been invited there by the widow of a man in the consular service who had been to Australia and had stayed with an uncle of ours. It was one of the names on Louise's list. Before she had been many weeks in Paris, she knew far more than I did about the hard chairs, cheerless lights, and gray-pink antique furniture of French rooms. The hobby of the late consul had been collecting costumes. The drawing room was lined with glass cases in which stood headless dummies wearing the beads and embroidery of Turkey, Macedonia, and Greece. It was a room intended not for people but for things—this was a feeling Louise said she often had about rooms in France. Thirty or forty guests drifted about, daunted by the museum display. They were given whiskey to drink and sticky cakes. Louise wore the gray wool dress that was her "best" and the turquoise bracelets our Melbourne grandfather brought back from a voyage to China. They were the only ornaments I have ever seen her wearing. She talked to a poet who carried in his pocket an essay about him that had been printed years before—yellow, brittle bits of paper, like beech leaves. She consoled a wild-haired woman who complained that her daughter had begun to carry on. "How old is your daughter?" said Louise. The woman replied, "Thirty-five. And you know how men are now. They have no respect for girlhood any more." "It is very difficult," Louise agreed. She was getting to know the people, and was pleased with her afternoon. The consul's widow looked toward the doors and muttered that Cocteau was coming, but he never came. All at once Louise heard her say, in answer to a low-toned question, "She's Australian," and then she heard, "She's like a coin, isn't she? Gold and cold. She's interested in music, and lives over on the Left Bank, just as you do—except that you don't give your address, little monkey, not even to your mother's friends. I had such a lot of trouble getting a message to you. Perhaps she's your sort, although she's much too old for you. She doesn't know how to talk to men." The consul's widow hadn't troubled to lower her voice—the well-bred Parisian voice that slices stone.

Louise accepted the summing up, which was inadequate, like any other. Possibly she did not know how to talk to men—at least the men she had met here. Because she thought people always said what they meant and no more than they intended, her replies were disconcerting; she never understood that the real, the unmentioned, topic was implicit between men and women. I had often watched her and seen the pattern—obtuseness followed by visible surprise—which made her seem more than ever an English Miss. She said to the young man who had asked the question about her, and who now was led across to be presented, "Yes, that's quite right. I don't talk to men much, although I do listen. I haven't any brothers and I went to Anglican convents."

That was abrupt and Australian and spinsterish, if you like, but she had been married. She had been married at eighteen to Collie Tate. After a few months his regiment was sent to Malaya, and before she'd had very many letters from him he was taken prisoner and died. He must have been twenty. Louise seemed to have forgotten Collie, obliterating, in her faithlessness, not only his death but the fact that he had ever lived. She wore the two rings he had given her. They had rubbed her fingers until calluses formed. She was at ease with the rings and with the protective thickening around them, but she had forgotten him.

The young actor gravely pointed out that the name he was introduced to her by—Patrick something—was a stage name, and after Louise had sat down on a gilt chair he sat down at her feet. She had never seen anyone sitting on the floor in France, and that made her look at him. She probably looked at his hands; most women think a man's character is shown in his hands. He was dressed like many of the students in the streets around our hotel, but her practical eye measured the cost and cut of the clothes, and she saw he was false-poor, pretending. There was something rootless and unclaimed in the way he dressed, the way he sprawled, and in his eagerness to explain himself; but for all that, he was French.

"You aren't what I think of as an Australian," he said, looking up at her. He must have learned to smile, and glance, and give his full attention, when he was still very young; perhaps he charmed his mother that way. "I didn't know there were any attractive women there."

"You might have met people from Sydney," Louise said. "I'm from Melbourne."

"Do the nice Australians come from Melbourne?"

"Yes, they do."

He looked at her briefly and suspiciously. Surely anyone so guileless seeming must be full of guile? If he had asked, she would have told him that, tired of clichés, she met each question as it came up. She returned his look, as if glancing out of shadows. There must have been something between them then—a mouse squeak of knowledge. She was not a little girl freshly out of school, wishing she had a brother; she was thirty-eight, and had been widowed nineteen years.

They discovered they lived in the same hotel. He thought he must have seen her, he said, particularly when she spoke of the bicycle. He remembered seeing a bicycle, someone guiding it up and down. "Perhaps your sister," he said, for she had told him about me. "Perhaps," said serpent Louise. She thought that terribly funny of him, funny enough to repeat to me. Then she told him that she was certain she had heard his voice. Wasn't he the person who had the room next to her sister? There was an actor in that room who real aloud—oh, admirably, said Louise. (He did read, and I had told her so; he read in the groaning, suffering French classical manner that is so excruciating to foreign ears.) He was that person, he said, delighted. They had recognized each other then; they had known each other for days. He said again that "Patrick" was a stage name. He was sorry he had taken it—I have forgotten why. He told her he was waiting for a visa so that he could join a repertory company that had gone to America. He had been tubercular once; there were scars, or shadows, on his lungs. That was why the visa was taking so long. He tumbled objects out of his pockets, as if everything had to be explained to her. He showed a letter from the embassy, telling him to wait, and a picture of a house in the Dordogne that belonged to his family, where he would live when he grew old. She looked at the stone house and the garden and the cherry trees, and her manner when she returned it to him was stiff and shy. She said nothing. He was young, but old enough to know what that sudden silence meant; and he woke up. When the consul's widow came to see how they were getting on and if one of them wanted rescuing, they said together, "We live in the same hotel!" Had anything as marvelous ever happened in Paris, and could it ever happen again?. The woman looked at Louise then and said, "I was wrong about you, was I? Discreet but sure—that's how Anglo-Saxons catch their fish."

It was enough to make Louise sit back in her chair. "What will people say?" has always been, to her, deeply real. In that light the gray wool dress she was wearing and the turquoise bracelets were cold as snow. She was a winter figure in the museum room. She was a thrifty widow; an abstemious traveler counting her comforts in shillings and pence. She was a blunt foreigner, not for an instant to be taken in. Her most profound belief about herself was that she was too honest to fall in love. She believed that men were basically faithless, and that women could not love more than once. She never forgave a friend who divorced. Having forgotten Collie, she thought she had never loved at all.

"Could you let me have some money?"

That was the first time Sylvie talked to Louise. Those were Sylvie's first words, on the winter afternoon, on the dark stairs. The girl was around the bend of a landing, looking down. Louise stopped, propping the bicycle on the wall, and stared up. Sylvie leaned into the stair well so that the dead light from the skylight was behind her; then she drew back, and there was a touch of winter light upon her, on the warm skin and inquisitive eyes.

I may say that giving money away to strangers was not the habit of my sister, our family, or the people we grew up with. Louise stood, in her tweed skirt, her arm aching with the weight of so many useful objects. The mention of money automatically evoked two columns of figures. In all financial matters, Louise was bound to the rows of numbers in her account books. These account books were wrapped in patent leather, and came from a certain shop in Melbourne; our father's ledgers had never been bought in any other place. The columns were headed "Paid" and "Received," in the old-fashioned way, but at the top of each page our father, and then Louise, crossed out the printed words and wrote "Necessary" and "Unnecessary." When Louise was obliged to buy a Christmas or birthday present for anyone, she marked the amount she had spent under "Unnecessary." I had never attached any significance to her doing this; she was closer to our parents than I, and that was how they had always reckoned. She guarded her books as jealously as a diary. What can be more intimate than a record of money and the way one spends it? Think of what Pepys has revealed. Nearly everything we know about Leonardo is summed up in his accounts.

"Well, I do need money," said the girl, rather cheerfully. "Monsieur Rablis wants to put me out of my room again. Sometimes he makes me pay and sometimes he doesn't. Oh, imagine being on top of the world on top of a pile of money!" This was not said plaintively but with an intense vitality that was like a third presence on the stairs. Her warmth and her energy communicated so easily that there was almost too much, and some fell away and had its own existence.

That was all Louise could tell me later on. She had been asked to put her hand in her pocket for a stranger, for someone who had no claim on her at all, and she was as deeply shocked as if she had been invited to take part in an orgy—a comparison I do not intend as a joke.

"What if *I* asked you for money?" I suddenly said.

She looked at me with that pale-eyed appraisal and gently said, "Why, Puss, you've got what you want, haven't you? Haven't you got what you wanted out of life?" I had two woolen scarves, one plaid and one blue, which meant I had one to lend. Perhaps Louise meant that.

The absence of sun in Paris brought on a kind of irrationality at times, just as too much sun can drive one mad. If it had been anyone but my sister talking to me, I would have said that Sylvie was nothing but an apparition on the stairs. Who ever has heard of asking strangers for money? And one woman to another, at that. I know that I had never become accustomed to the northern solstice. The whitish sky and the evil Paris roofs and the cold red sun suggested a destiny so final that I wondered why everyone did not rebel or run away. Often after Christmas there was a fall of snow, and one could be amazed by the confident tracks of birds. But in a few weeks it was forgotten, and the tramps, the drunks, the unrepentant poor (locked up by the police so that they would not freeze on the streets) were released once more, and settled down in doorways and on the grilles over the Métro, where fetid air rose from the trains below, to await the coming of spring. I could see that Louise was perplexed by all this. She had been warned of the damp, but nothing had prepared her for those lumps of bodies, or for the empty sky. At four o'clock every day the sun appeared. It hung over the northwest horizon for a few minutes, like a malediction, and then it vanished and the city sank into night.

This is the moment to talk about Patrick. I think of him in that season—something to do with chill in the bones, and thermometers, and the sound of the rain. I had often heard his voice through the wall, and had guessed he was an actor. I knew him by sight. But I came home tired every night, disinclined to talk. I saw that everyone in this hotel was as dingy, as stationary, as I was myself, and I knew we were tainted with the same incompetence. Besides giving music lessons, I worked in a small art gallery on the Ile de la Cité. I received a commission of one half of one per cent on the paintings I sold. I was a foreigner without a working permit, and had no legal recourse. Every day, ten people came into that filthy gallery and asked for my job. Louise often said, "But this is a rich country, Puss. Why are there no jobs, and why are people paid nothing?" I can only describe what I know.

Patrick: my sister's lover. Well, perhaps, but not for long. An epidemic of grippe came into the city, as it did every year. Patrick was instantly felled. He went into illness as if it were a haven, establishing himself in bed with a record-player and a pile of books and a tape recorder. I came down with it, too. Every day, Louise knocked on his door, and then on mine. She came down the stairs— her room was one flight above ours—pushing her bicycle, the plaid scarf tied under her chin. She was all wool and tweed and leather again. The turquoise bracelets had been laid in a drawer, the good gray dress put away. She fetched soup, aspirin, oranges, the afternoon papers. She was conscientious, and always had the right change. Louise was a minor heiress now, but I had never been pardoned. I inherited my christening silver and an income of fifteen shillings a month. They might have made it a pound. It was only fair; she had stayed home and carried trays and fetched the afternoon papers—just as she was doing now —while I had run away. Nevertheless, although she was rich and I was poor, she treated me as an equal. I mean by that that she never bought me a cheese sandwich or a thermos flask of soup without first taking the money for it out of the purse on my desk and counting out the correct change. I don't know if she made an equal of Patrick. The beginning had already rushed into the past and frozen there, as if, from the first afternoon, each had been thinking. This is how it will be remembered. After a few days she declined, or rose, to governess, nanny, errand girl, and dear old friend. What hurts me in the memory is the thought of all that golden virtue, that limpid will, gone to waste. He was such an insignificant young man. Long eyelashes, grave smile—I could have snapped him out between thumb and finger like a bug. Poor Louise! She asked so many questions but never the right kind. God help you if you lose your footing in this country. There are no second tries. Was there any difference between a music teacher without a working permit, a tubercular actor trying to get to America, and a man bundled in newspapers sleeping on the street? Louise never saw that. She was as careful in her human judgments as she was in her accounts. Unable to squander, she wondered where to deposit her treasures of pity, affection, and love.

Patrick was reading to himself in English, with the idea that it would be useful in New York. Surely he might have thought of it before? Incompetence was written upon him as plainly as on me, and that was one of the reasons I averted my eyes. Louise was expected to correct his accent, and once he asked me to choose his texts. He read

"End-game" and "Waiting for Godot," which I heard through the wall. Can you imagine listening to Beckett when you are lying in bed with a fever? I struggled up one day, and into a dressing gown, and dumped on his bed an armload of poetry. "If you *must* have Irish misery," I said, and I gave him Yeats. English had one good effect; he stopped declaiming. The roughness of it took the varnish off his tongue. "Nor dread nor hope attend a dying animal," I heard through the wall one Thursday afternoon, and the tone was so casual that he might have been asking for a cigarette or the time of a train. "Nor dread nor hope . . ." I saw the window and heard the rain and realized it was my thirty-third birthday. Patrick had great patience, and listened to his own voice again and again.

Louise nursed us, Patrick and me, as if we were one: one failing appetite, one cracked voice. She was accustomed to bad-tempered invalids, and it must have taken two of us to make one of Mother. She fed us on soup and oranges and soda biscuits. The soda biscuits were hard to find in Paris, but she crossed to the Right Bank on her bicycle and brought them back from the exotic food shops by the Madeleine. They were expensive, and neither of us could taste them, but she thought that soda biscuits were what we ought to have. She planned her days around our meals. Every noon she went out with an empty thermos flask, which she had filled with soup at the snack bar across the street. The oranges came from the market, rue St.-Jacques. Our grippe smelled of oranges, and of leek-and-potato soup.

Louise had known Patrick seventeen days, and he had been ailing for twelve, when she talked to Sylvie again. The door to Sylvie's room was open. She sat up in her bed, with her back to a filthy pillow, eating *pain-au-chocolat*. There were crumbs on the blanket and around her chin. She saw Louise going by with a string bag and a thermos, and she called, "Madame!" Louise paused, and Sylvie said, "If you are coming straight back, would you mind bringing me a cheese sandwich? There's money for it in the chrysanthemum box." This was a Japanese cigarette box in which she kept her savings. "I am studying for the stage," she went on, without giving Louise a chance to reply. This was to explain a large mirror that had been propped against the foot of the bed so that she could look at herself. "It's important for me to know just what I'm like," she said seriously. "In the theatre, everything is enlarged a hundred times. If you bend your little finger"—she showed how—"from the top gallery it must seem like a great arc."

"Aren't you talking about films?"said Louise.

Sylvie screwed her eyes shut, thought, and said, "Well, if it isn't films it's Brecht. Anyway, it's something I've heard." She laughed, with her hands to her face, but she was watching between her fingers. Then she folded her hands and began telling poor Louise how to sit, stand, and walk on the stage—rattling off what she had learned in some second-rate theatrical course. Patrick had told us that every unemployed actor in Paris believed he could teach.

They still had not told each other their names; and if Louise walked into that cupboard room, and bothered to hear Sylvie out, and troubled to reply, it must have been only because she had decided one could move quite easily into another life in France. She worked hard at understanding, but she was often mistaken. I know she believed the French had no conventions.

"I stay in bed because my room is so cold," said Sylvie, rapidly now, as if Louise might change her mind and turn away. "This room is an icebox—there isn't even a radiator —so I stay in bed and study and I leave the door open so as to get some of the heat from the stairs." A tattered book of horoscopes lay face down on the blanket. Tacked to the wall was a picture someone had taken of Sylvie asleep on a sofa, during or after a party, judging from the scene. The slit of window in the room gave on a court, but it was a bright court, with a brave tree whose roots had cracked the paving.

"My name is Sylvie Laval," she said, and, wiping her palm on the bedsheet, prepared to shake hands.

"Louise Tate." Louise set the thermos down on Sylvie's

table, between a full ashtray and a cardboard container of coagulated milk. She saw the Japanese box with the chrysanthemum painted on the lid, and picked it up.

"What a new element you are going to be for me," said Sylvie, settling back and watching with some amazement. "I shall observe you and become like you. Yes, that's the money box, and you must take whatever you need for the sandwich."

"Why do you want to observe me?" said Louise, turning and laughing at her.

"You look like an angel," Sylvie said. "I'm sure angels look like you."

"I was once told I looked like an English poet in first youth," said Louise, trying to pretend that Sylvie's intention had been ironical.

Sylvie tilted her little chin as if to say she knew what that was all about. "Your friends are poets," she said. "They must be like you, too—wise and calm. I wish I knew your friends."

"They are very plain people," said Louise, still smiling. "They wouldn't be much fun for a bright little thing like you."

"Foreigners?"

"Some. French, too." Louise was proud of her introductions.

Sylvie looked with her bold black eyes and said, "French. I knew it."

"Knew what?"

"You and the type upstairs. The great actor—the comedian." She bit her fingers, hesitating. Her features were coarse and sly. "You're so comic, the two of you, creeping about with your secret. But love is love, and everyone knows."

I have wondered since about that bit of mischief. I suppose Patrick had given Sylvie a role to play, because it was the only way he could control her. She had found out, or he had told, and he had warned her not to hurt Louise.

Louise was someone who must be spared. She must never guess that he and Sylvie had been lovers. They thought Louise could never stand up to the truth; they thought no one could bear to be told the truth about anything after a certain age.

Sylvie, launched in a piece of acting, could not help overloading. "Do you know any other French people?" she said. "Never mind. There's me." She flung out her arms suddenly—to the mirror, not to Louise—and cried, "I am your French friend."

"She's got a picture of herself sound asleep, curled up with no shoes on," said Louise, talking in a new, breathless voice. "It must be the first thing she looks at in the morning when she wakes up. And she seems terribly emotional and generous. I don't know why, but she gives you the feeling of generosity. I'm sure she does herself a lot of harm."

We were in Patrick's room. Louise poured the daily soup into pottery bowls. I have often tried to imagine how he must have seemed to Louise. I doubt if she could have told you. From the beginning they stood too close; his face was like a painting in which there are three eyes and a double profile. No matter how far she backed off, later on, she never made sense of him. Let me tell what *I* remember. I remember that it was easy for him to talk, easy for him to say anything, so that I can hear a voice, having ceased to think of a face. He seldom gestured. Only his voice, which was trained, and could never be disguised, told that he did not think he was an ordinary person; he did not believe he was like anyone else in the world, not for a minute. I asked myself a commonplace question: What does she see in him? I should have wondered if she saw him at all. As for me, I saw him twice. I saw him the first time when Louise described the meeting in the consul's widow's drawing room, and I understood that the dazzling boy was only that droning voice through the wall. From the time of our grippe, I can see a spiral of orange peel, a water glass with air bubbles on the side of the glass, but I cannot see him. There was the bluish smoke of his caporal cigarettes, and the shape of Louise, like something seen against the light ... None of it is sharp.

One day I saw Patrick and Sylvie together, and that was plain, and clear, and well remembered. I had gone out in the rain to give a music lesson to a spoiled child, the ward of a doting grandmother. I came up the stairs, and because I heard someone laughing, or because I was feverish and beyond despair, I went into Patrick's room instead of my own.

Sylvie was there. She knelt on the floor, wearing her nightdress (the time must have been close to noon), struggling with Patrick for a bottle of French vodka, which tastes of marsh water and smells like eau de cologne. "Louise says mustn't drink," said Sylvie, in a babyish voice; "and besides it's mine." They stopped their puppy play when they saw me; there was a mock scurry, as if it were Puss who had the governess role instead of Louise. Then I noticed Louise. She sat before the window, reading a novel, taking no notice of her brawling pair. Her face was calm and happy and the lines of moral obligation had disappeared. She said, "Well, Puss," with our mother's inflection, and she seemed so young—nineteen or so—that I remembered how Collie had been in love with her once, before going to Malaya to be killed. Sylvie must have been born that year, the year Louise was married. I hadn't thought of that until now.

"When Berlioz was living in Italy," I said, "he heard that Marie Pleyel was going to be married, and so he disguised himself as a lady's maid and started off for Paris. He intended to assassinate Marie and her mother and perhaps the fiancé as well. But he changed his mind for some reason, and I think he went to Nice." This story rushed to my lips without reason. Berlioz and Marie Pleyel seemed to me living people, and the facts contemporary gossip. While I was telling it, I remembered they had all of them died. I forgot every word I had ever known of French, and told it in English, which Sylvie could not understand.

"You ought to be in bed, my pet," I heard Louise say. Sylvie went on with something she had been telling before my arrival. She had an admirer who was a political cartoonist. His cartoons were ferocious, and one imagined him out on the boulevards of Paris doing battle with the police: but he was really a timid man, afraid of cats, and unable to cross most streets without trembling. "He spends thousands of francs," said Sylvie, sighing. She told how many francs she had seen him spending.

I said, "Money, money . . . it *does* bring happiness." I wondered if Louise recalled that Berlioz had written this, and that we had quarreled about it once.

Prone across the bed, leaning on his elbows, Patrick listened to Sylvie with grave attention, and I thought that here was a situation no amount of money could solve; for it must be evident to Louise, unless she were blind and had lost all feeling, that something existed between the two. The lark had stopped singing, but it had not died; it was alive and flying in the room. Sylvie, nibbling now on chocolates stuck to a paper bag, felt that I was staring at her, and turned her head.

"My room is so cold," she said humbly, "and I get so lonely, and finally I thought I'd come in to him."

"Quite right of you," I said, as if his time and his room were mine. But Sylvie seemed to think she had been dismissed. She licked the last of the chocolate from the paper, crumpled the bag, threw it at Patrick, and slammed the door. I sat down and leaned my head back and closed my eyes. I heard Patrick saying, "Read this," and when I looked again, Louise was on the edge of the bed with a letter in her hands. She bent over it. Her hair was like the sun—the real sun, not the sun we saw here.

"It says that your visa is refused," she said, in her flat, positive French. "It says that in six months you may apply again."

"That's what I understood. I thought you might understand more."

She smoothed the letter with both hands and made up her mind about saying something. She said, "Come to Australia."

"What?"

"Come to Australia. I'll see that they let you in; I can do that much for you. You can stay with me in Melbourne until you get settled. The house is enormous. It's too big for one person. The climate would be perfect for you."

Think of that courage: she'd have taken him home.

He looked as if she had said something completely empty of meaning, and then he appeared to understand; it was a splendid piece of mime. "What would I do in Australia? I can hardly talk the language."

"I've seen people arriving, without money, without English, without anything, and then they do as well as anyone."

"They were refugees," he said. "I've got my own country. I'm not a refugee."

"You were anxious enough to go to New York."

The apple never drops far from the tree; here was our mother all over again, saying something unpleasant but true. My dutiful sister, the good elder girl—I might have helped her then. I might have told her how men were, or what it was like in Paris. But I kept silent, and presently I heard him saying he was going home. He was going to the house in the Dordogne—the house he had shown her in the photograph. She may have been jealous of that house; in her place I should have been. He said that the winter in Paris had been bad for him; there hadn't been enough work. Next season he would try again.

"Your mother will be pleased to have you for a bit," said Louise, accepting it; but I doubt if any of us can accept humiliation so simply. She folded the letter and placed it quietly beside her on the blanket. She said, "I'd better put Puss to bed," and got to her feet. I don't believe they had much to say to each other after that. He went away for a week, came back to us for a fortnight, and then disappeared.

When I was recovering from that second attack of grippe, Louise made me go with her to the Faubourg St. Honoré to look at shops. Neither of us intended buying anything, but Louise thought the outing would do me good. Just as she was convinced invalids wanted soda biscuits, so she believed convalescents found a new purpose in living when they looked at pretty things. We looked at coats and ski boots and sweaters, and we stared at rare editions, and finally, fatigued and stupid, gazed endlessly at the brooches and strings of beads in an antique jewelry store.

"It can't be worth such an awful lot," said Louise, taking an interest in a necklace. The stones—agate, cornelian, red jasper—were rubbed and uneven, like glass that has been polished by waves. The charm of the necklace was in its rough, careless appearance and the warm color of the stones. I put one hand flat against the pane of the counter. When I took it away, I watched the imprint fade. I was accustomed to wanting what I could not have.

"Do you like it, Puss?" said Louise.

"Very much."

"So do I. It would be perfect for Sylvie."

That is all I can tell you: I am not Louise. She came out of the shop with a wrapped parcel in her hand, and said in a matter-of-fact tone that the stones were early-eighteenth-century seals, that the man had been most civil about taking her check, and that the necklace had cost a great deal of money. That was all until we reached the hotel, and then she said, "Puss, will you give it to her? She'll think it strange, coming from me."

"Why won't she think it just as odd if I give it?" I called, for Louise had simply moved on, leaving me outside Sylvie's door. I felt cross and foolish. Louise climbed slowly, one hand on the banister. I know now that she went straight upstairs to her room and marked the price of the necklace under "Necessary." It was not the real price but about a fifth of the truth. She absorbed the balance in the rest of her accounts by cheating heavily for a period of weeks. She charged herself an imaginary thousand francs for a sandwich and two thousand for a bunch of winter daisies, and inflated the cost of living until the cost of the necklace had disappeared.

I knocked on Sylvie's door, and heard her scuttling about behind it. "Come in!" she shouted. "Oh, it's you. I thought it was the horrible Rablis. I can't let him in when I'm not properly dressed, because . . . you know." She had pulled on a pair of slacks and a sweater I recognized as Patrick's.

"Louise wants you to have this," I said.

She took the box from me and sat down on the bed. She was terrified by this gift. Even the sight of the ribbons and tissue paper alarmed her. I saw that in terms of Sylvie's world Louise had made a mistake. The present was so extraordinary and it had been delivered in such a round-about fashion that the girl thought she was being bought.

"My sister chose it for you on an impulse," I said. I felt huge and uniformed, like a policeman. "It seems to me a ridiculous present for a girl who hasn't proper shoes or a decent winter coat, but she thought you'd like it."

She lifted the necklace out of its box and held it over her head and let it fall. She was an actress, true enough—Sarah Bernhardt to the life. But then she turned away from me, leaning on her hands, straining forward toward the mirror, and she stopped pretending. I saw on her impudent profile surprise and greed, and we understood, together, at the same moment, what could be had from women like Louise. Sylvie said, "Your sister must be very rich."

That jolted me. "Consider the necklace a kind of insurance if you want to," I said. "You can sell it if you need money. You can give it back when you don't want it any more." That stripped the giving of any intention; she was not obliged to admire Louise, or even be grateful.

She wore the necklace every day. It hung over her

plastic coat, and on top of Patrick's old sweater. One night she fell up the stairs wearing it, and a piece of jasper broke away. The necklace had a grin to it then, with a cracked tooth. Louise scarcely noticed. Now that she had given the necklace away, she scarcely saw it at all. Giving had altered her perceptions. She walked in her sleep, and part of her character, smothered until now, began to live and breathe in a dream. "I've hardly worn it," I can hear her telling Sylvie. "I bought it for myself, but it doesn't suit me." She said it about the tweed skirts, the quilted dressing gown, the stockings, the gloves, all purchased with Sylvie in mind. (She never felt the need to give me anything. She never so much as returned my scarf until she went back to Australia, and then it was simply a case of forgetting it, leaving it behind. She also left her trumped-up accounts. Sylvie abandoned her empty bottles and a diary and a dirty petticoat; my sister left my scarf and her false accounts. The stuff of her life is in those figures: "Dentist for S." "Shoes for S." "Oil stove for S." I was touched to find under "Necessary" "Aspirin for Puss." She had listed against it the price of a five-course meal. The two went together, the giving and the lying.)

The days drew out a quarter-second at a time. Patrick, who had been away (though not to the house in the Dordogne; he did not tell us where he was), returned to a different climate. Louise and Sylvie had become friends. They were silly and giggly, and had a private language and special jokes. The most unexpected remarks sent them off into fits of laughter. At times they hardly dared meet each other's eyes. It was maddening for anyone outside the society. I saw that Patrick was intrigued and then annoyed. The day he left (I mean, the day he left forever) he returned the books I'd lent him—Yeats, and the other poets —and he asked me what was happening between those two. I had never known him to be blunt. I gave him an explanation, but it was beside the truth. I could have said,

"You don't need her; you refused Australia; and now you're going home." Instead, I told him, "Louise likes looking after people. It doesn't matter which one of us she looks after, does it? Sylvie isn't worth less than you or me. She loves the stage as much as you do. She'd starve to pay for her lessons."

"But Louise mustn't take that seriously," he said. "There are thousands of girls like Sylvie in Paris. They all have natural charm, and they don't want to work. They imagine there's no work to acting. Nothing about her acting is real. Everything is copied. Look at the way she holds her arms, and that quick turn of the head. She never stops posing, trying things out; but acting is something else."

I took my books from him and put them on my table. I said, "This is between you and Sylvie. It's got nothing to do with me."

They were young and ambitious and frightened; and they were French, so that their learned behavior was all smoothness. There was no crevice where an emotion could hold. I was thinking about Louise. It is one thing to go away, but it is terrible to be left.

I wanted him to go away, or stop telling me about Sylvie and Louise, but he would continue and I had to hear him say, "The difference between Sylvie and me is that I work. I believe in work. Sylvie believes in one thing after the other. Now she believes in Louise, and one day she'll turn on her."

"Why should she turn on her?"

"Because Louise is good," he said. This was the only occasion I remember when he had trouble saying what he meant. We stood face to face in my room, with the table and books between us. We had never been as near. Twice in that conversation he slipped from "*vous*" to "*toi*," as if our tribal marks of incompetence gave us a right to intimacy. He stumbled over the words; stammered nearly. "She's so kind," he said. "She asks to be hurt."

"It's easy to be kind when you're an heiress."

"Aren't *you*?" I stared at him and he said, "Women

like Louise make you think they can do anything, solve all your problems. Sylvie believes in magic. She believes in the good fairy, the endless wishes, the bottomless purse. I don't believe in magic." He had stopped groping. His actor's voice was as fluid and persistent as the winter rain. "But Sylvie believes, and one day she'll turn on Louise and hurt her."

"What do you expect me to do?" I said. "You keep talking about hurting and being hurt. What do you think my life is like? It's got nothing to do with me."

"Sylvie would leave Louise alone if you told her to," he said. "She isn't a clinger. She's a tough little thing. She's had to be." There was the faintest coloration of class difference in his voice. I remembered that Louise had met him in a drawing room, even though he lived here, in the hotel, with Sylvie and me.

I said, "It's not my affair."

"Sylvie is good," he said suddenly. That was all. He said "Sylvie," but he must have meant "Louise."

He left alone and went to the station alone. I was the only one to watch him go. Sylvie was out and Louise upstairs in her room. Unless I have dreamed it, it was then he told me he was ill. He was not going home after all but to a place in the mountains—near Grenoble, I think he said. That was why he had been away for a week; that was where he'd been. As he said those words, water rushed between us and we stood on opposite shores. He was sick, but I was well. We were both incompetent, but I was well. And I smiled and shook hands with him, and said goodbye.

In a book or a film one of us would have gone with him as far as the station. If he had disappeared in a country as big as Russia, one of us would have learned where he was. But he didn't disappear; he went to a town a few hundred miles distant and we never saw him again. I remember the rain on the skylight over the stairs. Louise may have looked out of her window; I would rather not guess. She may have wanted to come down at the last minute; but he had refused Australia, which meant he had refused her, and so she kept away.

Later on that day, she did something foolish: she stood in the passage and watched as his room was turned out by a maid. I managed to get her to sit on a chair. That was where Sylvie found her. Sylvie had come in from the street. Rain stood on her hair in perfect drops. She knelt beside Louise and began chafing her hands. "Tell me what it is," she said softly, looking up into her face. "How do you feel? What is it like? It must be something quite real."

"Of course it's real," I said heartily. "Come *on*, old girl."

Louise was clinging to Sylvie: she barely listened to me. "I feel as though I had no more blood," she said.

"That feeling won't last," said the girl. "He couldn't help leaving, could he? Think of how it would be if he had stayed beside you and been somewhere else—as good as miles and miles away." But I knew it was not Patrick but Collie who had gone. It was Collie who vanished before everything was said, turning his back, stopping his ears. I was thirteen and they were the love of my life. Sylvie said, "I wish I could be you and you could be me, for just this one crisis. I have too much blood and it never stops moving—never." She squeezed my sister's hand so hard that when she took her fingers away the mark of them remained in white bands. "Do you know what you must do now?" she said. "You must make yourself wait. Try to expect something. That will get the blood going again."

When I awoke the next day, I knew we were all three waiting. We waited for a letter, a telegram, a knock on the door. When Collie died, Louise went on writing letters. The letters began, "I can't believe that you are dead," which was chatty of her, not dramatic, and they went on giving innocent news. Mother and I found them and read them and tore them to shreds. We were afraid she would put them in the post and that they would be returned to her. Soon after Patrick had gone, Louise said to Sylvie, "I've forgotten what he was like."

"Like an actor," said Sylvie, with a funny little face. But I knew it was Collie Louise had meant.

Our relations became queer and strained. The final person, the judge, toward whom we were always turning for confirmation, was no longer there. Sylvie asked Louise outright for money now. If Patrick had been there to hear her, she might not have dared. Everything Louise replied touched off a storm. Louise seemed to be using a language every word of which offended Sylvie's ears. Sylvie had courted her, but now it was Louise who haunted Sylvie, sat in her cupboard room, badgered her with bursts of questions and pleas for secrecy. She asked Sylvie never to talk about her, never to disclose—she did not say what. When I saw them quarreling together, aimless and bickering, whispering and bored, I thought that a cloistered convent must be like that: a house without men.

"Did you have to stop combing your hair just because he left?" I heard Sylvie say. "You're untidy as Puss."

If you listen at doors, you hear what you deserve. She must have seemed thunderstruck, because Sylvie said, "Oh my God, don't look so helpless."

"I'm not helpless," said Louise.

"Why didn't you leave us alone?" Sylvie said. "Why didn't you just leave us with our weakness and our mistakes? You do so much, and you're so kind and good, and you get in the way, and no one dares hurt you."

That might have been the end of them, but the same afternoon Louise gave Sylvie a bottle of Miss Dior and the lace petticoat and a piece of real amber, and they went on being friends

Soon after that scene, however, in March, Louise discovered two things. One was that Sylvie had an aunt and uncle living in Paris, so she was not as forsaken as she appeared to be. Sylvie told her this. The other had to do with Sylvie's social life, métier, and means. M. Rablis made one of his periodic announcements to the effect that Sylvie would have to leave the hotel—clothes, mirror, horoscopes, money box, and all. M. Rablis was, and is, a small truculent person. He keeps an underexercised dog chained to his desk. While the dog snarled and cringed, Louise said that she knew Sylvie had an aunt and uncle, and that she would make Sylvie go to them and ask them to pay their niece's back rent. Louise had an unshakable belief in the closeness of French families, having read about the welding influence of patriotism, the Church, and inherited property. She said that Sylvie would find some sort of employment. It was time to bring order into Sylvie's affairs, my sister said.

She was a type of client the hotel-keeper had often seen: the foreign, interfering, middle-aged female. He understood half she said, but was daunted by the voice, and the frozen eye, and the bird's-nest hair. The truth was that for long periods he forgot to claim Sylvie's rent. But he was not obsessed with her, and, in the long run, not French for nothing; he would as soon have had the money she owed. "She can stay," he said, perhaps afraid Louise might mention that he had been Sylvie's lover (although I doubt if she knew). "But I don't want her bringing her friends in at night. She never registers them, and whenever the police come around at night and find someone with Sylvie I have to pay a fine."

"Do you mean men?" said my wretched sister. "Do you mean the police come about men?"

Some of my sister's hardheaded common sense returned. She talked of making Sylvie a small regular allowance, which Sylvie was to supplement by finding a job, "Look at Puss," Louise said to her. "Look at how Puss works and supports herself." But Sylvie had already looked at me. Louise's last recorded present to Sylvie was a camera. Sylvie had told her some cocksure story about an advertising firm on the Rue Balzac, where someone had said she had gifts as a photographer. Later she changed her mind and said she was gifted as a model, but by that time Louise had bought the camera. She moved the listing in her books from "Necessary" to "Unnecessary." Mice, insects, and some birds have secret lives. She harped on the aunt and uncle, until one day I thought, She will drive Sylvie insane.

"Couldn't you ask them to make you a proper allowance?" Louise asked her.

"Not unless I worked for them, either cleaning for my aunt or in my uncle's shop. Needles and thread and mending wool. Just the thought of touching those old maid's things—no, I couldn't. And then, what about my lessons?"

"You used to sew for me," said Louise. "You darned beautifully. I can understand their point of view. You could make some arrangement to work half days. Then you would still have time for your lessons. You can't expect charity."

"I don't mind charity," said Sylvie. "You should know."

I remember that we were in the central market, in Les Halles, dodging among the barrows, pulling each other by the sleeve whenever a cart laden with vegetables came trundling toward us. This outing was a waste of time where I was concerned; but Sylvie hated being alone with Louise now. Louise had become so nagging, so dull. Louise took pictures of Sylvie with the new camera. Sylvie wanted a portfolio; she would take the photographs to the agency on the Rue Balzac, and then they would see how pretty she was and would give her a job. Louise had agreed, but she must have known it was foolish. Sylvie's bloom, divorced from her voice and her liveliness, simply disappeared. In any photograph I had ever seen of her she appeared unkempt and coarse and rather fat.

Her last words had been so bitter that I put my hand on the girl's shoulder, and at that her tension broke and she clutched Louise and cried, "I should be helped. Why shouldn't I be helped? I *should* be!"

When she saw how shocked Louise was, and how she looked to see if anyone had heard, Sylvie immediately laughed. "What will all those workmen say?" she said. It struck me how poor an actress she was; for the cry of "I should be helped" had been real, but nothing else had. All at once I had a strong instinct of revulsion. I felt that the new expenses in Louise's life were waste and pollution, and what had been set in motion by her giving was not goodness, innocence, courage, or generosity but something dark.

I would have run away then, literally fled, but Sylvie had taken my sleeve and she began dragging me toward a fruit stall. "What if Louise took my picture here?" she said. "I saw something like that once. I make up my eyes in a new way, have you noticed? It draws attention away from my mouth. If I want to get on as a model, I ought to have my teeth capped."

I remember thinking, as Louise adjusted the camera, Teeth capped. I wonder if Louise will pay for that.

I think it was that night I dreamed about them. I had been dream-haunted for days. I watched Louise searching for Patrick in railway stations and I saw him departing on ships while she ran along the edge of the shore. I heard his voice. He said, "Haven't you seen her wings? She never uses them now." Then I saw wings, small, neatly folded back. That scene faded, and the dream continued, a dream of labyrinths, of search, of missed chances, of people standing on opposite shores. Awaking, I remembered a verse from a folkloric poem I had tried, when I was Patrick's age, to set to music:

> Es warent zwei Königskinder
> Die hatten einander so lief
> Sie konnten zusammen nicht kommen
> Das Wasser, es war zu tief.

I had not thought of this for years. I would rather not think about all the verses and all the songs. Who was the poem about? There were two royal children, standing on opposite shores. I was no royal child, and neither was Louise. We were too old and blunt and plain. We had no public and private manners; we were all one. We had secrets—nothing but that. Patrick was one child. Sylvie must be the other. I was still not quite awake, and the power of the dream was so strong that I said to myself, "Sylvie has wings. She could fly."

Sylvie. When she had anything particularly foolish to say, she put her head on one side. She sucked her fingers and grinned and narrowed her eyes. The grime behind her ears faded to gray on her neck and vanished inside her collar, the rim of which was black. She said, "I wonder if it's true, you know, the thing I'm not to mention. Do you think he loved her? What do you think? It's like some beautiful story, isn't it? . . . [hand on cheek, treacle voice]. It's pure Claudel. Broken lives. I *think*."

Cold and dry, I said, "Don't be stupid, Sylvie, and don't play detective." Louise and Collie, Patrick and Louise: I was as bad as Sylvie. My imagination crawled, rampant, unguided, flowering between stones. Supposing Louise had never loved Collie at all? Supposing Patrick had felt nothing but concern and some pity? Sylvie knew. She knew everything by instinct. She munched sweets, listened to records, grimaced in her mirror, and knew everything about us all.

Patrick had been pushed to the very bottom of my thoughts. But I knew that Sylvie was talking. I could imagine her excited voice saying, "Patrick was an actor, although he hardly ever had a part, and she was good and clever, nothing of a man-eater . . ." I could imagine her saying it to the young men, the casual drifters, who stood on the pavement and gossiped and fingered coins, wondering if they dared go inside a café and sit down—wondering if they had enough money for a cup of coffee or a glass of beer. Sylvie knew everybody in Paris. She knew no one of any consequence, but she knew everyone, and her indiscretions spread like the track of a snail.

Patrick was behind a wall. I knew that something was living and stirring behind the wall, but it was impossible for me to dislodge the bricks. Louise never mentioned him. Once she spoke of her lost young husband, but Collie would never reveal his face again. He had been more thoroughly forgotten than anyone deserves to be. Patrick and Collie merged into one occasion, where someone had failed. The failure was Louise's; the infidelity of memory, the easy defeat were hers. It had nothing to do with me.

The tenants of the house in Melbourne wrote about

rotten beams, and asked Louise to find a new gardener. She instantly wrote letters and a gardener was found. It was April, and the ripped fabric of her life mended. One could no longer see the way she had come. There had been one letter from Patrick, addressed to all three.

A letter to Patrick that Sylvie never finished was among the papers I found in Sylvie's room after she had left the hotel. "I have been painting pictures in a friend's studio," it said. "Perhaps art is what I shall take up after all. My paintings are very violent but also very tender. Some of them are large but others are small. Now I am playing Mozart on your old record-player. Now I am eating chocolate. Alas."

Patrick wrote to Sylvie. I found his letter on M. Rablis' desk one day. I put my hand across the desk to reach for my key, which hung on a board on the wall behind the desk, and I saw the letter in a basket of mail. I saw the postmark and I recognized his hand. I put the letter in my purse and carried it upstairs. I sat down at the table in my room before opening it. I slit the envelope carefully and spread the letter flat. I began to read it. The first words were *"Mon amour."*

The new tenant of his room was a Brazilian student who played the guitar. The sun falling on the carpet brought the promise of summer and memories of home. Paris was like a dragonfly. The Seine, the houses, the trees, the wind, and the sky were like a dragonfly's wing. Patrick belonged to another season—to winter, and museums, and water running off the shoes, and steamy cafés. I held the letter under my palms. What if I went to find him now? I stepped into a toy plane that went any direction I chose. I arrived where he was, and walked toward him. I saw, on a winter's day (the only season in which we could meet), Patrick in sweaters. I saw his astonishment, and, in a likeness as vivid as a dream, I saw his dismay.

I sat until the room grew dark. Sylvie banged on the door and came in like a young tiger. She said gaily,

"Where's Louise? I think I've got a job. It's a funny job—I want to tell her. Why are you sitting in the dark?" She switched on a light. The spring evening came in through the open window. The room trembled with the passage of cars down the street. She looked at the letter and the envelope with her name upon it but made no effort to touch them.

She said, "Everything is so easy for people like Louise and you. You go on the assumption that no one will ever dare hurt you, and so nobody ever dares. Nobody dares because you don't expect it. It isn't fair."

I realized I had opened a letter. I had done it simply and naturally, as a fact of the day. I wondered if one could steal or kill with the same indifference—if one might actually do harm.

"Tell Louise not to do anything more for me," she said. "Not even if I ask."

That night she vanished. She took a few belongings and left the rest of her things behind. She owed much rent. The hotel was full of strangers, for with the spring the tourists came. M. Rablis had no difficulty in letting her room. Louise pushed her bicycle out to the street, and studied the history of music, and visited the people to whom she had introductions, and ate biscuits in her room. She stopped giving things away. Everything in her accounts was under "Necessary," and only necessary things were bought. One day, looking at the Seine from the Tuileries terrace, she said there was no place like home, was there? A week later, I put her on the boat train. After that, I had winter ghosts: Louise making tea, Sylvie singing, Patrick reading aloud.

Then, one summer morning, Sylvie passed me on the stairs. She climbed a few steps above me and stopped and turned. "Why, Puss!" she cried. "Are you still here?" She hung on the banister and smiled and said, "I've come back for my clothes. I've got the money to pay for them now. I've had a job." She was sunburned, and thinner than she had seemed in her clumsy winter garments. She wore a cotton dress, and sandals, and the necklace of seals. Her feet were filthy. While we were talking she casually picked up her skirt and scratched an insect bite inside her thigh. "I've been in a Christian coöperative community," she said. Her eyes shone. "It was wonderful! We are all young and we all believe in God. Have you read Maritain?" She fixed her black eyes on my face and I knew that my prestige hung on the reply.

"Not one word," I said.

"You could start with him," said Sylvie earnestly. "He is very materialistic, but so are you. I could guide you, but I haven't time. You must first dissolve your personality— are you listening to me?—and build it up again, only better. You must get rid of everything material. You must."

"Aren't you interested in the stage any more?" I said.

"That was just theatre," said Sylvie, and I was too puzzled to say anything more. I was not sure whether she meant that her interest had been a pose or that it was a worldly ambition with no place in her new life

"Oh," said Sylvie, as if suddenly remembering. "Did you ever hear from him?"

Everything was still, as still as snow, as still as a tracked mouse.

"Yes, of course," I said.

"I'm so glad," said Sylvie, with some of her old overplaying. She made motions as though perishing with relief, hand on her heart. "I was so silly, you know. I minded about the letter. Now I'm beyond all that. A person in love will do anything."

"I was never in love," I said.

She looked at me, searching for something, but gave me up. "I've left the community now," she said. "I've met a boy . . . oh, I wish you knew him! A saint. A modern saint. He belongs to a different group and I'm going off with them. They want to reclaim the lost villages in the South of France. You know? The villages that have been abandoned because there's no water or no electricity. Isn't that a good idea? We are all people for whom the theatre . . . [gesture] . . . and art . . . [gesture] . . . and music and all that have failed. We're trying something else. I don't know what the others will say when they see him arriving with me, because they don't want unattached women. They don't mind wives, but unattached women cause trouble, they say. *He* was against *all* women until he met *me*." Sylvie was beaming. "There won't be any trouble with me. All I want to do is work. I don't want anything . . ." She frowned. What was the word? ". . . anything material."

"In that case," I said, "you won't need the necklace."

She placed her hand flat against it, but there was nothing she could do. All the while she was lifting it off over her head and handing it down to me I saw she was regretting it, and for two pins would have taken back all she had said about God and materialism. I ought to have let her keep it, I suppose. But I thought of Louise, and everything spent with so little return. She had merged "Necessary" and "Unnecessary" into a single column, and when I added what she had paid out it came to a great deal. She must be living thinly now.

"I don't need it," said Sylvie, backing away. "I'd have been as well off without it. Everything I've done I've had to do. It never brought me *bonheur*."

I am sorry to use a French word here, but *"bonheur"* is ambiguous. It means what you think it does, but sometimes it just stands for luck; the meaning depends on the sense of things. If the necklace had done nothing for Sylvie, what would it do for me? I went on down the stairs with the necklace in my pocket, and I thought, Selfish child. After everything that was given her, she might have been more grateful. She might have bitten back the last word.

My Heart Is Broken

"When that Jean Harlow died," Mrs. Thompson said
to Jeannie, "I was on the 83 streetcar with a big, heavy
paper parcel in my arms. I hadn't been married for very
long, and when I used to visit my mother she'd give me a
lot of canned stuff and preserves. I was standing up in the
streetcar because nobody'd given me a seat. All the men
were unemployed in those days, and they just sat down
wherever they happened to be. You wouldn't remember
what Montreal was like then. *You* weren't even on earth.
To resume what I was saying to you, one of these men

sitting down had an American paper—the *Daily News*, I guess it was—and I was sort of leaning over him, and I saw in big print 'JEAN HARLOW DEAD.' You can believe me or not, just as you want to, but that was the most terrible shock I ever had in my life. I never got over it."

Jeannie had nothing to say to that. She lay flat on her back across the bed, with her head toward Mrs. Thompson and her heels just touching the crate that did as a bedside table. Balanced on her flat stomach was an open bottle of coral-pink Cutex nail polish. She held her hands up over her head and with some difficulty applied the brush to the nails of her right hand. Her legs were brown and thin. She wore nothing but shorts and one of her husband's shirts. Her feet were bare.

Mrs. Thompson was the wife of the paymaster in a road-construction camp in northern Quebec. Jeannie's husband was an engineer working on the same project. The road was being pushed through country where nothing had existed until now except rocks and lakes and muskeg. The camp was established between a wild lake and the line of raw dirt that was the road. There were no towns between the camp and the railway spur, sixty miles distant.

Mrs. Thompson, a good deal older than Jeannie, had become her best friend. She was a nice, plain, fat, consoling sort of person, with varicosed legs, shoes unlaced and slit for comfort, blue flannel dressing gown worn at all hours, pudding-bowl haircut, and coarse gray hair. She might have been Jeannie's own mother, or her Auntie Pearl. She rocked her fat self in the rocking chair and went on with what she had to say: "What I was starting off to tell you is you remind me of her, of Jean Harlow. You've got the same teeny mouth, Jeannie, and I think your hair was a whole lot prettier before you started fooling around with it. That peroxide's no good. It splits the ends. I know you're going to tell me it isn't peroxide but something more modern, but the result is the same."

Vern's shirt was spotted with coral-pink that had dropped off the brush. Vern wouldn't mind; at least, he wouldn't say that he minded. If he hadn't objected to anything Jeannie did until now, he wouldn't start off by complaining about a shirt. The campsite outside the uncurtained window was silent and dark. The waning moon would not appear until dawn. A passage of thought made Mrs. Thompson say, "Winter soon."

Jeannie moved sharply and caught the bottle of polish before it spilled. Mrs. Thompson was crazy; it wasn't even September.

"Pretty soon," Mrs. Thompson admitted. "Pretty soon. That's a long season up here, but I'm one person doesn't complain. I've been up here or around here every winter of my married life, except for that one winter Pops was occupying Germany."

"I've been up here seventy-two days," said Jeannie, in her soft voice. "Tomorrow makes seventy-three."

"Is that right?" said Mrs. Thompson, jerking the rocker forward, suddenly snappish. "Is that a fact? Well, who asked you to come up here? Who asked you to come and start counting days like you was in some kind of jail? When you got married to Vern, you must of known where he'd be taking you. He told you, didn't he, that he liked road jobs, construction jobs, and that? Did he tell you, or didn't he?"

"Oh, he told me," said Jeannie.

"You know what, Jeannie?" said Mrs. Thompson. "If you'd of just listened to me, none of this would have happened. I told you that first day, the day you arrived here in your high-heeled shoes, I said, 'I know this cabin doesn't look much, but all the married men have the same sort of place.' You remember I said that? I said, 'You just get some curtains up and some carpets down and it'll be home.' I took you over and showed you my place, and you said you'd never seen anything so lovely."

"I meant it," said Jeannie. "Your cabin is just lovely.

I don't know why, but I never managed to make this place look like yours."

Mrs. Thompson said, "That's plain enough." She looked at the cold grease spattered behind the stove, and the rag of towel over by the sink. "It's partly the experience," she said kindly. She and her husband knew exactly what to take with them when they went on a job, they had been doing it for so many years. They brought boxes for artificial flowers, a brass door knocker, a portable bar decorated with sea shells, a cardboard fireplace that looked real, and an electric fire that sent waves of light rippling over the ceiling and walls. A concealed gramophone played the records they loved and cherished—the good old tunes. They had comic records that dated back to the year 1, and sad soprano records about shipwrecks and broken promises and babies' graves. The first time Jeannie heard one of the funny records, she was scared to death. She was paying a formal call, sitting straight in her chair, with her skirt pulled around her knees. Vern and Pops Thompson were talking about the Army.

"I wish to God I was back," said old Pops.

"Don't I?" said Vern. He was fifteen years older than Jeannie and had been through a lot.

At first there were only scratching and whispering noises, and then a mosquito orchestra started to play, and a dwarf's voice came into the room. "Little Johnnie Green, little Sallie Brown," squealed the dwarf, higher and faster than any human ever could. "Spooning in the park with the grass all around."

"Where is he?" Jeannie cried, while the Thompsons screamed with laughter and Vern smiled. The dwarf sang on: "And each little bird in the treetop high/Sang 'Oh you kid!' and winked his eye."

It was a record that had belonged to Pops Thompson's mother. He had been laughing at it all his life. The Thompsons loved living up north and didn't miss cities or company. Their cabin smelled of cocoa and toast. Over their beds were oval photographs of each other as children, and they had some Teddy bears and about a dozen dolls.

Jeannie capped the bottle of polish, taking care not to press it against her wet nails. She sat up with a single movement and set the bottle down on the bedside crate. Then she turned to face Mrs. Thompson. She sat cross-legged, with her hands outspread before her. Her face was serene.

"Not an ounce of fat on you," said Mrs. Thompson. "You know something? I'm sorry you're going. I really am. Tomorrow you'll be gone. You know that, don't you? You've been counting days, but you won't have to any more. I guess Vern'll take you back to Montreal. What do you think?"

Jeannie dropped her gaze, and began smoothing wrinkles on the bedspread. She muttered something Mrs. Thompson could not understand.

"Tomorrow you'll be gone," Mrs. Thompson continued. "I know it for a fact. Vern is at this moment getting his pay, and borrowing a jeep from Mr. Sherman, and a Polack driver to take you to the train. He sure is loyal to *you*. You know what I heard Mr. Sherman say? He said to Vern, 'If you want to send her off, Vern, you can always stay,' and Vern said, 'I can't very well do that, Mr. Sherman.' And Mr. Sherman said, 'This is the second time you've had to leave a job on account of her, isn't it?,' and then Mr. Sherman said, 'In my opinion, no man by his own self can rape a girl, so there were either two men or else she's invented the whole story.' Then he said, 'Vern, you're either a saint or a damn fool.' That was all I heard. I came straight over here, Jeannie, because I thought you might be needing me." Mrs. Thompson waited to hear she was needed. She stopped rocking and sat with her feet flat and wide apart. She struck her knees with her open palms and cried, "I *told* you to keep away from the men. I told you it would make trouble, all that being cute and dancing around. I said to you, I remember saying it, I said nothing makes trouble faster in a place like this than a grown woman behaving like a little girl. Don't you remember?"

"I only went out for a walk," said Jeannie. "Nobody'll believe me, but that's all. I went down the road for a walk."

"In high heels?" said Mrs. Thompson. "With a purse on your arm, and a hat on your head? You don't go taking a walk in the bush that way. There's no place to walk *to*. Where'd you think you were going? I could smell Evening in Paris a quarter mile away."

"There's no place to go," said Jeannie, "but what else is there to do? I just felt like dressing up and going out."

"You could have cleaned up your home a bit," said Mrs. Thompson. "There was always that to do. Just look at that sink. That basket of ironing's been under the bed since July. I know it gets boring around here, but you had the best of it. You had the summer. In winter it gets dark around three o'clock. Then the wives have a right to go crazy. I knew one used to sleep the clock around. When her Nembutal ran out, she took about a hundred aspirin. I knew another learned to distill her own liquor, just to kill time. Sometimes the men get so's they don't like the life, and that's death for the wives. But here you had a nice summer, and Vern liked the life."

"He likes it better than anything," said Jeannie. "He liked the Army, but this was his favorite life after that."

"There," said Mrs. Thompson. "You had every reason to be happy. What'd you do if he sent you off alone, now, like Mr. Sherman advised? You'd be alone and you'd have to work. Women don't know when they're well off. Here you've got a good, sensible husband working for you and you don't appreciate it. You have to go and do a terrible thing."

"I only went for a walk," said Jeannie. "That's all I did."

"It's possible," said Mrs. Thompson, "but it's a terrible thing. It's about the worst thing that's ever happened around here. I don't know why you let it happen. A women can always defend what's precious, even if she's attacked. I hope you remembered to think about bacteria."

"What d'you mean?"

"I mean Javel, or something."

Jeannie looked uncomprehending and then shook her head.

"I wonder what it must be like," said Mrs. Thompson after a time, looking at the dark window. "I mean, think of Berlin and them Russians and all. Think of some disgusting fellow you don't know. Never said hello to, even. Some girls ask for it, though. You can't always blame the man. The man loses his job, his wife if he's got one, everything, all because of a silly girl."

Jeannie frowned, absently. She pressed her nails together, testing the polish. She licked her lips and said, "I was more beaten up, Mrs. Thompson. It wasn't exactly what you think. It was only afterwards I thought to myself, Why, I was raped and everything."

Mrs. Thompson gasped, hearing the word from Jeannie. She said, "Have you got any marks?"

"On my arms. That's why I'm wearing this shirt. The first thing I did was change my clothes."

Mrs. Thompson thought this over, and went on to another thing: "Do you ever think about your mother?"

"Sure."

"Do you pray? If this goes on at nineteen—"

"I'm twenty."

"—what'll you be by the time you're thirty? You've already got a terrible, terrible memory to haunt you all your life."

"I already can't remember it," said Jeannie. "Afterwards I started walking back to camp, but I was walking the wrong way. I met Mr. Sherman. The back of his car was full of coffee, flour, all that. I guess he'd been picking up supplies. He said, 'Well, get in.' He didn't ask any questions at first. I couldn't talk anyway."

"Shock," said Mrs. Thompson wisely.

"You know, I'd have to see it happening to know what happened. All I remember is that first we were only talking . . ."

"You and Mr. Sherman?"

"No, no, before. When I was taking my walk."

"Don't say who it was," said Mrs. Thompson. "We don't any of us need to know."

"We were just talking, and he got sore all of a sudden and grabbed my arm."

"Don't say the name!" Mrs. Thompson cried.

"Like when I was little, there was this Lana Turner movie. She had two twins. She was just there and then a nurse brought her in the two twins. I hadn't been married or anything, and I didn't know anything, and I used to think if I just kept on seeing the movie I'd know how she got the two twins, you know, and I went, oh, I must have seen it six times, the movie, but in the end I never knew any more. They just brought her the two twins."

Mrs. Thompson sat quite still, trying to make sense of this. "Taking advantage of a woman is a criminal offense," she observed. "I heard Mr. Sherman say another thing, Jeannie. He said, 'If your wife wants to press a charge and talk to some lawyer, let me tell you,' he said, 'you'll never work again anywhere,' he said. Vern said, 'I know that, Mr. Sherman.' And Mr. Sherman said, 'Let me tell you, if any reporters or any investigators start coming around here, they'll get their . . . they'll never . . .' Oh, he was mad. And Vern said, 'I came over to tell you I was quitting, Mr. Sherman.'" Mrs. Thompson had been acting this with spirit, using a quiet voice when she spoke for Vern and a blustering tone for Mr. Sherman. In her own voice, she said, "If you're wondering how I came to hear all this, I was strolling by Mr. Sherman's office window—his bungalow, that is. I had Maureen out in her pram." Maureen was the Thompsons' youngest doll.

Jeannie might not have been listening. She started to

tell something else: "You know, where we were before, on Vern's last job, we weren't in a camp. He was away a lot, and he left me in Amos, in a hotel. I liked it. Amos isn't all that big, but it's better than here. There was this German in the hotel. He was selling cars. He'd drive me around if I wanted to go to a movie or anything. Vern didn't like him, so we left. It wasn't anybody's fault."

"So he's given up two jobs," said Mrs. Thompson. "One because he couldn't leave you alone, and now this one. Two jobs, and you haven't been married five months. Why should another man be thrown out of work? We don't need to know a thing. I'll be sorry if it was Jimmy Quinn," she went on, slowly. "I like that boy. Don't say the name, dear. There's Evans. Susini. Palmer. But it might have been anybody, because you had them all on the boil. So it might have been Jimmy Quinn—let's say—and it could have been anyone else, too. Well, now let's hope they can get their minds back on the job."

"I thought they all liked me," said Jeannie sadly. "I get along with people. Vern never fights with me."

"Vern never fights with anyone. But he ought to have thrashed *you*."

"If he . . . you know. I won't say the name. If he'd liked me, I wouldn't have minded. If he'd been friendly. I really mean that. I wouldn't have gone wandering up the road, making all this fuss."

"Jeannie," said Mrs. Thompson, "you don't even know what you're saying."

"He could at least have liked me," said Jeannie. "He wasn't even friendly. It's the first time in my life somebody hasn't liked me. My heart is broken, Mrs. Thompson. My heart is just broken."

She has to cry, Mrs. Thompson thought. She has to have it out. She rocked slowly, tapping her foot, trying to remember how she'd felt about things when she was twenty, wondering if her heart had ever been broken, too.

Sunday Afternoon

On a wet February afternoon in the eighth winter of the Algerian war, two young Algerians sat at the window table of a café behind Montparnasse station. Between them, facing the quiet street, was a European girl. The men were dressed alike in the dark suits and maroon ties they wore once a week, on Sunday. Their leather jackets lay on the fourth chair. The girl was also dressed for an important day. Her taffeta dress and crocheted collar were new; the coat with its matching taffeta lining looked home-sewn. She had thrown back the coat so that the lining could be seen, but held the skirt around her knees. She was

an innocent from an inland place—Switzerland, Austria
perhaps. The slight thickness of her throat above the
crocheted collar might have been the start of a goiter.
She turned a gentle, stupid face to each of the men in turn,
trying to find a common language. Presently one of the
men stood up and the girl, without his help, pulled on her
coat. These two left the café together. The abandoned
North African sat passively with three empty coffee cups
and a heaped ashtray before him. He had either been told
to wait or had nothing better to do. The street lamps went
on. The rain turned to snow.

Watching the three people in the café across the street
had kept Veronica Baines occupied much of the afternoon.
Like the Algerian sitting alone, she had nothing more interesting to do. She left the window to start a phonograph
record over again. She looked for matches, and lit a Gitane
cigarette. It was late in the day, but she wore a dressing
gown that was much too large and that did not belong to
her, and last summer's sandals. Three plastic curlers along
her brow held the locks that, released, would become a
bouffant fringe. Her hair, which was light brown, straight,
and recently washed, hung to her shoulders. She was nineteen, and a Londoner, and had lived in Paris about a year.
She stood pushing back the curtain with one shoulder, a
hand flat on the pane. She seldom read the boring part of
newspapers, but she knew there was, or there had been,
a curfew for North Africans. She left the window for a
moment, and when she came back she was not surprised to
find the second Algerian gone.

She wanted to say something about the scene to the
two men in the room behind her. Surely it meant something—the Algerian boys and the ignorant girl? She held
still. One of the men in the room was Tunisian and very
touchy. He watched for signs of prejudice. When he
thought he saw them, he was pleased and cold. He could
be rude when he wanted to be; he had been educated in
Paris and was schooled in the cold attack.

Jim Bertrand, whose flat this was, and Ahmed had not stopped talking about politics since lunch. Their talk was a wall. It shut out young girls and girlish questions. For instance, Veronica could have asked if there was a curfew, and if it applied to Ahmed as well as the nameless and faceless North Africans you saw selling flowers or digging up the streets; but Ahmed might consider it a racial question. She never knew just where he drew his own personal line.

"I am not interested in theories," she had taught herself to say, for fear of being invaded by something other than a dream. But she was not certain what she meant, and not sure that it was true.

Jim turned on a light. The brief afternoon became, abruptly, a winter night. The window was a black mirror. She saw how the room must appear to anyone watching from across the street. But no one peeped at them. Up and down the street, persiennes were latched, curtains tightly drawn. The shops were a line of iron shutters broken only by the Arab café, from which spilled a brownish and hideous light. The curb was lined with cars; Paris was like a garage. Shivering at the cold, and the dead cold of the lined-up automobiles, she turned to the room. She imagined a garden filled with gardenias and a striped umbrella. Veronica was a London girl. At first her dreams had been of Paris, but now they were about a south she had not yet seen.

She moved across the room, scuffling her old sandals, dressed in Jim's dressing gown. She dropped her cigarette on the marble hearth, stepped on it, and kicked it under the gas heater in the fireplace. Then she knelt and lifted the arm of the record-player on the floor, starting again the Bach concerto she had been playing most of the day. Now she read the name of it for the first time: Concerto Italien en Fa Majeur BWV 971. She had played it until it was nothing more than a mosquito to the ear, and now that she was nearly through with it, about to discard it for something newer, she wanted to know what it had been called. Still kneeling, leaning on her fingertips, she reread the front page of a Sunday paper. Is Princess Paola sorry she has married a Belgian and has to live so far north? Deeply interested, Veronica examined the Princess's face, trying to read contentment or regret. Princess Paola, Farah of Iran, Grace of Monaco, and Princess Margaret were the objects of Veronica's solemn attention. Their beauty, their position, their attentive husbands should have been enough. According to *France Dimanche,* anonymous letters might still come in with the morning post. Their confidences went astray. None of them could say "Pass the salt" without wondering how far it would go.

When Jim and Ahmed talked on Sunday afternoon, Veronica was a shadow. If Princess Paola herself had lifted the coffeepot from the table between them, they would have taken no more notice than they now did of her. She picked up the empty pot and carried it to the kitchen. She saw herself in the looking glass over the sink: curlers, bathrobe—what a sight! Behind her was the music, the gas heater roaring away, and the drone of the men's talk.

Everything Jim had to say was eager and sounded as if it must be truthful. "Yes, I know," he would begin, "but look." He was too eager; he stammered. His Tunisian friend took over the idea, stated it, and demolished it. Ahmed was Paris-trained; he could be explicit about anything. He made sense.

"Sense out of hot air," said Veronica in the kitchen. "Perfect sense out of perfect hot air."

She took the coffeepot apart and knocked the wet grounds into the rest of the rubbish in the sink. She ran cold water over the pot and rinsed and filled it again; then she sat down on the low stepladder that was the only seat in the kitchen and ground new coffee, holding the grinder beween her knees. At lunch the men had dragged chairs into the kitchen and stopped talking politics. But the instant the meal was finished they wanted her away;

she sensed it. If only she could be dismissed, turned out to prowl like a kitten, even in the rain! But she lived here, with Jim; he had brought her here in November, four months ago, and she had no other home.

"I'm too young to remember," she heard Ahmed say, "and you weren't in Europe."

The coffeepot was Italian and composed of four aluminum parts that looked as if they never would fit one inside the other. Jim had written instructions for her, and tacked the instructions above the stove, but she was as frightened by the four strange shapes as she had been at the start. Somehow she got them together and set the pot on the gas flame. She put it on upside down, which was the right way. When the water began to boil, you turned the pot right way up, and the boiling water dripped through the coffee. You knew when the water was boiling because a thread of steam emerged from the upside-down spout. That was the most important moment.

Afraid of missing the moment, the girl leaned on the edge of the table, which was crowded with luncheon dishes; pushed together, behind her, were the remains of the rice-and-tomato, the bones and fat of the mutton chops. The Camembert dried in the kitchen air; the bread was already stale. She did not take her eyes from the spout of the coffee-pot. She might have been dreaming of love.

"You still haven't answered me," said Jim in the next room. "Will Algeria go Communist? Yes or no."

"Tunisia didn't."

"You had different leaders."

"The Algerians are religious—the opposite of materialists."

"They could use a little materialism in Algeria," said Jim. "I've never been there, but you've only got to read. I've got a book here . . ."

Those two could talk poverty the whole day and never weary. They thought they knew what it was. Jim had never taken her to a decent restaurant—not even at the begin-

ning, when he was courting her. He looked at the menu
posted outside the door and if the prices seemed more than
he thought simple working-class couples could pay he
turned away. He wanted everyone in the world to have
enough to eat, but he did not want them to enjoy what
they were eating—that was how it seemed to Veronica.
Ahmed lived in a cold room on the sixth floor of an old
building, but he needn't have. His father was a fashionable
doctor in Tunis. Ahmed said there was no difference between one North African and another, between Ahmed
talking of sacrifice and the nameless flower seller whose
existence was a sacrifice—that is to say, whose life appears
to have no meaning; whose faith makes it possible; of
whom one thinks he might as well be dead. All Veronica
knew was that Ahmed's father was better off than her
father had ever been. "I'm going to be an important personality," she had said to herself at the age of seventeen or
so. Soon after, she ran away and came to Paris; someone
got a job for her in a photographer's studio—a tidying-up
sort of job, and not modeling, as she had hoped. In the
office next to the studio, a drawer was open. She saw 100
Nouveaux Francs, a clean bill, on which the face of young
Napoleon dared her, said, "Take it." She bought a pair
of summer shoes for seventy francs and spent the rest on
silly presents for friends. Walking in the shoes, she was
new. She would never be the same unimportant Veronica
again. The shoes were beige linen, and when she wore
them in the rain they had to be thrown away. The friend
who had got her the job made up the loss when it was
discovered, but the story went round, and no photographer
would have her again.

The coffeepot spitting water brought Jim to the
kitchen. He got to the stove before Veronica knew what he
was doing there. "I'm sorry," she said. "I was thinking
about shoes."

"You need shoes?" He looked at her, as if trying to

remember why he had loved her and what she had been like. His glasses were thumb-printed and steamed; all his talk was fog. He looked at her beautiful ankles and the scuffed sandals on her feet. He had come from America to Paris because he had a year to spend—just like that. Imagine spending a whole year of life, when every minute mattered! He had to be sure about everything before he was twenty-six; it was the limit he had set. But Veronica was going to be a great personality, and it might happen any day. She wanted to be a great something, and she wanted to begin, but not like Jim—reading and thinking—and not like that girl in taffeta, starting *her* experience with the two Algerians.

"I think I could be nearly anything, you know." That was what Veronica had said five months ago, when Jim asked what she was doing, sitting in a sour café with ashes and bent straws around her feet. She was prettier than any of the girls at the other tables. She had spoken first; he would never have dared. Her wrists were chapped where her navy-blue coat had rubbed the skin. That was the first thing he saw when he fell in love with her. That was what he had forgotten when he looked at her so vaguely in the kitchen, trying to remember what he had loved.

When he met her, she was homeless. It was a cause-and-effect she had not foreseen. She knew that when you run away from home you are brave—braver than anyone; but then you have nowhere to live. Until Jim found her, fell in love with her, brought her here, she spent hours on the telephone, ringing up any casual person who might give her a bed for the night. She borrowed money for bus tickets, and borrowed a raincoat because she lost hers—left it in a cinema—and she borrowed books and forgot who belonged to the name on the flyleaf. She sold the borrowed books and felt businesslike and proud.

She stole without noticing she was stealing, at first. Walking with Jim, she strolled out of a bookshop with something in her hand. "You're at the Camus age," he said, thinking it was a book she had paid for. She saw she was holding "La Chute," which she had never read, and never would. They moved in the river of people down the Boulevard Saint-Michel, and he put his arm round her so she would not be carried away. The Boul'Mich was like a North African bazaar now; it was not the Latin Quarter of Baudelaire. Jim had been here three months and was homesick.

"It's wonderful to speak English," he said.

"You should practice your French." They agreed to talk French. "*Vous êtes bon*," she said, gravely.

"*Mais je ne suis pas beau.*" It was true, and that was the end of the French.

They held hands on the Pont des Arts and looked down at the black water. He wanted to take her home, to an apartment he had rented in Montparnasse. It was a step for him; it was an event. He had to discuss it: love, honesty, the present, the past.

Yes, but be quick, I am dying of hunger and cold, she wanted to say.

She knew more about men than he did about women, and had more patience. She understood his need to talk about a situation without making any part of the situation clear.

"You ought to get a job," he said, when she had been living with him a month. He thought working would be good for her. He believed she should be working or studying—preparing for life. He thought life began only after it was prepared, but Veronica thought it had to start with a miracle. That was the difference between them, and why the lovely beginning couldn't last, and why he couldn't remember what he had loved. One day she said she had found work selling magazine subscriptions. He had never heard of that in France; he started to say so, but she interrupted him: "I used to sell the *Herald Tribune* on the street."

Soon after that, Jim met Ahmed, and every Sunday Ahmed came to talk. Jim wondered why he had been so hurt and confused by love. He discovered that it was easier to talk than read, and that men were better company than girls. After Jim met Ahmed, and after Veronica began selling magazine subscriptions, Jim and Veronica were happier. It was never as lovely as it had been at the beginning; that never came back. But Veronica had a handbag, strings of beads, a pink sweater, and a velvet ribbon for her hair. Perhaps that was all she wanted—a ribbon or so, the symbols of love that he should have provided. Now she gave them to herself. Sometimes she came home with a treasure; once it was a jar of caviar for him. It was a mistake—the kind of extravagance he abhorred.

"You shouldn't spend that way," he said. "Not on me."

"What does it matter? We're together, aren't we? As good as married?" she said sadly.

If they had been married, he would never have let her sell magazine subscriptions. They both knew it. She was not his wife but a girl in Paris. She was a girl, and although he would not have let her know it, almost his first. He was not attractive to women. His ugliness was unpleasant; it was the kind of ugliness that can make women sadistic. Veronica was the first girl pretty enough for Jim to want and desperate enough to have him. He had never met desperation at home, although he supposed it must exist. She was the homeless, desperate girl in Paris against whom he might secretly measure, one future day, a plain but confident wife.

"What's the good of saving money? If they come, they'll shoot me. If they don't shoot me, I shall wait for their old-age pensions. Apparently they have these gorgeous pensions." That was Veronica on the Russians. She said this now, putting the hot coffeepot down on a folded newspaper between the two men.

For Ahmed this was why women existed: to come occasionally with fresh coffee, to say pretty, harmless things. Bach sent spirals of music around the room, music that to the Tunisian still sounded like a coffee grinder. His idea of Paris was nearly just this—couples in winter rooms; coffee and coffee-grinder music on Sunday afternoon. Records half out of their colored jackets lay on the floor where Veronica had scattered them. She treated them as if they were toys, and he saw that she loved her toys best dented and scratched. "Come next Sunday," Jim said to Ahmed every week. Nearly every childless marriage has a bachelor friend. Veronica and Jim lived as though they were married, and Ahmed was the Sunday friend. Ahmed and Jim had met at the Bibliothèque Nationale. They talked every Sunday that winter. Ahmed lay back in the iron-and-canvas garden chair, and Jim was straight as a judge in a hard Empire armchair, the seat of which was covered with plastic cloth. The flat had always been let to foreigners, and traces of other couples and their passage remained—the canvas chair from Switzerland, the American pink bathmat in the ridiculous bathroom, the railway posters of skiing in the Alps.

Ahmed liked talking to Jim, but he was uneasy with liberals. He liked the way Jim carefully said "A*k*med," having learned that was how it was pronounced; and he was almost touched by his questions. What did "Ben" mean? Was it the same as the Scottish "Mac"? However, Jim's liberalism brought Ahmed close to his mortal enemies; there were Jews, for instance, who wrote the kindest books possible about North Africa and the Algerian affair. Here was a novel by one of them. On the back of the jacket was the photograph of the author, a pipe-smoking earnest young intellectual—lighting his pipe, looking into the camera over the flame. "Well, yes, but still a Jew," said Ahmed frankly, and he saw the change in Jim—the face pink with embarrassment, the kind mouth opened to protest, to defend.

"I don't feel that way, I'm sorry." Jim brought out the useful answer. In his dismay he turned the book over and hid the author's face. He was sparing Ahmed now at the expense of the unknown writer; but the writer was only a photograph, and he looked an imbecile with that pipe.

Ahmed's attitudes were not acquired, like Jim's. They were as much part of him as his ears. He expected intellectual posturing from men but detested clever women. He judged women by merciless, frivolous, secret rules. First, a girl must never be plain.

Veronica was not an intellectual, nor was she plain. She moved like a young snake; like a swan. She put a new pot of coffee down upon the table. She started the same record again, the same coffee-grinder sound. She stretched her arms, sighing, in a bored, frantic gesture. He saw the rents in the dressing gown when she lifted her arms. He could have given her more than Jim; she was not even close to the things she wanted.

Jim knew Ahmed was looking at Veronica. He wondered if he would mind if Ahmed fell in love with her. She was not Jim's; she was free. He had told her so again and again, but it made her cry, and he stopped saying it. He had imagined her free and proud, but when he said "You're free" she just cried. Would the fact that Ahmed was his friend, and a North African, mean a betrayal? It was a useless exercise, as pointless as pacing a room, but it was the kind of problem he exercised his brain with. He thought back and forth for a minute: How would I feel? Hurt? Shocked?

In less than the minute it was played out. Ahmed looked at Veronica and thought she was not worth a quarrel with his friend. *"Pas pour une femme,"* Sartre had said. Jim was too active in his private debate to notice Ahmed's interest withdrawn. Ahmed's look and its meaning were felt only by the girl. She turned to the window, with her back to the room. Suffering miserably, humiliated, she pressed her hands on the glass. The men had forgotten her. They laughed, as if Ahmed's near betrayal had made them closer friends. Jim poured his friend's coffee and pushed the sugar toward him. She saw the movement in the black glass.

She knew what Jim's being an American and Ahmed a North African made their friendship unusual, but that was apart. She didn't care about politics and color. They had nothing to do with her life. No, the difficulty for Veronica was always the same: when a man was alone he wanted her, but when there were two men she was in the way. The admiration of men, when she was the center of attention, could not make up for their indifference when they had something to say to each other. She resented the indifference more than any amount of notice taken of another woman. She could have made pudding of a rival girl.

"The little things are so awful," said Jim. "Look, I was on the ninety-five bus. The bus stopped because they were changing drivers. There were two Algerians, and without even turning around to see why the bus stopped where it shouldn't, they pulled out their identity papers to show the police. It's automatic. Something unusual—the police."

"It is nearly finished," said Ahmed.

"Do you think so? That part?"

In one of the Sunday papers there was a new way of doing horoscopes. It was complicated and you needed a mathematician's brain, but anything was better than standing before the window with nothing to see. She found a pencil and sat down on the floor. I was born in '43 and Jim in '36. We're both the same month. That makes ten points in common. No, the ten points count against you.

"Ahmed, when were you born?"

"I am a Lion, a Leo, of the year 1939," Ahmed said. "It'll take a minute to work out."

Presently she straightened up with the paper in her hand and said, "I can't work it out. Ahmed, you're going to travel. Princess Margaret's a Leo and she's going to travel. It must be the same thing."

That made them laugh, and they looked at her. When they looked, she felt brave again. She stood over them, as if she were one of them. "I can't tell if I'm going to have twins or have rheumatism," she said. "I'm given both.

Actually, I think *I'll* travel. I've got to think of my future, as Jim says. I don't think Paris is the right place. Summer might be the time to move on. Somewhere like the Riviera."

"What would you do there?" said Ahmed.

"Sell magazine subscriptions," she said, smiling. "Do you know I used to sell the *Herald Tribune*? I really and truly did. I wore one of those ghastly sweaters they make you wear. If I sold something like a hundred and ninety-nine, I could pay for my hotel room. That was before I met Jim. I had to keep walking with the papers because of the law. If you stand still on a street with a pile of newspapers in your arms, you're what's called a kiosk, and you need a special permit. Now I sell magazine subscriptions and I can walk or stand still, just as I choose."

"I've never seen you," said Ahmed.

"She makes a fortune," said Jim. "No one refuses. It's her face."

"I'm not around where you are," said Veronica to Ahmed. "I'm around the Madeleine, where the tourists go."

"I'll come and see you there," said Ahmed. "I'd like to see you selling magazine subscriptions to tourists around the Madeleine."

"I earn enough for my clothes," said Veronica. "Jim needn't dress me."

She could not keep off her private grievances. As soon as his friend was attacked, Ahmed turned away. He looked at the books on the shelf over the table where Jim did his thinking and reading. Jim was mute with unhappiness. He tried to remember the beginning. Had either of them said a word about clothes?

She could go on standing there, holding the newspaper and the futures she had been unable to work out. There must be something she could do. In the kitchen, the washing up? The bedroom? She could dress. In the silence she had caused, she thought of questions she might ask: "Ahmed, are you the same as those Algerians in the café?" "Am I any better than that girl?"

They began to talk when Veronica was in the bedroom. Their voices were different. They were glad she was away. She knew it. Veronica thought she heard her name. They wanted her to be someone else. They didn't deserve her as she was. They wanted Brigitte Bardot and Joan of Arc. They want everything, she said to herself. In the bedroom there was nothing but a double bed and pictures of ballet dancers someone had left tacked to the walls.

She returned to them, dressed in a gray skirt and sweater and high-heeled black shoes. She had put her hair up in a neat plait, and her fringe was brushed out so that it nearly touched her eyelashes.

Jim was in the kitchen. He had closed the door. She heard him pulling the ladder about. He kept books and papers on the top shelf of the kitchen cupboard. She sat down in his chair, primly, and folded her hands.

"You are well dressed these days," said Ahmed, as if their conversation had never stopped.

"I'm not what you think," she said. "You know that. I said 'around the Madeleine' for a joke. I sometimes take things. That's all."

"What things? Money?" He looked at her without moving. His long womanish hands were often idle.

"Where would I ever see money? Not *here. He* doesn't leave it around. Nobody does, for that matter. I take little things, in the shops. Clothes, and little things. Once a jar of caviar for Jim, but he didn't want it."

"You'll get into trouble," Ahmed said.

"It's all here, all safe," said Jim, coming back, smiling. "I'm like an old maid, you know, and I hate keeping money in the house, especially an amount like this."

He put the paper package on the table. It was the size of a pound of coffee. They looked at it and she understood. She was older than she had ever been, even picking Jim up in a café. There it is: money. It makes no difference to them. It is life and death for me. "What is it, Jim?" she said carefully, pressing her hands together. "What is it for?

Is it for politics?" She remembered the two men in the café and the girl with the thick innocent throat. "Is it about politics? Is it for the Algerians? Was it in the kitchen a long time?" Slowly, carefully, she said, "What wouldn't you do for other people! Jim never spends anything. He needs a reason, and I'm not a reason. Ahmed, is it yours?"

"It isn't mine," said Ahmed.

"Why didn't you tell me it was here, Jim? Don't you trust me?"

"You can see we trust you," said Jim

"We're telling you now."

"You didn't tell me you had it here because you thought I'd spend it," she said. She looked at the paper as if it were a stuffed object—a dead animal.

"I never thought of it as money," said Jim. "That's the truth."

"It's anything except the truth," she said, her hands tight. "But it doesn't matter. There's never a moment money isn't money. You'd like me to say 'It isn't money,' but I won't. If I'd known, I'd have spent it. Wouldn't I just! Oh, wouldn't I!"

"It wasn't money," said Jim, as if it had stopped existing. "It was something I was keeping for other people." Collected for a reason, a cause. And hidden.

None of them touched it. Ahmed looked sleepy. This was a married scene in a winter room; the bachelor friend is exposed to this from time to time. He must never take sides.

"You both think you're so clever," said the girl. "You haven't even enough sense to draw the curtains." While they were still listening, she said, "It's not my fault if you don't like me. Both of you. I can't help it if you wish I was something else. Why don't you take better care of me?"

An Unmarried Man's Summer

The great age of the winter society Walter Henderson frequents on the French Riviera makes him seem young to himself and a stripling to his friends. In a world of elderly widows his relative youth appears a virtue, his existence as a bachelor a precious state. All winter long he drives his sporty little Singer over empty roads, on his way to parties at Beaulieu, or Roquebrune, or Cap Ferrat. From the sea he and his car must look like a drawing of insects: a firefly and a flea. He drives gaily, as if it were summer. He is often late. He has a disarming gesture of smoothing his hair as he makes his apologies. Sometimes his excuse has to do with Angelo, his hilarious and unpredictable manservant. Or else it is Mme. Rossi, the *femme de ménage*, who has been having a moody day. William of Orange, Walter's big old ginger tomcat, comes into the account. As Walter describes his household, he is the victim of servants and pet animals, he is chief player in an endless imbroglio of intrigue, swindle, cuckoldry—all of it funny, of course; haven't we laughed at Molière?

"*Darling* Walter," his great friend Mrs. Wiggott has often said to him. "*This* could only happen to *you*."

He tells his stories in peaceful dining rooms, to a circle of loving, attentive faces. He is surrounded by the faces of women. Their eyes are fixed on his dotingly, but in homage to another man: a young lover killed in the 1914 war; an adored but faithless son. "Naughty Walter," murmurs Mrs. Wiggott. "*Wicked* boy." Walter must be wicked, for part of the memory of every vanished husband or lover or son is the print of his cruelty. Walter's old friends are nursing bruised hearts. Mrs. Wiggott's injuries span four husbands, counted on four arthritic fingers—the gambler, the dipsomaniac, the dago, and poor Wiggott, who ate a good breakfast one morning and walked straight in front of a train. "None of my husbands was from my own walk of life," Mrs. Wiggott has said to Walter. "I made such mistakes with men, trying to bring them up to my level. I've often thought, Walter, if only I had met *you* forty years ago!"

"Yes, indeed," says Walter heartily, smoothing his hair.

They have lost their time sense in this easy climate; when Mrs. Wiggott was on the lookout for a second husband forty years ago, Walter was five.

"If your life isn't exactly the way you want it to be by the time you are forty-five," said Walter's father, whom he admired, "not much point in continuing. You might as well

hang yourself." He also said, "Parenthood is sacred. Don't
go about creating children right and left"; this when Walter
was twelve. Walter's Irish grandmother said, "Don't touch
the maids," which at least was practical. "I stick to the
women who respect and admire me," declared his god-
father. He was a bachelor, a great diner-out. "What good
is beauty to a boy?" Walter's mother lamented. "I have such
a plain little girl, poor little Eve. Couldn't it have been
shared?" "Nothing fades faster than the beauty of a boy."
Walter has read that, but cannot remember where.

A mosaic picture of Walter's life early in the summer
of his forty-fifth year would have shown him dead center,
where nothing can seem more upsetting than a punctured
tire or more thrilling than a sunny day. On his right is
Angelo, the comic valet. Years ago, Angelo followed Walter
through the streets of a shadeless, hideous town. He was
begging for coins; that was their introduction. Now he is
seventeen, and quick as a knife. In the mosaic image,
Walter's creation, he is indolent, capricious, more trouble
than he is worth. Mme. Rossi, the *femme de ménage*, is
made to smile. She is slovenly but good-tempered, she sings,
her feet are at ease in decaying shoes. Walter puts it about
that she is in love with a driver on the Monte Carlo bus.
That is the role he has given her in his dinner-party stories.
He has to say something about her to bring her to life. The
cat, William of Orange, is in Angelo's arms. As a cat, he is
film star, prize fighter, and stubbornness itself; as a personality, he lives in a cloud of black thoughts. The figures
make a balanced and nearly perfect design, supported by a
frieze of pallida iris in mauve, purple, and white.

The house in the background, the stucco façade with
yellow shutters, three brick steps, and Venetian door, is
called Les Anémones. It belongs to two spinsters, Miss
Cooper and Miss Le Chaine. They let Walter live here,
rent-free, with the understanding that he pay the property
taxes, which are small, and keep the garden alive and
the roof in repair. Miss Cooper is headmistress of a school

in England; Miss Le Chaine is her oldest friend. When Miss Cooper retires from her post fifteen years from now, she and Miss Le Chaine plan to come down to the Riviera and live in Les Anémones forever. Walter will then be sixty years of age and homeless. He supposes he ought to be doing something about it; he ought to start looking around for another place. He sees himself, aged sixty, Mrs. Wiggott's permanent guest, pushing her in a Bath chair along the Promenade des Anglais at Nice. It is such a disgusting prospect that he hates Mrs. Wiggott because of the imaginary chair.

Walter knows that pushing a Bath chair would be small return for everything Mrs. Wiggott has done for him: it was Mrs. Wiggott who persuaded Miss Cooper and Miss Le Chaine there might be a revolution here—nothing to do with politics, just a wild upheaval of some kind. (Among Walter's hostesses, chaos is expected from week to week, and in some seasons almost hourly.) With revolution a certain future, is it not wise to have someone like Walter in charge of one's house? Someone who will die on the brick doorstep, if need be, in the interests of Miss Cooper and Miss Le Chaine? Having had a free house for many years, and desiring the arrangement to continue, Walter will feel he has something to defend. So runs Mrs. Wiggott's reasoning, and it does sound sane. It sounded sane to the two ladies in England, luckily for him. He does not expect a revolution, because he does not expect anything; he would probably defend Les Anémones because he couldn't imagine where else he might go. This house is a godsend, because Walter is hard up. In spite of the total appearance of the mosaic, he has to live very carefully indeed, never wanting anything beyond the moment. He has a pension from the last war, and he shares the income of a small trust fund with his sister Eve, married and farming in South Africa. When anyone asks Walter why he has never married, he smiles and says he cannot support a wife. No argument there.

This picture belongs to the winter months. Summer is something else. In all seasons the sea is blocked from his view by a large hotel. From May to October, this hotel is festooned with drying bathing suits. Its kitchen sends the steam of tons of boiled potatoes over Walter's hedge. His hostesses have fled the heat; his telephone is still. He lolls on a garden chair, rereading his boyhood books—the Kipling, the bound albums of *Chums*. He tries to give Angelo lessons in English literature, using his old schoolbooks, but Angelo is silly, laughs; and if Walter persists in trying to teach him anything, he says he feels sick. Mme. Rossi carries ice up from the shop in a string bag. It is half melted when she arrives, and it leaves its trail along the path and over the terrace and through the house to the kitchen. In August, even she goes to the mountains, leaving Walter, Angelo, and the cat to get on as best they can. Walter wraps a sliver of ice in a handkerchief and presses the handkerchief to his wrists. He is deafened by cicadas and nauseated by the smell of jasmine. His skin does not sweat; most of his body is covered with puckered scars. Twenty years ago, he was badly burned. He reads, but does not quite know what he is reading. Fortunately, his old books were committed to memory years before.

At last the good weather fades, the crowds go away. The hotel closes its shutters. His hostesses return. They have survived the season in Scotland and Switzerland—somewhere rainy and cold. They are back now, in time for the winter rain. All at once Walter's garden seems handsome, with the great fig tree over the terrace, and the Judas tree waiting for its late-winter flowering. After Christmas the iris will bloom, and Walter will show his tottering visitors around. "I put in the iris," he explains, "but, of course, Miss Cooper shall have them when I go." This sounds as though he means to die on the stroke of sixty, leaving the iris as a mauve-and-white memorial along the path. "Naughty Walter," Mrs. Wiggott chides him. "Morbid boy." Yet the only morbid remark he has ever made in her

presence went unheard, or at least unanswered: "I wish
it had been finished off for me in the last war." That last
war, recalled by fragments of shell dug up in Riviera
gardens, was for many of his present friends the last
commerce with life, if life means discomfort, bad news.
They still see, without reading them, the slogans praising
Mussolini, relics of the Italian occupation of the coast.
Walter has a faded old *Viva* on the door to his garage. He
thought he might paint over it one day, but Mrs. Wiggot
asked him not to. Her third husband was a high-up Fascist,
close to Mussolini. Twenty years ago, she wore a smart
black uniform, tailored for her in Paris, and she had a
jaunty tasseled hat. She was the first foreign woman to
give her wedding ring to the great Italian gold collection;
at least she says she was. But Walter has met two other
women, one Belgian and one American, who claim the
same thing.

He lay in a garden chair that summer—the summer
he had not hanged himself, having arranged life exactly
as he wanted it—unshaven, surviving, when a letter arrived
that contained disagreeable news. His sister and brother-in-
law had sold their African farm, were flying to England,
and intended to stop off and have a short holiday with
him on the way. His eyes were bloodshot. He did not read
the letter more than twice. He had loved his sister, but she
had married a farmer, a Punch squire, blunt, ignorant,
Anglo-Irish. Walter, who had the same mixture in his blood,
liked to think that Frank Osborn had "the worst of both."
Frank was a countryman. He despised city life, yet the
country got the better of him every time. In twelve years in
Africa, he and Eve had started over twice. He attracted bad
luck. Once, Eve wrote Walter asking if he would let some
of the capital out of the trust whose income they shared.
She and Frank wanted to buy new equipment, expand. They
had two children now, a girl and a boy. She hinted that
halving the income was no longer quite fair. Walter an-

swered the letter without making any mention of her request, and was thankful to hear no more about it.

Now, dead center of summer, she was making a new claim: she was demanding a holiday. Walter saw pretty clearly what had happened. Although Frank and Eve had not yet been dispossessed in South Africa, they were leaving while the going was good. Eve wrote that no decent person could stand the situation down there, and Walter thought that might well be the truth, but only part of it; the rest of the truth was they had failed. They kept trying, which was possibly to their credit; but they had failed. Five days after the arrival of this letter came a second letter, giving the date of their arrival—August fifteenth.

On the fifteenth of August, Walter stood upon his terrace in an attitude of welcome. A little behind him was Angelo, excited as only an Italian can be by the idea of "family." William of Orange sat on the doorstep, between two tubs, each holding an orange tree. Walter had not met the family at the airport, because there was not room for them all in the Singer, and because Eve had written a third letter, telling him not to meet them. The Osborns were to be looked after by a man from Cook's, who was bringing to the airport a Citroën Frank had hired. In the Citroën they proposed to get from the airport to Walter, a distance of only thirty-odd miles, but through summer traffic and over unfamiliar roads. Walter thought of them hanging out the car windows, shouting questions. He knew there were two children, but pictured six. He thought of them lost, and the six children in tears.

Toward the end of the afternoon, when Walter had been pacing the terrace, or nervously listening, for the better part of the day, Angelo shouted that he heard children's voices on the other side of the hedge. Walter instantly took up a new position. He seemed to be protecting the house against the expected revolution. Then—there was no mistaking it—he heard car doors slammed, and the whole family calling out. He stared down the path to the

gate, between the clumps of iris Angelo had cut back after
the last flowering. The soil was dry and hard and clay. He
was still thinking of that, of the terrible soil he had to
contend with here, when Eve rushed at him. She was a
giantess, around his neck almost before he saw her face.
He had her damp cheek, her unsophisticated talcum smell.
She was crying, but that was probably due to fatigue. She
drew back and said to him, "You're not a minute older,
darling, except where you've gone gray." What remarkable
eyes she must have, Walter thought, and what gifts of
second sight; for his hair was *slightly* gray, but only at the
back. Eve was jolly and loud. It had been said in their childhood that she should have been a boy. Frank came along
with a suitcase in each hand. He put the cases down. "Well,
old Frank," said Walter. Frank replied with astonishment,
"Why, it's Walter!"

The two children stared at their uncle and then at
Angelo. They were not timid, but seemed to Walter without
manners or charm. Eve had written that Mary, the elder,
was the image of Walter in appearance and in character.
He saw a girl of about eleven with lank yellow hair, and
long feet in heavy sandals. Her face was brown, her lashes
rabbit white. The boy was half his sister's size, and entirely
Osborn; that is, he had his father's round red face. He
showed Walter a box he was holding. "There's a hamster
in it," he said, and explained in a piping voice that he had
bought it from a boy at the airport.

They don't waste any time when it comes to compli-
cating life," said Frank proudly.

Angelo stood by, smiling, waiting to be presented.
Keeping Angelo as a friend and yet not a social friend was
a great problem for Walter Angelo lacked the sophistication
required to make the change easily. Walter decided he
would not introduce him, but the little Osborn boy suddenly
turned to the valet and smiled. The two, Johnny and Angelo,
seemed to be struck shy. Until then, Walter had always
considered Angelo someone partly unreal, part of his per-

sonal mosaic. Once, Angelo had been a figure on the wall
of a baroque church; from the wall he came toward Walter,
with his hand out, cupped for coins. The church had been
intended from its beginnings to blister and crack, to set
off black hair, appraising black eyes. The four elements
of Angelo's childhood were southern baroque, malaria, idle-
ness, and hunger. They were what he would go back to
if Walter were to tire of him, or if he should decide to leave.
Now the wall of the church disappeared, and so did a
pretty, wheedling boy. Angelo was seventeen, dumpy,
nearly coarse. "Nothing fades faster than the beauty of a
boy." Angelo looked shrewd; he looked as if he might have
a certain amount of common sense—that most defeating
of qualities, that destroyer.

The family settled on the terrace, in the wicker chairs
that belonged with the house, around the chipped garden
table that was a loan from Mrs. Wiggott. They were sprawl-
ing, much at ease, like an old-fashioned *Chums* picture of
colonials. They praised Angelo, who carried in the luggage
and then gave them tea, and the children smiled at him,
shyly still.

"They've fallen for him," Eve said.

"What?" It seemed to Walter such an extraordinary
way to talk. The children slid down from their chairs (without permission, the bachelor uncle observed) and followed
Angelo around the side of the house.

"They don't love *us* much at the moment," Eve said.
"We've taken them away from their home. They don't think
anything of the idea. They'll get over it. But it's natural for
them to turn to someone else, don't you think? Tell Angelo
to watch himself with Mary. She's a seething mass of feminine wiles. She's always after something."

"She doesn't get anything out of *me*," said Mary's
father.

"You don't even notice when she does, that's how
clever she is," said Eve.

"I told her I'd buy her something at the airport, be-

cause Johnny had the hamster," said Frank. "She said she
didn't want anything."

"She doesn't want just anything you offer," said Eve.
"That's where she's wily. She thinks about what she wants
and then she goes after it without saying anything. It's a
game. I tell you, she's feminine. More power to her. I'm
glad."

"Angelo hasn't much to worry about," said Walter. "I
don't think she could get much out of him, because he
hasn't got anything. Although I do pay him; I'm a stickler
about that. He has his food and lodging and clothes, and
although many people would think that enough, I give him
pocket money as well." This had an effect he had not
expected. His sister and brother-in-law stared as if he had
said something puzzling and incomplete. Walter felt socially
obliged to go on speaking. In the dry afternoon he inspected
their tired faces. They had come thousands of miles by
plane, and then driven here in an unknown car. They were
still polite enough to listen and to talk. He remembered one
of his most amusing stories, which Mrs. Wiggott frequently
asked him to repeat. It was about how he had sent Angelo
and William of Orange to Calabria one summer so that
Angelo could visit his people and William of Orange have
a change of air. Halfway through the journey, Angelo had
to give it up and come back to Les Anémones. William of
Orange hadn't stopped howling from the time the train
started to move. "You understand," said Walter, "he couldn't
leave William of Orange shut up *in* his basket. It seemed
too cruel. William of Orange *wouldn't* keep still, Angelo
daren't let him *out*, because he was in such a fury he would
have attacked the other passengers. Also, William of Orange
was being desperately sick. It was an Italian train, third
class. You can imagine the counsel, the good advice! Angelo
tried leaving the basket partly open, so that William of
Orange could see what was going on but not jump out, but
he only screamed all the more. Finally Angelo bundled up
all his things, the presents he'd been taking his family

and William of Orange in his basket, and he got down at some stop and simply took the next train going the other direction. I shall never forget how they arrived early in the morning, having traveled the whole night and walked from the . . ."

"This is a dreadful story," said Eve, slowly turning her head. "It's sad."

Frank said nothing, but seemed to agree with his wife. Walter supposed they thought the cat and the valet should not have been traveling at all; they had come up from South Africa, where they had spent twelve years bullying blacks. He said, "They were traveling third class."

Mary, his niece, sauntered back to the table, as if she had just learned a new way of walking. She flung herself in a chair and picked up her father's cigarettes. She began playing with them, waiting to be told not to. Neither parent said a word.

"And how was your journey?" said Walter gravely.

The girl looked away from the cigarettes and said, "In a way, I've forgotten it."

"No showing off, please," said Eve.

"There's a kind of holiday tonight," said the girl. "There'll be fireworks, all that. Angelo says we can see them from here. He's making Johnny sleep now, on two chairs in the kitchen. He wanted me to sleep, too, but I wouldn't, of course. He's fixing a basket for the hamster up where the cat can't get it. We're going to have the fireworks at dinner, and then he'll take us down to the harbor, he says, to see the people throwing confetti and all that."

"The fireworks won't be seen from our dining room, I fear," said Walter.

"We're having our dinner out here, on the terrace," said the girl. "He says the mosquitoes are awful and you people will have to smoke."

"Do the children always dine with you?" said Walter.

There was no answer, because William of Orange came by, taking their attention. Mary put out her hand,

but the cat avoided it. Walter looked at the determined
child who was said to resemble him. She bent toward the
cat, idly calling. Her hair divided, revealing a delicate ear.
The angle of her head lent her expression something
thoughtful and sad; it was almost an exaggerated posture
of wistfulness. Her arms and hands were thin, but with
no suggestion of fragility. She smiled at the cat and said,
"*He* doesn't care. He doesn't care what we say." Her bones
were made of something tough and precious. She was not
pretty, no, but quite lovely, in spite of the straight yellow
hair, the plain way she was dressed. Walter knew instantly
what he would have given her to wear. He thought, Ballet
lessons . . . beautiful French, and saw himself the father
of a daughter. The mosaic expanded; there was room for
another figure, surely? Yes—but to have a daughter one
needed a wife. That brought everything down to normal
size again. He smiled to himself, thinking how grateful he
was that clods like Frank Osborn could cause enchanting
girls to appear, all for the enjoyment of vicarious fathers.
It was a new idea, one he would discuss next winter with
Mrs. Wiggott. He could develop it into a story. It would
keep the old dears laughing for weeks.

Angelo strung paper lanterns on wires between
branches of the fig tree. The children were fogged with
sleep, but bravely kept their heads up, waiting for the fireworks he had said would be set off over the sea. Neither of
them remarked that the sea was hidden by the hotel; they
trusted Angelo to produce the sea as he produced their
dinner. Walter's nephew slept with his eyes wide. Angelo's
lanterns were reflected in his eyes—pinpoints of cobalt
blue.

From the table they heard the crowd at the harbor,
cheering every burst. Colored smoke floated across the dark
sky. The smell of jasmine, which ordinarily made Walter
sick, was part of the children's night.

"Do you know my name?" said the little boy, as Angelo
moved around the table collecting plates. "It's Johnny."

He sighed, and put his head down where the plate had been. Presently Angelo came out of the house wearing a clean white pullover and with his hair well oiled. Johnny woke up as if he had heard a bell. "Are you taking us to the harbor?" he said. "Now?"

Mary, Johnny, and Angelo looked at Eve. It was plain to Walter that these children should not be anywhere except in bed. He was furious with Angelo.

"Is there polio or anything here?" said Eve lazily. Now it was Walter's turn. The children—all three—looked at him with something like terror. He was about to deny them the only pleasure they had ever been allowed; that was what their looks said. Without waiting for his answer about polio, Eve said the children could go.

The candles inside the paper lanterns guttered and had to be blown out. The Osborns smoked conscientiously to keep mosquitoes away. In the light of a struck match, Walter saw his sister's face, her short graying hair. "That's a nice lad," she said.

"The kids are mad about him," said Frank.

"They are besotted," said Eve. "I'm glad. You couldn't have planned a better welcome, Walter dear," and in the dark she briefly covered his hand with hers.

The family lived in Miss Cooper's house as if it were a normal place to be. They were more at home than Walter had ever been. Mornings, he heard them chattering on the terrace or laughing in the kitchen with Angelo. Eve and Angelo planned the meals, and sometimes they went to the market together. The Osborns took over the household food expenses, and Walter, tactfully, made no mention of it. Sometimes the children had their meals in the kitchen with Angelo and the hamster and the cat. But there was no order, no system, to their upbringing. They often dined with the adults. The parents rose late, but not so late as Walter. They seemed to feel it would be impolite to go off to the beach or the market until Walter's breakfast was over.

He was not accustomed to eating breakfast, particularly during the hot weather, but he managed to eat an egg and some cold toast, only because they appeared to expect it.

"Change has got to come in South Africa," said Eve one morning as Walter sat down to a boiled egg. The family had eaten. The table was covered with ashes, eggshells, and crumbs.

"Why at our expense?" said Frank.

"Frank is an anarchist, although you wouldn't think it at times," said Eve, with pride.

Married twelve years and still talking, Walter thought. Frank and Eve were in accord on one thing—that there was bad faith on all sides in South Africa. They interrupted each other, explaining *apartheid* to Walter, who did not want to hear anything about it. Frank repeated that no decent person could stand by and accept the situation, and Eve agreed; but she made no bones about the real reason for their having left. They had failed, failed. The word rolled around the table like a wooden ball.

So Frank was an anarchist, was he, Walter thought, snipping at his egg. Well, he could afford to be an anarchist, living down there, paying next to no income tax. He said, "You will find things different in England."

"An English farm, aha," said Frank, and looked at Eve.

"Just so long as it isn't a poultry farm," said Walter, getting on with his revolting breakfast. The egg had given him something to say. "I have seen people try that."

"As a matter of fact, it *is* a poultry farm," said Eve. Frank's face was earnest and red; this farm had a history of arguments about it. Eve went on, "You see, we try one thing after the other. We're obliged to try things, aren't we? We have two children to educate."

"I wouldn't want to live without doing something," said Frank. "Even if I could afford to. I mean to say that I'm not brainy and it's better for me if I have something to do."

"Walter used to think it better," said Eve. She went on, very lightly, "I did envy Walter once. Walter, think of

the money that was spent educating you. They wouldn't
do it for a girl. Ah, how I used to wish we could have exchanged, then." Having said this, she rounded on her
husband, as if it were Frank who had failed to give Walter
credit, had underestimated him, dragging schoolroom
jealousy across the lovely day. Frank must be told: Walter
in Hong Kong in a bank. Walter in amateur theatricals,
the image of Douglas Fairbanks. He was marvelous in the
war; he was burned from head to foot. He was hours
swimming in flames in the North Sea. He should have had
the Victoria Cross. Everyone said so.

The two children, sitting nearby sorting colored
pebbles they had brought up from the beach, scarcely
glanced at their courageous uncle. The impossibility of his
ever having done anything splendid was as clear to them
as it was to Walter. He agreed with the children—for it had
all of it gone, and he wanted nothing but the oasis of peace,
the admiration of undemanding old women, the winter
months. If he was irritated, it was only by his sister's
puritanical insistence on working. Would the world have
been a happier place if Walter had remained in Hong Kong
in a bank? Luckily, there was William of Orange to talk
about. There was William of Orange now, stalking an
invisible victim along the terrace wall. Up in the fig tree he
went, with his killer's face, his marigold eyes. "Oh, the
poor birds!" Eve cried. "He's after birds!" She saw him
stretch out his paw, spread like a hand, and then she saw
him detach ripe figs and let them fall on the paved terrace.
She had never seen a cat do that before. She said that
William of Orange was perfectly sweet.

"He doesn't care what you think about him," said Mary,
looking up from her heap of stones.

"You know, darling," said Eve, laughing at Walter, "if
you aren't careful, you'll become an old spinster with a
pussycat."

Frank sat on the terrace wall wearing a cotton shirt and
oversized Army shorts. He was burned reddish brown. His

arms and legs were covered with a coating of thick fair hair. "What is the appeal about cats?" he said kindly. "I've always wanted to know. I can understand having them on a farm, if they're good mousers." He wore a look of great sincerity most of the time, as if he wanted to say, Please tell me what you are thinking. I so much want to know.

"I like them because they are independent," said Walter. "They don't care what you think, just as Mary says. They don't care if you like them. They haven't the slightest notion of gratitude, and they never pretend. They take what you have to offer, and away they go."

"That's what all cat fanciers say," said Frank. "But it's hard for someone like me to understand. That isn't the way you feel about people, is it? Do you like people who just take what you can give them and go off?"

Angelo came out of the house with a shopping basket over one arm and a straw sun hat on his head. He took all his orders from Eve now. There had never been a discussion about it; she was the woman of the house, the mother.

"It would be interesting to see what role the cat fancier *is* trying on," said Walter, looking at Angelo. "He says he likes cats because they don't like anyone. I suppose he is proving he is so tough he can exist without affection."

"I couldn't," said Frank, "and I wouldn't want to try. Without Eve and the children and . . ."

The children jumped to their feet and begged to go to market with Angelo. They snatched at his basket, arguing whose turn it was to carry it. How Angelo strutted; how he grew tall! All this affection, this admiration, Walter thought—it was as bad as overtipping.

The family stayed two weeks, and then a fortnight more. They were brown, drowsy, and seemed reluctant to face England and the poultry farm. They were enjoying their holiday, no doubt about that. On the beach they met a professor of history who spoke a little English, and a retired consul who asked them to tea. They saw, without

knowing what to make of it, a monument to Queen Victoria.
They heard people being comic and noisy, they bought
rice-and-spinach pies to eat on the beach, and ice cream
that melted down to powder and water. They ate melons
and peaches nearly as good as the fruit back in Africa, and
they buried the peach stones and the melon skins and the
ice-cream sticks and the greasy piecrusts in the sand.
They drove along the coast as far as Cannes, in the Parma-
violet Citroën Frank had hired, sight unseen, from South
Africa. He had bought his new farm in the same way.
Walter was glad his friends were away, for he was ashamed
to be seen in the Citroën. It was a vulgar automobile. He
told Frank that the DS was considered exclusively the
property of concierges' sons and successful grocers.

"I'm not even that," said Frank.

The seats were covered with plastic leopard skin. At
every stop, the car gave a great sigh and sank down like
a tired dog. The children loved this. They sat behind, with
Eve between them, telling riddles, singing songs. They
quarreled across their mother as if she were a hedge. "Silly
old sow," Walter heard his nephew saying. He realized the
boy was saying it to Eve. His back stiffened. Eve saw.

"Why shouldn't he say it, if he wants to?" she said.
"He doesn't know what it means. Do you want me to treat
them the way we were treated? Would you like to see some
of that?"

"No," said Walter, after a moment.

"Well, then. I'm trying another way."

Walter said, "I don't believe one person should call
another a silly old sow." He spoke without turning his head.
The children were still as mice; then the little boy began to
cry.

They drove home in the dark. The children slept, and
the three adults looked at neon lights and floodlit palm
trees without saying much. Suddenly Eve said, "Oh, I like
that." Walter looked at a casino; at the sea; at the Anglican
church, which was thirty years old, Riviera Gothic. "That
church," she said. "It's like home."

"Alas," said Walter.

"Terrible, is it?" said his brother-in-law, who had not bothered to look.

"I think I'll make up my own mind," said Eve. So she had sat, with her face set, when Walter tried to introduce her to some of his friends and his ideas, fifteen years before. She had never wanted to be anything except a mother, and she would protect anyone who wanted protection—Walter as well. But nothing would persuade her that a church was ugly if it was familiar and reminded her of home.

Walter did not desire Eve's protection. He did not think he could use anything Eve had to give. Sometimes she persuaded him to come to the beach with the family, and then she fussed over him, seeing that the parasol was fixed so that he had full shade. She knew he did not expose his arms and legs to the sun, because of his scars. She made him sit on an arrangement of damp, sandy towels and said, "There. Isn't that nice?" In an odd way, she still admired him; he saw it, and was pleased. He answered her remarks (about Riviera people, French politics, the Mediterranean climate, and the cost of things) with his habitual social fluency, but it was the children who took his attention. He marveled at their singleness of purpose, the energy they could release just in tearing off their clothes. They flung into the water and had to be bullied out. Mauve-lipped, chattering, they said, "What's there to do now?"

"Have you ever wanted to be a ballet dancer?" Walter asked his niece.

"No," she said, with scorn.

One day Angelo spent the morning with them. Frank had taken the car to the Citroën garage and looked forward to half a day with the mechanics there. In a curious way Angelo seemed to replace the children's father. He organized a series of canals and waterways and kept the children digging for more than an hour. Walter noticed that Angelo was doing none of the work himself. He stood over them with his hand on one hip—peacock lad, cock of the walk. When an Italian marries, you see this change, Walter thought. He treats his servants that way, and then his wife. He said, "Angelo, put your clothes on and run up to the bar and bring us all some cold drinks."

"Oh, Uncle Walter," his niece complained.

"I'll go, Uncle Walter," said the little boy.

"Angelo will go," Walter said. "It's his job."

Angelo pulled his shorts over his bathing suit and stood, waiting for Walter to drop money in his hand.

"Don't walk about naked," Walter said. "Put on your shirt."

Eve was knitting furiously. She sat with her cotton skirt hitched up above her knees and a cotton bolero thown over her head to keep off the sun. From this shelter her sunglasses gleamed at him, and she said in her plain, loud voice, "I don't like this, Walter, and I haven't been liking it for some time. It's not the kind of world I want my children to see."

"I'm not responsible for the Riviera," said Walter.

"I mean that I don't like your bullying Angelo in front of them. They admire him so. I don't like any of it. I mean to say, the master-servant idea. I think it's bad taste, if you want my opinion."

"Are you trying to tell me you didn't have a servant in South Africa?"

"You know perfectly well what I mean. Walter, what *are* you up to?   That sad, crumbling house. Nothing has been changed or painted or made pretty in it for years. You don't seem to have any friends here. Your telephone never rings. It hasn't rung once since I've been here. And that poor boy."

"Poor?" said Walter. "Is that what he's been telling you? You should have seen the house I rescued him from. You should just see what he's left behind him. Twelve starving sisters and brothers, an old harridan of a mother —and a grandmother. He's so frightened of her even at this distance that he sends her every penny I give him. Twelve sisters and brothers . . ."

"He must miss them," said Eve.

"I've sent him home," Walter said. "I sent him for a visit with a first-class ticket. He sold the first-class ticket and traveled third. If I hadn't been certain he wanted to give the difference to his people, I should never have had him back. I hate deceit. If he didn't get home that time it was because the cat was worrying him. I've told you the story. You said it was sad. But it was his idea, taking the cat."

"He eyes the girls in the market," said Eve. "But he never speaks."

"Let him," said Walter. "He is free to do as he likes."

"Perhaps he doesn't think he is."

"I can assure you he is, and knows it. If he is devoted to me because I've been kind to him, it's his own affair."

"It's probably too subtle for me," she said. She pulled her skirts a little higher and stroked her veined, stretched legs. She was beyond vanity. "But I still think it's all wrong. He's sweet with the children, but he's a little afraid of me."

"Perhaps you think he should be familiar with women and call them silly old sows."

"No, not at his age," she said mildly. "Johnny is still a baby, you know. I don't expect much from him." She was veering away from a row.

"My telephone never rings because my friends are away for the summer," he said. "This summer crowd has nothing to do with my normal life." He had to go on with that; her remark about the telephone had annoyed him more than anything else.

Yet he wanted her to approve of him; he wanted even Frank to approve of him, too. He was pushed into seeing himself through their eyes. He preferred his own images, his own creations. Once, he had loved a woman much older than himself. He saw her, by chance, after many years, when she was sixty. What will happen when I am sixty, he wanted to say. He wondered if Eve, with her boundless concern for other people, had any answer to that. What will happen fifteen years from now, when Miss Cooper claims the house?

That night, William of Orange, who lost no love on anyone, pulled himself onto the terrace table, having first attained a chair, and allowed Walter to scratch his throat. When he had had enough, he slipped away and dropped off the table and prowled along the wall. Eve was upstairs, putting the children to bed. It was a task she usually left to Angelo. Walter understood he and Frank had been deliberately left together alone. He knew he was about to be asked a favor. Frank leaned over the table. His stupid, friendly face wore its habitual expression of deep attention: *I am so interested in you. I am trying to get the point of everything you say.* He was easy enough; he never suggested Walter should be married, or working at something. He began to say that he missed South Africa. They had sold their property at a loss. He said he was starting over again for the last time, or so he hoped. He was thirty-seven. He had two children to educate. His face was red as a balloon. Walter let him talk, thinking it was good for him.

"We can always use another person on a farm—another man, that is," said Frank.

"I wouldn't be much use to you, I'm afraid," said Walter.

"No. Well, I meant to say . . . We shall have to pack up soon. I think next week."

"We shall miss you," said Walter. "Angelo will be shattered."

"We're going to drive the Citroën up to Paris," said Frank, suddenly lively, "and turn it in to Cook's there We may never have a chance to do that trip again. Wonderful for the kids." He went off on one of his favorite topics—motors and mileage—and was diverted from whatever request he had been prodded by Eve to make. Walter was thankful it had been so easy.

Unloved, neglected, the hamster chewed newspaper in its cage. The cage hung from the kitchen ceiling, and rocked with every draft. Angelo remembered to feed the hamster, but as far as the children were concerned it might have been dead. William of Orange claimed them now; he threw up hair balls and string, and behaved as if he were poisoned. Angelo covered his coat with olive oil and pushed mashed garlic down his throat. He grew worse; Angelo found him on the steps one morning, dying, unable to move his legs. He sat with the cat on his knees and roared, as William of Orange had howled on the train in his basket. The cat was dying of old age. Walter assured everyone it was nothing more serious than that. "He came with the house," he repeated again and again. "He must be the equivalent of a hundred and two."

Angelo's grief terrified the children. Walter was frightened as well, but only because too much was taking place. The charming boy against the baroque wall had become this uncontrolled, bellowing adolescent. The sight of his niece's delicate ear, the lamps reflected in his nephew's eyes, his sister's disapproval of him on the beach, his brother-in-law's soulless exposition of his personal disaster—each was an event. Any would have been a stone to mark the season. Any would have been enough. He wanted nothing more distressing than a spoiled dinner, nothing more lively than a drive along the shore. He thought, In three days, four at the most, they will disappear. William of Orange is old and dying, but everything else will be as before. Angelo will be amusing and young. Mrs. Wiggot will invite me to dine. The telephone will ring.

The children recovered quickly, for they saw that William of Orange was wretched but not quite dead. They were prepared to leave him and go to the beach as usual, but Angelo said he would stay with the cat. The children were sorry for Angelo now. Johnny sat next to Angelo on the step, frowning in a grown-up way, rubbing his brown knees. "Tell me one thing," he said to Angelo from under his sun hat. "Is William of Orange your father or something like that?" That night the little boy wet his bed, and Walter had a new horror. It was the sight of a bedsheet with a great stain flapping on the line.

Fortunately for Walter, the family could no longer put off going away. "There is so much to do," said Eve. "We got the Citroën delivered, but we didn't do a thing about the children's schools. I wonder if the trunks have got to London? I expect there hasn't been time. I hope they get there before the cold weather. All the children's clothes are in them."

"You are preposterous parents," Walter said. "I suppose you know that."

"We are, aren't we?" said Eve cheerfully. "You don't understand how much one has to *do*. If only we could leave the children somewhere, even for a week, while we look at schools and everything."

"You had your children because you wanted them," said Walter. "I suppose."

"Yes, we did," said Frank. It was the only time Walter ever saw his easy manner outdistanced. "We wanted them. So let's hear no more about leaving them. Even for a week."

Only one rainy day marred the holiday, and as it was the last day, it scarcely counted. It was over—the breather between South Africa and England, between home for the children and a new home for Eve. They crowded into the sitting room, waiting for lunch. They had delayed leaving since early that morning, expecting, in their scatterbrained way, that the sky would clear. The room smelled of musty paper and of mice. Walter suddenly remembered what it was like in winter here, and how Angelo was often bored. His undisciplined relations began pulling books off the shelves and leaving them anywhere.

"Are all these yours?" Mary asked him. "Are they old?"

"These shelves hold every book I have ever bought or had given me since I was born," said Walter. And the children looked again at the dark-green and dark-wine covers.

"I know *Kim*," said Mary, and she opened it and began to read in a monotonous voice, " 'He sat, in defiance of municipal orders, astride the gun Zam-Zammeh on her brick platform opposite the old Ajaibgher.' "

"I can still see him," said Eve. "I can see Kim."

"I can't see him as I saw him," said Walter.

"Never could bear Kipling, personally," Frank said. "He's at the bottom of all the trouble we're having now. You only have to read something like 'Wee Willie Winkie' to understand that."

"Why is the gun 'her'?" Mary asked.

"Because in an English education it's the only thing allowed to be female," said Frank. "That and boats." He hadn't wanted the change; that was plain. For Eve's sake, Walter hoped it was a change for the good.

"This book is all scribbled in," Mary complained. She began to turn at random, reading the neat hand that had been Walter's at twelve: " 'Shows foresight,' " she read. " 'Local color. More color. Building up the color. Does not wish to let women interfere with his career.' That's underlined, Uncle Walter," she said, breaking off. " 'A deceiver. Kim's strong will—or white blood? Generous renunciation Sympathetic. Shows off. Sly. Easily imposed on. Devout. Persistent. Enterprising.' "

"That will do," said Frank. " 'Shows off' is the chief expression where you're concerned."

"Those notes were how Kipling was introduced to me, and I used them when I was teaching Angelo," said Walter. "Angelo doesn't like Kipling, either. You can keep the book, if you want it."

"Thank you very much," said Mary automatically. She placed the book more or less where it had been, as if she recognized that this was a bogus gesture.

"Thank you, darling Walter," said Eve, and she picked up the book and stroked the cover, dirtying her hand. "Johnny will love it, later on."

Walter's first dinner invitation of the autumn season arrived by post eight days after the Osborns had gone. In the same mail were three letters, each addressed by his sister. Eve thanked him for his great kindness; he would never know what it had meant, the holiday it had been. They were in a hotel, and it was a great change from the south. In a P.S. she said they were moving to the new farm soon. The children were their great worry. She went on about schools. The postscript was longer than the body of the letter.

The other two envelopes, although addressed by Eve, contained letters from Mary and Johnny. The boy spelled difficult words correctly, simple words hopelessly, and got his own name wrong.

"Dear Uncle Walter," he wrote. "Thank you for letting us stay at your house." A row of dots led out to the margin, where he had added, "and for Kim." The text of the letter went on, "It was the most exciting, and enjoyable time I have ever had. Please tell Angelo on the way back we were fined for overtaking in a village, but we got safley out of France. I hope the hamster is well and happy. Tell Angelo there are two very small kittens down in the kitchin of the hotel where we now rent two rooms. They are sweat, white, snowballs, also there is a huge golden labridore, he is very stuppid. Love from Johny."

The girl's letter had been written on a line guide. Her hand was firm. "Dear Uncle Walter," she said. "Thank you for letting us sleep in your house and for everything too. We had a lovely time. Will you please tell Angelo that on the way to Paris Daddy was fined 900 francs for over-taking in a village. He was livid. On Monday I had two teeth out, one on each side. I hope the hamster is healthy. Will you please tell Angelo that our trunks have arrived with my books and he can have one as a present from me, if he will tell me which one he likes best.

> Successful Show Jumping
> Bridle Wise
> Pink and Scarlet
> The Young Rider

"These are my favorites and so I would like him to have one. Also, here is a poem I have copied out for him from a book.

FROM THE DREAM OF AN OLD MELTONIAN
by W. Bromley Davenport
Though a rough-riding world may bespatter your breeches
Though sorrow may cross you, or slander revile,
Though you plunge overhead in misfortune's blind ditches,
Shun the gap of deception—the hand gate of guile.

"Tell Angelo we miss him, and William of Orange, and the hamster too. Thank you again for everything. Your affectionate niece, Mary."

Walking to the kitchen with the letters in his hand, he tried to see the passionate child—dancer, he had thought —on the summer beach. But although eight days had passed, no more, he had forgotten what she was like. He tried to think of England then. Someone had told him the elms were going, because of an American disease. He knew that all this thinking and drifting was covering one displeasure, one blister on his pride: it was Mary's letter he had been waiting for.

"These letters are intended for you," he said, and put them in Angelo's hands. "They were addressed to me by mistake. Or perhaps the family didn't know your full name. I didn't know you were interested in horses, by the way."

Angelo sat at the kitchen table, cleaning the hamster's cage. Mme. Rossi sat facing him. Neither of them rose. "Master-servant," Eve had said. She ought to have seen Angelo's casual manner now, the way he accepted his morning's post—as though Walter were the servant. The boy's secretive face bent over the letters. Already Angelo's tears were falling. Walter watched, exasperated, as the ink dissolved.

"You can't keep on crying every time I mention the children," he said. "Look at the letters now. You won't be able to read them."

"He is missing the family," Mme. Rossi said. "Even though they made more work for him. He cries the whole day."

Of course he was missing the family. He was missing the family, the children were missing him. Walter looked at the boy's face, which seemed as closed and vain as a cat's. "They meant more work for you," he said. "Did you hear that?"

"We could have kept the children," Angelo mumbled. His lips hung open. His face was Negroid, plump. One day he would certainly be fat.

"What, brought them up?"

"Only for one week," said Angelo, wiping his eyes.

"It seems to me you overheard rather a good deal." Another thought came to him: it would have been a great responsibility. He felt aggrieved that Angelo did not take into consideration the responsibilities Walter already had —for instance, he was responsible for Angelo's being in France. If Angelo were to steal a car and smash it, Walter would have to make good the loss. He was responsible for the house, which was not his, and for William of Orange, who was no better and no worse, but lay nearly paralyzed in a cardboard box, demanding much of Angelo's attention. Now he was responsible for a hamster in a cage.

"They would have taken me on the farm," Angelo said.

"Nonsense." Walter remembered how Eve avoided a brawl, and he imitated her deliberately mild manner. He understood now that they had been plotting behind his back. He had raised Angelo in cotton wool, taught him Kipling and gardening and how to wash the car, fed him the best food . . . "My brother-in-law is Irish," he said. "You mustn't think his promises are real."

The boy sat without moving, expressionless, sly. He was waiting for Walter to leave the room so that he could have the letters to himself.

"Would you like to go home, Angelo?" Walter said. "Would you like to go back and live in Italy, back with your family?" Angelo shook his head. Of course he would say no to that; for one thing, they relied on his pocket money—on the postal orders he sent them. An idea came to Walter. "We shall send for your mother," he said. The idea was radiant now. "We shall bring your old mother here for a visit. Why not? That's what we shall do. Bring your mother here. She can talk to you. I'm sure that is all you need."

"Can you imagine that lazy boy on an English farm?" said Walter to Mrs. Wiggott. "That is what I said to him: 'Have you ever worked as a farmer? Do you know what it means?'" He blotted imaginary tears with his sleeve to show how Angelo had listened. His face was swollen, limp.

"Stop it, Walter," said Mrs. Wiggott. "I shall *perish*."

"And so now the mother is coming," said Walter. "That is where the situation has got to. They will all sit in the kitchen eating my food, gossiping in Calabrian. I say 'all' because of course she is bound to come with a *covey* of cousins. But I am hoping that when I have explained the situation to the old woman she can reason with Angelo and make him see the light."

"Darling Walter," said Mrs. Wiggott. "This could only happen to you."

"If only I could explain things to Angelo in *our* terms," said Walter. "How to be a good friend, a decent host, all the rest. Not to expect too much. How to make the best of life, as we do."

"As we do," said Mrs. Wiggott, solemn now.

"Live for the minute, I would like to tell him. Look at the things I put up with, without complaint. The summer I've had! Children everywhere. Eggs and bacon in the *hottest* weather. High tea—my brother-in-law's influence, of course. Look at the house I live in. Ugly box, really. I never complain."

"That is true," said his old friend.

"No heat in winter. Not an anemone in the garden. Les Anémones, they called it, and not an anemone on the place. Nothing but a lot of iris, and I put those in myself."

The Ice Wagon
Going Down the Street

Now that they are out of world affairs and back where they started, Peter Frazier's wife says, "Everybody else did well in the international thing except us."

"You have to be crooked," he tells her.

"Or smart. Pity we weren't."

It is Sunday morning. They sit in the kitchen, drinking their coffee, slowly, remembering the past. They say the names of people as if they were magic. Peter thinks, *Agnes Brusen*, but there are hundreds of other names. As a private married joke, Peter and Sheilah wear the silk dressing gowns they bought in Hong Kong. Each thinks the other a peacock, rather splendid, but they pretend the dressing gowns are silly and worn in fun.

Peter and Sheilah and their two daughters, Sandra and Jennifer, are visiting Peter's unmarried sister, Lucille. They have been Lucille's guests seventeen weeks, ever since they returned to Toronto from the Far East. Their big old steamer trunk blocks a corner of the kitchen, making a problem of the refrigerator door; but even Lucille says the trunk may as well stay where it is, for the present. The Fraziers' future is so unsettled; everything is still in the air.

Lucille has given her bedroom to her two nieces, and sleeps on a camp cot in the hall. The parents have the living-room divan. They have no privileges here; they sleep after Lucille has seen the last television show that interests her. In the hall closet their clothes are crushed by winter overcoats. They know they are being judged for the first time. Sandra and Jennifer are waiting for Sheilah and Peter to decide. They are waiting to learn where these exotic parents will fly to next. What sort of climate will Sheilah consider? What job will Peter consent to accept? When the parents are ready, the children will make a decision of their own. It is just possible that Sandra and Jennifer will choose to stay with their aunt.

The peacock parents are watched by wrens. Lucille and her nieces are much the same—sandy-colored, proudly plain. Neither of the girls has the father's insouciance or the mother's appearance—her height, her carriage, her thick hair, and sky-blue eyes. The children are more cautious than their parents; more Canadian. When they saw their aunt's apartment they had been away from Canada nine years, ever since they were two and four; and Jennifer, the elder, said, "Well, now we're home." Her voice is nasal and flat. Where did she learn that voice? And why should this be home? Peter's answer to anything about his mystifying children is, "It must be in the blood."

Cn Sunday morning Lucille takes her nieces to

church. It seems to be the only condition she imposes on
her relations: the children must be decent. The girls go
willingly, with their new hats and purses and gloves and
coral bracelets and strings of pearls. The parents, ram-
shackle, sleepy, dim in the brain because it is Sunday, sit
down to their coffee and privacy and talk of the past.

"We weren't crooked," says Peter. "We weren't even
smart."

Sheilah's head bobs up; she is no drowner. It is wrong
to say they have nothing to show for time. Sheilah has the
Balenciaga. It is a black afternoon dress, stiff and boned at
the waist, long for the fashions of now, but neither Sheilah
nor Peter would change a thread. The Balenciaga is their
talisman, their treasure; and after they remember it they
touch hands and think that the years are not behind them
but hazy and marvelous and still to be lived.

The first place they went to was Paris. In the early
fifties the pick of the international jobs was there. Peter had
inherited the last scrap of money he knew he was ever likely
to see, and it was enough to get them over: Sheilah and
Peter and the babies and the steamer trunk. To their joy
and astonishment they had money in the bank. They said
to each other, "It should last a year." Peter was fastidious
about the new job; he hadn't come all this distance to accept just anything. In Paris he met Hugh Taylor, who was
earning enough smuggling gasoline to keep his wife in
Paris and a girl in Rome. That impressed Peter, because
he remembered Taylor as a sour scholarship student without the slightest talent for life. Taylor had a job, of course.
He hadn't said to himself, I'll go over to Europe and smuggle
gasoline. It gave Peter an idea; he saw the shape of things.
First you catch your fish. Later, at an international party,
he met Johnny Hertzberg, who told him Germany was
the place. Hertzberg said that anyone who came out of
Germany broke now was too stupid to be here, and deserved
to be back home at a desk. Peter nodded, as if he had already
thought of that. He began to think about Germany. Paris

was fine for a holiday, but it had been picked clean. Yes,
Germany. His money was running low. He thought about
Germany quite a lot.

That winter was moist and delicate; so fragile that
they daren't speak of it now. There seemed to be plenty of
everything and plenty of time. They were living the dream
of a marriage, the fabric uncut, nothing slashed or spoiled.
All winter they spent their money, and went to parties,
and talked about Peter's future job. It lasted four months.
They spent their money, lived in the future, and were
never as happy again.

After four months they were suddenly moved away
from Paris, but not to Germany—to Geneva. Peter thinks
it was because of the incident at the Trudeau wedding at
the Ritz. Paul Trudeau was a French-Canadian Peter had
known at school and in the Navy. Trudeau had turned into
a snob, proud of his career and his Paris connections. He
tried to make the difference felt, but Peter thought the
difference was only for strangers. At the wedding recep-
tion Peter lay down on the floor and said he was dead. He
held a white azalea in a brass pot on his chest, and sang,
"Oh, hear us when we cry to Thee for those in peril on the
sea." Sheilah bent over him and said, "Pete, darling, get up.
Pete, listen, every single person who can do something for
you is in this room. If you love me, you'll get up."

"I do love you," he said, ready to engage in a serious
conversation. "She's so beautiful," he told a second face.
"She's nearly as tall as I am. She was a model in London.
I met her over in London in the war. I met her there in the
war." He lay on his back with the azalea on his chest, explaining their history. A waiter took the brass pot away,
and after Peter had been hauled to his feet he knocked the
waiter down. Trudeau's bride, who was freshly out of an
Ursuline convent, became hysterical; and even though Paul
Trudeau and Peter were old acquaintances, Trudeau never
spoke to him again. Peter says now that French-Canadians
always have that bit of spite. He says Trudeau asked the

Embassy to interfere. Luckily, back home there were still a few people to whom the name "Frazier" meant something, and it was to these people that Peter appealed. He wrote letters saying that a French-Canadian combine was preventing his getting a decent job, and could anything be done? No one answered directly, but it was clear that what they settled for was exile to Geneva: a season of meditation and remorse, as he explained to Sheilah, and it was managed tactfully, through Lucille. Lucille wrote that a friend of hers, May Fergus, now a secretary in Geneva, had heard about a job. The job was filing pictures in the information service of an international agency in the Palais des Nations. The pay was so-so, but Lucille thought Peter must be getting fed up doing nothing.

Peter often asks his sister now who put her up to it—what important person told her to write that letter suggesting Peter go to Geneva?

"Nobody," says Lucille. "I mean, nobody in the way *you* mean. I really did have this girl friend working there, and I knew you must be running through your money pretty fast in Paris."

"It must have been somebody pretty high up," Peter says. He looks at his sister admiringly, as he has often looked at his wife.

Peter's wife had loved him in Paris. Whatever she wanted in marriage she found that winter, there. In Geneva, where Peter was a file clerk and they lived in a furnished flat, she pretended they were in Paris and life was still the same. Often, when the children were at supper, she changed as though she and Peter were dining out. She wore the Balenciaga, and put candles on the card table where she and Peter ate their meal. The neckline of the dress was soiled with make-up. Peter remembers her dabbing on the make-up with a wet sponge. He remembers her in the kitchen, in the soiled Balenciaga, patting on the make-up with a filthy sponge. Behind her, at the kitchen table, Sandra and Jennifer, in buttonless pajamas and bunny slippers, ate their supper of marmalade sandwiches and milk. When the children were asleep, the parents dined solemnly, ritually, Sheilah sitting straight as a queen.

It was a mysterious period of exile, and he had to wait for signs, or signals, to know when he was free to leave. He never saw the job any other way. He forgot he had applied for it. He thought he had been sent to Geneva because of a misdemeanor and had to wait to be released. Nobody pressed him at work. His immediate boss had resigned, and he was alone for months in a room with two desks. He read the *Herald-Tribune*, and tried to discover how things were here—how the others ran their lives on the pay they were officially getting. But it was a closed conspiracy. He was not dealing with adventurers now but civil servants waiting for pension day. No one ever answered his questions. They pretended to think his questions were a form of wit. His only solace in exile was the few happy weekends he had in the late spring and early summer. He had met another old acquaintance, Mike Burleigh. Mike was a serious liberal who had married a serious heiress. The Burleighs had two guest lists. The first was composed of stuffy people they felt obliged to entertain, while the second was made up of their real friends, the friends they wanted. The real friends strove hard to become stuffy and dull and thus achieve the first guest list, but few succeeded. Peter went on the first list straight away. Possibly Mike didn't understand, at the beginning, why Peter was pretending to be a file clerk. Peter had such an air— he might have been sent by a universal inspector to see how things in Geneva were being run.

Every Friday in May and June and part of July, the Fraziers rented a sky-blue Fiat and drove forty miles east of Geneva to the Burleighs' summer house. They brought the children, a suitcase, the children's tattered picture books, and a token bottle of gin. This, in memory, is a period of water and water birds; swans, roses, and singing

birds. The children were small and still belonged to them.
If they remember too much, their mouths water, their
stomachs hurt. Peter says, "It was fine while it lasted."
Enough. While it lasted Sheilah and Madge Burleigh were
close. They abandoned their husbands and spent long summer afternoons comparing their mothers and praising each
other's skin and hair. To Madge, and not to Peter, Sheilah
opened her Liverpool childhood with the words "rat poor."
Peter heard about it later, from Mike. The women's friendship seemed to Peter a bad beginning. He trusted women
but not with each other. It lasted ten weeks. One Sunday,
Madge said she needed the two bedrooms the Fraziers
usually occupied for a party of sociologists from Pakistan,
and that was the end. In November, the Fraziers heard that
the summer house had been closed, and that the Burleighs
were in Geneva, in their winter flat; they gave no sign.
There was no help for it, and no appeal.

Now Peter began firing letters to anyone who had
ever known his late father. He was living in a mild yellow
autumn. Why does he remember the streets of the city
dark, and the windows everywhere black with rain? He
remembers being with Sheilah and the children as if they
clung together while just outside their small shelter it
rained and rained. The children slept in the bedroom of
the flat because the window gave on the street and they
could breathe air. Peter and Sheilah had the living-room
couch. Their window was not a real window but a square
on a well of cement. The flat seemed damp as a cave. Peter
remembers steam in the kitchen, pools under the sink,
sweat on the pipes. Water streamed on him from the children's clothes, washed and dripping overhead. The trunk,
upended in the children's room, was not quite unpacked.
Sheilah had not signed her name to this life; she had not
given in. Once Peter heard her drop her aitches. "You kids
are lucky," she said to the girls "I never 'ad so much as a
sit-down meal. I ate chips out of a paper or I 'ad a butty
out on the stairs." He never asked her what a butty was.
He thinks it means bread and cheese.

The day he heard "You kids are lucky" he understood they were becoming in fact something they had only *appeared* to be until now—the shabby civil servant and his brood. If he had been European he would have ridden to work on a bicycle, in the uniform of his class and condition. He would have worn a tight coat, a turned collar, and a dirty tie. He wondered then if coming here had been a mistake, and if he should not, after all, still be in a place where his name meant something. Surely Peter Frazier should live where "Frazier" counts? In Ontario even now when he says "Frazier" an absent look comes over his hearer's face, as if its owner were consulting an interior guide. What is Frazier? What does it mean? Oil? Power? Politics? Wheat? Real estate? The creditors had the house sealed when Peter's father died. His aunt collapsed with a heart attack in somebody's bachelor apartment, leaving three sons and a widower to surmise they had never known her. Her will was a disappointment. None of that generation left enough. One made it: the granite Presbyterian immigrants from Scotland. Their children, a generation of daunted women and maiden men, held still. Peter's father's crowd spent: they were not afraid of their fathers, and their grandfathers were old. Peter and his sister and his cousins lived on the remains. They were left the rinds of income, of notions, and the memories of ideas rather than ideas intact. If Peter can choose his reincarnation, let him be the oppressed son of a Scottish parson. Let Peter grow up on cuffs and iron principles. Let him make the fortune! Let him flee the manse! When he was small his patrimony was squandered under his nose. He remembers people dancing in his father's house. He remembers seeing and nearly understanding adultery in a guest room, among a pile of wraps. He thought he had seen a murder; he never told. He remembers licking glasses wherever he found them—on window sills, on stairs, in the pantry. In his room he listened while Lucille read Beatrix Potter. The bad rabbit stole the carrot from the good rabbit without saying please, and downstairs was the noise of the party—the roar of the

crouched lion. When his father died he saw the chairs upside down and the bailiff's chalk marks. Then the doors
were sealed.

He has often tried to tell Sheilah why he cannot be
defeated. He remembers his father saying, "Nothing can
touch us," and Peter believed it and still does. It has prevented his taking his troubles too seriously. "Nothing can
be as bad as this," he will tell himself. "It is happening to
me." Even in Geneva, where his status was file clerk, where
he sank and stopped on the level of the men who never
emigrated, the men on the bicycles—even there he had a
manner of strolling to work as if his office were a pastime,
and his real life a secret so splendid he could share it with
no one except himself.

In Geneva Peter worked for a woman—a girl. She
was a Norwegian from a small town in Saskatchewan. He
supposed they had been put together because they were
Canadians; but they were as strange to each other as if
"Canadian" meant any number of things, or had no real
meaning. Soon after Agnes Brusen came to the office she
hung her framed university degree on the wall. It was one
of the gritty, prideful gestures that stand for push, toil,
and family sacrifice. He thought, then, that she must be
one of a family of immigrants for whom education is everything. Hugh Taylor had told him that in some families the
older children never marry until the youngest have finished
school. Sometimes every second child is sacrificed and
made to work for the education of the next born. Those
who finish college spend years paying back. They are
white-hot Protestants, and they live with a load of work
and debt and obligation. Peter placed his new colleague on
scraps of information. He had never been in the West.

She came to the office on a Monday morning in October. The office was overheated and painted cream. It contained two desks, the filing cabinets, a map of the world
as it had been in 1945, and the Charter of the United Na-

tions left behind by Agnes Brusen's predecessor. (She took down the Charter without asking Peter if he minded, with the impudence of gesture you find in women who wouldn't say boo *to* a goose; and then she hung her college degree on the nail where the Charter had been.) Three people brought her in—a whole committee. One of them said, "Agnes, this is Pete Frazier. Pete, Agnes Brusen. Pete's Canadian, too, Agnes. He knows all about the office, so ask him anything."

Of course he knew all about the office: he knew the exact spot where the cord of the venetian blind was frayed, obliging one to give an extra tug to the right.

The girl might have been twenty-three: no more. She wore a brown tweed suit with bone buttons, and a new silk scarf and new shoes. She clutched an unscratched brown purse. She seemed dressed in going-away presents. She said, "Oh, I never smoke," with a convulsive movement of her hand, when Peter offered his case. He was courteous, hiding his disappointment. The people he worked with had told him a Scandinavian girl was arriving, and he had expected a stunner. Agnes was a mole: she was small and brown, and round-shouldered as if she had always carried parcels or younger children in her arms. A mole's profile was turned when she said goodbye to her committee. If she had been foreign, ill-favored though she was, he might have flirted a little, just to show that he was friendly; but their being Canadian, and suddenly left together, was a sexual damper. He sat down and lit his own cigarette. She smiled at him, questioningly, he thought, and sat as if she had never seen a chair before. He wondered if his smoking was annoying her. He wondered if she was fidgety about drafts, or allergic to anything, and whether she would want the blind up or down. His social compass was out of order because the others couldn't tell Peter and Agnes apart. There was a world of difference between them, yet it was she who had been brought in to sit at the larger of the two desks.

While he was thinking this she got up and walked around the office, almost on tiptoe, opening the doors of closets and pulling out the filing trays. She looked inside everything except the drawers of Peter's desk. (In any case, Peter's desk was locked His desk is locked wherever he works. In Geneva he went into Personnel one morning, early, and pinched his application form. He had stated on the form that he had seven years' experience in public relations and could speak French, German, Spanish, and Italian. He has always collected anything important about himself—anything useful But he can never get on with the final act, which is getting rid of the information. He has kept papers about for years, a constant source of worry.)

"I know this looks funny, Mr. Ferris," said the girl. "I'm not really snooping or anything. I just can't feel easy in a new place unless I know where everything is. In a new place everything seems so hidden."

If she had called him "Ferris" and pretended not to know he was Frazier, it could only be because they had sent her here to spy on him and see if he had repented and was fit for a better place in life. "You'll be all right here," he said. "Nothing's hidden. Most of us haven't got brains enough to have secrets. This is Rainbow Valley." Depressed by the thought that they were having him watched now, he passed his hand over his hair and looked outside to the lawn and the parking lot and the peacocks someone gave the Palais des Nations years ago. The peacocks love no one. They wander about the parked cars looking elderly. bad-tempered. mournful, and lost.

Agnes had settled down again. She folded her silk scarf and placed it just so, with her gloves beside it. She opened her new purse and took out a notebook and a shiny gold pencil. She may have written

Duster for desk
Kleenex

Glass jar for flowers
Air-Wick because he smokes
Paper for lining drawers

because the next day she brought each of these articles to
work. She also brought a large black Bible, which she un-
wrapped lovingly and placed on the left-hand corner of her
desk. The flower vase—empty—stood in the middle, and
the Kleenex made a counterpoise for the Bible on the right.

When he saw the Bible he knew she had not been
sent to spy on his work. The conspiracy was deeper. She
might have been dispatched by ghosts. He knew everything
about her, all in a moment: he saw the ambition, the terror,
the dry pride. She was the true heir of the men from Scotland; she was at the start. She had been sent to tell him,
"You can begin, but not begin again." She never opened the
Bible, but she dusted it as she dusted her desk, her chair,
and any surface the cleaning staff had overlooked. And
Peter, the first days, watching her timid movements, her
insignificant little face, felt, as you feel the approach of a
storm, the charge of moral certainty round her, the belief
in work, the faith in undertakings, the bread of the Black
Sunday. He recognized and tasted all of it: ashes in the
mouth.

After five days their working relations were settled.
Of course, there was the Bible and all that went with it, but
his tongue had never held the taste of ashes long. She was
an inferior girl of poor quality She had nothing in her
favor except the degree on the wall. In the real world, he
would not have invited her to his house except to mind the
children. That was what he said to Sheilah. He said that
Agnes was a mole, and a virgin, and that her tics and man-
nerisms were sending him round the bend. She had an
infuriating habit of covering her mouth when she talked.
Even at the telephone she put up her hand as if afraid of
losing anything, even a word. Her voice was nasal and flat.

She had two working costumes, both dull as the wall. One was the brown suit, the other a navy-blue dress with changable collars. She dressed for no one; she dressed for her desk, her jar of flowers, her Bible, and her box of Kleenex. One day she crossed the space between the two desks and stood over Peter, who was reading a newspaper. She could have spoken to him from her desk, but she may have felt that being on her feet gave her authority. She had plenty of courage, but authority was something else.

"I thought—I mean, they told me you were the person . . ." She got on with it bravely: "If you don't want to do the filing or any work, all right, Mr. Frazier. I'm not saying anything about that. You might have poor health or your personal reasons. But it's got to be done, so if you'll kindly show me about the filing I'll do it. I've worked in Information before, but it was a different office, and every office is different."

"My dear girl," said Peter. He pushed back his chair and looked at her, astonished. "You've been sitting there fretting, worrying. How insensitive of me. How trying for you. Usually I file on the last Wednesday of the month, so you see, you just haven't been around long enough to see a last Wednesday. Not another word, please. And let us not waste another minute." He emptied the heaped baskets of photographs so swiftly, pushing "Iran—Smallpox Control" into "Irish Red Cross" (close enough), that the girl looked frightened, as if she had raised a whirlwind. She said slowly, "If you'll only show me, Mr. Frazier, instead of doing it so fast, I'll gladly look after it, because you might want to be doing other things, and I feel the filing should be done every day." But Peter was too busy to answer, and so she sat down, holding the edge of her desk.

"There," he said, beaming. "All done." His smile, his sunburst, was wasted, for the girl was staring round the room as if she feared she had not inspected everything the first day after all; some drawer, some cupboard, hid a monster. That evening Peter unlocked one of the drawers

of his desk and took away the application form he had
stolen from Personnel. The girl had not finished her search.

"How could you *not* know?" wailed Sheilah. "You sit
looking at her every day. You must talk about *something*.
She must have told you."

"She did tell me," said Peter, "and I've just told you."

It was this: Agnes Brusen was on the Burleighs' guest
list. How had the Burleighs met her? What did they see in
her? Peter could not reply. He knew that Agnes lived in a
bed-sitting room with a Swiss family and had her meals
with them. She had been in Geneva three months, but no
one had ever seen her outside the office. "You *should* know,"
said Sheilah. "She must have something, more than you
can see. Is she pretty? Is she brilliant? What is it?"

"We don't really talk," Peter said. They talked in a
way: Peter teased her and she took no notice. Agnes was
not a sulker. She had taken her defeat like a sport. She did
her work and a good deal of his. She sat behind her Bible,
her flowers, and her Kleenex, and answered when Peter
spoke. That was how he learned about the Burleighs—just
by teasing and being bored. It was a January afternoon.
He said, "*Miss* Brusen. Talk to me. Tell me everything.
Pretend we have perfect rapport. Do you like Geneva?"

"It's a nice clean town." she said. He can see to this
day the red and blue anemones in the glass jar, and her
bent head, and her small untended hands.

"Are you learning beautiful French with your Swiss
family?"

"They speak English."

"Why don't you take an apartment of your own?" he
said. Peter was not usually impertinent. He was bored.
"You'd be independent then."

"I am independent," she said. "I earn my living. I don't
think it proves anything if you live by yourself. Mrs. Burleigh wants me to live alone, too. She's looking for something for me. It mustn't be dear. I send money home."

Here was the extraordinary thing about Agnes
Brusen: she refused the use of Christian names and never
spoke to Peter unless he spoke first, but she would tell
anything, as if to say, "Don't waste time fishing. Here it
is."

He learned all in one minute that she sent her salary
home, and that she was a friend of the Burleighs. The first
he had expected; the second knocked him flat.

"She's got to come to dinner," Sheilah said. "We should
have had her right from the beginning. If only I'd known!
But *you* were the one. You said she looked like—oh, I don't
even remember. A Norwegian mole."

She came to dinner one Saturday night in January, in
her navy-blue dress, to which she had pinned an organdy
gardenia. She sat upright on the edge of the sofa. Sheilah
had ordered the meal from a restaurant. There was lobster,
good wine, and a *pièce-montée* full of kirsch and cream.
Agnes refused the lobster; she had never eaten anything
from the sea unless it had been sterilized and tinned, and
said so. She was afraid of skin poisoning. Someone in her
family had skin poisoning after having eaten oysters. She
touched her cheeks and neck to show where the poisoning
had erupted. She sniffed her wine and put the glass down
without tasting it. She could not eat the cake because of
the alcohol it contained. She ate an egg, bread and butter,
a sliced tomato, and drank a glass of ginger ale. She seemed
unaware she was creating disaster and pain. She did not
help clear away the dinner plates. She sat, adequately
nourished, decently dressed, and waited to learn why she
had been invited here—that was the feeling Peter had. He
folded the card table on which they had dined, and opened
the window to air the room.

"It's not the same cold as Canada, but you feel it
more," he said, for something to say.

"Your blood has gotten thin," said Agnes.

Sheilah returned from the kitchen and let herself fall
into an armchair. With her eyes closed she held out her

hand for a cigarette. She was performing the haughty-lady act that was a family joke. She flung her head back and looked at Agnes through half-closed lids; then she suddenly brought her head forward, widening her eyes.

"Are you skiing madly?" she said.

"Well, in the first place there hasn't been any snow," said Agnes. "So nobody's doing any skiing so far as I know. All I hear is people complaining because there's no snow. Personally, I don't ski. There isn't much skiing in the part of Canada I come from. Besides, my family never had that kind of leisure."

"Heavens," said Sheilah, as if her family had every kind.

I'll bet they had, thought Peter. On the dole.

Sheilah was wasting her act. He had a suspicion that Agnes knew it was an act but did not know it was also a joke. If so, it made Sheilah seem a fool, and he loved Sheilah too much to enjoy it.

"The Burleighs have been wonderful to me," said Agnes. She seemed to have divined why she was here, and decided to give them all the information they wanted, so that she could put on her coat and go home to bed. "They had me out to their place on the lake every weekend until the weather got cold and they moved back to town. They've rented a chalet for the winter, and they want me to come there, too. But I don't know if I will or not. I don't ski, and, oh, I don't know—I don't drink, either, and I don't always see the point. Their friends are too rich and I'm too Canadian."

She had delivered everything Sheilah wanted and more: Agnes was on the first guest list and didn't care. No, Peter corrected; doesn't know. Doesn't care and doesn't know.

"I thought with you Norwegians it was in the blood, skiing. And drinking," Sheilah murmured.

"Drinking, maybe," said Agnes. She covered her mouth and said behind her spread fingers, "In our family we were religious. We didn't drink or smoke. My brother was in Norway in the war. He saw some cousins. Oh," she said, unexpectedly loud, "Harry said it was just terrible. They were so poor. They had flies in their kitchen. They gave him something to eat a fly had been on. They didn't have a real toilet, and they'd been in the same house about two hundred years. We've only recently built our own home, and we have a bathroom and two toilets. I'm from Saskatchewan," she said. "I'm not from any other place."

Surely one winter here had been punishment enough? In the spring they would remember him and free him. He wrote Lucille, who said he was lucky to have a job at all. The Burleighs had sent the Fraziers a second-guest list Christmas card. It showed a Moslem refugee child weeping outside a tent. They treasured the card and left it standing long after the others had been given the children to cut up. Peter had discovered by now what had gone wrong in the friendship—Sheilah had charged a skirt at a dressmaker to Madge's account. Madge had told her she might, and then changed her mind. Poor Sheilah! She was new to this part of it—to the changing humors of independent friends. Paris was already a year in the past. At Mardi Gras, the Burleighs gave their annual party. They invited everyone, the damned and the dropped, with the prodigality of a child at prayers. The invitation said "in costume," but the Fraziers were too happy to wear a disguise. They might not be recognized. Like many of the guests they expected to meet at the party, they had been disgraced, forgotten, and rehabilitated. They would be anxious to see one another as they were.

On the night of the party, the Fraziers rented a car they had never seen before and drove through the first snowstorm of the year. Peter had not driven since last summer's blissful trips in the Fiat. He could not find the switch for the windshield wiper in this car. He leaned over the wheel. "Can you see on your side?" he asked.

"Can I make a left turn here? Does it look like a one-way?"

"I can't imagine why you took a car with a right-hand drive," said Sheilah.

He had trouble finding a place to park; they crawled up and down unknown streets whose curbs were packed with snow-covered cars. When they stood at last on the pavement, safe and sound, Peter said, "This is the first snow."

"I can see that," said Sheilah. "Hurry, darling. My hair."

"It's the first snow."

"You're repeating yourself," she said. "Please hurry darling. Think of my poor shoes. My *hair*."

She was born in an ugly city, and so was Peter, but they have this difference: she does not know the importance of the first snow—the first clean thing in a dirty year. He would have told her then that this storm, which was wetting her feet and destroying her hair, was like the first day of the English spring, but she made a frightened gesture, trying to shield her head. The gesture told him he did not understand her beauty.

"Let me," she said. He was fumbling with the key, trying to lock the car. She took the key without impatience and locked the door on the driver's side; and then, to show Peter she treasured him and was not afraid of wasting her life or her beauty, she took his arm and they walked in the snow down a street and around a corner to the apartment house where the Burleighs lived. They were, and are, a united couple. They were afraid of the party, and each of them knew it. When they walk together, holding arms, they give each other whatever each can spare.

Only six people had arrived in costume. Madge Burleigh was disguised as Manet's "Lola de Valence," which everyone mistook for Carmen. Mike was an Impressionist painter, with a straw hat and a glued-on beard. "I am all of them," he said. He would rather have dressed as a den-

tist, he said, welcoming the Fraziers as if he had parted
from them the day before, but Madge wanted him to look
as if he had created her. "You know?" he said.

"Perfectly," said Sheilah. Her shoes were stained and
the snow had softened her lacquered hair. She was not
wasted; she was the most beautiful woman here.

About an hour after their arrival, Peter found himself
with no one to talk to. He had told about the Trudeau
wedding in Paris and the pot of azaleas, and after he mis-
laid his audience he began to look round for Sheilah. She
was on a window seat, partly concealed by a green velvet
curtain. Facing her, so that their profiles were neat and
perfect against the night, was a man. Their conversation
was private and enclosed, as if they had in minutes covered
leagues of time and arrived at the place where everything
was implied, understood. Peter began working his way
across the room, toward his wife, when he saw Agnes.
He was granted the sight of her drowning face. She had
dressed with comic intention, obviously with care, and now
she was a ragged hobo, half tramp, half clown. Her hair
was tucked up under a bowler hat. The six costumed guests
who had made the same mistake—the ghost, the gypsy,
the Athenian maiden, the geisha, the Martian, and the
apache—were delighted to find a seventh; but Agnes was
not amused; she was gasping for life. When a waiter
passed with a crowded tray, she took a glass without seeing
it; then a wave of the party took her away.

Sheilah's new friend was named Simpson. After Simpson said he thought perhaps he'd better circulate, Peter
sat down where he had been. "Now look, Sheilah," he
began. Their most intimate conversations have taken place
at parties. Once at a party she told him she was leaving
him; she didn't, of course. Smiling, blue-eyed, she gazed
lovingly at Peter and said rapidly, "Pete, shut up and listen.
That man. The man you scared away. He's a big wheel in
a company out in India or someplace like that. It's gorgeous
out there. Pete, the *servants*. And it's warm. It never never

snows. He says there's heaps of jobs. You pick them off the trees like . . . orchids. He says it's even easier now than when we owned all those places, because now the poor pets can't run anything and they'll pay *fortunes*. Pete, he says it's warm, it's heaven, and Pete, they pay."

A few minutes later, Peter was alone again and Sheilah part of a closed, laughing group. Holding her elbow was the man from the place where jobs grew like orchids. Peter edged into the group and laughed at a story he hadn't heard. He heard only the last line, which was, "Here comes another tunnel." Looking out from the tight laughing ring, he saw Agnes again, and he thought, I'd be like Agnes if I didn't have Sheilah. Agnes put her glass down on a table and lurched toward the doorway, head forward. Madge Burleigh, who never stopped moving around the room and smiling, was still smiling when she paused and said in Peter's ear, "Go with Agnes, Pete. See that she gets home. People will notice if Mike leaves."

"She probably just wants to walk around the block," said Peter. "She'll be back."

"Oh, stop thinking about yourself, for once, and see that that poor girl gets home," said Madge. "You've still got your Fiat, haven't you?"

He turned away as if he had been pushed. Any command is a release, in a way. He may not want to go in that particular direction, but at least he is going somewhere. And now Sheilah, who had moved inches nearer to hear what Madge and Peter were murmuring, said, "Yes, go, darling," as if he were leaving the gates of Troy.

Peter was to find Agnes and see that she reached home: this he repeated to himself as he stood on the landing, outside the Burleighs' flat, ringing for the elevator. Bored with waiting for it, he ran down the stairs, four flights, and saw that Agnes had stalled the lift by leaving the door open. She was crouched on the floor, propped on her fingertips. Her eyes were closed.

"Agnes," said Peter. "*Miss* Brusen, I mean. That's no

way to leave a party. Don't you know you're supposed to curtsey and say thanks? My God, Agnes, anybody going by here just now might have seen you! Come on, be a good girl. Time to go home."

She got up without his help and, moving between invisible crevasses, shut the elevator door. Then she left the building and Peter followed, remembering he was to see that she got home. They walked along the snowy pavement, Peter a few steps behind her. When she turned right for no reason, he turned, too. He had no clear idea where they were going. Perhaps she lived close by. He had forgotten where the hired car was parked, or what it looked like; he could not remember its make or its color. In any case, Sheilah had the key. Agnes walked on steadily, as if she knew their destination, and he thought, Agnes Brusen is drunk in the street in Geneva and dressed like a tramp. He wanted to say, "This is the best thing that ever happened to you, Agnes; it will help you understand how things are for some of the rest of us." But she stopped and turned and, leaning over a low hedge, retched on a frozen lawn. He held her clammy forehead and rested his hand on her arched back, on muscles as tight as a fist. She straightened up and drew a breath but the cold air made her cough. "Don't breathe too deeply," he said. "It's the worst thing you can do. Have you got a handkerchief?" He passed his own handkerchief over her wet weeping face, upturned like the face of one of his little girls. "I'm out without a coat," he said, noticing it. "We're a pair."

"I never drink," said Agnes. "I'm just not used to it." Her voice was sweet and quiet. He had never seen her so peaceful, so composed. He thought she must surely be all right, now, and perhaps he might leave her here. The trust in her tilted face had perplexed him. He wanted to get back to Sheilah and have her explain something. He had forgotten what it was, but Sheilah would know. "Do you live around here?" he said. As he spoke, she let herself fall. He had wiped her face and now she trusted him to pick her up, set her on her feet, take her wherever she ought to be. He pulled her up and she stood, wordless, humble, as he brushed the snow from her tramp's clothes. Snow horizontally crossed the lamplight. The street was silent. Agnes had lost her hat. Snow, which he tasted, melted on her hands. His gesture of licking snow from her hands was formal as a handshake. He tasted snow on her hands and then they walked on.

"I never drink," she said. They stood on the edge of a broad avenue. The wrong turning now could lead them anywhere; it was the changable avenue at the edge of towns that loses its houses and becomes a highway. She held his arm and spoke in a gentle voice. She said, "In our house we didn't smoke or drink. My mother was ambitious for me, more than for Harry and the others." She said, "I've never been alone before. When I was a kid I would get up in the summer before the others, and I'd see the ice wagon going down the street. I'm alone now. Mrs. Burleigh's found me an apartment. It's only one room. She likes it because it's in the old part of town. I don't like old houses. Old houses are dirty. You don't know who was there before."

"I should have a car somewhere," Peter said. "I'm not sure where we are."

He remembers that on this avenue they climbed into a taxi, but nothing about the drive. Perhaps he fell asleep. He does remember that when he paid the driver Agnes clutched his arm, trying to stop him. She pressed extra coins into the driver's palm. The driver was paid twice.

"I'll tell you one thing about us," said Peter. "We pay everything twice." This was part of a much longer theory concerning North American behavior, and it was not Peter's own. Mike Burleigh had held forth about it on summer afternoons.

Agnes pushed open a door between a stationer's shop and a grocery, and led the way up a narrow inside stair. They climbed one flight, frightening beetles. She had to search every pocket for the latchkey. She was shaking with cold. Her apartment seemed little warmer than the street. Without speaking to Peter she turned on all the lights. She looked inside the kitchen and the bathroom and then got down on her hands and knees and looked under the sofa. The room was neat and belonged to no one. She left him standing in this unclaimed room—she had forgotten him —and closed a door behind her. He looked for something to do—some useful action he could repeat to Madge. He turned on the electric radiator in the fireplace. Perhaps Agnes wouldn't thank him for it; perhaps she would rather undress in the cold. "I'll be on my way," he called to the bathroom door.

She had taken off the tramp's clothes and put on a dressing gown of orphanage wool. She came out of the bathroom and straight toward him. She pressed her face and rubbed her cheek on his shoulder as if hoping the contact would leave a scar. He saw her back and her profile and his own face in the mirror over the fireplace. He thought, This is how disasters happen. He saw floods of sea water moving with perfect punitive justice over reclaimed land; he saw lava covering vineyards and overtaking of dogs and stragglers. A bridge over an abyss snapped in two and the long express train, suddenly V-shaped, floated like snow. He thought amiably of every kind of disaster and thought, This is how they occur.

Her eyes were closed. She said, "I shouldn't be over here. In my family we didn't drink or smoke. My mother wanted a lot from me, more than from Harry and the others." But he knew all that; he had known from the day of the Bible, and because once, at the beginning, she had made him afraid. He was not afraid of her now.

She said, "It's no use staying here, is it?"

"If you mean what I think, no."

"It wouldn't be better anywhere."

She let him see full on her blotched face. He was not expected to do anything. He was not required to pick her up when she fell or wipe her tears. She was poor quality, really—he remembered having thought that once. She left him and went quietly into the bathroom and locked the door. He heard taps running and supposed it was a hot bath. He was pretty certain there would be no more tears. He looked at his watch: Sheilah must be home, now, wondering what had become of him. He descended the beetles' staircase and for forty minutes crossed the city under a windless fall of snow.

The neighbor's child who had stayed with Peter's children was asleep on the living-room sofa. Peter woke her and sent her, sleepwalking, to her own door. He sat down, wet to the bone, thinking, I'll call the Burleighs. In half an hour I'll call the police. He heard a car stop and the engine running and a confusion of two voices laughing and calling goodnight. Presently Sheilah let herself in, rosy-faced, smiling. She carried his trenchcoat over her arm. She said, "How's Agnes?"

"Where were you?" he said. "Whose car was that?"

Sheilah had gone into the children's room. He heard her shutting their window. She returned, undoing her dress, and said, "Was Agnes all right?"

"Agnes is all right. Sheilah, this is about the worst . . ."

She stepped out of the Balenciaga and threw it over a chair. She stopped and looked at him and said, "Poor old Pete, are you in love with Agnes?" And then, as if the answer were of so little importance she hadn't time for it, she locked her arms around him and said, "My love, we're going to Ceylon."

Two days later, when Peter strolled into his office, Agnes was at her desk. She wore the blue dress, with a spotless collar. White and yellow freesias were symmetrically arranged in the glass jar. The room was hot, and the spring snow, glued for a second when it touched the window, blurred the view of parked cars.

"Quite a party," Peter said.

She did not look up. He sighed, sat down, and thought if the snow held he would be skiing at the Burleighs' very soon. Impressed by his kindness to Agnes, Madge had invited the family for the first possible weekend.

Presently Agnes said, "I'll never drink again or go to a house where people are drinking. And I'll never bother anyone the way I bothered you."

"You didn't bother me," he said. "I took you home. You were alone and it was late. It's normal."

"Normal for you, maybe, but I'm used to getting home by myself. Please never tell what happened."

He stared at her. He can still remember the freesias and the Bible and the heat in the room. She looked as if the elements had no power. She felt neither heat nor cold. "Nothing happened," he said.

"I behaved in a silly way. I had no right to. I led you to think I might do something wrong."

"I might have tried something," he said gallantly. "But that would be my fault and not yours."

She put her knuckle to her mouth and he could scarcely hear. "It was because of you. I was afraid you might be blamed, or else you'd blame yourself."

"There's no question of any blame," he said. "Nothing happened. We'd both had a lot to drink. Forget about it. Nothing *happened*. You'd remember if it had."

She put down her hand. There was an expression on her face. Now she sees me, he thought. She had never looked at him after the first day. (He has since tried to put a name to the look on her face; but how can he, now, after so many voyages, after Ceylon, and Hong Kong, and Sheilah's nearly leaving him, and all their difficulties—the money owed, the rows with hotel managers, the lost and found steamer trunk, the children throwing up the foreign food?) She sees me now, he thought. What does she see?

She said, "I'm from a big family. I'm not used to being alone. I'm not a suicidal person, but I could have done something after that party, just not to see any more, or think or listen or expect anything. What can I think when I see these people? All my life I heard, Educated people don't do this, educated people don't do that. And now I'm here, and you're all educated people, and you're nothing but pigs. You're educated and you drink and do everything wrong and you know what you're doing, and that makes you worse than pigs. My family worked to make me an educated person, but they didn't know you. But what if I didn't see and hear and expect anything any more? It wouldn't change anything. You'd all be still the same. Only *you* might have thought it was your fault. You might have thought you were to blame. It could worry you all your life. It would have been wrong for me to worry you."

He remembered that the rented car was still along a snowy curb somewhere in Geneva. He wondered if Sheilah had the key in her purse and if she remembered where they'd parked.

"I told you about the ice wagon," Agnes said. "I don't remember everything, so you're wrong about remembering. But I remember telling you that. That was the best. It's the best you can hope to have. In a big family, if you want to be alone, you have to get up before the rest of them. You get up early in the morning in the summer and it's you, you, once in your life alone in the universe. You think you know everything that can happen . . . Nothing is ever like that again."

He looked at the smeared window and wondered if this day could end without disaster. In his mind he saw her falling in the snow wearing a tramp's costume, and he saw her coming to him in the orphanage dressing gown. He saw her drowning face at the party. He was afraid for himself. The story was still unfinished. It had to come to a climax, something threatening to him. But there was no climax. They talked that day, and afterward nothing else was said. They went on in the same office for a short time, until Peter left for Ceylon; until somebody read the right letter, passed it on for the right initials, and the Fraziers began the Oriental tour that should have made their fortune. Agnes and Peter were too tired to speak after that morning. They were like a married couple in danger, taking care.

But what were they talking about that day, so quietly, such old friends? They talked about dying, about being ambitious, about being religious, about different kinds of love. What did she see when she looked at him—taking her knuckle slowly away from her mouth, bringing her hand down to the desk, letting it rest there? They were both Canadians, so they had this much together—the knowledge of the little you dare admit. Death, near-death, the best thing, the wrong thing—God knows what they were telling each other. Anyway, nothing happened.

When, on Sunday mornings, Sheilah and Peter talk about those times, they take on the glamor of something still to come. It is then he remembers Agnes Brusen. He never says her name. Sheilah wouldn't remember Agnes. Agnes is the only secret Peter has from his wife, the only puzzle he pieces together without her help. He thinks about families in the West as they were fifteen, twenty years ago —the iron-cold ambition, and every member pushing the next one on. He thinks of his father's parties. When he thinks of his father he imagines him with Sheilah, in a crowd. Actually, Sheilah and Peter's father never met, but they might have liked each other. His father admired good-looking women. Peter wonders what they were doing over there in Geneva—not Sheilah and Peter, *Agnes* and Peter. It is almost as if they had once run away together, silly as children, irresponsible as lovers. Peter and Sheilah are back where they started. While they were out in world affairs picking up microbes and debts, always on the fringe of disaster, the fringe of a fortune, Agnes went on and did— what? They lost each other. He thinks of the ice wagon going down the street. He sees something he has never seen in his life—a Western town that belongs to Agnes. Here is

Agnes—small, mole-faced, round-shouldered because she has always carried a younger child. She watches the ice wagon and the trail of ice water in a morning invented for her: hers. He sees the weak prairie trees and the shadows on the sidewalk. Nothing moves except the shadows and the ice wagon and the changing amber of the child's eyes. The child is Peter. He has seen the grain of the cement sidewalk and the grass in the cracks, and the dust, and the dandelions at the edge of the road. He is there. He has taken the morning that belongs to Agnes, he is up before the others, and he knows everything. There is nothing he doesn't know. He could keep the morning, if he wanted to, but what can Peter do with the start of a summer day? Sheilah is here, it is a true Sunday morning, with its dimness and headache and remorse and regrets, and this is life. He says, "We have the Balenciaga." He touches Sheilah's hand. The children have their aunt now, and he and Sheilah have each other. Everything works out, somehow or other. Let Agnes have the start of the day. Let Agnes think it was invented for her. Who wants to be alone in the universe? No, begin at the beginning: Peter lost Agnes. Agnes says to herself somewhere, Peter is lost.

FOR THE BEST IN PAPERBACKS, LOOK FOR THE

In every corner of the world, on every subject under the sun, Penguin represents quality and variety—the very best in publishing today.

For complete information about books available from Penguin—including Pelicans, Puffins, Peregrines, and Penguin Classics—and how to order them, write to us at the appropriate address below. Please note that for copyright reasons the selection of books varies from country to country.

In the United Kingdom: For a complete list of books available from Penguin in the U.K., please write to *Dept E.P., Penguin Books Ltd, Harmondsworth, Middlesex, UB7 0DA.*

In the United States: For a complete list of books available from Penguin in the U.S., please write to *Dept BA, Penguin,* Box 120, Bergenfield, New Jersey 07621-0120.

In Canada: For a complete list of books available from Penguin in Canada, please write to *Penguin Books Ltd, 2801 John Street, Markham, Ontario L3R 1B4.*

In Australia: For a complete list of books available from Penguin in Australia, please write to the *Marketing Department, Penguin Books Ltd, P.O. Box 257, Ringwood, Victoria 3134.*

In New Zealand: For a complete list of books available from Penguin in New Zealand, please write to the *Marketing Department, Penguin Books (NZ) Ltd, Private Bag, Takapuna, Auckland 9.*

In India: For a complete list of books available from Penguin, please write to *Penguin Overseas Ltd, 706 Eros Apartments, 56 Nehru Place, New Delhi, 110019.*

In Holland: For a complete list of books available from Penguin in Holland, please write to *Penguin Books Nederland B.V., Postbus 195, NL-1380AD Weesp, Netherlands.*

In Germany: For a complete list of books available from Penguin, please write to *Penguin Books Ltd, Friedrichstrasse 10-12, D-6000 Frankfurt Main 1, Federal Republic of Germany.*

In Spain: For a complete list of books available from Penguin in Spain, please write to *Longman, Penguin España, Calle San Nicolas 15, E-28013 Madrid, Spain.*

In Japan: For a complete list of books available from Penguin in Japan, please write to *Longman Penguin Japan Co Ltd, Yamaguchi Building, 2-12-9 Kanda Jimbocho, Chiyoda-Ku, Tokyo 101, Japan.*

FOR THE BEST LITERATURE, LOOK FOR THE

☐ **THE BOOK AND THE BROTHERHOOD**
Iris Murdoch

Many years ago Gerard Hernshaw and his friends banded together to finance a political and philosophical book by a monomaniacal Marxist genius. Now opinions have changed, and support for the book comes at the price of moral indignation; the resulting disagreements lead to passion, hatred, a duel, murder, and a suicide pact.   *602 pages   ISBN: 0-14-010470-4   **$8.95***

☐ **GRAVITY'S RAINBOW**
Thomas Pynchon

Thomas Pynchon's classic antihero is Tyrone Slothrop, an American lieutenant in London whose body anticipates German rocket launchings. Surely one of the most important works of fiction produced in the twentieth century, *Gravity's Rainbow* is a complex and awesome novel in the great tradition of James Joyce's *Ulysses*.   *768 pages   ISBN: 0-14-010661-8   **$10.95***

☐ **FIFTH BUSINESS**
Robertson Davies

The first novel in the celebrated "Deptford Trilogy," which also includes *The Manticore* and *World of Wonders*, *Fifth Business* stands alone as the story of a rational man who discovers that the marvelous is only another aspect of the real.   *266 pages   ISBN: 0-14-004387-X   **$4.95***

☐ **WHITE NOISE**
Don DeLillo

Jack Gladney, a professor of Hitler Studies in Middle America, and his fourth wife, Babette, navigate the usual rocky passages of family life in the television age. Then, their lives are threatened by an "airborne toxic event"—a more urgent and menacing version of the "white noise" of transmissions that typically engulfs them.   *326 pages   ISBN: 0-14-007702-2   **$7.95***

You can find all these books at your local bookstore, or use this handy coupon for ordering:

Penguin Books By Mail
Dept. BA Box 999
Bergenfield, NJ 07621-0999

Please send me the above title(s). I am enclosing ―――――――――
(please add sales tax if appropriate and $1.50 to cover postage and handling). Send check or money order—no CODs. Please allow four weeks for shipping. We cannot ship to post office boxes or addresses outside the USA. *Prices subject to change without notice.*

Ms./Mrs./Mr. ――――――――――――――――――――――――――――――

Address ――――――――――――――――――――――――――――――――――

City/State ――――――――――――――――――――――― Zip ――――――――

Sales tax: CA: 6.5%   NY: 8.25%   NJ: 6%   PA: 6%   TN: 5.5%

FOR THE BEST LITERATURE, LOOK FOR THE

☐ **A SPORT OF NATURE**
Nadine Gordimer

Hillela, Nadine Gordimer's "sport of nature," is seductive and intuitively gifted at life. Casting herself adrift from her family at seventeen, she lives among political exiles on an East African beach, marries a black revolutionary, and ultimately plays a heroic role in the overthrow of apartheid.

354 pages   *ISBN: 0-14-008470-3*   **$7.95**

☐ **THE COUNTERLIFE**
Philip Roth

By far Philip Roth's most radical work of fiction, *The Counterlife* is a book of conflicting perspectives and points of view about people living out dreams of renewal and escape. Illuminating these lives is the skeptical, enveloping intelligence of the novelist Nathan Zuckerman, who calculates the price and examines the results of his characters' struggles for a change of personal fortune.

372 pages   *ISBN: 0-14-009769-4*   **$4.95**

☐ **THE MONKEY'S WRENCH**
Primo Levi

Through the mesmerizing tales told by two characters—one, a construction worker/philosopher who has built towers and bridges in India and Alaska; the other, a writer/chemist, rigger of words and molecules—Primo Levi celebrates the joys of work and the art of storytelling.

174 pages   *ISBN: 0-14-010357-0*   **$6.95**

☐ **IRONWEED**
William Kennedy

"Riding up the winding road of Saint Agnes Cemetery in the back of the rattling old truck, Francis Phelan became aware that the dead, even more than the living, settled down in neighborhoods." So begins William Kennedy's Pulitzer-Prize winning novel about an ex-ballplayer, part-time gravedigger, and full-time drunk, whose return to the haunts of his youth arouses the ghosts of his past and present.   *228 pages*   *ISBN: 0-14-007020-6*   **$6.95**

☐ **THE COMEDIANS**
Graham Greene

Set in Haiti under Duvalier's dictatorship, *The Comedians* is a story about the committed and the uncommitted. Actors with no control over their destiny, they play their parts in the foreground; experience love affairs rather than love; have enthusiasms but not faith; and if they die, they die like Mr. Jones, by accident.

288 pages   *ISBN: 0-14-002766-1*   **$4.95**

FOR THE BEST LITERATURE, LOOK FOR THE

☐ **HERZOG**
Saul Bellow

Winner of the National Book Award, *Herzog* is the imaginative and critically acclaimed story of Moses Herzog: joker, moaner, cuckhold, charmer, and truly an Everyman for our time.

      342 pages   *ISBN: 0-14-007270-5*   **$6.95**

☐ **FOOLS OF FORTUNE**
William Trevor

The deeply affecting story of two cousins—one English, one Irish—brought together and then torn apart by the tide of Anglo-Irish hatred, *Fools of Fortune* presents a profound symbol of the tragic entanglements of England and Ireland in this century.   *240 pages*   *ISBN: 0-14-006982-8*   **$6.95**

☐ **THE SONGLINES**
Bruce Chatwin

Venturing into the desolate land of Outback Australia—along timeless paths, and among fortune hunters, redneck Australians, racist policemen, and mysterious Aboriginal holy men—Bruce Chatwin discovers a wondrous vision of man's place in the world.   *296 pages*   *ISBN: 0-14-009429-6*   **$7.95**

☐ **THE GUIDE: A NOVEL**
R. K. Narayan

Raju was once India's most corrupt tourist guide; now, after a peasant mistakes him for a holy man, he gradually begins to play the part. His succeeds so well that God himself intervenes to put Raju's new holiness to the test.

      220 pages   *ISBN: 0-14-009657-4*   **$5.95**

FOR THE BEST LITERATURE, LOOK FOR THE

☐ **THE LAST SONG OF MANUEL SENDERO**
Ariel Dorfman

In an unnamed country, in a time that might be now, the son of Manuel Sendero refuses to be born, beginning a revolution where generations of the future wait for a world without victims or oppressors.

464 pages   *ISBN: 0-14-008896-2*   **$7.95**

☐ **THE BOOK OF LAUGHTER AND FORGETTING**
Milan Kundera

In this collection of stories and sketches, Kundera addresses themes including sex and love, poetry and music, sadness and the power of laughter. "*The Book of Laughter and Forgetting* calls itself a novel," writes John Leonard of *The New York Times*, "although it is part fairly tale, part literary criticism, part political tract, part musicology, part autobiography. It can call itself whatever it wants to, because the whole is genius."

240 pages   *ISBN: 0-14-009693-0*   **$6.95**

☐ **TIRRA LIRRA BY THE RIVER**
Jessica Anderson

Winner of the Miles Franklin Award, Australia's most prestigious literary prize, *Tirra Lirra by the River* is the story of a woman's seventy-year search for the place where she truly belongs. Nora Porteous's series of escapes takes her from a small Australia town to the suburbs of Sydney to London, where she seems finally to become the woman she always wanted to be.

142 pages   *ISBN: 0-14-006945-3*   **$4.95**

☐ **LOVE UNKNOWN**
A. N. Wilson

In their sweetly wild youth, Monica, Belinda, and Richeldis shared a bachelor-girl flat and became friends for life. Now, twenty years later, A. N. Wilson charts the intersecting lives of the three women through the perilous waters of love, marriage, and adultery in this wry and moving modern comedy of manners.

202 pages   *ISBN: 0-14-010190-X*   **$6.95**

☐ **THE WELL**
Elizabeth Jolley

Against the stark beauty of the Australian farmlands, Elizabeth Jolley portrays an eccentric, affectionate relationship between the two women—Hester, a lonely spinster, and Katherine, a young orphan. Their pleasant, satisfyingly simple life is nearly perfect until a dark stranger invades their world in a most horrifying way.

176 pages   *ISBN: 0-14-008901-2*   **$6.95**

FOR THE BEST LITERATURE, LOOK FOR THE

☐ **VOSS**
Patrick White

Set in nineteenth-century Australia, *Voss* is the story of the secret passion between an explorer and a young orphan. From the careful delineation of Victorian society to the stark narrative of adventure in the Australian desert, Patrick White's novel is one of extraordinary power and virtuosity. White won the Nobel Prize for Literature in 1973.

448 pages   *ISBN: 0-14-001438-1*   **$7.95**

☐ **STONES FOR IBARRA**
Harriet Doerr

An American couple, the only foreigners in the Mexican village of Ibarra, have come to reopen a long-dormant copper mine. Their plan is to live out their lives here, connected to the place and to each other. Along the way, they learn much about life, death, and the tide of fate from the Mexican people around them.

214 pages   *ISBN: 0-14-007562-3*   **$6.95**

You can find all these books at your local bookstore, or use this handy coupon for ordering:

Penguin Books By Mail
Dept. BA Box 999
Bergenfield, NJ 07621-0999

Please send me the above title(s). I am enclosing _____
(please add sales tax if appropriate and $1.50 to cover postage and handling). Send check or money order—no CODs. Please allow four weeks for shipping. We cannot ship to post office boxes or addresses outside the USA. *Prices subject to change without notice.*

Ms./Mrs./Mr. _____

Address _____

City/State _____ Zip _____

Sales tax: CA: 6.5%   NY: 8.25%   NJ: 6%   PA: 6%   TN: 5.5%